P9-CCQ-681

ALSO BY LAURELL K. HAMILTON

Published by The Random House Publishing Group

SWALLOWING DARKNESS

A LICK OF FROST

MISTRAL'S KISS

A STROKE OF MIDNIGHT

SEDUCED BY MOONLIGHT

A CARESS OF TWILIGHT

A KISS OF SHADOWS

DIVINE MISDEMEANORS

LAUREL K.

Ballantine Books New York

HAMILTON

DIVINE

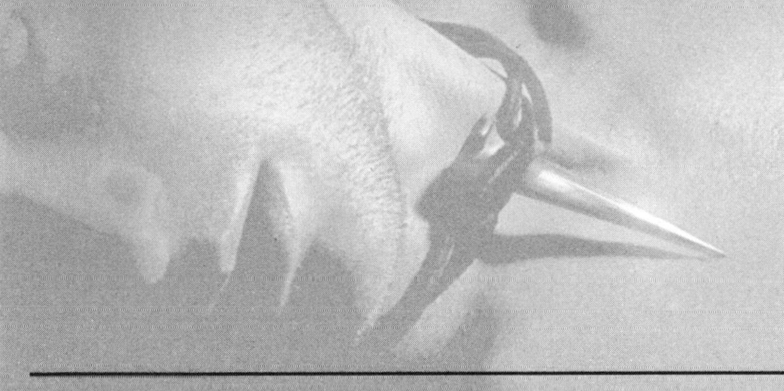

MISDEMEANORS

A Novel

Divine Misdemeanors is a work of fiction. Names, characters, places, and incidents are the products of the author's imagination or are used fictitiously. Any resemblance to actual events, locales, or persons, living or dead, is entirely coincidental.

Published in the United States by Ballantine Books, an imprint of The Random House Publishing Group, a division of Random House, Inc., New York.

BALLANTINE and colophon are registered trademarks of Random House, Inc.

Library of Congress Cataloging-in-Publication Data
Hamilton, Laurell K.
Divine misdemeanors : a novel / Laurell K. Hamilton.
p. cm.
ISBN 978-0-345-49596-9 (alk. paper)
1. Gentry, Meredith (Fictitious character)—Fiction. 2. Women private investigators—Fiction. 3. Supernatural—Fiction. 4. Fairies—Fiction. I. Title.
PS3558.A443357D58 2009
813'.54—dc22 2009043078

Printed in the United States of America on acid-free paper

www.ballantinebooks.com

2 4 6 8 9 7 5 3 1

First Edition

To Jonathon—I could not have invented you, because I did not know I needed you by my side until you were there. No amount of poetry can explain both the surprise of you, and the warm familiarity of you in my arms.

ACKNOWLEDGMENTS

This one has to be for Carri, who saw O-dark-thirty with me on this book, and she still came in to work the next day. I also have to acknowledge all the bumps along the road to this book, because without all the bad, would I have come to all the good? But really, guys, can it be a little less bumpy next time, please?

DIVINE MISDEMEANORS

CHAPTER ONE

THE SMELL OF EUCALYPTUS ALWAYS MADE ME THINK OF SOUTHERN California, my home away from home; now it might forever be entwined with the scent of blood. I stood there with the strangely hot wind rustling through the high leaves. It blew my summer dress in a tangle around my legs, and spread my shoulder-length hair in a scarlet web across my face. I grabbed my hair in handfuls so I could see, though maybe not being able to see would have been better. The plastic gloves pulled at my hair. They were designed so I didn't contaminate evidence, not for comfort. We were surrounded by a nearly perfect circle of the tall, pale tree trunks. In the middle of that natural circle were the bodies.

The spicy smell of the Eucalyptus could almost hide the scent of blood. If it had been this many adult human-sized bodies the Eucalyptus wouldn't have had a chance, but they weren't adult-sized. They were tiny by human standards, so tiny, the size of dolls; none of the corpses were even a foot tall, and some were less than five inches. They lay on the ground with their bright butterfly and moth wings frozen as if in mid-movement. Their dead hands were wrapped around wilted flowers like a cheerful game gone horribly wrong. They looked like so many broken Barbie dolls, except that Barbie dolls never lay so lifelike, or so perfectly poised. No matter how hard

I'd tried as a little girl, their limbs remained stiff and unyielding. The bodies on the ground were stiff with rigor mortis, but they'd been laid out carefully, so they had stiffened in strangely graceful, almost dancing poses.

Detective Lucy Tate came to stand beside me. She was wearing a pants suit complete with jacket and a white button-up shirt that strained a little across the front because Lucy, like me, had too much figure for most button-up shirts. But I wasn't a police detective so I didn't have to pretend I was a man to try to fit in. I worked at a private detective agency that used the fact that I was Princess Meredith, the only American-born fey royal, and back working for the Grey Detective Agency: Supernatural Problems; Magical Solutions. People loved paying money to see the princess, and have her hear their problems; I'd begun to feel a little like a freak show until today. Today I would have loved to be back in the office listening to some mundane matter that didn't really need my special brand of help, but was just a human rich enough to pay for my time. I'd have rather been doing a lot of things than standing here staring down at a dozen dead fey.

"What do you think?" she asked.

What I really thought was that I was glad the bodies were small so that the trees covered most of the smell, but that would be admitting weakness, and you didn't do that on the rare occasions you got to work with the police. You had to be professional and tough or they thought less of you, even the female cops, maybe especially them.

"They're laid out like something from a children's storybook down to the dancing poses and the flowers in their hands."

Lucy nodded. "It's not just like, it is."

"Is what?" I asked, looking at her. Her dark brunette hair was cut shorter than mine, and held back by a thick band so that nothing obscured her vision, as I still fought with my own hair. She looked cool and professional.

She used one plastic-gloved hand to hold out a plastic-wrapped page. She held it out to me, though I knew not to touch it even with the gloves. I was a civilian, and I had been very aware of that as I walked through all the police on the way to the center of all this activity. The police were never that fond of the private detective, no matter what you see on television, and I wasn't even human. Of course, if I'd been human they wouldn't have called me down to the murder scene in the first place. I was here because I was a trained detective and a faerie princess. One without the other wouldn't have gotten me under the police tape.

I stared at the page. The wind tried to snatch it from her hand, and she used both hands to hold it steady for me. It was an illustration from a children's book. It was dancing faeries with flowers in their hands. I stared at it for a second more, then looked down at the bodies on the ground. I forced myself to study their dead forms, then looked at the illustration.

"They're identical," I said.

"I believe so, though we'll have to have some kind of flower expert tell us if the flowers match up bloom for bloom, but except for that our killer has duplicated the scene."

I stared from one to the other again, those laughing happy faces in the picture and the very still, very dead ones on the ground. Their skin had begun to change color already, turning that bluish-purple cast of the dead.

"He, or she, had to dress them," I pointed out. "No matter how many illustrations you see with these little blousy dresses and loincloth things, most demi-fey outside of faerie don't dress like this. I've seen them in three-piece suits and formal evening wear."

"You're sure they didn't wear the clothes here?" she asked.

I shook my head. "They wouldn't have matched perfectly without planning it this way."

"We were thinking he lured them down here with a promise of an acting part, a short film," she said.

I thought about it, then shrugged. "Maybe, but they'd have come to the circle anyway."

"Why?"

"The demi-fey, the small winged fey, have a particular fondness for natural circles."

"Explain."

"The stories only tell humans not to step into a ring of toadstools, or a ring of actual dancing fey, but it can be any natural circle. Flowers, stones, hills, or trees, like this circle. They come to dance in the circle."

"So they came down here to dance and he brought the clothes?" She frowned at me.

"You think that it works better if he lured them down here to film them," I said.

"Yes."

"Either that or he watched them," I said, "so he knew they came down here on certain nights to dance."

"That would mean he or she was stalking them," Lucy said.

"It would."

"If I go after the film angle, I can find the costume rental and the advertisement for actors for his short film." She made little quote marks in the air for the word film.

"If he's just a stalker and he made the costumes, then you have fewer leads to follow."

"Don't say he. You don't know that the killer is a he."

"You're right, I don't. Are you assuming that the killer isn't human?"

"Should we be?" she asked, her voice neutral.

"I don't know. I can't imagine a human strong enough or fast enough to grab six demi-fey and slit their throats before the others could escape or attack him."

"Are they as delicate as they look?" she asked.

I almost smiled, and then didn't feel like finishing it. "No, Detective, they aren't. They're much stronger than they look, and incredibly fast."

"So we aren't looking for a human?"

"I didn't say that. I said that physically humans couldn't do this, but there is some magic that might help them do it."

"What kind of magic?"

"I don't have a spell in mind. I'm not human. I don't need spells to use against other fey, but I know there are stories of magic that can make us weak, catchable, and hurtable."

"Yeah, aren't these kind of fey supposed to be immortal?"

I stared down at the tiny lifeless bodies. Once the answer would have simply been yes, but I'd learned from some of the lesser fey at the Unseelie Court that some of them had died falling down stairs, and other mundane causes. Their immortality wasn't what it used to be, but we had not publicized that to the humans. One of the things that kept us safe was that the humans thought they couldn't hurt us easily. Had some human learned the truth and exploited it? Was the mortality among the lesser fey getting worse? Or had they been immortal and magic had stolen it away?

"Merry, you in there?"

I nodded and looked at her, glad to look away from the bodies. "Sorry, I just never get used to seeing this kind of thing."

"Oh, you get used to it," she said, "but I hope you don't see enough dead bodies to be that jaded." She sighed, as if she wished she wasn't that jaded either.

"You asked me if the demi-fey are immortal, and the answer is yes." It was all I could say to her until I found out if the mortality of the fey was spreading. So far it had only been a few cases inside faerie.

"Then how did the killer do this?"

I'd only seen one other demi-fey killed by a blade that wasn't cold iron. A noble of the Unseelie Court had wielded that one. A noble of faerie, and my blood kin. We'd killed the sidhe who did it, although he said that he hadn't meant to kill her. He had just meant to wound her through the heart as her desertion of him had wounded his heart—poetic and the kind of romantic drivel you get when you're used to being surrounded by beings who can have their heads chopped off and still live. That last bit hasn't worked in a long time even among the sidhe, but we haven't shared that either. No one likes to talk about the fact that their people are losing their magic and their power.

Was the killer a sidhe? Somehow I didn't think so. They might kill a lesser fey out of arrogance or a sense of privilege, but this had the taste of something much more convoluted than that—a motive that only the killer would understand.

I looked carefully at my own reasoning to make certain I wasn't talking myself out of the Unseelie Court, the Darkling Throng, being suspects. The court that I had been offered rulership of and given up for love. The tabloids were still talking about the fairy-tale ending, but people had died, some of them by my hand, and, like most fairy tales, it had been more about blood and being true to yourself than about love. Love had just been the emotion that had led me to what I truly wanted, and who I truly was. I guess there are worse emotions to follow.

"What are you thinking, Merry?"

"I'm thinking that I wonder what emotion led the killer to do this, to want to do this."

"What do you mean?"

"It takes something like love to put this much attention into the details. Did the killer love this book or did he love the small fey? Did he hate this book as a child? Is it the clue to some horrible trauma that twisted him to do this?"

"Don't start profiling on me, Merry; we've got people paid to do that."

"I'm just doing what you taught me, Lucy. Murder is like any skill; it doesn't fall out of the box perfect. This is perfect."

"The killer probably spent years fantasizing about this scene, Merry. They wanted, needed it to be perfect."

"But it never is. That's what serial killers say when the police interview them. Some of them try again and again for the real-life kill to match the fantasy, but it never does, so they kill again and again to try to make it perfect."

Lucy smiled at me. "You know, that's one of the things I always liked about you."

"What?" I asked.

"You don't just rely on the magic; you actually try to be a good detective."

"Isn't that what I'm supposed to do?" I asked.

"Yeah, but you'd be surprised how many psychics and wizards are great at the magic but suck at the actual detecting part."

"No, I wouldn't, but remember, I didn't have that much magic until a few months ago."

"That's right, you were a late bloomer." And she smiled again. Once I'd thought it was strange that the police could smile over a body, but I'd learned that you either lighten up about it or you transfer out of homicide, or better yet, you get out of police work.

"I've already checked, Merry. There are no other homicides even close to this one. No demi-fey killed in a group. No costumes. No book illustration left. This is one of a kind."

"Maybe it is, but you helped teach me that killers don't start out this good. Maybe they just planned it perfectly and got lucky that it was this perfect, or maybe they've had other kills that weren't this good, this thought-out, but it would be staged, and it would have this feel to it."

"What kind of feel?" she asked.

"You thought film not just because it would give you more leads, but because there's something dramatic about it all. The setting, the choice of victims, the display, the book illustration; it's showy."

She nodded. "Exactly," she said.

The wind played with my purple sundress until I had to hold it to keep it from flipping up and flashing the police line behind us.

"I'm sorry to drag you out to something like this on a Saturday, Merry," she said. "I did try to call Jeremy."

"He's got a new girlfriend and keeps turning off his phone." I didn't begrudge my boss, the first semi-serious lover he'd had in years. Not really.

"You look like you had a picnic planned."

"Something like that," I said, "but this didn't do your Saturday any good either."

She smiled ruefully. "I didn't have any plans." She stabbed a thumb in the direction of the other police. "Your boyfriends are mad at me for making you look at dead bodies while you're pregnant."

My hands automatically went to my stomach, which was still very flat. I wasn't showing yet, though with twins the doctor had warned me that it could go from nothing to a lot almost overnight.

I glanced back to see Doyle and Frost, standing with the policemen. My two men were no taller than some of the police—six feet and some inches isn't that unusual—but the rest stood out painfully. Doyle had been called the Queen's Darkness for a thousand years, and he fit his name, black from skin to hair to the eyes behind their black wraparound sunglasses. His black hair was in a tight braid down his back. Only the silver earrings that climbed from lobe to the pointed tip of his ears relieved the black-on-black of his jeans, T-shirt, and leather jacket. The last was to hide the weapons he was carrying. He was the captain of my bodyguards, as well as one of the fathers to my unborn children, and one of my dearest loves. The other dearest love stood beside him like a pale negative, skin as white as my own, but Frost's hair was actually silver, like Christmas tree tinsel, shining in the sunlight. The wind played with his hair so that it floated outward in a shimmering wave, looking like some model with a wind machine, but even though his hair was near ankle-length and unbound, it did not tangle in the wind. I'd asked him about that, and he'd said simply, "The wind likes my hair." I hadn't known what to say to that so I hadn't tried.

His sunglasses were gunmetal gray with darker gray lenses to hide the paler gray of his eyes, the most unremarkable part of him, really. He favored designer suits, but he was actually in one of the few pairs of blue jeans he owned, with a silk T-shirt and a suit jacket to hide his own weapons, all in grays. We actually had been planning on an outing to the beach, or I'd have never gotten Frost out of slacks and into jeans. His face might have been the more traditionally handsome of the two, but it wasn't by much. They were as they had been for centuries, the light and dark of each other.

The policemen in their uniforms, suits, and more casual clothes seemed like shadows not as bright, not as alive as my two men, but maybe everyone in love thought the same thing. Maybe it was not being immortal warriors of the sidhe but simply love that made them stand out to my eye.

Lucy had gotten me through the police line because I'd worked with the police before, and I was actually a licensed private detective in this state. Doyle and Frost weren't, and they had never worked with the police on a case, so they had to stay behind the line away from any would-be clues.

"If I find out anything for certain that seems pertinent about this kind of magic, I will let you know." It wasn't a lie, not the way I worded it. The fey, and especially the sidhe, are known for never lying, but we'll deceive you until you'll think the sky is green and the grass is blue. We won't *tell* you the sky is green and the grass is blue; but we will leave you with that definite impression.

"You think there'll be an earlier murder," she said.

"If not, this guy, or girl, got very lucky."

Lucy motioned at the bodies. "I'm not sure I'd call this lucky."

"No murderer is this good the first time, or did you get a new flavor of killer while I was away in faerie?"

"Nope. Most murders are pretty standard. Violence level and victim differs but you're about eighty to ninety percent more likely to be killed by your nearest and dearest than by a stranger, and most killing is depressingly ordinary."

"This one's depressing," I said, "but it's not ordinary."

"No, it's not ordinary. I'm hoping this one perfect scene kind of got it out of the killer's system."

"You think it will?" I asked.

"No," she said. "No, I don't."

"Can I alert the local demi-fey to be careful, or are you trying to withhold the victim profile from the media?"

"Warn them, because if we don't and it happens again, we'll get accused of being racists, or is that speciesist?" She shook her head, walking back toward the police line. I followed her, glad to be leaving the bodies behind.

"Humans can interbreed with the demi-fey, so I don't think speciesist applies."

"I couldn't breed with something the size of a doll. That's just wrong."

"Some of them have two forms, one small and one not much shorter than me."

"Five feet? Really, from eight inches tall to five feet?"

"Yes, really. It's a rare ability, but it happens, and the babies are fertile, so I don't think it's quite a different species."

"I didn't mean any offense," she said.

"None taken, I'm just explaining."

We were almost to the police line and my visibly anxious boyfriends. "Enjoy your Saturday," she said.

"I'd say you too, but I know you'll be here for hours."

"Yeah, I think your Saturday will be a lot more fun than mine." She looked at Doyle and Frost as the police finally let them move forward. Lucy was giving them an admiring look behind her sunglasses. I didn't blame her.

I slipped the gloves off even though I hadn't touched a thing. I dropped them onto the mass of other discarded gloves that was on this side of the tape. Lucy held the tape up for me and I didn't even have to stoop. Sometimes short is good.

"Oh, check out the flowers, florists," I said.

"Already on it," she said.

"Sorry, sometimes I get carried away with you letting me help."

"No, all ideas are welcome, Merry, you know that. It's why I called you down here." She waved at me and went back to her murder scene. We couldn't shake because she was still wearing gloves and carrying evidence.

Doyle and Frost were almost to me, but we weren't going to get to the beach right away either. I had to warn the local demi-fey, and try to figure out a way to see if the mortality had spread to them, or if there was magic here in Los Angeles that could steal their immortality. There were things that would kill us eventually, but there wasn't much that would allow you to slit the throat of the winged-kin. They were the essence of faerie, more so even than the high court nobles. If I found out anything certain I'd tell Lucy, but until I had something that was useful I'd keep my secrets. I was only part human; most of me was pure fey, and we know how to keep a secret. The trick was how to warn the local demi-fey without causing a panic. Then I realized that there wasn't a way. The fey are just like humans—they understand fear. Some magic, a little near-immortality, doesn't make you unafraid; it just gives you a different list of fears.

CHAPTER TWO

FROST TRIED TO HUG ME, BUT I PUT A HAND ON HIS STOMACH, TOO short to really touch his chest. Doyle said, "She's trying to appear strong in front of the policemen."

"We shouldn't have let you come see this now," Frost said.

"Jeremy could have given a fey's opinion."

"Jeremy is the boss and he's allowed to turn his phone off on a Saturday," I said.

"Then Jordan or Julian Kane. They are psychics and practicing wizards."

"They're only human, Frost. Lucy wanted a fey to see this crime scene."

"You shouldn't have to see this in your condition."

I leaned in and spoke low. "I am a detective. It's my job, and it's our people up there dead on the hillside. I may never be queen, but I'm the closest they have here in L.A. Where else should a ruler be when her people are threatened?"

Frost started to say something else, but Doyle touched his arm. "Let it go, my friend. Let us just get her back to the vehicle and begone."

I put my arm through Doyle's leather-clad arm, though I thought it was too hot for the leather. Frost trailed us, and a glance showed that he was doing his job of searching the area for threats. Unlike a human bodyguard, Frost looked from sky to ground, because when faerie is your potential enemy, danger can come from nearly anywhere.

Doyle was keeping an eye out too, but his attention was divided by trying to keep me from twisting an ankle in the sandals that looked great with the dress but sucked for uneven ground. They didn't have too tall a heel, they were just very open and not supportive. I wondered what I'd wear when I got really pregnant. Did I have any practical shoes except for jogging ones?

The major danger had passed when I'd killed my main rival for the throne and given up the crown. I'd done everything I could to make myself both too dangerous to tempt anyone and harmless to the nobles and their way of life. I was in voluntary exile, and I'd made it clear that it was a permanent move. I didn't want the throne; I just wanted to be left alone. But since some of the nobles had spent the last thousand years plotting to get closer to the throne, they found my decision a little hard to believe.

So far no one had tried to kill me, or anyone close to me, but Doyle was the Queen's Darkness, and Frost was the Killing Frost. They had earned their names, and now that we were all in love and I was carrying their children, it would be a shame to let something go wrong. This was the end of our fairy tale, and maybe we had no enemies left, but old habits aren't always a bad thing. I felt safe with them, except that while I loved them more than life itself, if they died trying to protect me I'd never recover from it. There are all sorts of ways to die without dying.

When we were out of hearing of the human police, I told them all my fears about the killings.

"How do we find out if the lesser fey here are easier to kill?" Frost asked.

Doyle said, "In other days it would have been easy enough."

I stopped walking, which forced him to stop. "You'd just pick a few and see if you could slit their throats?"

"If my queen had asked it, yes," he said.

I started to pull away from him, but he held my arm in his. "You knew what I was before you took me to your bed, Meredith. It is a little late for shock and innocence."

"The queen would say, 'Where is my Darkness? Someone bring me my Darkness.' You would appear, or simply step closer to her, and then someone would bleed or die," I said.

"I was her weapon and her general. I did what I was bid."

I studied his face, and I knew it wasn't just the black wraparound sunglasses that kept me from reading him. He could hide everything behind his face. He had spent too many years beside a mad queen, where the wrong look at the wrong moment could get you sent to the Hallway of Mortality, the torture chamber. Torture could last a long time for the immortal, especially if you healed well.

"I was lesser fey once, Meredith," Frost said. He'd been Jack Frost, and, literally, human belief plus needing to be stronger to protect the woman he loved had turned him into the Killing Frost. But once he had been simply little Jackie Frost, just one minor being in the entourage of Winter's power. The woman he had changed himself completely for was centuries in her human grave, and now he loved me: the only non-aging, non-immortal sidhe royal ever. Poor Frost—he couldn't seem to love people who would outlive him.

"I know you were not always sidhe."

"But I remember when he was the Darkness to me, and I feared him as much as any. Now he is my truest friend and my captain, because that other Doyle was centuries before you were born."

I studied his face, and even around his sunglasses I saw the gentleness—a piece of softness that he'd only let me see in the last few weeks. I realized that just as he would have had Doyle's back in battle, he did the same now. He had distracted me from my anger, and put himself in the way of it, as if I were a blade to be avoided.

I held out a hand to him, and he took it. I stopped pulling against Doyle's arm, and just held them both. "You are right. You are both right. I knew Doyle's history before he came to my side. Let me try this again." I looked up at Doyle, still with Frost's hand in mine. "You aren't suggesting that we test our theory on random fey?"

"No, but in honesty I do not have another way to test."

I thought about it, and then shook my head. "Neither do I."

"Then what are we to do?" Frost asked.

"We warn the demi-fey, and then we go to the beach."

"I thought this would end our day out," Doyle said.

"When you can't do anything else, you go about your day. Besides, everyone is meeting us at the beach. We can talk about this problem there as well as at the house. Why not let some of us enjoy the sand and water while the rest of us debate immortality and murder?"

"Very practical," Doyle said.

I nodded. "We'll stop off at the Fael Tea Shop on the way to the beach."

"The Fael is not on the way to the beach," Doyle said.

"No, but if we leave word there about the demi-fey, the news will spread."

"We could leave word with Gilda, the Fairy Godmother," Frost said.

"No, she might keep the knowledge to herself so she can say later that I didn't warn the demi-fey because I thought I was too good to care."

"Do you truly think she hates you more than she loves her people?" Frost asked.

"She was the ruling power among the fey exiles in Los Angeles. The lesser fey went to her to settle disputes. Now they come to me."

"Not all of them," Frost said.

"No, but enough that she thinks I'm trying to take over her business."

"We want no part of her businesses, legal or illegal," Doyle said.

"She was human once, Doyle. It makes her insecure."

"Her power does not feel human," Frost said, and he shivered.

I studied his face. "You don't like her."

"Do you?"

I shook my head. "No."

"There is always something twisted inside the minds and bodies of humans who are given access to the wild magic of faerie," Doyle said.

"She got a wish granted," I said, "and she wished to be a fairy godmother, because she didn't understand that there is no such thing among us."

"She's made herself into a power to be reckoned with in this city," Doyle said.

"You've scouted her, haven't you?"

"She all but threatened you outright if you kept trying to steal her people away. I investigated a potential enemy's stronghold."

"And?" I asked.

"She should be frightened of us," he said, and his voice was that voice of before, when he'd been only a weapon and not a person to me.

"We stop by the Fael, and then we'll talk about what to do with the other godmother. If we tell her and she tells no one, then it is we who can say that she cares more about her jealousy of me than about her own people."

"Clever," Doyle said.

"Ruthless," Frost said.

"It would only be ruthless if I didn't warn the demi-fey some other way. I won't risk another life for some stupid power play."

"It is not stupid to her, Meredith," Doyle said. "It is all the power she has ever had, or will ever have. People will do very bad things to keep their perceived power intact."

"Is she dangerous to us?"

"In a full frontal assault, no, but if it is trickery and deceit, then she has fey who are loyal to her and hate the sidhe."

"Then we keep an eye on them."

"We are," he said.

"Are you spying on people without telling me?" I asked.

"Of course I am," he said.

"Shouldn't you run things like that by me first?"

"Why?"

I looked at Frost. "Can you explain to him why I should know these things?"

"I think he is treating you like most royals want to be treated," said Frost.

"What does that mean?" I asked.

"Plausible deniability is very important among monarchs," he said.

"You see Gilda as a fellow monarch?" I asked.

"She sees herself as such," Doyle said. "It is always better to let petty kings keep their crowns until we want the crown and the head it sits upon."

"This is the twenty-first century, Doyle. You can't run our life like it's the tenth century."

"I have been watching your news programs and reading books on governments that are present-day, Merry. Things have not changed so very much. It is just more secret now."

I wanted to ask him how he knew that. I wanted to ask him if he knew government secrets that would make me doubt my government, and my country. But in the end, I didn't ask. For one thing, I wasn't certain he'd tell me the truth if he thought it would upset me. And for another, one mass murder seemed like enough for one day. I had Frost call home and warn our own demi-fey to stay close to the house and to be wary of strangers, because the only thing I was sure of was that it wasn't one of us. Beyond that I had no ideas. I'd worry about spies and governments on another day, when the image of the winged dead weren't still dancing behind my eyes.

CHAPTER THREE

I DROVE TO THE FAEL TEA SHOP, AND DOYLE WAS RIGHT. IT WASN'T close to the beach, where everyone would be waiting. It was blocks away in a part of town that had once been a bad area but had been gentrified, which used to simply mean claimed by the yuppies, but had come to mean a place that the faeries had moved into and made more magical. It would then become a tourist stronghold, and a place for teens and college students to hang out. The young have always been drawn to the fey. It's why for centuries you put charms on your children to keep us from taking the best and brightest and the most creative. We like artists.

Doyle had his usual death grip on the door and the dashboard. He always rode that way in the front seat. Frost was less afraid of the car and L.A. traffic, but Doyle insisted that as captain he should be beside me. The fact that it was an act of bravery to him just made it cute, though I kept the cute comment to myself. I wasn't certain how he would take it.

He managed to say, "I do like this car better than the other one you drive. It's higher from the ground."

"It's an SUV," I said, "more a truck than a car." I was looking for a parking spot, and not having much luck. This was a section of town where people came to stroll on a lovely Saturday, and there were lots of people, which meant lots of cars. It was L.A. Everyone drove everywhere.

The SUV actually belonged to Maeve Reed, like so much of our stuff. Her chauffeur had offered to drive us around, but the moment the police called, the limo stayed at home. I had enough problems with the police not taking me seriously without showing up in a limo. I'd never live that down, and Lucy wouldn't live it down either, and that mattered more. It was her job. In a sense, the other police were right; I was just sightseeing.

I knew that part of the problem was the car itself, all that technology and metal. Except that I knew several lesser fey who owned cars and drove. Most of the sidhe had no trouble in the big modern skyscrapers, and they had plenty of metal and technology. Doyle was also afraid of airplanes. It was one of his few weaknesses.

Frost called out, "Parking spot." He pointed and I maneuvered the huge SUV toward it. I had to speed up and almost hit a smaller car that was trying to outmuscle me for the spot. It made Doyle swallow hard and let out a shaky breath. I wanted to ask him why riding in the back of the limo didn't bother him to this degree, but refrained. I wasn't sure if pointing out that he was only this afraid in the front seat of a car would make him more afraid in the limo. That we did not need.

I got the parking spot, though parallel parking the Escalade wasn't my favorite thing to do. Parking the Escalade was never easy, and parallel parking was like getting a master's degree in parking. Would that make parking a semi the doctoral test? I really never wanted to drive anything bulkier than this SUV, so I'd probably never find out.

I could see Fael's sign from the car, just a few storefronts down. We hadn't even had to go around the block once; perfect.

I waited for Doyle to make his shaky way out of the car, and for Frost to unbuckle and come around to my door. I knew better than to simply get out without one of them beside me. They had all made very certain that I understood that part of being a good bodyguard was to train your guardee how to be guarded. Their tall bodies blocked me at almost every turn when we were on the street. If there had been a credible threat I'd have had more guards. Two was minimum and precautionary. I liked precautionary—it meant no one was trying to kill me. The fact that it was a novelty that no one was trying said a lot about the last few years of my life. Maybe it wasn't the happily ever after the tabloids were painting, but it was definitely happier.

Frost helped me down from the SUV, which I needed. I always had a moment of feeling childlike when I had to climb in or out of the Escalade. It was like sitting in a chair where your feet swing. It made me feel like I was six again, but Frost's arm under mine, the height and solidness of him, reminded me that I was no longer a child, and decades from six.

Doyle's voice came. "Fear Dearg, what are you doing here?"

Frost stopped in mid-motion and put his body more solidly in front of me, shielding me, because Fear Dearg was not a name. The Fear Dearg were very old, the remnants of a faerie kingdom that had predated the Seelie and the Unseelie courts. That made the Fear Dearg more than three thousand years old, at minimum. Since they did not breed, for they had no females, they were all simply that old. They were somewhere between a brownie, a hobgoblin, and a nightmare—a nightmare that could make a man think that a stone was his wife, or that a cliff into the sea a path of safety. And some delighted in the kind of torture that would have pleased my aunt. I'd once seen her skin a sidhe noble until he was unrecognizable and then she made him follow her on a leash like a dog.

The Fear Dearg could be taller than an average human or they could be shorter than me by a foot, and almost any size in between. The only sameness from one to the other was that they were not humanly handsome and they wore red.

The voice that answered Doyle's question was high pitched though definitely male, but it was querulous with that tone that usually means great age in a human. I'd never heard that tone in the voice of a fey. "Why, I saved a parking spot for you, cousin."

"We are not kin, and how did you know to save a parking place for us?" Doyle asked, and there was now no hint of his weakness in the car in his deep voice.

He ignored the question. "Oh, come. I'm a shape-shifting, illusion-using goblin, and so was your father. Phouka is not so far from Fear Dearg."

"I am the Queen's Darkness, not some nameless Fear Dearg."

"Ah, and there's the rub," he said in his thin voice. "It's a name I'm wanting."

"What does that mean, Fear Dearg?" Doyle asked.

"It means I ha' a story to tell, and it would best be told inside the Fael, where your host and my boss awaits ye. Or would ye deny the hospitality of our establishment?"

"You work at the Fael?" Doyle asked.

"I do."

"What is your job there?"

"I am security."

"I didn't know the Fael needed extra security."

"Me boss felt the need. Now I will ask once more, will you refuse our hospitality? And think long on this one, cousin, for the old rules still apply to my kind. I have no choice."

That was a tricky question, because one of the things that some Fear Deargs were known for was appearing on a dark, wet night and asking to warm before the fire. Or the Fear Dearg could be the only shelter on a stormy night, and a human might wander in, attracted by their fire. If the Fear Dearg were refused or treated discourteously, they would use their glamour for ill. If treated well, they left you unharmed, and sometimes did chores around the house as a thank-you, or left the human with a gift of luck for a time, but usually the best you could hope for was to be left in peace.

But I could not hide behind Frost's broad body forever, and I was beginning to feel a little silly. I knew the reputation of the Fear Dearg, and I also knew that for some reason the other fey, especially the old ones, didn't care for them. I touched Frost's chest, but he wouldn't move until Doyle told him to, or I made a fuss. I didn't want to make a fuss in front of strangers. The fact that my guards sometimes listened more to each other than to me was still something we were working out.

"Doyle, he has done nothing but be courteous to us."

"I have seen what his kind does to mortals."

"Is it worse than what I've seen our kind do to each other?"

Frost actually looked down at me then, being alert for whatever threat might, or might not, be coming. The look even through his glasses said that I was oversharing in front of someone who was not a member of our court.

"We heard what the gold king did to you, Queen Meredith."

I took a deep breath and let it out slowly. The gold king was my maternal uncle Taranis, more a great-uncle, and king of the Seelie Court, the golden throng. He'd used magic as a date-rape drug, and I had evidence in a forensic storage unit somewhere that he had raped me. We were trying to get him tried among the humans for that rape. It was some of the worst publicity the Seelie court had ever had.

I tried to peer around Frost's body and see who I was talking to, but Doyle's body blocked me, too, so I talked to the empty air. "I am not queen."

"You are not queen of the Unseelie Court, but you are queen of the sluagh, and if I belong to any court left outside the Summerlands, it is King Sholto's sluagh."

Faerie, or the Goddess, or both, had crowned me twice that last night. The first crown had been with Sholto inside his faerie mound. I had been crowned with him as King and Queen of the Sluagh, the dark host, the nightmares of faerie so dark that even the Unseelie would not let them skulk about their own mound, but in a fight they were always the first called. The crown had vanished from me when the second crown, which would have made me high queen of all the Unseelie lands, had appeared on my head. Doyle would have been king to my queen there, and it was once traditional that all the kings of Ireland had married the same woman, the Goddess, who had once been a real queen whom each king "married," at least for a night. We had not always played by the traditional human rules of monogamy.

Sholto was one of the fathers of the children I carried, so the Goddess had shown all of us. So technically I was still his queen. Sholto had not pressed that idea in this month back home; he seemed to understand that I was struggling to find my footing in this new, more-permanent exile.

All I could think to say aloud was, "I didn't think the Fear Dearg owed allegiance to any court."

"Some of us fought with the sluagh in the last wars. It allowed us to bring death and pain without the rest of you good folk"—and he made sure the last phrase held bitterness and contempt in it—"hunting us down and passing sentence on us for doing what is in our nature. The sidhe of either court have no lawful call on the Fear Dearg, do they, kinsman?"

"I will not acknowledge kinship with you, Fear Dearg, but Meredith is right. You have acted with courtesy. I can do no less." It was interesting that Doyle had dropped the "Princess" he normally used in front of all lesser fey, but he had not used queen either, so he was interested in the Fear Dearg acknowledging me as queen, and that was very interesting to me.

"Good," the Fear Dearg said. "Then I will take you to Dobbin, ah, Robert, he now calls himself. Such richness to be able to name yerself twice. It's a waste when there are others nameless and left wanting."

"We will listen to your tale, Fear Dearg, but first we must talk to any demi-fey who are at the Fael," I said.

"Why?" he asked, and there was far too much curiosity in that one word. I remembered then that some Fear Dearg demand a story from their human hosts, and if the story isn't good enough, they torture and kill them, but if the story is good enough they leave them with a blessing. What would make a being thousands of years old care that much for stray stories, and what was his obsession with names?

"That is not your business, Fear Dearg," Doyle said.

"It's all right, Doyle. Everyone will know soon enough."

"No, Meredith, not here, not on the street." There was something in the way he said it that made me pause. But it was Frost's hand squeezing my arm, making me look at him, that made me realize that a Fear Dearg might be able to kill the demi-fey. He might be our killer, for the Fear Dearg walked outside many of the normal rules of our kind, for all this one's talk of belonging to the kingdom of the sluagh.

Was our mass murderer standing on the other side of my boyfriends? Wouldn't that have been convenient? I felt a flash of hope flare inside me, but let it die as quickly as it had risen. I'd worked murder cases before, and it was never that easy. Murderers did not meet you on the street just after you'd left the scene of their crime. But it would be nifty if just this once it really was that easy. Then I realized that Doyle had realized the possibility that the Fear Dearg might be our murderer the moment he saw him; that was why the extreme caution.

I felt suddenly slow, and not up to the job. I was supposed to be the detective, and Lucy had called me in because of my expertise on faeries. Some expert I turned out to be.

CHAPTER FOUR

THIS FEAR DEARG WAS SMALLER THAN I BUT ONLY BY A FEW INCHES. He was just under five feet. Once he'd have probably been average size for a human. His face was wizened, with grayish whiskers sticking out from his cheeks like fuzzy muttonchop sideburns. His nose was thin, long, and pointed. His eyes were large for his face and uptilted at the corners. They were black, and seemed to have no iris until you realized that, like Doyle's, his irises were simply as black as his pupils, so you had trouble seeing them.

He walked ahead of us up the sidewalk, with its happy couples walking hand in hand and its families all smiling, all laughing. The children stared openly at the Fear Dearg. The adults took quick looks at him, but it was us that they stared at. I realized that we looked like ourselves. I hadn't thought to use glamour to make us look human, or at least less noticeable. I had been too careless for words.

The parents did double takes, then smiled, and tried to make eye contact. If I did that, they might want to talk, and we really needed to warn the demi-fey. Normally I tried to be friendly, but not today.

Glamour was the ability to cloud the minds of others so that they saw what you wished them to see, not what was actually there. It had always been my strongest magic, until a few months ago. It was still the magic I was most familiar with, and it flowed easily across my skin now.

I spoke low to Doyle and Frost. "We're getting stared at, and the press isn't here to complain."

"I can hide."

"Not in this light you can't," I said. Doyle had this uncanny ability to hide like some kind of movie ninja. I'd known he was the Darkness, and you never see the dark before it gets you, but I hadn't realized that it was more than just centuries of practice. He could actually wrap shadows around himself and hide. But he couldn't hide us, and he needed something other than bright sunlight to wrap around himself.

I pictured my hair simply red, human auburn, but not the spun garnet of my true color. I made my skin the paleness to go with the hair, but not the near pearlescent white of my own skin. I spread the glamour out to flow over Frost's skin as we walked. His skin was the same moonlight white as my own, so it was easier to change his color at the same time. I darkened his hair to a rich gray and kept darkening it as we moved until it was a brunette shade that was black with gray undertones. It matched the white skin and made him look like he'd gone Goth. He was dressed wrong for it, but for some reason I found this color to be the easiest for me on him. I could have chosen almost any color if I had had enough time, but we were attracting attention, and I didn't want that today. Once too many people "saw" us as us, the glamour might break under their knowledge. So it was down and dirty, change as we walked, and a thought out to the people who had recognized us, so that they would do a double take and think they'd been mistaken.

The trick was to change hair and skin gradually, smoothly, and to make people not notice that you were doing it, so it was really two types of glamour in one. The first just simply an illusion of our appearance changing, and the second an Obi Wan moment where the people just didn't see what they thought they saw.

Changing Doyle's appearance was always harder for some reason. I wasn't sure why, but it took just a little more concentration to turn his black skin to a deep, rich brown, and the oh-so-dark hair to a brown that matched the skin. The best I could do quickly was to make him look vaguely Indian, as in American Indian. I left the graceful curves of his ears with their earrings, even though now that I'd changed his skin to a human shade, the pointed ears marked him as a faerie wannabe, no, a sidhe wannabe. They all seemed to think that the sidhe had pointy ears like something out of fiction, when in fact it marked Doyle as not pure-blooded, but part lesser fey. He almost never hid his ears, a defiant gesture, a finger in the eye of the court. The wannabes were also fond of calling the sidhe elves. I blamed Tolkien and his elves for that.

I'd toned us down, but we were still eye-catching, and the men were still exotic, but I would have had to stop moving and concentrate fully to change them more completely.

The Fear Dearg had enough glamour that he could have changed his appearance, too. He simply didn't care if they stared. But then a phone call to the right number wouldn't make the press descend on him until we had to call other bodyguards to get us to our car. That had happened twice since we came back to Los Angeles. I didn't want a repeat.

The Fear Dearg dropped back to talk to us. "I have never seen a sidhe able to use glamour so well."

"That's high praise coming from you," I said. "Your people are known for their ability at glamour."

"The lesser fey are all better at glamour than the bigger folk."

"I've seen sidhe make garbage look like a feast and have people eat it," I said.

Doyle said, "And the Fear Dearg need a leaf to create money, a cracker to be a cake, a log to be a purse of gold. You need something to pin the glamour to for it to work."

"So do I," I said. I thought about it. "So do the sidhe that I've seen able to do it."

"Oh, but once the sidhe could conjure castles out of thin air, and food to tempt any mortal that was mere air," the Fear Dearg said.

"I've not seen . . ." Then I stopped, because the sidhe didn't like admitting out loud that their magic was fading. It was considered rude, and if the Queen of Air and Darkness heard you, the punishment would be a slap, if you were lucky, and if you weren't, you'd bleed for reminding her that her kingdom was lessening.

The Fear Dearg gave a little skip, and Frost was forced a little back from my side, or he would have stepped on the smaller fey. Doyle growled at him, a deep rumbling bass that matched the huge black dog he could shift into. Frost stepped forward, forcing the Fear Dearg to step ahead or be stepped on.

"The sidhe have always been petty," he said, as if it didn't bother him at all, "but you were saying, my queen, that you'd never seen such glamour from the sidhe. Not in your lifetime, eh?"

The door of the Fael was in front of us now. It was all glass and wood, very quaint and old-fashioned, as if it were a store from decades before this one.

"I need to speak with one of the demi-fey," I said.

"About the murders, eh?" he asked.

We all stopped moving for a heartbeat, then I was suddenly behind the men and could only glimpse the edge of his red coat around their bodies.

"Oh, ho," the Fear Dearg said with a chuckle. "You think it's me. You think I slit their throats for them."

"We do now," Doyle said.

The Fear Dearg laughed, and it was the kind of laugh that if you heard it in the dark, you'd be afraid. It was the kind of laugh that enjoyed pain.

"You can talk to the demi-fey who fled here to tell the tale. She was full of all sorts of details. Hysterical she was, babbling about the dead being dressed like some child's story complete with picked flowers in their hands." He made a disgusted sound. "Every faery knows that no flower faery would ever pick a flower and kill it. They tend them."

I hadn't thought of that. He was absolutely right. It was a human mistake, just like the illustration in the first place. Some fey could keep a picked flower alive, but it was not a common talent. Most demi-fey didn't like bouquets of flowers. They smelled of death.

Whoever our killer was, they were human. I needed to tell Lucy. But I had another thought. I tried to push past Doyle, but it was like trying to move a small mountain; you could push, but you didn't make much progress. I spoke around him. "Did this demi-fey see the killings?"

"Nay"—and what I could see of the Fear Dearg's small wizened face seemed truly sad—"she went to tend the plants that are hers on the hillside and found the police already there."

"We still need to talk to her," I said.

He nodded the slip of his face that I could see between Doyle and Frost's bodies. "She's in the back with Dobbin having a spot of something to calm her nerves."

"How long has she been here?"

"Ask her yourself. You said you wanted to talk to a demi-fey, not her specifically. Why did you want one to speak with, my queen?"

"I wanted to warn the others that they might be in danger."

He turned so that one eye stared through the opening the men had left us. The black eye curled around the edges, and I realized he was grinning. "Since when did the sidhe give a rat's ass how many flower faeries were lost in L.A.? A dozen fade every year from too much metal and technology, but neither faerie court will let them back in even to save their lives." The grin faded as he finished, and left him angry.

I fought to keep the surprise off my face. If what he'd just said was true, I hadn't known it. "I care or I wouldn't be here."

He nodded, solemn. "I hope you care, Meredith, daughter of Essus, I hope you truly do."

Frost turned and Doyle was left to give the Fear Dearg his full attention. Frost was looking behind us, and I realized we had a little line forming.

"Do you mind?" a man asked.

"Sorry," I said, and smiled. "We were catching up with old friends."

He smiled before he could catch himself, and his voice was less irritated as he said, "Well, can you catch up inside?"

"Yes, of course," I said. Doyle opened the door, made the Fear Dearg go first, and in we went.

CHAPTER FIVE

THE FAEL WAS ALL POLISHED WOOD, LOVINGLY HAND CARVED. I knew that most of the interior woodwork had been recovered from an old West saloon/bar that was being demolished. The scent of some herbal and sweet musk polish blended with the rich aroma of tea, and overall was the scent of coffee, so rich you could taste it on your tongue. They must have just finished grinding some fresh for a customer, because Robert insisted that the coffee be tightly covered. He wanted to keep the freshness in, but it was more so that the coffee didn't overwhelm the gentler scent of his teas.

Every table was full, and there were people sitting at the curved edge of the bar, waiting for tables or taking their tea at the bar. There was almost an even number of humans to fey, but they were all lesser fey. If I dropped the glamour we would have been the only sidhe. There weren't that many sidhe in exile in Los Angeles, but the ones who were here saw the Fael as a hangout for the lesser beings. There were a couple of clubs far away from here that catered to the sidhe and the sidhe wannabes. Now that I'd lightened Doyle's skin, the ears marked him as a possible wannabe who'd gotten those pointy ear implants so he'd look like an "elf." There was actually another tall man sitting at a far table with his own implants. He'd even grown his blond hair long and straight. He was handsome, but there was a shape to his broad shoulders that said he hit the gym a lot, and just a roughness to him that marked him as human and not sidhe, like a sculpture that hadn't been smoothed quite enough.

The blond wannabe stared at us. Most of the patrons were looking, but then most looked away. The blond stared at us over the rim of his teacup, and I didn't like the level of attention. He was too human to see through the glamour, but I didn't like him. I wasn't sure why. It was almost as if I'd seen him somewhere before, or should know him. It was just a niggling sensation. I was probably just being jumpy. Murder scenes do that sometimes, make you see bad guys everywhere.

Doyle touched my arm. "What is wrong?" he whispered against my hair.

"Nothing. I just thought I recognized someone."

"The blond with the implants?" he asked.

"Hm-hm," I said, not moving my lips, because I really didn't like how he was staring at us.

"Good of you to join us this fine morning." It was a hale and hearty voice, one to greet you and make you happy that you'd come. Robert Thrasher, as in thrashing wheat, stood behind the counter polishing the wood with a clean white cloth. He was smiling at us, his nut-brown face handsome. He'd let modern surgery give him a nose, and make the cheekbones and chin graceful, though tiny. He was tall for a brownie, my own height, but he was still small of bone, and the doctor who had done his face had kept that in mind so that if you hadn't known that he'd begun life with only empty holes where the nose was, and a face closer to that of the Fear Dearg, you'd never have known that he hadn't been this delicate, handsome man all his life.

If anyone ever asked for a plastic surgeon recommendation, I'd send them to Robert's doctor.

He smiled, only his dark brown eyes showing the edge of his worry, but none of the customers would see it. "I've got your order in the back. Come back and have a cup before you approve it."

"Sounds good," I said, all happy to go with his tone. I'd lived in the Unseelie Court when the only magic I could do was glamour. I knew how to pretend to feel things that I wasn't feeling at all. It had made me good at undercover work for the Grey Detective Agency.

Robert handed the cloth to a young woman who looked like a pinup girl for *Goth Monthly*, from her black hair to her black velvet minidress, striped hose, and clunky retroish shoes. She sported a neck tattoo and a piercing through her dark lipsticked mouth.

"Mind the front for me, Alice."

"Will do," she said and smiled brightly at him. Ah, a perky Goth, not a gloomy one. Positive attitude makes better counter help.

The Fear Dearg stayed behind, twisting his face into a smile for the tall human girl. She smiled down at him, and there wasn't a shadow in her face that saw anything but attraction in the small fey.

Robert was moving and we were following, so I left off speculating on whether Alice and the Fear Dearg were a couple, or at least hooked up. He wouldn't have been my cup of tea, but then I knew what he was capable of; did she?

I shook my head and pushed it all away. Their love life was not my business. The office space was neat and modern but all warm earth tones, and had a wall of photographs from home so that all the staff, even those without a desk, could bring family photos in and see them during the day. Robert and his partner were pictured in tropical shirts in front of a beautiful sunset. Goth Alice had several pictures, each with a different friend; maybe she was just friendly. There was a partition, still in that warm shade between tan and brown, that separated the break area from the office space. We heard the voices before we could see around the partition. One was low and masculine, the other high-pitched and feminine.

Robert called out in a cheerful voice, "We have visitors, Bittersweet."

There was a little scream, and the sound of china breaking, and then we were around the corner of the partition. There was nice leather furniture with cushions, a large coffee table, some drink and snack machines almost hidden by an oriental screen, a man, and a small flying faery.

"You promised," she shrieked, and her voice was thin with anger so that there was an edge of buzz to it, as if she were the insect she resembled. "You promised you wouldn't tell!"

The man was standing, trying to comfort her as she hovered near the ceiling. Her wings were a blur, and I knew when she stopped moving that it wouldn't be butterfly wings on her back, but rather something faster, slimmer. Her wings caught the artificial light with little winks of rainbow color. Her dress was purple, only a little darker than my own. Her hair fell around her shoulders in white-blond waves. She would barely fill my hand, tiny even by demi-fey standards.

The man trying to calm her was Robert's partner, Eric, who was five foot eight, slender, neatly dressed, tanned, and handsome in a preppie sort of way. They'd been a couple for more than ten years. Before Eric, Robert's last love of his life had been a woman who he'd been faithful to until she died at eighty-something. I thought it was brave of Robert to love another human so soon.

Robert spoke sharply. "Bittersweet, we promised not to tell everyone, but you were the one who flew in here babbling hysterically. Did you think no one would talk? You're lucky that the princess and her men are here before the police."

She flew at him, tiny hands balled into tiny fists, and her eyes blazed with rage. She hit him. You would think that something smaller than a Barbie doll wouldn't pack much punch, but you'd be wrong.

She hit him, and I was behind him, so I felt the wave of energy that came before and around her fist like a small explosion. Robert was airborne, and pitched backward toward me. Only Doyle's speed put him between me and the falling man. Frost yanked me out of the way of both as they hit the floor.

Bittersweet turned on us, and I watched the ripple of power around her like heat on a summer's day. Her hair formed a pale halo around her face, raised by the wind of her own energy. It was the magic that kept a "human" that small alive without her having to eat multiple times her own body weight every day like a hummingbird or a shrew.

"Do not be rash," Frost said. His skin ran cold against mine as his magic woke in a skin-tingling winter's chill. The glamour that I'd used to hide us fell away, partly because to hold it with his magic coming was harder, and partly because I hoped it would help bring the small fey to her senses.

Her wings stopped, and I had a moment to see the crystal of dragonfly wings on her tiny body as she did the airborne equivalent of a human stumbling on uneven ground. It made her dip toward the ground before she caught herself and rose to eye level with both Frost and Doyle. She'd turned sideways so she could see both of them. Her energy quieted around her as she hovered.

She bobbed an awkward curtsey in the air. "If you hide yourself with glamour, Princess, then how's a fey to know how to act?"

I started to come around Frost's body, but he stopped me partway with his arm, so I had to speak from the shield of him. "Would you have harmed us if we had simply been humans who were part fey?"

"You looked like those pretend elves that the humans dress up as."

"You mean the wannabes," I said.

She nodded. Her blond curls had fallen around her tiny shoulders in beautiful ringlets, as if the power had curled her hair tighter.

"Why would human wannabes frighten you?" Doyle asked.

Her eyes flicked to him, and then back to me as if the very sight of him frightened her. Doyle had been the queen's assassin for centuries; the fact that he was with me now didn't take away his past.

She answered his question while looking at me. "I saw them coming down the hill from where my friends were . . ." Here she stopped, put her hands in front of her eyes, and began to weep.

"Bittersweet," I said, "I'm sorry for your loss, but are you saying you saw the killers?"

She just nodded without moving her hands from her face, and began to weep louder, an amazing amount of noise from a being so small. The weeping had an edge of hysteria to it, but I guess I couldn't blame her.

Robert moved around her to Eric, and they held hands as Eric asked Robert if he was hurt. Robert just shook his head.

"I have to make a call," I said.

Robert nodded, and something in his eyes let me know that he understood both who I was going to call and why I wasn't doing so in this room. The little fey didn't seem to want anyone to know what she'd seen, and I was about to call the police.

Robert let us go back into the storage room that was behind the offices, but not before he had the Fear Dearg come in and sit with Eric and the demi-fey. Extra security seemed like a really good idea.

Frost and Doyle started to come with me, but I said, "One of you stay with her."

Doyle ordered Frost to do so, while he stayed with me. Frost didn't argue; he'd had centuries of orders followed from the other sidhe. It was habit for most of the guards to do what Doyle said.

Doyle let the door close behind us as I dialed Lucy's cell phone. "Detective Tate."

"It's Merry."

"You think of something?"

"How about a witness who says she saw the killers?"

"Don't tease," she said.

"No tease, I plan to put out."

She almost laughed. "Where are you, and who is it? We can send a car down and pick them up."

"It's a demi-fey, and a tiny one. She probably can't ride in a car without being hurt by the metal and tech."

"Shit. Is she going to have problems just coming in the buildings at headquarters?"

"Probably."

"Double shit. Tell me where you are and we'll come to her. Do they have a room where we can question her?"

"Yes."

"Give me your address. We're on our way." I heard her moving through the grass fast enough that her slacks made that *whish-whish* sound.

I gave her the address.

"Sit tight. I'll have the closest uniforms come babysit, but they won't have magic, just guns."

"We'll wait."

"We'll be there in twenty if the traffic actually gets out of the way of the lights and sirens."

I smiled, even though she couldn't see it. "Then we'll see you in thirty. No one moves in traffic here."

"Hold the fort. We're on our way." I heard the wail of the sirens before the phone went dead.

"They're on their way. She wants us to stay here even after the closest uniforms arrive," I said.

"Because they do not have magic, and this killer does," Doyle said.

I nodded.

"I do not like that the detective asks you to put yourself in harm's way for her case."

"It's not for her case. It's to keep any more of our people from dying, Doyle."

He looked down at me, studying my face, as if he hadn't seen it before. "You would have stayed anyway."

"Until they kicked us out, yes."

"Why?" he asked.

"No one slaughters our people and gets away with it."

"When we know who did this thing, are you determined to see them stand trial in human court?"

"You mean, just send you out to take care of them the old-fashioned way?" It was my turn to study his face.

He nodded.

"I think we'll go with the court."

"Why?" he asked.

I didn't try to tell him that it was the right thing to do. He'd seen me kill people for revenge. It was a little too late to hide behind the sanctity of life now. "Because we're in permanent exile here in the human world and we need to adapt to their laws."

"It would be easier to kill them, and save the taxpayers' money."

I smiled, and shook my head. "Yes, it would be fiscally responsible, but I'm not the mayor, and I don't manage the budget."

"If you did, would we kill them?"

"No," I said.

"Because we are playing by human rules now," he said.

"Yes."

"We won't be able to play by human rules all the time, Merry."

"Probably not, but today we are, and we will."

"Is that an order, my princess?"

"If you need it to be," I said.

He thought about it, then nodded. "It will take some time to get used to this."

"What?"

"That I am no longer just a bringer of death, and that you are also interested in justice."

"The killer could still get off on some technicality," I said. "The law isn't really about justice here, it's about the letter of the law and who has the best lawyer."

"If the killer gets off on a technicality, then what would my orders be?"

"That's months or years down the road, Doyle. Justice moves slowly out here."

"The question stands, Meredith." He was studying my face again.

I met his eyes behind their dark glasses, and said the truth. "He, or they, either spend the rest of their lives in prison, or they die."

"By my hand?" he asked.

I shrugged, and looked away. "By someone's hand." I moved past him to touch the door. He grabbed my arm, and made me look back at him.

"Would you do it yourself?"

"My father taught me to never ask of anyone what I'm not willing to do myself."

"Your aunt, the Queen of Air and Darkness, is quite willing to get her own lily-white hands bloody."

"She's a sadist. I'd just kill them."

He raised my hands in his and kissed them both gently. "I would rather your hands hold more tender things than death. Let that be my task."

"Why?"

"I think if you drench yourself in blood it may change the children you carry."

"Do you believe that?" I asked.

He nodded. "Killing changes things."

"I'll do my best not to kill anyone while I'm still pregnant."

He kissed me on the forehead, and then leaned down to touch his lips to mine. "That is all I ask."

"You know that what happens to the mother while pregnant doesn't really affect the babies, right?"

"Humor me," he said, rising to his full height, but keeping my hands in his. I don't know if I would have told him he was being superstitious because a knock on the door interrupted us. Frost opened the door. He said, "Uniformed police are here."

Bittersweet began screaming again, "Police can't help! Police can't protect us from magic!"

Doyle and I sighed at the same time, glanced at each other, and smiled. His smile was a small one, just a bare lift of his lips, but we went through the door smiling. The smiles slipped and we hurried as Frost turned back and said, "Bittersweet, do not harm the officers."

We went to join him in trying to keep the tiny fey from throwing the big, bad policemen across the room.

CHAPTER SIX

IT WASN'T BIG, BAD POLICEMEN. IT WAS BIG, BAD POLICE OFFICERS, because one of the uniforms was a woman, and they were both perfectly nice, but Bittersweet would not be comforted.

The policewoman did not like the Fear Dearg. I suppose if you hadn't spent your life around beings who made him look like a GQ cover boy he might be worth a little fear. The problem really was that the Fear Dearg liked that she was afraid of him. He kept an eye on the hysterical Bittersweet, but he also managed to inch ever closer to the blonde woman in her pressed uniform. Her hair was back in a tight ponytail. Every bit of shiny on her was shined. Her partner was a little older, and a lot less spit and polish. I was betting she was new on the force. Rookies tended to take it all much more to heart at first.

Robert had asked Eric to man the front with Alice. I was also guessing that he had sent his human lover away from Bittersweet just in case she lost control of her power again. If she hit Eric the way she had hit Robert and Doyle, he might have been hurt. Better to surround hysterical fey with people who were tougher than pure human blood could make you.

Bittersweet was sitting on the coffee table crying softly. She'd exhausted herself with hysterics, the energy burst, and crying; all of it had taken its toll. It was actually possible for a really tiny fey to deplete their energy so badly that they could fade away. It was especially hazardous outside of faerie. The more metal and tech around a fey, the harder it could be on them. How had such a tiny thing come to Los Angeles? Why had she been exiled, or had she simply followed her wildflower across the country like the insect she resembled? Some flower faeries were very devoted to their plants, especially if they were species specific. They were like any fanatic: the narrower your focus, the more devoted you could be.

Robert had taken one of the overstuffed leather chairs and given us the couch. The couch was actually a nice intermediate size between my and Robert's height, and the average height of a human worker. Which meant it fit me well enough, but probably didn't fit Doyle or Frost quite right, but they weren't interested in sitting down, so it didn't matter.

Frost sat on the arm of the couch by me. Doyle stood near the "door" of the half-partitioned room and kept an eye on the outer door. Because my guards wouldn't sit down, the two uniforms didn't want to sit either. The older cop, Officer Wright, did not like my men. He was six feet and in good shape, from his short brown hair to his comfortable and well-chosen boots. He kept looking from Frost to Doyle to the little faery on the table, but mostly at Frost and Doyle. I was betting that Wright had learned a thing or two about physical potential in his years on the job. Anyone who could judge that never liked my men much. No policeman likes to think that they may not be the biggest dog in the room just in case a dogfight breaks out.

O'Brian, the female rookie, was five foot eight at least, which was tall to me, but not standing there with her partner and my guards. But I was betting that she was used to that on the force; what she wasn't used to was the Fear Dearg at her side. He'd worked himself within inches of her. He'd done nothing wrong, nothing she could complain about except invade her personal space, but I was betting that she'd taken to heart the lectures on human/fey relations. One of the cultural differences between us and most Americans was that we didn't have the personal-space boundaries that most did, so if Officer O'Brian complained, then she was being insensitive to our people with Princess Meredith sitting right there. I watched her try not to be nervous as the Fear Dearg moved just a fraction closer to her. I watched the thought in her blue eyes as she tried to work out the political implications of telling the Fear Dearg to back off.

There was a polite knock on the door, which meant it wasn't Lucy and her people. Most police have very authoritative knocks. Robert called, "Come in."

Alice pushed through the door with a small tray of pastries. "Here's something for you to munch on while I take your orders." She'd flashed a smile at everyone, showing dimples in the corners of her full red mouth. The red lipstick was the only deviation to her black-and-white outfit. Did her smile linger a little on the Fear Dearg? Did her eyes harden just a little at his closeness to O'Brian? Perhaps, or maybe I was looking for it.

She hesitated with the sweets as if unsure who to serve first. I helped her make the decision. "Is Bittersweet cool to the touch, Robert?"

Robert had moved over to sit with the demi-fey and she was still sobbing quietly on his shoulder, huddled against the smooth line of his neck. "Yes. She needs something sweet."

Alice gave me a thankful smile, then offered the tray first to her boss and the little fey. Robert took an iced cake and held it up toward the little fey. She seemed not to notice it.

"Is she hurt?" Officer Wright asked, and he was suddenly more alert, more something. I'd seen other police do that, and some of my guards. One minute they're just standing there, the next they are "on"; they are cop, or warrior. It's like some internal switch is hit and they are just suddenly more.

Officer O'Brian tried to follow suit, but she was too new. She didn't know how to turn on the hyperalert mode yet. She'd learn.

I felt Frost tense beside me on the couch arm. I knew that if Doyle had been on my other side, I'd have felt the same from him. They were all warriors, and it was hard for them not to react to the other man.

"Bittersweet has used up a lot of energy," I said, "and needs to refuel."

Alice was now offering the tray of sweets to Frost and me. I took the second frosted cake, which was somewhere between a cupcake and something smaller, but the frosting was white and frothy, and I was suddenly hungry. I'd noticed that since I got pregnant. I'd be fine, and then I'd suddenly be ravenous.

Frost shook his head. He was keeping his hands free. Was he hungry? How often had he and Doyle both stood at a banquet at the Queen's side and guarded her safety while the rest of us ate? Had that been hard for them? It had never occurred to me to ask, and I couldn't ask now in front of so many outsiders. I filed the thought away for later and began to eat my cake by licking off the frosting.

"She looks like she's had a hard day," Wright said.

I realized that they might not even know why they were here to guard Bittersweet. They might simply have been told that there was a witness to guard, or maybe even less. They'd been told to show up and keep an eye on her, and that's what they were doing.

"She has, but it's more than that. She needs fuel." I ran a finger through the icing and licked the tip of my finger. It was homemade-frosting sweet, but not too sweet.

"You mean eat?" O'Brian asked.

I nodded. "Yes, but it's more than that. We don't eat and we just get hungry, maybe a little sick. When you're warm-blooded, the smaller you are the harder it is to maintain your body temperature and your energy level. Shrews have to eat about five times their own body weight every day just to keep from starving to death."

I gave up with my finger and just licked the icing off the cake. Officer Wright glanced at me, then quickly away and ignored me. Neither officer took anything off the tray, wanting to keep their hands free, too, maybe, or were they told not to take food from the faeries?

That was only a rule if you were inside faerie and were human. But I didn't say anything, because if they were passing on the cakes because of fear of faery magic, it was an insult to Robert.

The Fear Dearg took a piece of carrot cake from the tray, smiling his wicked smile up at Alice. Then he stared at me. There was no glancing out of the corners of his eyes; he simply stared. Among the fey if you were trying to be sexy and someone didn't notice, it was an insult. Was I trying to be sexy? I hadn't meant to. I just wanted my icing first, and without silverware there were only so many options.

Robert was still holding the iced cake up to the small fey on his shoulder. "For me, Bittersweet, just a taste."

"You mean she could die just from not eating enough?" O'Brian asked.

"Not just from that. The hysteria and her use of magic all eat up some of the power that enables her to function at this size and still be a reasoning being."

"I'm just a cop, you need to uses smaller words, or more of them," Wright said. He looked at me as he said it, then quickly away. I was making him uncomfortable. Among the humans I was being rude. Among the fey, he was being rude.

Frost slid one arm around me, his fingers lingering on the bare skin of my shoulder. He was still watching the room, but his touch let me know that he'd noticed, and that he was thinking what it would mean to have me use the same skills on his body. Humans who try to play by these rules often get it wrong and are too sexual about it. It's polite to notice, not to grope.

I talked to the officers as Frost's fingers traced my shoulder in delicate circles. Doyle was at a disadvantage. He was too far away to touch me, but he needed to keep his attention on the far door, so how could he acknowledge my behavior and not be a bad guard? I realized that this was the dilemma that the queen had put him in for centuries. He'd shown nothing to her; the cold, unmovable Darkness. I left the icing to itself while I talked to the police and thought about that.

"It takes energy to use a complicated brain. It takes energy to be bipedal, and to do all the things we do at our size. Now shrink us down and it takes magic to make fey like Bittersweet able to exist."

"You mean without magic she couldn't survive?" O'Brian asked.

"I mean she has a magical aura, for lack of a better term, that encircles her and keeps her working. She is by all laws of physics and biology impossible; only magic sustains the smallest of us."

Both officers were looking at the little faery as she scooped icing off the cake and ate it as delicately as a cat with cream on its paw.

Alice said, "I've never heard it explained that clearly before." She gave a nod to Robert. "Sorry, boss man, but it's the truth."

Robert said, "No, you're right." He looked at me, and it was a more intent look than before. "I forgot that you were educated at human schools. You have a bachelor of science in biology, correct?"

I nodded.

"It makes you uniquely able to explain our world to their world."

I thought about shrugging but just said, "I've been explaining my world to their world since I was six and my father took me out of faerie to be educated in public school."

"Those of us who were exiled when that happened always wondered why Prince Essus did it."

I smiled. "I'm sure there were plenty of rumors."

"Yes, but not the truth, I think."

I did shrug then. My father had taken me into exile because his sister, my aunt, the Queen of Air and Darkness, had tried to drown me. If I'd been truly sidhe and immortal, I couldn't have died by drowning. The fact that my father had to save me meant that I wasn't immortal, and to my aunt Andais that meant that I was no different than if someone's purebred dog had accidentally gotten pregnant by the neighbors' mongrel. If I could be drowned, then I should be.

My father had taken me and his household into exile to keep me safe. To the human media he did it so I would know my country of birth, and not just be a creature of faerie. It was some of the most positive publicity the Unseelie Court had ever gotten.

Robert was watching me. I went back to my icing, because I did not dare share the truth with anyone outside the court. Family secrets are something the sidhe, both flavors, take seriously.

Alice had set the tray on the coffee table and was taking orders, starting at the opposite side of the room with Doyle. He ordered an exotic coffee that he'd ordered the first time we'd come here, and that he liked to have at the house. It wasn't a coffee that I'd ever seen in faerie, which meant that he'd been outside enough to grow fond of it. He was also the only sidhe I'd ever seen with a nipple piercing to go with all his earrings. Again, it spoke of time outside faerie, but when? In my lifetime he hadn't been that far from the queen's side for any length of time that I remembered.

I loved him dearly, but it was one of those moments when I realized, again, that I honestly didn't know that much about him, not really.

The Fear Dearg ordered one of those coffee drinks that has so much in it that it's more milk shake than coffee. The officers passed, and then it was my turn. I wanted Earl Grey tea, but the doctor had made me give up caffeine for the duration of the pregnancy. Earl Grey without caffeine seemed wrong, so I ordered green tea with jasmine. Frost ordered straight Assam, but took cream and sugar with it. He liked black teas brewed strong, then made sweet and pale.

Robert ordered cream tea for himself and Bittersweet. It would come with real scones, clotted cream thick as butter, and fresh strawberry jam. They were famous for their cream teas at the Fael.

I almost ordered one, but scones don't go well with green tea. It just wasn't the same, and I suddenly didn't want anything else sweet. Protein sounded good. Was I starting to get cravings? I leaned to the table and laid the half-eaten cake on a napkin. The icing was totally unappealing now.

Robert said, "Go back to the officers, Alice. They need at least coffee."

Wright said, "We're on duty."

"So are we," Doyle said in that deep, thicker-than-molasses voice.

"Are you implying that we hold our duty less dear than you hold yours, Officer Wright?"

They ordered coffee. O'Brian went first and ordered black, but Wright ordered frozen coffee with cream and chocolate—a coffee shake even sweeter than the Fear Dearg had ordered. O'Brian did that quick look at Wright, and the look was enough. If she'd known he was going to order something so girlie, she'd have ordered something besides black coffee. I watched the thought go over her face; could she change her order?

"Officer O'Brian, would you like to change your order?" I asked. I wiped my fingers on another napkin. I suddenly didn't even want the sticky residue of the icing.

She said, "I . . . no, thank you, Princess Meredith."

Wright made a sound in his throat. She looked at him, confused. "You don't say that to the fey."

"Say what?" she asked.

"Thank you," I said. "Some of the older fey take thanks as a grave insult."

She blushed through her tan. "I'm sorry," she said, then she stopped in confusion and looked at Wright.

"It's okay," I said. "I'm not old enough to see 'thank you' as an insult, but it is a good general rule when dealing with us."

"I am old enough," Robert said, "but I've been running this place too long to be insulted about much of anything." He smiled, and it was a good smile, all white, perfect teeth and handsome face. I wondered how much all the work had cost. My grandmother had been half brownie, so I knew just how much he'd had changed.

Alice went to get our orders. The door shut behind her, and then there was a very firm, loud knock. It made Bittersweet jump and touch Robert's shirt with her icing-covered hands. Now *that* was the police. Lucy came through the door without waiting for an invitation.

CHAPTER SEVEN

"THEY RAN DOWN THE HILL," BITTERSWEET SAID IN A HIGH, ALMOST musical voice, but it was music that was off-key today. It was her stress showing through even as she tried to answer questions.

She was hiding between Robert's collar and his neck, peeking at the two plainclothes detectives like a scared toddler. Maybe she was that frightened, or maybe she was playing to her size. Most humans treat the demi-fey like children, and the tinier they are, the more childlike humans view them. I knew better.

The two uniforms, Wright and O'Brian, had taken up posts by the far door, where the detectives had told them to stand. The Fear Dearg had gone back into the outer room to help in the shop, though I had given a thought to how much help he would be with customers. He seemed more likely to frighten than to take orders.

"How many ran down the hill?" Lucy asked in a patient voice. Her partner had his notebook out writing things down. Lucy had once explained to me that some people got nervous watching their words being written down. It could help you intimidate suspects, but it could also intimidate witnesses when that was the last thing you wanted. The compromise was that Lucy let her partner write down when she interrogated. She did the same for him on occasion.

"Four, five. I'm not sure." She hid her face against Robert's neck. Her thin shoulders began to shake, and we realized she was crying again.

All we'd learned so far was that they'd been male elf wannabes complete with long hair and ear implants. There were anywhere between four and six of them, though there could have been more. Bittersweet was only certain of four, or more. She was very fuzzy on time, because most fey, especially ones who still do their original nature-oriented jobs, use light, not clocks, to judge time.

Robert got the demi-fey to eat a little more cake. We'd already explained to the detectives why the sweets were important. Oh, and why were we still here? When we'd gotten up to leave, Bittersweet had gotten hysterical again. She seemed convinced that without the princess and royal guards to make the human police behave, they would drag her off to the police station and all that metal and technology, and they would kill her by accident.

I'd tried to vouch for Lucy being one of the good guys, but Bittersweet had lost someone she loved to just such an accident decades ago when she and he first came out to Los Angeles. I guess if I'd lost one of my loves to police carelessness, I might have trouble trusting too.

Lucy tried again, "Can you describe the wannabes who ran down the hill?"

Bittersweet peeked out with frosting smeared on her tiny mouth. It was very innocent, very victim-looking, yet I knew that most demi-fey would take fresh blood over sweets.

"Everyone is tall to me, so they were tall," she said in that little piping voice. It was not the voice that had screamed at us. She was playing the humans. It might be suspicious, or it might simply be habit, camouflage so the big people didn't hurt her.

"What color was their hair?" Lucy asked.

"One was black as night, one was yellow like maple leaves before they fall, one was paler yellow like roses when they fade from the sun, one had hair like leaves when they've fallen and lost all color save brown, though it's the brown after a rain."

We all waited, but she went back to the cake that Robert held up for her.

"What were they wearing, Bittersweet?"

"Plastic," she said, at last.

"What do you mean, 'plastic'?" Lucy asked.

"Clear plastic like you wrap leftover food in."

"You mean they wore plastic wrap?"

She shook her head. "They had plastic over their hair and clothes, and their hands."

I watched Lucy and her partner both fight not to give away the fact that the news excited them. This bit of description must help explain something at the crime scene, which gave credence to Bittersweet's statement. "What color was the plastic?"

I sipped my tea and tried not to draw attention to myself. Frost, Doyle, and I were here because Bittersweet trusted us to keep her out of the clutches of the human police. She trusted as most of the lesser fey did that the nobles of her court would be noble. We would try. Lucy had insisted that Doyle sit on the couch with me rather than looming over them. So I sat on the couch between the two of them. Frost had even moved from the couch arm to the actual couch, so he wouldn't loom either.

"It had no color," Bittersweet said, and whispered something in Robert's ear. He reached carefully to bring the china teacup up so she could drink from it. It was large enough for her to bathe in.

"Do you mean," asked Lucy, "that it was colorless?"

"That is what I said," and she sounded a little more irritated. Was it glamour, which the demi-fey were very, very good at, that gave an edge of bee buzzing to her words?

"So you could see their clothes underneath the plastic?"

She seemed to think about that, then nodded.

"Can you describe the clothes?"

"Clothes, they were clothes, squished behind the plastic." She rose suddenly upward, her clear dragonfly wings buzzing around her like a moving rainbow halo. "They are big people. They are humans. They all look alike to me." The high angry buzzing was louder, like an undercurrent to her words.

Lucy's partner said, "Does anyone else hear bees?"

Robert stood, raising his hand toward the hovering fey like you would to encourage a bird to land on your hand. "Bittersweet, they want to help find the men who did this terrible thing. They are here to help you."

The sound of angry bees rose high and higher, loud and louder. If I'd been outside, I'd have been running. The tension level in the room had gone way up. Even Frost and Doyle were tense beside me, though we all knew it was a sound illusion that would keep curious big people from coming too close to the small fey, or her plants. It was a noise designed to make you nervous, to make you want to be elsewhere. That was the point of it.

There was another loud knock on the door. Lucy said, "Not now." She kept her eyes on the hovering demi-fey. She wasn't treating Bittersweet like a child now. Lucy was like anyone who had been on the job long enough; they get a sense for danger. All the best cops I know listen to that crawling sensation on the back of their necks. It's how they stay alive.

Robert tried again, "Bittersweet, please, we are here to help you."

Wright opened the door enough to relay Lucy's message. There was urgent whispering back and forth.

Doyle's leg was tensed under my hand, ready to spring him forward. The line of Frost's body had a slight tremor up its entire length where it touched mine like an eager horse. They were right. If Bittersweet used the same power on the detectives that had knocked Doyle and Robert down, they could be badly hurt.

For the first time I wondered if Bittersweet was more than just scared. Once was lashing out in hysteria, but twice? I wondered, was she crazy? It happened to the fey just like humans. Some fey went a little mad in exile from faerie. Had our star witness hallucinated the killers? Was this all for nothing?

Robert moved forward, his hand still upraised. "Bittersweet, my sweet, please. There's more cake, and I'll send for fresh tea."

The angry buzz of bees grew louder. The tension in the room rose on the strength of the sound like a musical note drawn out too long so you almost wanted it to change at any cost rather than simply continuing.

She turned in midair, her wings making a silver and rainbow blur around her body. Tiny as she was, all I could think was that she hovered like one of those fighter planes. The analogy should have been ridiculous for someone four inches tall, but malice rolled off of her in waves.

"I am not some foolish brownie to be calmed by sweets and tea," she said.

Robert lowered his arm, slowly, because the insult was a true one. Brownies had often taken their payment in sweets and tea, or good liquor in the olden days.

There was some kind of commotion outside the door, raised voices, as if a crowd was trying to get past the policemen whom I knew had to be on the other side. Bittersweet did another of those precise, almost mechanical turns, this time toward the door and the noise. "The killers are here. I won't let them take my magic and destroy me." If someone forced the door now she would hurt them, or at least hurt Wright and O'Brian, who were on our side of the door.

I did the only thing I could think of. I spoke. "You asked for my help, Bittersweet."

The malignant hovering doll turned toward me. Doyle moved slightly forward on the couch, minutely, so that if she had another burst of power he could shield me. Frost's body was so tense beside me it felt like his muscles should ache with it. I fought not to tense, to be calm, and to send calm out to Bittersweet. She was a buzzing, rage-filled thing, and I wondered again if she was mad.

"You begged me to stay here and keep you safe. I stayed, and I have made certain that the police did not take you somewhere with more metal and technology."

She dipped toward the ground, and then hovered again, but not as high, and not as precise. I knew enough of winged beings to know that that was puzzlement, a hesitation. The sound of bees began to fade.

She scrunched her tiny face up and said, "You stayed because I was afraid. You stayed because I asked."

"Yes," I said, "that's exactly right, Bittersweet."

The voices outside grew louder, more strident. "It's too late, Queen Meredith. They've come." Bittersweet turned toward the door. "They've come to get me." Her voice sounded distant, and not right. Danu save us, she was mad. The question was, had the madness come before or after she saw her friends dead? The sound of bees began to grow louder again, and there was the smell of summer and sun beating down on the grass.

"They aren't coming to get you, Bittersweet," I said, and I sent calming thoughts to her. I wished we'd had Galen or Abeloec with us; they could both project positive emotions. Abe could make warriors stop in the middle of the battle and have a drink together. Galen just made everyone happy to be around him. None of the three of us sitting here could do any of that. We could kill Bittersweet to save the humans from harm, but could we stop her short of that?

"Bittersweet, you called me your queen. As your queen I command you not to harm anyone in this place."

She looked back over her shoulder at me and her almond-shaped eyes glinted blue with her magic. "I'm not Bittersweet anymore. I'm just Bitter, and we have no queen," she said. She began to fly toward the door.

O'Brian said, "Detectives?"

We all stood and began to move carefully after the demi-fey. Lucy came close to me and whispered, "What kind of damage can she really do?"

"Enough to blast the door off its hinges," I said.

"With my people between her and the door," Lucy said.

"Yes," I said.

"Well, shit."

I agreed.

CHAPTER EIGHT

A VOICE CAME THROUGH THE DOOR, HIGH AND MUSICAL; JUST HEARING it made me start to smile. "Bittersweet, my child, do not fear. Your fairy godmother is here."

Bittersweet dipped toward the floor again. "Gilda," she said in an uncertain voice. The bee sounds were fading along with the scent of summer-browned grass.

"Yes, dearie, it's Gilda. Calm down in there and the nice policeman will let me through."

Bittersweet floated to the floor in front of the surprised Wright and O'Brian. The little fey laughed and the two officers laughed with her. The demi-fey were our smallest people, but some of them had glamour to rival the sidhe, though most of my people would never admit it.

I found myself wanting to help Gilda get through that door. I glanced at the detectives to see the glamour working on them, but it wasn't. They just looked puzzled, as if they heard a song but it was too distant to understand the words. I could hear the song too, something like a music box, or the tinkling of chimes, or bells, or . . . I shielded harder, a flexing of the mind and will, and the song was pushed away. I didn't want to smile like a fool or help Gilda get through that door.

Bittersweet laughed again and Lucy's partner did too, nervously, as if he knew he shouldn't. Lucy said, "Did you leave your anti-charm at home again?"

He shrugged.

She reached into her pocket and handed him a small cloth bag. "I brought extra today." She flicked her eyes at me as if wondering if I'd take offense.

"Sometimes even I wear protection," I said. I didn't add out loud, "but usually only around my own relatives."

Lucy gave me a quick smile of thanks.

I whispered to Doyle and Frost, "Do you feel Gilda's persuasion?"

"Yes," Frost said.

"It's aimed at fey only," Doyle said, "but she has not the precision to aim only at Bittersweet."

I glanced behind me at Robert. He seemed fine, but he came closer to us at my glance. "You know brownies are solitary faeries, Princess. We're not so easily taken by such things."

I nodded. I did know that, but somehow the plastic surgery made me think of Robert as less than pure brownie.

"But just because I can fight it off doesn't mean I don't feel it," he said, and shivered. "She's an abomination, but she's got juice."

I was a little startled at his using the word "abomination." It was reserved for humans who had fallen afoul of wild magic and been changed to something monstrous. I'd met Gilda, and "monstrous" wasn't a word I would have used to describe her. But I'd only met her once, briefly, in the days when everyone in L.A. thought I was just another human with a lot of fey blood in my family tree somewhere. I wasn't important enough or a big enough toadie for her to be interested in me then.

The detectives moved out of the little partitioned area. Robert motioned for us to go first. I gave him a look, and he whispered, "She will make this about queens. I want it clear which queen I would choose."

I whispered back, "I am not queen."

"I know you and tall, dark, and handsome gave it all up for love." He grinned and there was something of the old brownie in that grin;

it needed less-than-perfect teeth and a less-than-perfect face, but it was still a leer.

It made me smile back.

"I've got it on good authority that Goddess herself came down and crowned you both."

"Exaggerations," I said. "The power of faerie and Goddess, but there was no physical materialization of Deity."

He waved it away. "You're splitting hairs, Merry, if it's still all right to call you that, or do you prefer Meredith?"

"Merry is fine."

He grinned up at my two men, who were intent on the far door and its opening. "The last time I saw these two they were the queen's guard dogs." He looked at me with those shrewd brown eyes. "Some men are drawn to power, Merry, and some women are more queen without a crown than others are with one."

As if on cue the door opened and Gilda, Fairy Godmother of Los Angeles, swept into the room.

CHAPTER NINE

GILDA WAS A VISION OF LIGHT, LACE, AND SPARKLES. HER FLOOR-length dress seemed to have been scattered with diamonds that caught the light so that she moved in a circle of bright white sparkles. The dress itself was pale blue, but the diamond flashes were so numerous they almost made an overdress that covered the pale blue lace, so the illusion was that there was a dress made of light and movement over the actual dress. It seemed a little flashy to me, but it matched the rest of her, from her crystal-and-glass crown towering over her blond ringlets to the two-foot-long wand complete with a starred tip.

She was like a magical version of a movie fairy godmother, but then she'd been a wardrobe mistress in the movies in the 1940s, so when the wild magic found her and offered her a wish, clothes were important to her. No one knew the truth about how she'd been offered the magic. She'd told more than one version over the years. Every version made her look more heroic. The last story was something about rescuing children from a burning car, I think.

She waved the wand around the room like a queen waving her scepter at her subjects. But there was a prickling of power as the wand moved past us. Whatever else was illusion about Gilda, the wand was real. It was faerie workmanship, but beyond that no one had been able to say what the wand was, and where it had come from. Magic wands were very rare among us, because we didn't need them.

When Gilda had made her wish, she hadn't realized that almost everything she wanted marked her as fake. Her magic was real enough, but the way she did it, everything about her was more fairy tale than faery.

"Come here, little one," she said, and just like that Bittersweet flew to her. Whatever sort of compulsion spell she had in her voice, it was strong. Bittersweet nestled into those golden ringlets, lost in the dazzle of light. Gilda turned as if to leave the room.

Lucy called, "Excuse me, Gilda, but you can't take our witness just yet."

"I am her queen. I have to protect her."

"Protect her from what?" Lucy asked.

The light show made Gilda's face hard to read. I thought she looked annoyed. Her perfectly bowed mouth made an unhappy moue. Her perfectly blue eyes narrowed a little around her long diamond-sparkled lashes. When I'd last seen her, she'd been covered in gold dust, from her eyelashes to a more formfitting formal dress. Gilda was always gilded, but it changed substance with her clothes.

"Police harassment," she said. Again she turned as if to leave.

"We aren't done with our witness," Lucy said.

Robert said, "You seem in a hurry to leave, Godmother, almost as if you don't want Bittersweet to speak with the police."

She turned back then, and even through all the silly lights and sparkles she was angry. "You have never had a civil tongue in your head, brownie."

"You liked my tongue well enough once, Gilda," he said.

She blushed in that way that some blonds and redheads do, all the way into her hairline. "The police wouldn't let me bring all my people inside here. If Oberon were here you wouldn't dare say such things."

Frost said, "Oberon? Who's Oberon?"

She frowned at him. "He is my king, my consort." Her eyes narrowed again, but more like she was squinting. I wondered if the diamond lights were bright enough to affect her vision. She was acting as if they were.

Her face softened suddenly. "The Killing Frost. I had heard you were in L.A. I've been waiting for you to visit me." Her voice was suddenly sweet and teasing. There was some power to her voice, but it washed over me like the sea on a stone. I didn't think it was my improved shields. I think this compulsion spell was simply not meant for me.

She turned and said, "Darkness, the Queen's Darkness, now exiled to our fair land. I'd hoped that you would both pay court to me. It has been so long since I've seen anyone from faerie. I would dearly love it if you would visit me."

"Your magic will not work on us," Doyle said in his deep voice.

A little shiver ran down her, making the top of her crown shake, the blue lace quiver, and the diamonds send little rainbows around the room. "Come over here and bring that big, deep voice with you."

Frost said, "She's insulting you."

"More than us," Doyle said.

I took in a lot of air, let it out slowly, and moved forward past the police. My men moved with me, and I felt that Gilda genuinely thought her spell was working. Now that we'd seen what she did to Bittersweet, and what she had tried to do to my men, we were going to have to take a harder look at how she got the other lesser fey to obey her. If it was all magic and compulsion and no free will, then that was bad.

"Both of you coming to me, how marvelous," she said.

"Am I missing something?" Lucy asked as I passed her.

I whispered, "A pissing contest of sorts."

Gilda couldn't keep acting as if she didn't see me. She kept smiling past me at Doyle and Frost, as if pretending still that they were coming closer for her. She actually held out her hand at a higher angle than I would need, as if she'd just bypass me.

"Gilda, Godmother of Los Angeles, greetings," I said, voice low but clear.

She made a little *humph* sound, then looked at me, lowering her hand as she did so. "Merry Gentry. Back in town, I see."

"All the royal of faerie know that if another royal gives you your title, you must give them back their own, or it's an insult that can only be settled by a duel." That was half true—there were other options—but a duel was at the end of all the other options. But Gilda wouldn't know that.

"Duels are illegal," she said primly.

"As are compulsion spells that steal the free will of any legal citizen of these United States."

She blinked at me, frowning. Bittersweet cuddled against Gilda's curls with a face gone half sleepy, as if touching Gilda made the godmother's spell even stronger. "I don't know what you're talking about."

"Yes, you do," I said, and I leaned closer, so that the light around her dress reflected in my tricolor eyes and moonlight skin. "I don't remember you being this powerful last time we met, Gilda. What have you been doing to gain such power?"

I was close enough to see the flash of fear in her perfect blue eyes. She masked it, but it had been there. What had she been doing that she didn't want anyone to know about? I had the thought that maybe she really didn't want Bittersweet to talk to the police. Maybe Gilda knew more about the murders than she wanted to let on. There were spells—evil spells, forbidden spells—that allowed a fey to steal power from those less powerful. I'd even seen a human wizard who had perfected it so that he could steal power from other humans who had only the faintest trace of faerie blood. He'd died trying to rape me. No, I didn't kill him. The sidhe traitor who had given the human the power killed him before we could use him to trace the power back to its master. The traitor was dead now, too, so it had all evened out.

Then I realized why I'd noticed the blond wannabe in the café. We'd killed the main wizard of that ring of magic thiefs and rapists, but we hadn't caught all of them. One of them had been described to me as an uncircumcised wannabe with long blond hair named Donald. It would be a huge coincidence, but I'd seen bigger coincidences in real life. Was stealing magic slowly over months that much of a step up to stealing the demi-fey's magic all at once? It was only magic that kept the smallest of us alive outside of faerie.

Something must have shown on my face, because Gilda asked, "What's wrong with you? Why are you looking at me like that?"

"Do you know an elf wannabe named Donald?"

"I would never consort with the false elves. They are an abomination."

I thought her choice of words was interesting. "Do you have a sidhe lover?"

"That is none of your business."

I studied her offended face. Would she not know the difference between a really well-done wannabe and the real thing? I doubted that she'd ever been with a true sidhe of the courts, and if you've never had the real thing you might have trouble spotting a fake.

I smiled, and said, "Hold that thought." I started for the door behind her. Doyle and Frost followed like shadows. Lucy called after me, "Merry, where are you going?"

"Need to check something in the café," I called back but kept moving. The room was thick with people, police of different flavors, and the court retinue that followed Gilda everywhere, but that the police hadn't allowed into the back room. They were a pretty lot, almost as shiny and spectacular as their mistress. There were still customers at the tables, a mix of human and fey. Some had stayed to have tea and cakes, but others were just there to gawk.

I pushed my way through the crowd, until Doyle moved a little forward of me and people just seemed to move out of his way. When he wanted to he could be very intimidating. I'd seen men step out of his way without even knowing why they'd done so. But when Doyle got me through the crowd, the table that had held the blond wannabe was empty.

CHAPTER TEN

I WENT TO ALICE, WHO WAS BEHIND THE COUNTER, AND ASKED, "The man with long blond hair, ear implants, and muscles at that table—when did he leave?"

"He left with most of the customers when the police came in," she said, and her gaze was serious and intelligent.

"Do you know his name?"

"Donal," she said.

"Donald?" I made it a question.

She shook her head. "No, he's very insistent about it being Donal, not after that stupid duck. His quote, not mine. I love classic Disney."

The comment made me smile, but I let it go, and asked the next question. "Is he a regular?"

She nodded, making her black pigtails bounce. "Yep, he comes in at least once a week, sometimes twice."

"What's he like?"

She narrowed her eyes and gave me a look. "Why do you want to know?"

"Humor me," I said.

"Well, he's one of those men who are rude until he wants to charm a woman; then he's sweet."

"Has he hit on you?"

"Nope, I'm too human. He only dates fey. He's very insistent on that."

"Is he fond of any particular kind of fey?"

Again, she gave me that look. "Just as full-blooded as he can get them. He's dated a lot of different fey."

"Can you give me some names?"

Lucy's voice came from behind me, "And why do you want the names, Merry?"

Frost and Doyle parted so I could see the detective. She was giving me a look that made Alice's suspicious look pale in comparison, but then Lucy was a cop. They give great suspicious looks.

She spoke more quietly. "What's up, Merry? What do you think you've figured out?"

The attempted rape and the perpetrator's death were public record, so I told her my suspicions.

"Do you really think this Donal is the Donald that the client told you about?" she asked.

"I'd love to get a picture of him and see if they could pick him out. It would be easy to hear Donal and just put the 'd' on the end to make it a more familiar name, especially if you were scared."

Lucy nodded. "Fair enough. I'll see about getting someone to snap a picture, discreetly."

"Grey's would be happy to help."

She shook her finger at me. "No, you are not involved in this from now on. If these are the same people, you almost got killed the last time you came up against them." She looked up at Frost and Doyle. "Come on, big guys, back me up on this."

"I would love to tell her to stay away from such dangerous people," Doyle said, "but she's made it clear that her job as a detective requires risk. If we do not like that, then we can send other guards with her and we can stay home."

Lucy raised her eyebrows at them. Frost nodded and said, "We had this talk again before we went to the murder scene this morning."

"The only card, as you would say, that we have to play is potential harm to the babes she carries, and even that must be a card carefully played," Doyle said. His lips gave that bare movement of a smile, as if he were both amused and not amused by it all.

"Yeah, that's what I've learned. She looks all soft and feminine, but push her and it's like trying to shove through a brick wall. It doesn't move, and neither does she," Lucy said.

"You do know our princess," Doyle said, and his words were so dry that it took me a moment to hear the humor in them.

Lucy nodded, then looked at me. "We'll get names of who this guy dated. We'll do some district checking. We'll get the picture and hunt up your old client. And by 'we' I mean the police, not you or anyone else from your agency or your entourage." She pointed her finger at me as if I were a stubborn child.

"You've used me on decoy assignments where the danger was a lot more real than checking a few facts," I said.

"I didn't know you were Princess Meredith back then, and you weren't pregnant." She held up a hand before I could do more than take a breath to protest. "First, before I could even bring you to see today's crime scene, I got warnings from my upper brass that I was, under no circumstances, to endanger you. That if anything happened to you because of involvement in a case of mine, it was my ass on the chopping block."

I sighed. "I'm sorry, Lucy."

She waved it away. "But more important to me, I've known you for about four years, and this is the happiest I've ever seen you. I don't want you to fuck that up because you're helping me on a case. You're not a cop. You don't have to put everything on the line for a case. That's my job."

"But this person is killing my people . . ."

A shrill voice came. "They are not your people! They are mine! They've been mine for sixty years!" She was screaming the last at me as she pushed her way closer.

Lucy must have made some sign because uniformed officers moved in to stop her forward progress. They blocked her until all I could see were the sparkles of light and the trembling top of her crystal crown.

"Get out of my way!" she yelled. They were police; they didn't get out of her way.

I heard someone shout, "Gilda, no!" then one of the uniforms fell straight down as if his knees had just buckled. He made no move to catch himself, and it was left to other officers to keep him from hitting the floor.

The cops began to shout, "Drop the wand! Drop it now!"

Doyle and Frost were suddenly in front of me and moving me farther away from the action. Doyle said, "Door."

I didn't understand at first, and then Frost was leading me toward a second smaller door leading outside. I glanced back to see Doyle close behind us, but facing the police and Gilda. I protested, "The door is alarmed. The noise could make it all worse."

Frost's hand was on the handle as he said, "It says for emergencies. This is an emergency." Then he was pulling me by one arm through the door with the alarm screeching and Doyle spilling out behind us. We were on the sidewalk in the bright sunshine and warm, but not too warm, Southern California air.

Doyle took my other arm and kept us moving. "Bullets travel. I don't want you close to them."

I tried to pull free of their hands, but I might as well have been trying to pry metal away from my skin.

"I am a detective. You can't just pull me out of a case when it gets dangerous."

"We are your bodyguards first and foremost," Doyle said.

I let my legs collapse under me so that they had to either stop or drag my bare legs and feet on the concrete. They stopped, but only long enough for Doyle to say, "Pick her up."

Frost picked me up and kept walking away from the police and the potential fey riot. Gilda's retinue would not take kindly to their queen being arrested, but what else could they do?

"Fine," I said, "you've made your point."

"Have we?" Doyle asked, and then he was suddenly in front of Frost and me. He glared down at me, and I could feel the weight of his anger behind the dark glasses. "I don't think we have made our point at all, or you would have been the first one out that door."

"Doyle," Frost began.

"No," he said, and pointed his finger at both of us. With Lucy it had reminded me of a child being scolded, but there was something ominous about Doyle reaching out with the anger riding his body. "What if you had caught a stray bullet? What if you had caught a stray bullet in the stomach? What if you had killed our children because you simply won't run away?"

I didn't know what to say to that. I just stared at him. He was right, of course he was right, but . . . "I can't do my job like this."

"No," he said, "you can't."

Then suddenly I felt the first tear slide down my face.

"No crying," he said.

Another tear joined the first. I fought not to wipe at them.

His hand dropped to his side and he took a deep breath. "That's not fair. Don't cry."

"I'm sorry, I don't mean to, but you're right, I think. I'm pregnant, damn it, not crippled."

"But you carry the future of the Unseelie Court in your body." He leaned in so that his arms went around Frost's until their faces touched and both of them were looking down at me. "You and the babies are too important to risk like this, Meredith."

I wiped at the tears, angry now that I had cried at all. I'd been doing that more lately. The doctor said it was hormones. More emotions I did not need right now.

"You are right, but I didn't know we'd end up with police all around us and guns."

"If you simply avoid cases with the police involved, it will guarantee that you do not end up surrounded by police with guns," he said.

Again I couldn't argue with his logic, but I wanted to. "First, put me down; we're attracting attention."

They glanced out from the circle of their arms over me, and there were people staring, whispering among themselves. I didn't have to hear them to know what they were saying. "Is that her?" "Is that Princess Meredith?" "Is that them?" "Is that the Darkness?" "Is that the Killing Frost?" If we weren't careful, someone would call the press and we'd be besieged.

Frost put me down, and we started to walk. A moving target was always harder to photograph. I tried to keep my voice low as I said, "I can't avoid this case, Doyle. They're killing fey here in the only home we have left. We're nobles of the court; the lesser fey are watching us, waiting to see what we'll do."

A couple came up to us, the woman saying, "Are you Princess Meredith? You are, aren't you?"

I nodded.

"Can we take your picture?"

There was a sound to the side as someone else used their phone to take a picture without asking. If they had the right phone, the photo could be on the Internet almost instantly. We had to get to the car and get out of here before the press descended.

"The princess is feeling unwell," Doyle said. "We need to get her to the car."

The woman touched my arm and said, "Oh, I know how hard the baby thing can be. I had terrible pregnancies every time. Didn't I, dear?"

Her husband nodded, and said, "Just a quick picture?"

We let them take their "quick" picture, which is rarely quick, then moved away. We'd have to double back for the car. But the voluntary picture had been a mistake, because other tourists wanted a picture and Doyle said, no, which upset them. "*They* got a picture," they said.

We kept moving, but a car stopped in the middle of the street, a window glided down and a camera lens came out. The paparazzi had arrived. But it was like the first hit in a shark attack. They came in to hit you to see what you'd do and whether you were edible. If you were, the next hit used teeth. We had to get out of sight and onto private property before more of them arrived.

A man was yelling from the car, "Princess Meredith, look this way! Why are you crying?"

That was all we needed, not only pictures of us but some caption about how I was crying. They'd feel free to speculate on why, but I'd learned that trying to explain was worse. We made ourselves a moving target. It was the best we could do as the first photographer ran up the sidewalk toward us, from the direction we'd been heading. We were trapped.

CHAPTER ELEVEN

DOYLE USED HIS MORE-THAN-HUMAN SPEED TO PICK ME UP AND take us inside the nearest shop. Frost locked the door behind us. A man protested, "Hey, this is my business."

Doyle set my feet on the floor of the small family-run deli. The man behind the counter was balding, and round under his white apron. The entire store matched him, old-fashioned, with cut meats, cheeses and unhealthy sides in little containers. I didn't think anything like this could have survived in L.A., land of the health obsessed.

Then I saw that the short line of customers was made up almost entirely of fey. There was one elderly man who looked full human, but the short woman behind him was small and plump with red curly hair and eyes like a hawk's, and I mean that literally. They were yellow, and her pupils spiraled up and down as she tried to get the best look at me. A little boy of about four clung to her skirts, staring at me with blue eyes and white-blond hair, cut modern; short and neat. The last person in line had a multicolored Mohawk with a long tail of hair trailing down his back. He wore a white T-shirt with a band logo on it, but his pants and vest were black leather. He was pierced, and looked out of place in the line, but then so did we.

They stared at us, and I stared back. Staring wasn't considered rude among us. Most fey didn't sweat high cholesterol or high blood sugar or any of a myriad of illnesses that might kill a human being eating foods with salt and preservatives. Immortals don't really sweat heart disease. I had a sudden craving for roast beef.

The door rattled behind us. One of the reporters was banging on the door angrily, shouting at us to open up, saying that this was a public area. We had no right to do this.

Cameras were shoved in front of the glass so that the daylight was gone in a brilliance of flashes. I turned, shielding my eyes. Apparently, I'd left my sunglasses in the break area of the Fael.

The slender fey male with his Mohawk, who most would have thought in his teens, came forward. He made a rough bow. "Princess Meredith, may I get you a seat?" I looked into his slender face with its pale greenish skin. There was something about his face that simply wasn't human. I couldn't have put my finger on it, but the bone structure was simply a little off for a human. He looked like a pixie drawn to short human size by some mix of genetics. His pointed ears had almost as many earrings as Doyle's did. But the earrings in his lobes were dangling and had multicolored feathers brushing the shoulders of his leather vest.

"That would be lovely," I said.

He drew up one of the few small chairs and held it for me. I sank into it gratefully. I was suddenly very tired. Was it being pregnant, or was it the day?

Doyle went to the shopkeeper. "Where does the back way empty out to?" Not was there a back way, but where did it go.

A woman spoke as she came out of the back. "You'll not be getting out back there, I'm afraid, Princess and Princes. I had to bar the door to keep the hounds of the press from outflanking you."

At first glance she matched her husband, all soft folds and comfortable roundness, human, then I realized that she'd had the same kind of surgery that Robert at the Fael had had done, though she had only done enough to pass for human, not tried to make herself gorgeous. Pretty had been enough for her, and when she came around the counter and looked at me with those brown eyes, it reminded me so much of my grandmother that it made my chest and throat tight. I would not cry, damn it.

She knelt in front of me and put her hands over mine. Her hands were cool to the touch as if she'd been working with something cold in the back.

Her husband said, "Get up, Matilda. They're taking pictures."

"Let them," she said over her shoulder, then turned back to me. She looked up at me with those eyes that echoed Gran's.

"I'm cousin to Maggie Mae what cooks in the Unseelie Court."

It took me a moment to realize what that meant for me personally. Once I knew that I had no sidhe relatives exiled outside faerie, I'd not thought that there might be other relatives here who weren't sidhe. I smiled. "Then you're cousin to my Gran."

She nodded. "Aye," and there was an accent in that one word thick enough to walk on. "If it's a brownie from Scotland who came to the new world, then we're cousins. Robert down the way, well he's Welsh, so not related to me."

"To us," I said.

She gave me a brilliant smile that flashed teeth too white to be anything but dentist whitened, but then we were in L.A. "So you would own me as kin?"

I nodded. "Of course," I said. Some tension that I hadn't even realized just went out of them all, as if until that moment they'd been nervous, or even afraid. It seemed to free them all up to come closer.

"Most of the highborn like to pretend there's nothing but pure sidhe in their veins," she said.

"He doesn't pretend," the punk pixie said. He nodded toward Doyle. "Nice rings. You got anything else pierced?"

"Yes," Doyle said.

The boy smiled, making the rings in the edge of his nose and his bottom lip curl cheerfully with it. "Me too," he said.

Matilda patted my hands. "You look pale. Are you having a hungry pregnancy or a starving one?"

I frowned at the phrasing. "I don't understand."

"Some women are hungry all the time and some don't want to look at food when they carry babes."

The frown eased and I said, "I'm craving roast beef. Protein."

She flashed that brilliant smile again. "That we have." She called back over her shoulder to the man. "Harvey, get some roast beef for the princess."

He started to protest about the photographers and such, but she turned and gave him such a look that he just turned away and did what she said. But apparently he wasn't doing it fast enough, because she patted my hand again and got up to oversee, or help.

We were all pretending that there wasn't a growing crowd of people pressed against the windows and door. I kept my back to the flashes against the glass and wished for my sunglasses.

The young-looking man, who was probably older than me by a century, sidled closer to Doyle and Frost. "Are you hiding pointy ears?"

It took Frost a moment to realize that he was the one being addressed. "No," he said.

The boy gazed up at him. "So you're what pure sidhe looks like?"

"No," Frost said.

"I know you don't all look the same," the boy said.

"I am not pure sidhe any more than Doyle."

I turned in the chair and said, "Or me."

The boy looked from one to the other of us. He was smiling, and pleased.

A throat-clearing sound made me turn to see the woman with her human-looking child. The woman dropped a bobbing curtsey, blinking her hawk eyes at me. The boy with her started to try to do the same, but she caught him by the arm.

"No, no, Felix, she's a fey princess, not a human one. You don't bow to her."

The boy frowned, trying to understand.

"I'm his nanny," she said, as if she needed to explain. "Fey nannies have become quite popular here."

"I didn't know," I said.

She smiled brightly. "I would never leave Felix here. I've been with him since he was three months old, but I can recommend a few others if they're between charges, or are willing to leave their charges."

I hadn't thought that far ahead, but . . . "Do you have a business card?" I asked.

She smiled and got one out of her purse. She put it on the table and wrote on the back of it. "This is my home phone so you don't have to go through the agency. They won't understand that you need different things than most clients."

I took the card and put it in the small wristlet wallet that was all I'd brought with me. We'd been headed to the beach; I'd wanted my ID and not much more.

Matilda brought me a small plate with roast beef folded artfully on it. "I'd put something else with it but when a lady's expecting you never know what to add."

I smiled at her. "It's perfect. Tha—sorry. I know better."

"Oh, don't worry about it. I've been out among the humans for centuries. It takes more than a thank-you to lay this brownie, eh, Harvey?" She laughed at her own joke. Harvey behind the counter looked both embarrassed and pleased.

The roast beef was tender, just the right side of rare, and exactly what I wanted. Even the little hint of salt was perfect. I'd noticed that about the cravings, that if I gave in to them the food tasted amazing. I wondered if that was typical.

Matilda pulled up a chair, and the nanny, whose name was Agnes, did the same. It wasn't like any of us could leave. We were walled in with the press. In fact, the reporters and paparazzi in the front were being squashed against the windows and door. They were beginning to try to push back, but there was too much weight behind them.

Doyle and Frost stayed standing, keeping an eye on the people outside. The young-looking man stood with them. He was obviously enjoying being one of the guys, and was showing his shoulder tattoo to Doyle and Frost.

Matilda had told Harvey to put coffee on. I realized with a start that this was the first time in weeks that I'd sat down with other women and not felt either like a princess, a detective, or someone else in charge of everyone I was dealing with. We'd brought sidhe women with us out of faerie, but they'd all been part of the prince's guard. They'd spent centuries serving my father, Prince Essus, and he'd been friendly, but not overly so; he'd been as careful of the boundaries as the queen, his sister, had been careless. Where she'd treated her guard as her harem and her toys to torment, he'd treated his guard with respect. He'd had lovers among them, but sex wasn't looked down on among the fey. It was just normal.

The female guards would give their lives to keep me safe, but they were meant to guard a prince, and there were no more princes in the Unseelie Court in or out of faerie. I'd killed the last one before he could kill me. The guards didn't mourn their lost prince. He'd been a sexual sadist like his mother. One thing we'd managed to hide from the media so far was how many of the guard, both male and female, were traumatized from the tortures they'd endured.

Some of them wanted Doyle, or Frost, or one of the other fathers to be named prince so they could be their guard. Traditionally, making me pregnant would have made the father a prince and future king, or at least royal consort. But with so many fathers, there was no precedent for making them all princes.

I sat with the women and just listened to them talk about normal things, and realized that sitting in the kitchen at my Gran's or in the kitchen with Maggie Mae had been the closest to normal I'd ever known.

For the third time that day I felt tears at the back of my eyes, in my throat. It was that way every time I thought about Gran. It had only been a month since her death. I guess I was entitled.

Matilda said, "Are you well, Princess?"

"Merry," I said. "Call me Merry."

That earned me another bright smile. Then there was a sound behind us.

We all turned to see the glass begin to crack under the weight of the reporters crushing one another against it.

Doyle and Frost were at my side. They got me to my feet, and we were running for the counter and the back area. Agnes picked up the little boy and we ran for cover. We heard screams, and the glass gave with a high, thin cracking.

CHAPTER TWELVE

THERE WERE AMBULANCES, POLICE, AND GLASS EVERYWHERE. NONE of us in the shop were hurt, but some of the paparazzi were taken to the hospital. Most of the people plastered against the glass had been photographers trying to get that one special picture that would make them rich. Certain shots were rumored to go for hundreds of thousands of dollars. After today, I believed the rumors.

Lucy was standing over me as the ambulance medic checked me out. My protests of, "I'm fine. I wasn't hurt," fell on deaf ears. When Lucy had found me inside the glass-covered deli she'd been pale. I looked up at the tall brunette and realized that though we might never go shopping together, she was my friend.

The emergency medical technician pulled the blood pressure cuff off my arm and pronounced, "Everything seems fine. Blood pressure, all of it. But I'm not a doctor, and I'm sure as heck not a baby doc."

"So you think she should go to the hospital?" Lucy asked.

The EMT frowned and I felt his dilemma. If he said no and he was wrong, he was fucked. But there were other people who were actually injured, and if he left one behind to take me, just in case, and the one left behind died, he was also screwed.

She turned to Doyle and Frost for backup. "Tell her she needs to go to the hospital."

They exchanged a look, then Doyle gave a small nod as if to say "Go ahead," and Frost answered, "We don't 'tell' Merry what to do, Detective. She is our princess."

"But she's also carrying your babies," Lucy said.

"That doesn't give us the right to order her around," he said.

Doyle added, "I expected you to understand that better than most, Detective Tate."

She frowned at both of them, then turned back to me. "You promise me you never fell or had something fall on you?"

"I promise," I said.

She took in a lot of air, let it out slowly, then nodded. "Fine. Okay. I'll let it go. If none of you are worried, I don't know why I bother."

I smiled up at her. "Because you are my friend, and friends worry about each other."

She looked almost embarrassed, then grinned at me. "Fine. Go enjoy what's left of your Saturday."

Doyle reached out a hand and I let him help me stand though I really didn't need it. They'd both been calmer than Lucy, but then they'd been with me the entire time. They knew nothing had happened to me physically, but they were still more careful of me than they had been before. It was both touching and a little irritating. I was worried that as the pregnancy progressed it might become a lot less touching and a lot more irritating, but that was a worry for another day. We were free to head for the beach, and there was still daylight to enjoy it. It was all good.

The EMT asked, "So I'm done here with the princess?"

"Yeah," Lucy said, "go find someone who's bleeding to take for a ride."

He smiled, obviously relieved, and hurried off to find someone who really did need a ride to the hospital.

"I'll give you uniforms to escort you back to your car." She sort of nodded toward the press that was being held back by tape and barriers. Oddly, the paparazzi who had gotten injured were now news themselves. I wondered if they were enjoying being on the other side of the camera.

"Some of them will follow us to the beach," Frost said.

"I can try to lose them."

"No, I do not want to see what that would mean on the roads to the beach." Doyle said it very quickly and even Lucy picked up his unease.

"So tall, dark, and deadly is still not comfy riding in regular cars." She addressed the comment to me.

I smiled and shook my head.

"I prefer the limo; at least then I can't see the road so clearly."

Lucy smiled and shook her head. "You know, it makes me like you better that you're afraid of something, Doyle."

He frowned at her, and probably would have commented, but her phone rang. She checked, and saw that she needed to answer it. She held up a finger for us to wait.

"Tell me this is a joke," she said. Her tone was anything but amused.

"How," she asked, then listened and said, "Sorry doesn't fix this." She got off the phone and cursed softly but completely under her breath.

"What's wrong?" I asked.

"While we were down here cleaning up this mess our witness fled the scene. We can't find her."

"When did she get . . . ?"

"He doesn't know. Apparently when there were fewer of us, Gilda's entourage got braver, and when they calmed it down the witness was gone." I noticed that she was careful not to say Bittersweet's name out in public. It was a good precaution when murders are magical; you never know who, or how, someone is listening.

"Lucy, I'm sorry. If you hadn't come down here to help us this wouldn't have happened."

She gave a glare to the paparazzi who were not hurt but whom the police had forced to wait for questioning. "You wouldn't have needed help if these bastards hadn't mobbed you."

"I'm not even sure you can charge them with anything," I said.

"We'll find something," she said, her voice full of anger. The anger was probably more about Bittersweet fleeing the scene and having to tell her bosses that she'd been rescuing the faery princess from the big, bad reporters when it had happened, but the uninjured paparazzi would make a nice target for that anger.

"Go, enjoy your weekend. I'll take care of this bunch and give you an escort to your car. I'll have some cars make sure that no one follows you from the Fael, but if they're waiting for you farther away"—she shrugged—"afraid there's not much I can do."

I took her hand and squeezed it. "Thank you for everything, and I'm sorry that you're going to take grief about the witness."

She smiled, but her eyes weren't happy enough for it. "I'll deal with it. Go, have your picnic or whatever." She turned away, then back to frowning. She moved closer to us and whispered, "How do we find someone who is only four inches high in a city the size of Los Angeles?"

It was a good question, but I had a helpful answer. "She's one of the smallest of us, so she's very sensitive to metal and technology. So look for her at parks, vacant lots, street sides with trees like today's scene. She needs nature to survive here."

"What kind of flower faery is she?" Frost asked.

"I don't know," Lucy said.

"Good idea, Frost," I said. "Find out, Lucy, because she'll be attracted to her plant. Some of them are so tied to a bit of land that if their plant goes extinct they die with it."

"Wow, that'd make you environmentally active," Lucy said.

I nodded.

"Who would know what flower she likes?"

"Robert might know," I said.

"Gilda would know," Doyle said.

Lucy frowned at him. "She's already called for her lawyer. She's not going to talk to us."

"She might if you tell her that not cooperating endangers her people," Doyle said.

"I don't think she cares that much," Lucy said.

He gave that small smile. "Tell her that Meredith cares more than she does, obviously. Imply that Meredith is a better, kinder ruler and I think Gilda will at least tell you the plant."

She looked up at him with a nod of approval. "They're both handsome and smart. It's so not fair. Why can't I find a Prince Charming like these guys?"

I wasn't sure what to say to that, but Doyle was. "We are not the Prince Charming of our story, Detective Tate. Meredith rode to our rescue and saved us from our sad fates."

"So she's what, Princess Charming?"

He smiled and this time it was that bright flash that he didn't give often. It made Lucy blush just a little, and I realized that she liked Doyle. I couldn't blame her. "Yes, Detective, she's our Princess Charming."

Frost took one of my hands in his, and looked down at me with everything in his eyes. "She is."

"So instead of waiting for the prince to find me, I need to find one to save and bring him home?"

"It worked for me," I said.

She shook her head. "I save people all day, or try to, Merry. Just once I'd like to be the one being saved."

I shook my head. "I've been both, Lucy. Trust me, it's better to do the saving."

"If you say so. I gotta go see if Robert knows where to find our little friend." She waved at us as she made her way toward the crowd.

Two uniformed officers appeared as if she'd told them to step up when she left us; she probably had. It was our old friends Wright and O'Brian. "We're supposed to see you safely to your car," Wright said.

"Let's do it," I said.

We started the trip back the way we'd come, through a barrage of new camera flashes from yet more and different paparazzi and reporters.

CHAPTER THIRTEEN

WE ENDED UP WITH AN IMPROMPTU ENTOURAGE OF REPORTERS AND uniformed police. At one point the reporters were such a solid mass that Wright and O'Brian couldn't move us forward without laying hands on them, and apparently they'd been ordered not to manhandle the press. They were experiencing the problem that my bodyguards had been having for weeks. How do you stay politically correct with strangers shouting in your face, flashes going off like blinding bombs, and the crowd turning into a mass of bodies that you were not allowed to touch?

The reporters yelled questions. "Are you helping the police with a case, Princess?" "What investigation are you helping the police with?" "Why were you crying?" "Is the shop owner really a relative of yours?"

Wright and O'Brian tried to push a way through without actually pushing, which is a lot harder than it sounds. Doyle and Frost stayed on either side of me, because the crowd had grown beyond the reporters. Human and fey had come out of the shops and restaurants to see what the commotion was about. It was "human" nature to be curious but they began to add to the press around us so that forward movement stopped.

Then suddenly the reporters fell silent, not all at once, but gradually. First one went quiet, then another, and they began to look around, as if they'd heard a noise, a disturbing noise. Then I felt it, too: fear. Fear like a cold, clammy wind across your skin. I had a moment to stand there in the bright California sunshine and feel a shiver creep down my spine.

Doyle squeezed my arm and that helped me think. It helped me tighten my magical shields, and the moment I did, the fear washed away from me, but I could still see it on the reporters' faces.

Wright and O'Brian had their hands on their guns, looking around apprehensively. I spilled my shields outward to them, the way I'd done the glamour over Doyle and Frost earlier. Wright's shoulders dropped as if a weight had gone from him. O'Brian said, "What was that?"

"*Is* that," Doyle said.

"What?" she asked.

The reporters parted like a curtain. They simply didn't want to be near whatever was walking between them. The Fear Dearg walked toward us grinning his snaggletoothed grin. I'd been right; it was an evil grin. His enjoyment of the reporters' fear showed in his face and the jaunty roll of his walk.

He came to stand in front of us, and then went down on one knee before us. "My queen," he said.

A camera flashed, freezing the image for tomorrow's news, or tonight's. The Fear Dearg looked in the direction of the flash and there was a yell, then a man went running down the sidewalk. His many cameras jangled as he raced away screaming, as if all the devil's Dandy Dogs were chasing him.

The other reporters took a collective step back. The Fear Dearg gave an evil chuckle, and just the sound of it was enough to make me break out in goose bumps. If I'd been alone on some dark road it would have been terrifying.

"You must practice that laugh," I said. "It's positively evil."

He grinned up at me. "A fey likes to know his work is appreciated, my queen."

A reporter called out in a shaking voice, "He called you his queen. Does that mean you did keep the throne?"

The Fear Dearg got to his feet and bounced at them, hands up, and said, "Boo!" The reporters fled on that side. He made a move toward the other group, but most of them backed away, hands held out, as if to show that they meant no harm.

One woman asked in a breathless voice, "Meredith, are you queen of the Unseelie Court?"

"No," I answered.

The Fear Dearg looked at me. "Shall I tell her the crown that sat upon your head first?"

"Not here," Doyle said.

The Fear Dearg glared up at him. "I did not ask you, Darkness. If we were kin, then it would be different, but I owe you nothing, only her."

I realized that Doyle refusing to acknowledge that his ancestry was similar to the Fear Dearg's had insulted the fey.

Doyle seemed to figure it out then too, because he said, "I do not hide my mixed heritage, Fear Dearg. I only meant that I had none of your blood in my veins, which is only truth."

"Ay, but you've had our blood on your sword, haven't you? Before you were the Queen's Darkness, before you were Nudons and healed at your magic spring, you were other things, other names." The Fear Dearg lowered his voice with each word, until the remaining reporters began to come closer trying to hear. I had known that Doyle had been something before he was worshipped as a god, and that he had not sprung full grown at the side of Queen Andais, but I had never asked. The older of the sidhe did not like to talk about the time before, when our people were greater.

The Fear Dearg whirled and jumped at the reporters with a loud "Hah!" They ran, some falling down and others trampling them underfoot in a mad panic to be away from him. The ones on the ground got up and raced after the others.

O'Brian said, "It's not strictly legal to use magic on the press."

The Fear Dearg cocked his head to one side like a bird that has spied a worm. The look made O'Brian swallow a little harder, but with my shields around her she held her ground. "And how would you have moved them, girlie?"

"Officer O'Brian," she said.

He grinned at her, and I felt her flinch, but she didn't move back. It earned her a point for bravery, but I wasn't certain that taunting him after he'd shown such obvious sexual interest in her during Bittersweet's questioning was a good idea. Sometimes a little fear is a wise thing.

He started to invade her personal space, and I stepped between them. "What do you want, Fear Dearg? I appreciate the help, I do, but you did not do it out of the goodness of your heart."

He leered at O'Brian, then turned the leer to me. It didn't bother me. "I have no goodness in my heart, my queen, only evil."

"No one is only evil," I said.

The leer grew until his face was a mask of evil intent, but it was the kind of evil they put on Halloween masks. "You're too young to understand what I am."

"I know what evil is," I said, "and it does not come with a cartoon mask and a leer. Evil comes in the face of those who are supposed to love and care for you, but they don't. Evil comes with a slap, or a hand holding you underwater until you can't breathe, and all the time her face is serene, not angry, not mad, because she believes that she has the right."

His evil face began to fold down into something more serious. He gazed up at me, and said, "Rumors say you endured much abuse at the hands of your sidhe relatives."

Doyle turned to the police officers. "Give us some privacy, please?"

Wright and O'Brian exchanged glances, then Wright shrugged. "We were just told to get you safely into your car, so fine, we'll wait over here."

O'Brian tried to protest, but her partner insisted. They argued quietly as they gave us our privacy.

Doyle's hand on my arm tightened, and Frost moved closer. They were telling me silently not to share stories out of court, but the queen had never cared that I talked about some things. "And their friends, never forget their friends, I never could," I said.

He looked from Frost to Doyle, and asked, "Did they torment you before they became your lovers?"

I shook my head. "No, I have taken no lover who ever raised a hand to me."

"You have cleared out the Unseelie sithen. They've all come to L.A. with you. Who is left, who tormented you so?"

"I've taken only the guards away, not the nobles," I said.

"But all guards are noble among the sidhe, or they are not worthy of guarding a queen, or a king."

I shrugged. "I have called to me that which is mine."

He went to his knees again, but closer to my feet, so that I had to fight the urge to back up a step. Earlier I would have, but something about this moment made me want to be the queen that the Fear Dearg needed. Doyle seemed to feel me think it, because he put a hand on my back as if to help me not give ground. Frost simply moved to my other side, so that he almost touched me, but he was keeping his hands free for weapons, just in case. In public they tried to keep one of them free for that, though sometimes it was hard to comfort me and guard me at the same time.

"You have not called the Fear Dearg, Queen Meredith."

"I did not know they were mine to call."

"We were cursed and our women destroyed so we would cease to be a people. No matter how long-lived we are, the Fear Dearg are a dying race."

"I have never heard even a hint that the Fear Dearg have women, or of a curse."

He turned those black, uptilted eyes to Doyle at my side. "Ask that one if I speak the truth."

I looked at Doyle. He simply nodded.

"We and the Red Caps almost beat the sidhe. We were two proud races, and we existed on bloodshed. The sidhe came to help the humans, to save them." His voice was bitter.

"You would have killed every man, woman, and child on the isle," Doyle said.

"Mayhap we would have," he said, "but it was our right to do it. They were our worshippers before they were yours, sidhe."

"And what is a god if he destroys all those who worship him, Fear Dearg?"

"What is a god who has lost all his followers, Nudons?"

"I am no god, nor was I ever."

"But we all thought we were, didn't we, Darkness?" He gave that disturbing chuckle again.

Doyle nodded, his hand on my back tensing. "We thought many things that turned out not to be true."

"Ay, that we did, Darkness." The Fear Dearg sounded sad.

"I will tell you truth, Fear Dearg. I had forgotten you and your people and what happened so long ago."

He looked up at Doyle. "Oh, ay, the sidhe do so many things that they simply forget. They wash their hands not in water, or even blood, but forgetfulness and time."

"Meredith cannot do what you want."

"She is crowned queen of the sluagh, and for a brief moment queen of the Unseelie. Crowned by faerie and Goddess, that's what you made us wait for, Darkness. You and your people, we were cursed to be nameless, childless, homeless, until a queen crowned rightly by Goddesses and faerie itself granted us a name again." He looked up at me. "It was a way for them to curse us forever without sounding like it was forever. It was a way to torment us. We used to come before every new queen and ask for our names back, and they all refused."

"They remembered what you were, Fear Dearg," Doyle said.

The Fear Dearg turned to Frost. "And you, Killing Frost, why so silent? Do you have no opinions but the ones that Darkness gives you? That's the rumor, you're his sub."

I wasn't entirely sure that Frost would understand that last part, but he knew he was being taunted. "I do not remember the Fear Dearg's fate. I woke to winter, and your people were gone."

"That's right, that's right, once you were but wee Jackie Frost, just one more retainer in the court of the Winter Queen." He did that head cock to one side again. "How did you turn into a sidhe, Frost? How did you grow in power while all the rest of us faded?"

"People believe in me. I am Jack Frost. They talk, they write books and stories, and children look out their window and see the frost on their windows and think I did it." Frost took a step toward the smaller kneeling man. "And what do the human children say of you, Fear Dearg? You are barely a whisper in the human's minds these days, all forgotten."

The Fear Dearg gave him a look that was frightening, for real, because it held such hate. "They remember us, Jackie, they remember us. We live in their memories and in their hearts. They are still what we made of them."

"Lies will not help you, only truth," Doyle said.

"It's not lies, Darkness, go into any theater and watch their slasher flicks. Their serial killers, their wars, the slaughter on the evening news when a man kills his whole family so they won't know he's lost his job, or the woman who drowns her children so she can have another man. Oh, no, Darkness, humans remember us. We were the voices in the blackest night of the human soul, and what we planted there still lives. The Red Caps gave them war, but the Fear Dearg gave them pain and torment. They are still our children, Darkness, make no mistake about that."

"And we gave them music, stories, art, and beauty," Doyle said.

"You are Unseelie sidhe; you gave them slaughter, too."

"We gave them both," Doyle said. "You hated us because we offered more than just blood, death, and fear. No Red Cap, no Fear Dearg ever wrote a poem, painted a picture, or designed something new and fresh. You have no ability to create, only to destroy, Fear Dearg."

He nodded. "I have spent centuries, more centuries than most acknowledge, learning the lesson you set us, Darkness."

"And what lesson have you learned?" I asked. My voice was soft, as if I wasn't sure I wanted to know the answer.

"That people are real. That the humans aren't just for our pleasure and slaughter, and that they are a people, too." He glared up at Doyle. "But the Fear Dearg survived long enough to see the mighty fall as we fell. We watched the sidhe diminish in power and glory, and the few of us left rejoiced."

"Yet you bend knee to us again," Doyle said.

He shook his head. "I bend knee to the queen of the sluagh, not of the Unseelie, or the Seelie Court. I bend knee to Queen Meredith, and if King Sholto were here I would acknowledge him. He has kept the faith with his other side."

"Sholto's tentacles are only a tattoo unless he calls them forth. He looks as sidhe as any of us standing here," Doyle said.

"And if I want a fair young maiden, don't I use my glamour to make myself look a bit better?"

"It's illegal to use magic to trick someone into bed," O'Brian said.

I started. I hadn't realized that the police had moved back into hearing range.

The Fear Dearg glared at her. "And do you wear makeup on your dates, Officer? Do you put on a pretty dress?"

She didn't answer him.

"But there's no makeup that will cover this." He motioned at his own face. "There's no suit to hide my body. It's magic or nothing for me. I could make you understand what it's like to be twisted in the eyes of the other humans."

"You will not harm her," Doyle said.

"Ah, the great sidhe speaks and we all must listen."

"You have learned nothing, Fear Dearg," Doyle said.

"You did just threaten to use magic to deform O'Brian," I said.

"No, my magic is all glamour; to deform I'd have to use something more solid."

"Do not end their curse, Meredith. They would be a plague on the humans."

"Someone explain to me what the curse was, exactly."

"I will, in the car," Doyle said, and he stepped forward, putting me behind him. "Fear Dearg, we might have taken pity on you after so very long, but you have shown in just a few words to a human woman that you are still dangerous, still too evil to be given back your powers."

The Fear Dearg reached out to me, past Doyle's leg. "But give me a name, my queen, I beg you. Give me a name and I can have a life again."

"Do not, Meredith, not until you understand what they were and what they might be again."

"There are only a handful of us left in the world, Darkness." His voice was rising. "What harm could we do now?"

"If you did not need Meredith to free you from the curse, if you did not need her goodwill, the goodwill of some queen of faerie, what would you do to some human woman tonight, Fear Dearg?"

The Fear Dearg's eyes held such hate. I actually stepped back behind Doyle, and Frost moved so that I only saw the Fear Dearg between their bodies as I had at the beginning.

He looked at me between the two of them, and it was a look that made me truly afraid. He got to his feet, a little heavily, as if his knees ached from being on the sidewalk so long. "Not just human women, Darkness, or have you forgotten that once we rivaled your magic, and the sidhe were no more safe than the humans?"

"I have not forgotten that." Doyle's voice held rage. I'd never heard quite that tone in his voice before. It sounded of something more personal.

"There is no rule to how we get our naming from the queen," he said. "I have asked nicely, but she would name me to save herself and those babes inside her. You would let her name me to save them."

The two men closed ranks and I lost sight of the Fear Dearg. "Do not come near her, Fear Dearg, for it will be your death. And if we hear of any crimes on humans that smack of your work, we will see that you no longer have to mourn your lost greatness, for the dead mourn nothing."

"Ah, but how will you tell what is my work and what is the work of humans who carry the spirit of the Fear Dearg in their souls? It is not music and poetry that I see on the news, Darkness."

"We are leaving," Doyle said. We said good-bye to Wright and O'Brian, and the men got me into the truck. We started the engine but didn't leave until O'Brian and Wright were lost in the mass of police down the way. I think none of us wanted to leave O'Brian close to the Fear Dearg.

It was Alice in her Goth outfit who came out of the Fael and went to the Fear Dearg. She hugged him, and he hugged her back. They went back into the tea shop hand in hand, but he cast a look back over his shoulder as I put the SUV in gear. The look was a challenge, a sort of Stop Me If You Can. They vanished into the shop. I pulled carefully out into the street and the traffic, then said, "What the hell was all that about?"

"I don't wish to tell the tale in the car," Doyle said, with his death grip on the door and the dashboard. "You do not tell tales of the Fear Dearg when you are afraid. It calls them to you, gives them power over you."

To that I didn't know what to say, because I remembered a time when I thought the Queen's Darkness felt nothing, least of all fear. I knew that Doyle felt all the emotions everyone else felt, but admitting weakness, that he didn't do often. He'd said the only thing that could have kept me from questioning him on the way to the beach. I used the bluetooth to call ahead to the beach house and the main house to let everyone know that we were fine. That the only ones wounded were the paparazzi. Some days karma balances out instantly.

CHAPTER FOURTEEN

MAEVE REED'S BEACH HOUSE SAT ABOVE THE OCEAN, HALF ON THE cliff and half resting on wood and concrete supports designed to stand up to earthquakes, mudslides, and anything else the Southern California climate could throw at the house. It sat in a gated community complete with a uniformed guard and a gatehouse. It was what kept the press from following us. Because they'd found us. It was almost a type of magic how they always found us again, like a dog on a scent. There weren't as many on the narrow curving road, but enough to stop and look disappointed as we went through the gates.

Ernie was at the gate. He was an older African American who had once been a soldier, but had been injured badly enough that his army career had gone away. He would never tell me what the injury had been, and I knew enough human culture not to ask outright.

He frowned at the cars parked out of reach of the gate. "I'll call the police so we'll have the trespassing on record."

"They stay away from the gate when you're on duty, Ernie," I said.

He smiled at me. "Thank you, Princess. I do my best." He tipped an imaginary hat at Doyle and Frost, and said, "Gentlemen."

They nodded back and away we went. If the beach house hadn't been behind a gate, we'd have been at the mercy of the media, and after watching the windows crack at Matilda's deli, I didn't think that would be a good idea tonight. It would have been nice to think that the accident would make the paparazzi back off, but it would probably make me bigger news, more of a target. It was ironic, but almost certainly true.

The car's phone sounded. Doyle started, and I spoke into the air toward the microphone. "Hello."

"Merry, how close to the house are you guys?" Rhys asked.

"Almost there," I said.

He gave a chuckle that sounded tinny because of the bluetooth. "Good, our cook is getting nervous that the food will get cold before you arrive."

"Galen?" I made it a question.

"Yep, he hasn't even taken anything off the stove, but he's fretting about that so he won't fret about you. Barinthus told me you called and shared some excitement. Are you okay?"

"Fine, but tired," I said.

Doyle spoke loudly, "We are almost to the turnoff."

"The bluetooth only works for the driver," I said, not for the first time.

Doyle said, "Why doesn't it work for everyone in the front seat?"

"Merry, what did you say?" Rhys asked.

"Doyle said something." More quietly to Doyle, I said, "I don't know."

"You don't know what?" Rhys asked.

"Sorry, still not used to the bluetooth. We're almost there, Rhys."

A huge black raven perched on an ancient fence post by the road. It cawed and flexed its wings. "Tell Cathbodua we're fine, too."

"You see one of her pets?" he asked.

"Yes." The raven winged skyward and began to circle the car.

"She'll know more about you than I do then," he said, and sounded a little discouraged.

"Are you all right? You sound tired," I said.

"Fine, like you," he said, and laughed again, then added, "but I just got here myself. The simple case Jeremy sent me on turned out to be not so simple."

"We can talk about it over dinner," I said.

"I'd like your opinion, but I think there's a different agenda for dinner."

"What do you mean?"

Frost leaned up as far as the seat belt would let him, and asked, "Has something else happened? Rhys sounds worried."

"Did something else happen while we were gone?" I asked. I was looking for the turnoff to the house. The light was beginning to fade. It wasn't quite twilight, but it was still a turn I missed if I wasn't paying attention.

"Nothing new, Merry. I swear."

I braked sharply for the turnoff, which made Doyle grab the car tightly enough that I heard the door frame protest. He was strong enough to tear the door off its hinges. I just hoped he didn't dent it because of his phobia.

I spoke as I eased the SUV over the rise at the top of the road and down the steep lip of the private driveway. "I'm on the driveway. See you in a few."

"We'll be waiting." He hung up and I concentrated on the steep drive. I wasn't the only one who didn't like it. It was hard to tell behind the dark glasses, but I think Doyle had closed his eyes as I wound the SUV around the turns.

The outside lights were already on, and the shortest guard I had was pacing outside the front of the house, white trench coat flapping in the ocean breeze. Rhys was the only one of the guards who had gotten his own private detective license. He'd always loved old film noir movies, and when he wasn't doing undercover work he liked his trench coat and fedoras. They were just usually white or cream to match his waist-length curls. His hair was flying in the wind along with his coat. I realized that his hair was tangling in the wind like mine had earlier.

"Rhys's hair tangles in the wind," I said.

"Yes," Frost said.

"Is that why he only has it to his waist?"

"I believe so," he said.

"Why does his hair tangle and yours doesn't?"

"Doyle's doesn't either. He just likes the braid."

"Same question. Why?"

I pulled the car to a stop beside Rhys's car. He started striding toward us. He was smiling, but I knew his body language well enough to see the anxiety. He was wearing a white eye patch to match his coat today. He wore them when he was meeting with clients, or out in the world at large. Most people, and some fey, found the scars where his right eye had once been disturbing. At home when it was just us, he didn't bother with the patch.

"We don't know why some of our hair does not tangle," Frost said. "It's just the way it's always been."

With that unsatisfying answer, Rhys was at my door. I unlocked it so he could help me out of the car, but the anxiety had turned his one blue eye with its three circles of blue—cornflower blue, sky blue, and winter white—to spinning slowly like a lazy storm. It meant that his magic was close to the surface, which usually took a lot of emotion, or concentration. Was it anxiety about my safety today, or was it something the Grey Detective Agency and he were working on? I couldn't even remember, except that it had something to do with corporate sabotage using magic.

Rhys opened the door, and I offered my hand automatically. He took it and raised it to his lips to put a kiss on my fingers that made my skin tingle. Anxiety for me then, not the case, was making his magic swirl closer to the surface. I wondered how much worse the pictures on TV had looked from the outside looking in; it hadn't seemed that bad at the time, had it?

He wrapped his arms around me and drew me in against his body. He squeezed and I had a moment of feeling just how very strong he was, and that there was a slight tremor to his body. I tried to push back enough to see his face, and for a moment he held me more tightly so that I had no choice but to stay against him. I let myself feel his body underneath his clothes. Bare skin would have been like his kiss; it would have tingled against my skin, but even through his clothes I could feel the pulse and beat of his power like some finely tuned engine purring against my body from cheek to thigh. I let myself sink into that sensation. Let myself sink into the strength of his arms, the muscled firmness of his body, and for just a moment I allowed myself to let go of all that had happened and all that I had seen today. I let it be chased away by the strength of the man holding me.

I thought of him nude and holding me, and letting the promise of that deep vibrating power sink into my body. The thought made me press my groin more tightly against him, and I felt his body begin to respond.

He was the one who raised his head enough to allow me to gaze up into his face. He was smiling, and he kept his arms tight across my back. "If you're thinking about sex, then you can't be that traumatized." He grinned.

I smiled back. "I'm better now."

Hafwyn's voice turned us toward the door. She came out of the house with her long yellow hair in a thick, single braid to one side of her slender form. She was everything a Seelie sidhe woman should have been. She was an inch under six feet, slender but feminine, with eyes like spring skies. When I had been a little girl this was what I had wanted to look like instead of my all-too-human height and curves. My hair, eyes, and skin were sidhe, but the rest of me had never measured up. Many of the sidhe of both courts had made certain that I knew I was too human looking, not sidhe enough. Hafwyn had not been one of those. She had never been cruel to me when I was just Meredith, Daughter of Essus, and not likely to sit any throne. In fact, she had been nearly invisible to me in the courts, just one of my cousin Cel's guards.

Standing there in Rhys's arms with Doyle and Frost moving up behind us, I did not envy anyone. How could I want to change anything about myself when I had so many people who loved me?

Hafwyn wore a white sundress, simpler than mine, almost a shift like something they once wore under dresses, but the simplicity of the cloth could not hide her beauty. The beauty of all the sidhe reminded me often why we'd once been worshipped as gods. It was only partly the magic. Humans have a tendency to either worship or revile beauty.

She dropped a curtsy as she came to me. I'd almost broken the new guards from such public displays but a century's worth of habits are hard to break.

"Do you need healing, my lady?"

"I am unharmed," I said.

She was one of the few true healers that faerie had left. She could lay hands on a wound or illness and simply magick it away. Outside of faerie her powers were lessened, but then many of our powers were less in the human world.

"Goddess be praised," she said, and touched my arm where it lay against Rhys's body. I'd noticed that the longer we were outside of the high courts of faerie the more touchy-feely the guards became. Touching someone when anxious was considered something that lesser fey did. We sidhe were supposed to be above such petty comforts, but I had never found the touch of a friend a petty comfort. I valued the people who drew strength from touching me, or gave me peace with their own touch.

Her touch was brief, because the Queen of Air and Darkness, my aunt, would have either laughed at her for the need, or turned that kind gesture into something sexual and/or threatening. All weaknesses were to be exploited; all kindness was to be stamped out.

Galen came out of the house still wearing an apron that was all white and very TV chef, unlike the sheer white one we had in the house. He wore that one without a shirt, because he knew I enjoyed watching him. But he'd fallen in love with the food channel and had some more useful aprons now. He was wearing a dark green tank top and cargo shorts under the apron. The shirt brought out the slight green tinge in his skin and short curly hair. His only sop to the long hair that the other sidhe men kept at the Unseelie Court was a long, thin braid of hair that fell to his knees. He was the only sidhe I'd ever known to voluntarily cut his hair so short.

Rhys let me go so I could be wrapped up in Galen's six feet worth of lean body. I was suddenly airborne as he picked me up. His green eyes were so worried. "We turned the TV on just a little bit ago. All that glass; you could have been hurt."

I touched his face, trying to smooth out the worry lines that would never leave a trace on his perfect skin. The sidhe did age in a way, but they didn't really grow old. But then immortal things don't, do they?

I leaned up for a kiss, and he leaned down to help me reach him. We kissed and there was magic to Galen's kiss as there had been to Rhys's touch, but where the other man's touch had been deep and almost electric, like some kind of distant motor humming, Galen's energy was like having my skin caressed by a soft spring wind. His kiss filled my mind with the perfume of flowers, and that first warmth that comes when the snow has finally left and the earth wakes once more. All that poured over my skin from one kiss. It drew me back from him with wide, startled eyes, and I had to fight to catch my breath.

He looked embarrassed. "I'm sorry, Merry, I was just so worried, and so glad to see you safe."

I gazed up into his eyes and found them just the same lovely green color. He didn't give as many clues as the rest of us did when his magic was upon him, but that kiss said better than any glowing eyes or shining skin that his magic was very close to the surface. If we'd been inside faerie there might have been flowers growing at his feet, but the asphalt driveway was untouched underneath us. Man-made technology was proof against so much of our magic.

There was a man's voice from inside. "Galen, something's boiling over. I don't know how to stop it!"

Galen turned grinning toward the house with me still in his arms. "Let's go rescue the kitchen before Amatheon and Adair set it on fire."

"You left them in charge of dinner?" I asked.

He nodded happily as he began to walk toward the still-open door. He carried me effortlessly, as if he could have walked with me in his arms forever and never tired. Maybe he could have.

Doyle and Frost fell into step on one side, and Rhys on the other. Doyle asked, "How did you get them to agree to help cook?"

Galen flashed that hail-fellow-well-met smile of his that made everyone want to smile back. Even Doyle was not immune to the charm, because he flashed white teeth in his dark face, responding to the sheer goodwill of Galen.

"I asked," he said.

"And they just agreed?" Frost asked.

He nodded.

"You should have seen Ivi peeling potatoes," Rhys said. "That was something the queen had to threaten torture to get him to do."

All of us but Galen glanced at him. "Are you saying that Galen simply asked them and they agreed?" Doyle said.

"Yes," Rhys said.

We all exchanged a look. I wondered if they were all thinking what I was thinking, that at least some of our magic was doing just fine outside faerie. In fact, Galen's seemed to be growing stronger. That was almost as interesting and surprising as anything that had happened today, because just as it was "impossible" for the fey to be killed in the manner that they seemed to have been killed, so sidhe magic growing stronger outside faerie was just as impossible. Two impossible things in one day, I would have said it was like being Alice in Wonderland, but her Wonderland was fairyland, and none of the impossibilities survived Alice's trip back to the "real" world. Our impossibilities were on the wrong end of the rabbit hole. Curiouser and curiouser, I thought, quoting the little girl who got to go to fairy-tale land twice, and come home in one piece. That's one of the biggest reasons that no one ever thought Alice's adventures were real. Fairyland doesn't give second chances. But maybe the outside world was a little more forgiving. Maybe you have to be somewhere that isn't full of too many immortal things to have the hope of second chances. But since Galen and I were the only two of the exiled sidhe who had never been worshipped in the human world, maybe it wasn't second chances, but a first chance. The question was, a chance to do what?, because if he could convince fellow sidhe to do his bidding, humans wouldn't stand a chance.

CHAPTER FIFTEEN

THE ONLY LIGHT IN THE HUGE GREAT ROOM OF THE BEACH HOUSE was the glow of the roomy kitchen to one side, like a glowing cave in the growing dimness. Amatheon and Adair were in that glow panicking. They were both a little over six feet tall with broad shoulders, their bare arms in the modern T-shirts muscular from centuries of weapon practice. Adair's honey-brown hair was knotted and braided into a complicated club between his shoulder blades; unleashed, it hit his ankles. Amatheon's hair was a deep copper red, and curled enough so that the ponytail of knee-length hair was a foam of burnished red as he leaned down toward the chiming oven. They had kilts on instead of pants, but you just didn't see six feet-plus of immortal warrior panicking about anything often, but panicking in a kitchen with pots in their hands and the oven open while they peered inside in a puzzled manner was a very special and endearing type of panic.

Galen put me down gently but quickly, striding toward the kitchen to save the meal from their well-meaning but ineffectual ministrations. They weren't actually wringing their hands, but their body language said clearly that they'd run away if they could convince themselves it wouldn't be cowardly.

Galen entered the fray totally calm and in control. He liked to cook, and he'd taken well to modern conveniences, but then he'd visited the outside world often all his life. The other two men had only been outside faerie for a month. Galen took the pot out of Adair's hands and put it back on the stove on low heat. He got a towel, leaned in past Amatheon's waterfall of hair, and began taking pies out of the oven. In moments everything was under control.

Amatheon and Adair stood just outside the glow of the kitchen, looking crestfallen and relieved. "Please, never leave us in charge of a meal again," Adair said.

"I can cook over an open fire if I have to," Amatheon said, "but these modern contrivances are too different."

"Can either of you grill steaks?" Galen asked.

They looked at each other. "Do you mean over an open fire?" Amatheon asked.

"Yes, with a wire rack so the meat sits above the flames, but it's real fire and it's outside."

They both nodded. "We can do that." They sounded relieved. Adair added, "But Amatheon is the better cook of the two of us."

Galen got a platter out of the refrigerator, took plastic wrap off it, and handed it to Amatheon. "The steaks have been marinating. All you have to do is ask everyone how they like their steaks cooked."

"How they like them cooked?" he asked.

"Bloody, not so bloody, brown in the middle, gray in the middle," Galen said, wisely not even trying to explain rare, medium, and well done for the men. The last time either of them had been out of fairyland one of the Henrys was king of England. And that had been a brief outing into the human world, then back they'd gone to the only life they'd ever known. They'd had one month of modern kitchens and not having servants to do all the grunt work. They were actually doing better than some of the others who were new to the human world. Mistral was, unfortunately, not taking well at all to modern America. Since he was one of the fathers of my babies, that was a problem, but he wasn't here tonight. He didn't like traveling outside the walled estate in Holmby Hills that we called home. Amatheon,

Adair, and many of the other guards were cuter about it, and not so frustrating to the rest of us, which was nice.

Hafwyn joined Galen in the kitchen. Her long yellow braid moved in rhythm against the back of her body as she walked. She began to take things from him and hand things to him as if they'd done this before. Was Hafwyn helping in the kitchen more? As a healer, she didn't have guard duty, and as a healer we didn't feel that her having a job outside of that was a good idea, but she could heal with her hands, so no hospital or doctor would take her. Magic healing was still considered fraud in the United States. There had been too many charlatans over the centuries, so the law didn't leave much room for the genuine article.

Rhys was still beside me in the dimness of the huge living room, but Doyle and Frost had moved across the room past the huge dining room table that was all pale wood gleaming in the moonlight. They were silhouetted against the huge glass wall that looked directly out onto the ocean. There was a third silhouette that stood a foot taller than them. Barinthus was seven feet tall, the tallest sidhe I'd ever met. He was bending that height over the shorter men, and without hearing a word, I knew they were reporting the day's events. Barinthus had been my father's closest friend and advisor. The queen had feared him as both a kingmaker and a rival for the throne. He'd only been allowed to join the Unseelie Court on the promise that he would never try to rule there. But we weren't in the Unseelie Court anymore, and for the first time I was seeing what my aunt Andais might have seen. The men reported to him and asked his advice; even Doyle and Frost did. It was as if he had an aura of leadership wrapped around him that no crown, title, or bloodline could truly bestow. He was simply a point that people rallied around. I wasn't even sure how aware the other sidhe were that they were doing it.

Barinthus's ankle-length hair was unbound and spilled around his body like a cloak made of water, for his hair was every shade that ocean can be, from darkest blue to tropical turquoise to the gray of storm and everything in between. You couldn't see the extraordinary play of colors in the low light from the moonlit windows, but there was something of movement and flow to his hair even in the dark that made it ripple in the glow of what little light was available as if it were indeed water. His hair actually hid his body so I couldn't tell anything of his clothes.

He lived at the beach house to be near the ocean, and it was as if the longer he was near it, the stronger he grew, the more confident. He had once been Mannan Mac Lir, and there was still a sea god in there trying to get out. It was as if fairyland had drained him of his powers, but being near the ocean gave him back what most of the sidhe had lost when they had left faerie.

Rhys put an arm around my shoulders, and whispered, "Even Doyle treats him as a superior."

I nodded. "Does Doyle realize that yet?"

Rhys kissed me on the cheek, and he'd gotten his power under control enough that it was just a kiss, nice, but not so overwhelming. "I don't think so."

I turned and looked at him; he was only six inches taller than I, so it was almost direct eye contact. "But you noticed," I said.

He smiled and traced the edge of my face with one finger, like a child drawing in the sand. I leaned into that touch and he gave me more of his hand so that he cupped part of the side of my face in his hand. There were other men in my bed who could cup the entire side of my face in one hand, but Rhys was like me, not so big, and sometimes that was nice, too. Variety was not a bad thing.

Amatheon and Adair followed Hafwyn out the sliding-glass doors that led to the huge deck and the huge grill. The ocean rolled underneath that deck. Even without being able to see clearly, you could somehow feel all that power pulsing and moving against the pilings of the house.

Rhys put his forehead against mine and whispered, "How do you feel about the big guy taking over?"

"I don't know. There are so many other problems to solve."

His hand moved to the back of my neck and he moved our faces apart so he could move in for a kiss, but he spoke as he did it. "If you want to stop the power he is building you must do it soon, Merry." He kissed me as he said my name, and I let myself sink into that kiss. I let the warmth of his lips, the tenderness of his touch, hold me in a way that nothing else had today. Maybe it was finally being inside, away from the prying eyes that seemed to be everywhere, but something hard and unhappy loosened inside me as he kissed me.

He hugged me to him, and our bodies touched from shoulder to thigh as close as we could. I could feel his body growing hard and happy to see me against the front of my own. I don't know if we would have tried for a little predinner privacy in the bedrooms, because Caswyn came down the hallway from the bedrooms, and suddenly a lot of the happy seeped away from me.

It wasn't that he was not lovely, for he was, handsome, tall, slender, and muscular as most sidhe warriors were, but the air of sorrow that clung to him made my heart ache. He'd been a minor noble at the Unseelie Court. His hair was straight and raven black like Cathbodua's or even Queen Andais herself. His skin as pale as mine, or Frost's. His eyes were still circles of red, red-orange, and finally true orange, like a fire banked down in his eyes. Andais had quieted that fire in him by the torture she'd done to him, the night her son died and we fled faerie. Caswyn had been brought to us by a cloaked woman who told us only that Caswyn's mind would not survive any more of the Queen's Mercy. I wasn't entirely certain his mind wasn't already broken beyond repair. But since Caswyn had been the whipping boy for Andais's anger at us we took him in. His body had healed because he was sidhe, but his mind and heart were more fragile things.

He came down the hallway like a raven-haired ghost in an oversized white dress shirt untucked and billowing over a pair of cream dress slacks. The clothes were borrowed, but surely Frost's shirt had fit him better last week? Was he still not eating?

He came straight for me as if Rhys wasn't holding me. Rhys moved aside so that I could embrace Caswyn. He wrapped himself around me with a sigh that was almost a sob. I held him and let the fierceness of his grip envelop me. He'd been clingy and overly emotional since he had been rescued from the queen's bloody bed. She'd tortured him to punish me in a way, and because my lovers had been out of reach. She'd picked him at random. He'd never been anything to me, not friend or enemy. Caswyn had been as neutral as the courts allowed and centuries of diplomacy had crashed against Andais's madness. The cloaked noblewoman had said, "The queen asked him to bed her and as he was not one of her guards to be ordered so, he politely refused." Caswyn had been one rejection too many for her sanity. She'd turned him into a red ruin on her sheets and made certain to show it to me with a spell that turned a mirror into a video phone better than anything human technology had yet created. When I'd first seen him, he'd been so unrecognizable that I thought he was someone I cared for.

When she told me who it was I'd been puzzled. He was nothing to me. I could still hear Andais's voice, "Then you don't care what I do to him?"

I didn't know how to answer that, but finally I'd said, "He is a noble of the Unseelie Court and deserves protection from its queen."

"You refused the crown, Meredith, and this queen says he deserves nothing for his years of hiding. He's no one's enemy and no one's friend. I always hated that about him." She'd grabbed his hair and made him beg while we watched.

"I will distroy him."

"Why?" I'd asked.

"Because I can."

I'd told him to come to us if ever he could. Days later, with the help of a sidhe who wanted no one to know her identity, he had come. I could not take responsibility for my aunt's deeds. It was her evil and I was just an excuse for her to let out all her demons at once. I think and Doyle agreed, Andais was trying to force the nobles to assassinate her. It was a queen's version of "Suicide by cop."

Moments like that weren't uncommon for Queen Andais, my aunt, and that was one of the reasons that so many of the guards had agreed to exile rather than stay with her once they had a choice. Most of them liked a little tie-me-up-tie-me-down, but there was a line that few would cross willingly, and Andais wasn't a dominant in the sense of modern bondage and submission. She was a dominant in the old sense of might makes right, and being absolute ruler meant absolutely that. The old adage "Power corrupts and absolute power corrupts absolutely" applied to both of my royal relatives on both thrones. What I hadn't foreseen was her idea of pain and sex spreading to outside her personal guard, or that the nobles would keep taking the abuse. Why hadn't someone tried to kill her by now? Why didn't they fight back?

"I thought you were gone," Caswyn said. "I thought you were hurt, or worse; we all did."

"Doyle and Frost wouldn't let that happen," Rhys said.

Caswyn looked at him, still trying to drape all of that six-feet-plus frame around my much smaller one. "And how would they keep Princess Meredith from being cut to pieces with glass? Weapon skill and bravery won't stop every threat. Even the Queen's Darkness and the Killing Frost cannot stop the perils of modern life like man-made glass. It would have cut them all to pieces, not just the princess."

He spoke the truth. Old-fashioned glass made of naturally occurring substances with heat added could fall on my guards all day and not harm them, but anything with artificial additives, or metals, would cut them as much as me.

Doyle came across the room, speaking as he moved. "You are right, Wyn, but we would have shielded her body with ours. Meredith would have been unhurt no matter what happened to us." Aloud we'd started calling him Wyn because my aunt had made his full name a thing whispered in the dark with blood and pain.

I pushed gently on Wyn's chest to make him ease up and not lean so heavily on me. I couldn't take that kind of hugging forever without it beginning to hurt a little. The angle of my neck wasn't right for it.

"And the deli is owned by one of my Gran's cousins, a brownie named Matilda. She would have kept me safe."

Wyn unbent enough for his shoulder to go across mine, and my arm to encircle his waist. I could stand like that for hours, and he just seemed to need to touch me a lot. He was six feet of muscled warrior, but the queen had truly broken him in every way. His body had healed, as the sidhe do, but he only seemed to feel truly safe when he was with me, Doyle, Frost, Barinthus, Rhys, or anyone he perceived as powerful enough to keep him safe. The others made him afraid, as if he feared that Andais would snatch him away if he wasn't with someone strong.

"One brownie does not seem enough protection," he said in that uncertain voice that he'd had since he came to us. He'd never been the boldest of men, but now his fear was always there trembling below his skin, as if it ran in his blood now, so that fear was everywhere inside him.

I smiled up at him, trying to get him to smile back. "Brownies are a lot tougher than they look."

He didn't smile; he looked horrified. "Oh, Princess, forgive me." He actually dropped to one knee and bowed his head, all that pale hair sweeping out and around his body. "I forgot that you are yourself part brownie. I did not mean to imply that you were not powerful." He said all of it with his head bowed, and his gaze fixed on the floor, or at best my sandaled feet.

"Get up, Wyn. I took no offense."

He dropped lower so that he could lay his hands on the floor by my feet. His hair covered his face, so all I had was his ever-more-frantic voice. "Please, your majesty, I meant no offense."

"Wyn, I said that I took no offense."

"Please, please, I didn't mean any harm . . ."

Rhys knelt down by him. "Did you hear what Merry said, Wyn? She's not mad at you."

His forehead touched his hands on the floor so that he was in a position of abject abasement. He was saying "Please, please, don't," over and over again.

I knelt beside Rhys, and touched the long unbound hair. Caswyn actually screamed and laid himself flat on his stomach, hands out before him beseeching.

Doyle and Frost came to kneel on either side of him with us. They tried to calm him, but it was as if he couldn't hear us or see us, and whatever he was hearing and seeing was terrible.

I finally yelled at him. "Wyn, Wyn, its Merry! It's Merry!" I lay flat on the hardwood floor near his head. I could see nothing through all that hair, so I reached to smooth it back from his face.

He screamed, and scrambled back from my touch. The men tried to touch him, too, but he screamed at every touch, and scrambled away from us on hands and knees until he found a wall to huddle against. He held his hands out in front of him as if warding off blows.

In that moment I hated my aunt.

CHAPTER SIXTEEN

IT WAS HAFWYN WHO MOVED FORWARD, ARMS OUTSTRETCHED. "LET me help you, Caswyn."

He was shaking his head over and over, his hair in a wild profusion across his face so that his wide, staring eyes were framed by strands of his hair. It made him look wild, feral, and a little mad.

She started to bend and touch him, but he screamed again, and Galen was suddenly at her side, taking her wrist and saying "Make sure he sees you and not her before you touch him."

"He would never hurt me," she said.

"He may not know it's you," Galen said.

I started to get up off my knees and Rhys's hand was there to help me stand. Doyle and Frost were standing there staring at Caswyn. Their faces showed such grief.

I started toward them with Rhys's hand in mine. He drew back, and I looked at him. "My powers bring death, Merry. That won't help here."

I looked at Doyle and Frost, and even Barinthus still standing against the sliding-glass doors. I could see Amatheon and Adair out on the deck. They looked away when I made eye contact, as if they were happy to be outside cooking steaks, and not inside trying to make this better. That did seem easier, but the point to being a royal, a real one, was that you couldn't just do the easy things. Sometimes you had to do what was hardest if that was what your people needed. Caswyn needed something right now, and I was all we had.

I prayed, "Goddess, help me help him. Give me the power I need to heal him." I smelled roses, which was the scent that I smelled when the Goddess was answering prayers, or trying to get my attention.

Galen said, "Does anyone else smell flowers?"

"No," said Hafwyn.

"Does anyone else smell flowers or plants?" Rhys asked.

There was a chorus of deep bass "nos" throughout the room. I moved toward Galen and Hafwyn where they stood in front of Caswyn. The scent of roses was stronger as I moved toward them. That was one way I knew that the Goddess was saying yes. Inside faerie or a dream I got to see her, but in everyday life it was often perfume, or other less-dramatic signs.

Hafwyn moved away from Galen and Caswyn. Her blue eyes were wide as she said to me, "I can only heal the body, not the mind."

I nodded, and went to stand beside Galen. He looked down at me. "I'm not a healer."

"Me either," I said. I reached for his hand, nervous. The moment his hand wrapped around mine the scent of roses was even stronger, as if I stood beside a bank of wild roses thick with summer's heat.

"Flowers again," he said, "stronger than before."

"Yes," I said.

"How do we help him?" he asked.

And that was the question. How did we help him even with the scent of flowers around us, and the presence of the Goddess on the very air? How did we heal Caswyn outside of faerie?

The scent of roses was so thick it was as if I'd drunken rose water, so that it sat sweet and clean on my tongue. "May wine," Galen said, "I can taste May wine."

"Rose water," I said softly.

I started to kneel, and Galen knelt with me. "Goddess, let Caswyn see us. Let him know that we are his friends."

Galen's hand grew warm in mine, not heat warm, but as if he had been out in the sunshine and his skin held that warmth. He was smiling that welcoming, good-natured smile of his, and Caswyn was looking at him. His wide eyes began to lose their complete panic.

He said, "Galen."

"Yes, Wyn, it's me."

He looked frantically around the room, but he ended up staring at me. "Princess, where did she go?"

"Where did who go?" I asked, but I was pretty certain who "she" was.

Caswyn shook his head, making his hair slide over his face again. "I dare not speak her name after dark. She'll find me again."

"She's not in Los Angeles."

"Los Angeles?" he made it a question.

Galen asked, "Wyn, do you know where you are?"

Caswyn licked his lips, his eyes looking afraid again, but it was a different kind of fear now. It wasn't fear of some post-traumatic-stress vision, it was fear that he didn't know where he was, and he didn't know why he didn't know.

His eyes were wide and frightened as he whispered, "No, I don't know." He reached out to us and we both reached for him together with our unclasped hands. Was it accident or design that we touched him simultaneously, and both touched the bare skin of lower arms where the sleeves had been rolled back? Whatever the cause, the moment we all made skin contact magic breathed through us. It wasn't the overwhelming magic that it might have been inside faerie, but maybe that wasn't what Caswyn needed. Maybe what he needed to heal was something gentle, something like the touch of spring, or the first heat of summer when the roses fill the meadows.

Tears filled his eyes as he gazed at us, and we drew him into our arms and held him while he wept. We held him and the scent of flowers was everywhere.

CHAPTER SEVENTEEN

I SLEPT THAT NIGHT BETWEEN GALEN AND CASWYN WITH RHYS ON the far side of the big bed. There had been no sex, because Wyn needed to be held more than he needed to be fucked. In a very real way he'd been fucked up enough already, and the hands that held him as he drifted off to sleep were there to try to heal that. It had not been the restful end to the day that I'd wanted, but as I drifted off to sleep with Wyn spooned in my arms, and Galen spooned against my back, I realized that there were worse ways to end a day.

The dream started with me in the military Hummer. It was the one that the National Guard had rescued me with when I'd called for help so that my relatives couldn't take me back to either court. But none of the soldiers were in the Hummer. None of my guards. I was alone in the back with the Hummer driving itself. I knew that wasn't right, so I knew it was a dream. I'd dreamed about the bomb going off before, but always before it had been closer to the reality. Then I realized that the Hummer was black, completely, utterly black, and I knew it wasn't a military anything, but a new form of the Black Coach. It was the coach that had been coming to the beck and call of the ruler of the Unseelie Court for centuries. Once it had been a coach and four with horses blacker than any moonless night and eyes filled with fire that had never warmed anyone by a campfire. Then it had changed on its own and become a long black limousine with unholy fire under its hood. The Black Coach was a force of its own, a thing of its own, older than any of the fey courts, older than anyone could remember, which meant that it had existed for thousands of years or else it had simply appeared one day. Either way, it was somewhere between a living being and a magical construct, and it definitely had a mind of its own.

The question was, why was it in my dream? And was it just a dream, or did the Black Coach exist for "real" inside the dreamscape? It didn't talk, so I couldn't ask it, and I was alone so I couldn't ask anyone else.

The car drove itself over the narrow road. We were coming to the open meadow where the bomb had gone off. I'd ended up with shrapnel in one arm and shoulder, huge nails that had fallen out as I magically healed the wounded soldiers. I had never before had the gift of healing by the laying on of hands, but that night I did. But first there was the explosion.

The cold winter air came through the open window. I'd lowered it to use magic against our enemies because the soldiers were dying, dying to protect me, and I couldn't let that happen. They weren't my soldiers, my guards, and somehow giving their life to protect me hadn't seemed right. Not if I could stop it.

The explosion ripped the world apart with noise and force. I waited for the blow and the pain, but it didn't come. The world wavered with the vibration, and suddenly it was daylight, bright hot daylight. I was blinded by the glare of it all, and sand was everywhere. I had never been anywhere with so much sand and rock. The heat through the open window was like peering into a broiling oven.

The only things that were the same were the explosions. The world reverberated with their impact, and the Hummer's wheels rocked on the uneven ground of what had been a road before a bomb had put a crater in the middle of it.

There was another Hummer in desert camouflage colors, and there were soliders on one side of it using it for cover as something too big for a bullet and too small for a rocket whirred past. It made another impact crater in the road.

I heard a voice shouting, "They're getting into our range. They're getting into our range!"

The soldier on one end tried to move out from the Hummer but a bullet whizzed by him and hit the dirt of the road. They were pinned down and about to die.

Then the soldier at the other end of the line turned and saw the black Hummer. He had his rifle across his lap, one hand on it, but his other hand was wrapped around something at his neck. I thought it would be a cross, but then I saw his face, and knew it was a nail. A nail on the end of a leather cord tied around his neck.

He stared at me with large brown eyes, his skin dark enough with the sun's heat that he looked changed from the paler version I remembered. It was Brennan, one of the soldiers whom I had healed at the beginning of it all.

His mouth moved, and I saw the shape of my name. There was no sound over the cry of the weapons. "Meredith," he mouthed.

The Hummer drove to him, and the bullets seemed to not quite hit it, and when the next rocket came, it was just to one side of it. I felt the impact in my gut, as if the vibration ran through my body and hit me in the stomach. Sand and dirt fell like dry rain on the shiny black metal of the Hummer.

I opened the door, but it was as if only Brennan could see me. None of the others were mine. He said my name, and even over the ringing in my ears I heard the whisper of it, "Meredith." He reached up with the hand that had been clutching the nail around his throat. The others asked, "What are you doing?"

It was only as his hand wrapped around mine that the others saw me, saw the car. There were gasps of amazement and guns pointed at me, but Brennan said, "She's a friend. Now get in the Humvee!"

One of the other soldiers said, "Where did she come from? How did it . . ."

Brennan pushed him toward the front door. "Questions later."

Another rocket hit just on the other side of their Hummer, and suddenly there were no more questions. There was an exclamation of, "No one's driving!" But everyone piled in, Brennan squeezing beside me in the back, and the moment we were all inside the Hummer drove away. We drove farther down the road, which was intact enough to drive on, and the next moment the Humvee behind us exploded.

One of the new men said, "They got into our range."

The man from the front seat turned around and asked, "What the fuck is going on, Brennan?"

He looked at me as he said, "I prayed for help."

"Well, God hears you good," the other man said.

"It wasn't God I was praying to," Brennan said, and he looked into my eyes and reached out one hand as if afraid to touch me.

I put his hand against my face. There was grit and dirt and blood. He had a wound in his hand that he'd touched to the nail.

"I was praying to Goddess," Brennan said.

"You called me with blood, metal, and magic," I whispered.

"Where are you?" he asked.

"Los Angeles," I said.

I felt the dream, or vision, or whatever it was begin to soften and waver, and I spoke into the air, "Black Coach of mine, take them to safety. See that no harm comes to my people."

The radio in the front of the Humvee crackled to life, which made us all startle, and then give nervous laughs. The song was "Take it Easy" by The Eagles.

One of the soldiers said, "What is this, a Transformer movie?"

Their laughter was the last thing I heard as the dream faded, and I woke sitting bolt upright in the bed between the men. The bed was covered in pink rose petals.

CHAPTER EIGHTEEN

RHYS WAS THE ONLY ONE AWAKE FOR SOME REASON. GALEN AND WYN slept as if nothing was happening. The petals decorated their hair and faces, but they slept on.

Rhys said, "There's something on your face." He reached out and came away with dirt and fresh blood. "Are you hurt?" he asked.

"It's not my blood."

"Whose is it, then?" he asked.

"Brennan's."

"Corporal Brennan—the soldier you healed, who helped us fight?"

"Yes," I said. I wanted to know if Rhys had watched me dream. I wanted to know if my body had stayed here in the bed, or if I'd vanished, but I was half afraid to find out. But I had to know.

"How long have you been watching me?"

"I felt the touch of the Goddess. She woke me, and I kept guard over your sleep, though if you could come away with Brennan's blood on you, maybe I wasn't guarding the right part of you."

"Why are Galen and Wyn not awake?" I asked, my voice soft the way you do when people nearby are sleeping.

"I'm not sure. Let's leave them sleep and talk in the living room."

I didn't argue. I simply slipped out from the petal-covered sheet and the warmth of their bodies. Wyn snuggled into the hole I'd made. When he touched Galen, he stopped moving and settled back into deeper sleep. Galen never moved. That wasn't entirely unusual; he was a heavy sleeper, but not this heavy.

I stared down at him as Rhys gathered his holster, gun, and a short sword that he usually wore at his back. He was licensed to carry the gun here, but the sword was only allowed because technically he was still the bodyguard of Princess Meredith, and some things that might attack me respected a blade more than a bullet.

He gathered his weapons, but he didn't bother with clothes. He held out a hand to me, completely nude, with his weapons in his other hand.

I scooped up a short silk robe that had been lost to the floor. Sometimes I got cold; Rhys seldom did. He, like Frost, had once been a deity of colder things than a Southern California night.

He laid his weapons on the kitchen counter and turned on the light over the oven, making a small glow in the dark, quiet house. He turned on the coffeemaker, which was ready to go for the morning.

I chided him. "You just wanted coffee."

He smiled at me. "I always want coffee, but I think this may be a long talk, and I worked today, too."

"It's industrial espionage using magic, right?" I asked.

"Yes, but the Goddess didn't wake us up to talk about a case."

I slipped the robe on and tied it. It was black with red and green flowers on it here and there. I seldom wore all black if I could help it. It was too much my aunt Andais's signature color. My hair had gotten long enough that I had to sweep it out of the robe to settle the collar.

I enjoyed watching Rhys move around the kitchen nude. I admired the tight line of his ass as he stood on tiptoe to reach mugs from the cabinet.

"The problem with a seven-foot-tall man being the main one who lives here is that he puts things you use every day too damn high."

"He doesn't think about it," I said, and slid onto the bar stool near the front of the outside counter.

He got the mugs down, and turned with a grin. "Were you watching my ass?"

"Yes, and the rest of you. I'm enjoying watching you move around the kitchen in nothing but your smile."

That made him grin again as he put the mugs by the coffeemaker, which was now making the happy noises that said coffee was on its way.

He came to me, face going solemn. He gave me the full attention of that one blue-ringed eye. He raised his hand again, and touched the blood and grit on my face.

"I take it Brennan was injured."

"A small cut on his palm, and it was that hand that he gripped the nail with."

"He's still wearing it around his neck," Rhys said.

I nodded.

"You know the rumors about the soldiers who fought beside us?"

"No," I said.

"They're healing people, Merry. They're laying on hands."

I stared at him. "I thought that was just for that night, just with faerie's magic bleeding all over everything."

"Apparently not," he said. He studied my face, as if looking for something specific.

"What?" I asked, nervous under his so-serious scrutiny.

"You never left the bed, Merry. I swear to that, but Brennan touched you physically. Enough to leave dirt from his location and his blood, and that scares me."

He turned and started searching the drawers of the cabinets for something. He came up with ziplock bags and a spoon.

I must have given him a suspicious look, because he chuckled and explained. "I'm going to take a sample of the dirt and blood. I want to know what a modern lab will make of it."

"To get the Grey Detective Agency to pay for it you'll have to explain."

"Jeremy is a good boss, a good fey, and a good man. He'll let me put it through as part of a case."

I couldn't argue with anything he said about Jeremy. He'd been one of my few friends when I first came to Los Angeles.

Rhys opened one of the bags and leaned toward my cheek with the spoon. "This isn't exactly chain of evidence. If it was a real case the ziplock bag might let the other side argue that it was contaminated by anything and everything."

"I wasn't thinking when I touched it, so my skin is in there, and you're right about the method of collection, but this isn't a real case, Merry." He very carefully scraped some dirt into one of the open bags. He was so gentle I felt only a slight pressure.

When he had enough dirt he closed the bag. He got a new spoon and a new bag, and scraped some of the dirt, but I was betting that he had more blood in this one. He took more time with this one, and it actually scraped my skin a little. It didn't hurt, but it might have if he'd kept doing it long enough.

"What do you hope to gain by testing these?"

"I don't know, but we'll know more than we do right this minute." He started opening drawers until he found a Sharpie in the drawer closest to the phone. He wrote on the bags, dated them, signed his name, and had me sign them, too.

The rich smell of coffee filled the kitchen. It always smelled good. He poured coffee into one of the mugs, but I stopped him from doing it twice.

"No caffeine, remember?"

He hung his head enough for the white curls to fall forward. "I'm an idiot. I'm sorry, Merry. I'll put on water for tea."

"I should have said something earlier, but honestly, the dream spooked me."

He filled the kettle with water and put it on the stove, then came back to stand beside me. "Tell me about it while we wait for the water to boil."

"You can drink your coffee," I said.

He shook his head. "I'll get fresh when you can have tea."

"You don't have to do that," I said.

"I know." He put his hand over mine. "Your hands are cold." He took my hands in his and raised them to his mouth to lay a gentle kiss on them. "Tell me about the dream."

I took a deep breath and told him. He listened, made encouraging noises here and there, and held my hands, when he wasn't making tea. When I finished telling the story, my hands were a little warmer, and there was a pot of tea steeping on the counter.

"Traveling through a dream or vision isn't unheard-of for us in the far past, but to manifest physically so that a follower could touch us and be touched or rescued from danger, that is really rare, even when we were in our prime as a people."

"How rare?" I asked.

The timer went off for the tea, and he went to hit the button. "I was willing to believe that we'd been quiet enough not to wake anyone, but I purposefully put on that annoying buzzer for the tea." He used small tongs to fish out the tea toddy with the loose-leaf jasmine in it. "No one woke up, Merry."

I thought about that. "Doyle and Frost should have been up when we walked past the door to the bedroom they're in, but they didn't."

"This buzzer would wake the dead." He seemed to find that funny, laughed at his own joke, shook his head, and put a small strainer over my mug before he poured the tea.

"I'm not sure I get the joke," I said.

"Death deity," he said, half pointing at himself as he put the teapot down.

I nodded, as if that made perfect sense, which it didn't, but . . . "I still don't get the joke."

"Sorry, it's an insider sort of thing. You aren't a death deity, so you wouldn't get it."

"Okay."

He brought my mug of tea to me, then went back to pour out his cold coffee, and pour fresh for himself. He took a sip, closed his eye, and just looked happy. I raised my tea so I could smell the jasmine before I tasted it. With some of the gentler teas, scent was as important as taste.

"Why do you think that no one else has woken up? I mean, Galen and Wyn were right there through all of it."

"I think Goddess isn't done with you tonight, and it's something she wants us to do together."

"Do you think it's because you're the only death deity we have out here?"

He shrugged. "I'm not the only death deity in Los Angeles, I'm just the only Celtic one in Los Angeles."

I frowned at him. "Who do you mean?"

"Other religions have deities, Merry, and some of them like to walk around pretending to be people."

"You make it sound like they're not the same kind of deity that you and the others are."

He shrugged again. "I know that this particular deity is choosing to walk around in human shape, but he can be simply spirit. If you see me walking around without being in human form, I'm dead."

"So you mean not just something else with magic over the dead, but something that is truly a deity, a god with a capital 'G' like the Goddess and the Consort."

He nodded, sipping his coffee.

"Who is it? I mean, what is it? I mean, . . ."

"Nope, not going to tell you. I know you too well. You'll tell Doyle and he won't be able to resist a closer look. I've already spoken to the deity in question and he and I have a deal. I'll leave him alone and he'll leave us alone."

"Is he that scary?"

"Yes and no. Let's just say that I'd rather not test his limits when all we have to do is leave him alone."

"He's not harming anyone in the city, is he?"

"Leave it alone." He frowned. "I should have kept my big mouth shut."

I sipped my tea, enjoying the jasmine flavor, but honestly, the scent of Rhys's coffee overpowered the delicate perfume of flowers. Coffee would have been nice. I could try caffeine free.

"What are you thinking about so hard?" he asked suspiciously.

"I'm wondering if I could get caffeine-free coffee and how it would taste."

He laughed then, and leaned up to kiss my cheek. "We should clean you up."

He went to the sink again, and got a paper towel off the roll by the sink. He set his coffee down so he could get it wet. But the moment he came toward me with the towel, I smelled roses, not jasmine.

"No," I said, "we don't clean it off like this."

"What do you mean?" he asked.

I just knew the answer. "The ocean, Rhys, we clean it off in the ocean at the place where the water meets the shore."

"That's an in-between place," he said. "A place where faerie and a lot of other places meet the mundane world."

"It can be," I said.

"What do you have in mind?"

I took a deep breath and could smell jasmine again more than roses. "I'm not sure it's what *I* have in mind."

"All right, then what does the Goddess have in mind?"

"I don't know," I said.

"We're saying that a lot tonight. I don't like it."

"Me, either, but she's the Goddess. A real one like your nameless death deity."

"You're not going to let that go, are you?"

"No, because when I asked if he was harming people here, you wouldn't answer me."

"Fine, let's go down to the sea." He put his coffee down and held a hand out to me.

"Just like that, you'll go with me without knowing why."

"Yes."

"Because you don't want to talk about the death deity anymore," I said.

He smiled and made a wobbling motion with his head. "Partly, but the Goddess helped you save Brennan and his men. The Black Coach has chosen a new shape that will allow it to move through the war zone. The Goddess covered our bed with pink rose petals. She's never done that outside of faerie, or on nights when the wild magic is loose. Soldiers are healing people in your name. I think after all that that I'll take it on faith that she wants us down by the surf for a good reason."

I slid off the stool and put a hand in his. He grabbed his weapons as he moved past, and we went for the sliding-glass doors. He did add just before he let go of my hand to open the door, "If you get salt water on that silk robe it's ruined."

"You're right," I said, and undid the sash and let the robe fall to the floor.

He gave me the look that he'd been giving me since I was about sixteen, but now the look held knowledge and not just lust, but love. It was a good look.

"I don't think I'll need the robe," I said.

"The water's cold," he said.

I laughed. "Then I'm on top."

"There may be other problems with the cold."

"Ah, the guy problem with cold water," I said.

He nodded.

"Fertility deity, sort of. I think I can help you work around it," I said.

"Why does the Goddess want death and fertility at the water's edge?"

"She hasn't told me that part."

"Will she?"

I shrugged. "I don't know."

That made him shake his head, but he took my hand in his and we went out into the cool night air and the smell of the sea. We went out to do as the Goddess bid without knowing why, because sometimes faith is about that blind trust even if you were once worshipped as a god yourself.

CHAPTER NINETEEN

THE SAND WAS COOL UNDER OUR BARE FEET, WHICH DIDN'T PROMISE well for the water. I shivered, and Rhys put an arm across my shoulders, drawing me in against his muscled firmness. More than any of the other guards he was honed down to his essence, all muscle. He didn't have a six-pack, he had an eight-pack, which I hadn't known was possible.

He wrapped me in his arms and held me in the warmth of his embrace, though the metal of his gun was not warm against my bare back. He had the leather sheath of the short sword in the same hand, so it swung gently against my body. I clung to his warmth, wiggling a little closer and away from the hard press of the gun's lines.

"Sorry," he said, and moved the gun a little so it wouldn't dig into me. He laid his face against my hair. "I have weapons, but once we start having sex I won't be able to use them. I'll be too busy using my favorite weapon to worry about guns and swords."

"Weapon, is it?" I said smiling.

I felt his smile just by the flexing of his lips against my head. "Well, I don't mean to brag."

I laughed and looked up at him. He was grinning down at me. His face was half in moonlight and half in shadow. It hid his good eye and left his scars painted silver, his face looking smooth and perfect except for that glimmer of scar, so that the scar simply became another part of that perfection.

"Why so solemn?" he asked.

"Kiss me and find out."

"Wait. Before we get distracted, my point was a good one."

"Why, yes it is," I said, and I traced my fingers over the firm muscles of his stomach toward lower things.

He caught my hands in his empty hand, and used the hand full of weapons to help hold me still. "No, Merry, not until you hear me on this." He moved his face so all of him was in the bright, soft moonlight. The light grayed his eye so that it was no longer blue at all.

"Once the sex starts I will be too distracted to guard you. Everyone else is in what amounts to an enchanted sleep, so there will be no help if we need it."

I thought about what he'd said, and finally nodded. "You're right, but first we've made it clear to all of faerie that we want no throne of either kingdom, so killing me gains them nothing. Second, I don't believe the Goddess brought us out here to be attacked."

"You think she'll keep us safe?"

"Have you no faith left, Rhys?" I studied his face as I asked it.

He looked very sad and sighed. "Once I did."

"Let us go down to the sea and find it again for you."

He smiled, but it was sad around the edges. I wanted that sorrow gone.

I pulled gently on his hand and he let me pull away. I leaned up and kissed him, soft and full of lips, and let my body fall against his so he made a small surprised sound, still kissing me. Then his arms came up with gun and sword still in one, so I could feel the press of them against my back again.

I drew back from the kiss to find him a little breathless, lips parted, eye wide. I could feel his body growing hard and firm against mine.

He didn't protest again, but let me lead him toward the sighing of the sea.

CHAPTER TWENTY

THE SURF BECKONED LIKE WHITE FOAMING LACE, THE WATER BLACK and silver in the moonlight. The tide had grown and deepened around the bottom steps, so that I walked into the cold foam of the sea to find it spilling around my knees, while I could still touch the railing. It was cold enough to make me shiver, but the sight of Rhys there nude, suspicious, and very Rhys helped the shiver be more. The pull of the ocean made my legs move and the sand shift, as if the very world wasn't certain it would hold still.

"I'll have to pin everything down so the tide doesn't take it, Merry. Once I do that the weapons will be slow to draw."

I should have said no, or cautioned him, or tried to wake other guards, but I didn't. I said, "It will be all right, Rhys." Somehow, I knew it would be.

He didn't say a word, just moved down into the swirling water until he could touch my outstretched hand. The moment our hands touched, there was power, magic.

"We stand in a place betwixt and between neither land nor sea," I said.

"The closest we'll get to faerie here on the Western sea," he said.

I nodded.

Rhys threaded the straps of the sword sheath around the gun, and used the naked blade to pin the sheath to the sand. He knelt in the water, so that it was above his waist, to thrust the sword almost hilt deep into the shifting sand, so that it would not be pulled away by the sea.

He grinned up at me, still kneeling in the water, and the edge of it playing with the ends of his curls. "Most of the positions I'm thinking of will drown one of us."

"You can't drown, you're sidhe."

"Maybe I can't die from drowning, Merry, but trust me, it hurts like a son of a bitch to swallow that kind of water." He made a face and shivered, and I didn't think it was entirely the chill of the water.

I wondered what old memory was shaking him. I almost asked, but the scent of roses came mingled with the salt of the next wave. No bad memories tonight; we would make new and better ones.

I went to stand so that I could touch his shoulders and his face, and made him look up at me. There was a moment where the shadow of that old hurt was there in his face, and then he smiled up at me, wrapped his strong arms around my hips, and drew me in against his body. He kissed his way up my stomach, my chest, and my neck, as if the kisses themselves drew him to his feet until he could lay his lips against mine.

He kissed me. He kissed me as the water swirled and moved around us so that the pull and push of it was like more hands to caress our bodies, as our lips, hands, and arms explored the skin above the water's edge.

He leaned down, and used his hand to mound my breast up so his mouth could lick and suck, until just the pull of his mouth on my nipple made me cry out for him. He mounded the other breast with his other hand, and did the same again. He went back and forth between them as the water rose around us, until I cried out his name. Only then did he drop back to his knees, chest deep in the water, and lift me so that my knees were on his shoulders, and his face was between my legs.

I protested, "You can't hold this position long enough."

He gazed up the line of my body, his mouth close to that most intimate part, but not quite touching me yet. "Probably not," he said.

"Then why do it?"

He grinned. "Because I want to try." And that was very Rhys. It made me smile, and then his mouth found me, and it wasn't smiles he got from me.

He bowed my body backward with the strength of his hands and arms so that he could reach all of me to lick and suck. His hands were actually supporting my weight at the small of my back, my legs on his shoulders like some impossible act. I kept meaning to tell him to put me down, to be reasonable, but every time I came close to saying it, he would do something with his mouth, his tongue, and he would steal my words away with pleasure.

I felt his arms begin to tremble, ever so slightly, as that delicious pressure began to build between my legs, so that it would be a race to see if he could spill me over that edge before he had to put me down. A few sensations earlier and I would have told him to put me down when I felt his muscles begin to tremble, but the pleasure had passed to that point of selfishness so that I wanted release more than I wanted to be kind or generous. I wanted him to finish what he had begun. I wanted him to spill me over that wet, warm edge.

My skin had begun to glow as if I was some still pool that could reflect the moon's glow to herself. Rhys had called my magic to life.

In the end he moved on his knees, so that my back touched the railing. The water was high enough that the lower steps were underwater, and I leaned back against the wood, using the railing as I would have used the headboard of a bed to support my weight, to keep me at the angle he needed. He moved up the water-covered steps so that they helped him support my weight as he licked and sucked, and made love to me there with his mouth as he would make love to me later with other things.

I caught the glow of my own hair and eyes; crimson, emerald, and gold. His own skin had begun to glow white with a play of light underneath it as if clouds or something else moved inside his body, things I couldn't see or understand.

I was almost there, almost there, almost there, then between one caress of his tongue and the next that building warmth between my legs spilled out and over and through me in a warm rush that danced over my body, and made me grind my hips against his face. He sucked harder, drawing the pleasure out, making it last, growing one orgasm into another, into another, until I shrieked, and screamed at the moon above us.

Only when I sagged, limp, and couldn't quite make my hands keep their hold on the railing did he stop and stand on the steps to lift me with his arms, and let the rising water buoy me up. I felt him push against the front of my body. The cold water had done him no harm, because he was long and hard and eager as he pushed against my opening.

The sea came spilling between our legs. It was too soon since his kiss there, so that it made me cry out as he pushed his way inside me, as if the sea and Rhys were both making love to me at the same time.

Then he was inside me, as deep as he could go, pinning me against the railing, his hands holding onto the wood to keep the waves from chasing us down into the sea. I wrapped my legs around his waist, my arms around his shoulders, and I kissed him. I kissed him and tasted me on his lips, fresh and salty, my body mingled with the ocean so that it was different, as if he'd gone down on someone else, someone who tasted of the sea.

His eye with its three circles of color had regained its blue, because his magic had its own light to show me the day's blue sky in his eye, if the sky could burn blue.

He slid in and out of me, with the waves helping some of the time, and some of the time they seemed determined to pull us apart, as if they were jealous of what we were doing. I began to feel that growing weight of pleasure again, but deeper inside me this time.

I wasn't sure if I shouted or whispered against his face, "Soon, soon."

He understood, and he began to work his hips faster, driving himself deeper and quicker, so that each thrust ran over that part of me, and the waves tried to help find that spot inside me, but Rhys gave them no room. He filled me up, and then between one thrust and the next I was screaming his name again, my nails pinning into his back, tracing my pleasure in half-moons on his pale skin.

I screamed his name as he rode me, in the sea and the steps leading up. I felt him fight his body to keep the rhythm that had brought me so that he could bring me again and again, and only when I'd lost count did he finally allow himself that last deep thrust that spasmed him backward, so that he was staring at the sky as he finally let himself go.

That last deep thrust brought me one final time, and it was then that the scent of roses fell around us in a shower of pink petals that glided out to sea with the waves. The magic rushed across our skin like a different kind of orgasm, so that our skin ran in shivers, but it was warm, so warm. Warm enough that the sea could not be cold for us. The twin glow of our bodies merged and became one, as if together we could make a new moon to send into the sky—a moon that had eyes of liquid fire, burning emeralds, spun garnets, melting gold, and sapphires so blue they would make you weep to see them. His hair was white foam around his face, across his shoulders, merging with the white glow of our bodies.

It was only then that I realized we should have put up a circle to keep in the power, or to control it, but it was too late. The power surged through us and went up and out into the night. I'd felt a release of power before, but never one with such purpose. Always before it had been almost accidental, but I felt our merged energies seeking something, like a magical missile aimed at a target.

We felt it hit, and I half expected to hear the echo of some great explosion, but there was no sound. The impact of it shook us, and sent Rhys thrusting inside me one last time, as we both cried out at the release of our bodies and the release of the magic miles away.

Only when our skin began to fade, glowing around the edges, instead of that white-hot light, only then did he let himself slide to his knees, still holding me, as I slid down the railing. The sea held our weight, and then tried to spill us down the steps. He moved us up in a kind of crawl until he had us safe on a drier step. He had fallen out of me somewhere in the climb but we were both ready to be done. It had been enough.

He gave a shaky laugh as he cradled me against him, and we leaned back against the steps.

"What was that magic?" I asked, my voice still breathless.

"It was the power of faerie creating a sithen."

"A hollow hill here in Los Angeles," I said.

He nodded, still trying to catch his own breath. "I caught a glimpse of it. It's a building, a new building that wasn't there before."

"Wasn't where before?" I asked.

"On a street."

"What street?" I asked.

"I don't know, but tomorrow I'll be able to find it. It will call to me."

"Rhys, how will you explain a new building appearing?"

"I won't have to, just as the hollow hills would appear and the people would think the hill had been there forever. If the magic works as it always has, everyone will accept that it's been there. I'll be new moving in, but the building won't look new, and people will remember it."

I laid my head on his chest, and his heart was still thudding fast. "A sithen is like a new court of faerie, right?"

"Yes," he said.

"So, in essence, faerie just made you a king."

"Not the Ard-ri, but a lesser king, yes."

"But I didn't see the building. I didn't feel it."

"You are the high queen, Merry. You don't have just one sithen; in a way they're all yours."

"Are you saying that the other men will get them, too?"

"I don't know. Maybe only those of us who had one once upon a time."

"Which would be you, and who?"

"Barinthus for one. I'll have to think about the others. It's been so long for most, so many centuries. You try to forget what you were before, because you don't ever think you'll get it back. You try to forget."

"First my dream or vision and being able to save Brennan and his men when they have to be hundreds of miles away, and then them being able to heal with my blessing, or whatever you want to call it. Now this. What does it all mean?"

"The sidhe didn't appreciate the Goddess coming back through you. I think she's decided to find out if the humans are more grateful than the fey."

"And what exactly does that mean?" I asked.

He laughed again. "I don't know, but I can hardly wait to see this new modern sithen, or try to explain all this to Doyle and Frost." He pushed to his feet, grabbing onto the railing to steady himself.

"I can't walk yet," I said.

He grinned. "High praise for me."

I smiled at him. "Very."

"I'm going to rescue my weapons before the tide rises any more. I'll have to clean everything. Salt water rusts like nothing else." He waded down into the water, and finally had to dive out of sight in the waves to find where he'd pierced the sand and left his weapons.

I had a moment of being alone with the sea and the wind and the moon full and glowing above me. I whispered, "Thank you, Mother."

Then I heard Rhys surface, taking a deep breath, splashing toward the steps, his weapons dangling from his hand, his curls plastered to his face and shoulders. He walked up beside me, the water running down his skin in shining rivulets.

"Can you walk yet?"

"With help, I think so."

He grinned again. "That was amazing."

"The sex or the magic?" I asked as he helped me to my feet. My knees were still weak enough that I grabbed for the railing even with his arm on mine.

"Both," he said. "Consort save us, but it was both."

We walked a little shakily up the steps laughing. The wind from the water seemed much warmer than before we'd made love, as if the weather had changed its mind and decided that summer was a better idea than autumn.

CHAPTER TWENTY-ONE

SALT WATER IS ONE THING YOU HAVE TO RINSE OFF YOUR BODY BEfore you fall into bed. I was in the big shower doing just that when the door burst open and Ivi and Brii, short for Briac, were in the doorway, breathing hard, and weapons naked in their hands.

I froze in the middle of rinsing the conditioner out of my hair, blinking at them through the glass of the shower doors.

I caught movement from the corner of my eye, and Rhys was just suddenly sliding in low through the door they had left open behind them. He had his newly oiled sword at Brii's throat, and his newly cleaned gun pointed at Ivi as the other man froze in mid-motion of bringing his own gun up.

"Sloppy," Rhys said, "both of you. Why did you leave your posts?"

They were both breathing so hard I could see their chests fighting for air, so much so that they couldn't get enough air to talk. Brii might have been having trouble talking around the sword point that never wavered from his skin, and the short bow in his hand with its half-cocked arrow and a hand full of arrows fanned in his fingers were completely useless.

Brii blinked brilliant green eyes, his hair the yellow of cherry leaves in the fall, tied back in a long braid. His clothing was leather and could have looked like club wear, but was actually pieces of armor older than most people's history books.

Rhys's sword point seemed to be shoved up against the thudding pulse in his throat.

He looked at the other man, who was still frozen, unmoving under the point of his gun; only the frantic rise and fall of his chest betrayed him. His green and white hair was loose and swirled around his legs, but like Doyle and Frost, it never seemed to tangle. Unlike them, Ivi had a pattern of vines and leaves like a print upon his hair. His namesake on his hair was like a work of art, and his eyes were starbursts of green and white, so that people would ask him if it was fancy contacts, but it was just Ivi. He wore modern clothes, and the vest on his chest was modern body armor.

Rhys said, "Ivi, explain, and it better be good." He never took his gun off the other man.

Ivi fought his own breath and pounding heart rate to speak. "We woke . . . on guard duty. Enchanted sleep . . . thought enemies." He coughed, sharply trying to clear his throat, or take a deeper breath. He was being very careful about keeping the naked gun unmoving in his hand. "Thought we'd find Princess dead, or taken."

"I could kill you both for falling asleep on duty," Rhys said.

Ivi gave a small nod. "You're third in command, you have that right."

Brii finally managed to talk around the sword point and his pulse. "We failed the princess."

Rhys moved in one motion, taking the sword from Brii's throat, lowering his gun to the floor, and standing in the doorway as if he'd just walked through. With Frost and Doyle around me, I sometimes forgot that there was more than one reason that Rhys had been third in command of the Queen's Ravens. When everyone is this good, it's hard to remember just how good that is.

"It was the Goddess herself who did the enchanted sleep," Rhys said. "None of us can fight that, so I guess I won't kill you tonight."

Ivi said, "Shit." He went to his knees outside the shower doors, laying his head on his arm that held the gun. Brii leaned his back against the half wall by the shower. He had to adjust the long bow at his back so it didn't get damaged against the tile. He was one of the guards who hadn't embraced guns yet, but when you were as good with a bow as he was, it wasn't as big a problem as it might have been, according to Doyle.

I leaned my hair back into the water enough to finish rinsing off. It was Rhys's turn in the shower anyway. He'd cleaned his weapons first.

"What do you mean, the Goddess herself?" Brii asked.

Rhys started to explain, a much edited version of things. I turned off the shower, and opened the door to get the towels that always seemed to be hanging where we needed them. I had a moment to wonder if Barinthus put out the towels, but I doubted it. He didn't strike me as that domestic.

Brii handed me the first towel, but his eyes were all for Rhys and the story. I bent over to wrap my hair, and it was Ivi's hand that traced my back and slid lower. It made me look at him, because I would have thought that talk of the Goddess would have distracted him from such things. But, unlike Brii, his eyes were on me. There was a heat in his eyes that shouldn't have been there after a month of freedom—a month when we had almost an even number of male and female sidhe guards.

"Ivi," Rhys said, "you aren't listening to me." He didn't sound angry, but rather puzzled.

Ivi blinked and shook himself like a bird settling its feathers. "I would say apologies, but we're both so old that that's an insult, so what do I say, that the sight of the princess naked distracted me from anything you could say?" He smiled at the end but it wasn't a completely happy smile.

"You and the others were supposed to talk to Merry at dinner about this."

"The Fear Dearg are back," Ivi said. "I remember them, oh Lord of Death. It was they I first thought of when we woke and found that both of us were asleep on duty." Ivi made a face; it was anger, disgust, and other things I couldn't read.

"I am too young to remember, for I was not yet aware," Brii said, "but I came to true life not long after the end of it and I remember the stories. I saw the wounds and the damage done. When such enemies are about, what good soldier complains about anything else?"

I stood there with my hair in its towel, but the other towel loose in my hands. "I'm missing something here," I said.

"Tell her," Rhys said, making a little go-ahead motion with his gun.

Brii looked embarrassed, and that was a rare emotion for the sidhe. Ivi lowered his bold eyes, but said, "I have failed at my post this night. How can I ask for more after that?"

"Galen and Wyn were still deep asleep when I came in here. This should have woken them?" I asked.

The three men looked at each other, and then Brii and Rhys both moved out through the door enough to see the big bed. They came back into the bathroom, with Rhys shaking his head. "They haven't moved." He seemed to think about that. "In fact, Doyle and Frost should be in here. All the rest of the guards should be in here with weapons drawn. These two"—and he motioned with his sword at them—"made a hell of a lot of noise rushing to save you."

"But no one else woke up," I said.

Rhys smiled. "The Goddess has kept everyone but the two of you asleep. I think that means you get to have your talk with Merry. My weapons are clean. Now it's my turn in the shower."

"Wait," I said, "what talk?"

Rhys kissed me on the forehead. "Your guards are afraid of you, Merry. They're afraid you'll be like your aunt, and your cousin, or uncle, or grandfather." He looked up as if thinking over the list.

"There's a lot of bad crazy in my family tree," I said.

"Most of the new guard who followed you out of faerie have stayed celibate."

I stared at him, and then turned slowly to stare from Brii to Ivi.

"Why, in the name of the Danu? I told you my aunt's celibacy rule didn't hold anymore."

"She said that in the past," Brii said slowly, "and she was fine if it was casual lusts, but if we found someone we cared for . . ." He stopped and looked to Ivi.

"I never fell in love with anyone," Ivi said, "and after seeing what she did to some of the lady loves, I had never been so happy that I was a cad and a bounder in my existence."

"I have six fathers and six consorts. I'm okay that the rest of you have sex, make friends, fall in love. It would be wonderful if more of you fell in love."

"You seem to mean that," Ivi said, "but your relatives have seemed sane over the centuries, but they weren't."

I realized what he was saying. "You think I'm going to go crazy like my aunt, and cousin, and uncle, and . . ." I thought about it, and could only nod. "I guess I see your point."

"None of them but your grandfather was always cruel and horrible," Ivi said.

"There's a reason his name is Uar the Cruel," I said, and I didn't try to keep the look of disgust off my face. He'd never had any use for me, nor I for him.

"It always seemed that jealousy was what undid your relatives—jealousy of affection, of power, of possessions even," Brii said. "You have a relative on both thrones of faerie, and they are both vain and hate anyone who even hints that they may not be the most beautiful, the most handsome, the most powerful."

"You believe that if you go to other lovers I will see it as a rejection of my beauty?"

"Something like that, yes," he said.

I looked from one to the other of them, frowning. "I don't know how to reassure you, because you're right about my blood relatives. My father and grandmother were sane, but even my own mother isn't quite right. So I don't know how to reassure you."

"It's the fact that you haven't touched any of them that's creeping them out," Rhys said.

"What?"

"The queen would only let the guards she hadn't slept with find other lovers. If she'd had sex with you then you were hers forever even if she never touched you again."

I stared at him. "You mean before the celibacy nonsense that was her rule?"

"Her law," Ivi said.

"She was always a very possessive woman," Rhys said.

"She was always crazy, you mean," I said.

"No, not always," Rhys said.

The other men agreed.

"And the very fact that once the queen wasn't mad, but just ruthless, is what frightens us about you, Princess Meredith," Ivi said.

"You see," Brii said, "if she had always been mad then we would trust that your reasonableness would last, but once the queen was reasonable. Once she was a good ruler or faerie and the Goddess wouldn't have chosen her."

"I see the problem," I said, and wrapped the almost forgotten towel around me. I felt a little cold all of a sudden. I hadn't thought about my family quite like this. What if it was genetic? What if sadistic craziness was inside me somewhere, waiting for a chance to come out? Was it possible? Well, yes, but . . . My hand went to my stomach, still so flat, but there were babies in there. Would they take after me and my father, or . . . That was the most frightening of all. I trusted myself, but the babies were unknown.

"What can I do?" I asked. I wasn't even sure which fear I was asking about, but the men had only one fear to focus on.

"We failed you tonight, Princess Meredith," Brii said. "We do not deserve any more consideration than our lives."

"When the Goddess moves among us none can stand in her way," Rhys said.

"Do you really think that the Darkness or the Killing Frost would see it that way if something had happened to her?" Ivi asked.

"If something had happened to her, neither would I," Rhys said, and there was that hardness to him that he hid most of the time behind jokes and his love of film noir, but more and more I glimpsed it. He'd come back into a lot of his power that had been gone for centuries, and there is something about that much power that makes you harder.

"See," Ivi said.

"Again, I feel like I'm missing something. Rhys, just tell me what they keep tiptoeing around."

Rhys looked from one man to the other. "You have to ask for yourselves. That's always been the rule."

"Because if you won't ask for yourself, you don't want it that badly," Brii finished for him, a little sadly. He began to put all his arrows away, and turned for the still-open door.

"Stay, for if I ask it can be for both of us," Ivi said.

Brii hesitated in the doorway.

"I want it badly enough to ask," Ivi said.

"Ask what?" I said.

"Make love to us, have sex with us, fuck us. I don't care what you call it, but please touch us. If you touch us tonight and let us have other lovers tomorrow and are calm about it, then it will be proof that you are not your aunt, or even your uncle of the Bright court. He wouldn't kill lovers who went to another bed, but he destroyed them politically at court, because to go directly to another bed after a night with him said, to him at least, that he wasn't good enough to make you not want someone else."

"See why I would not ask tonight?" Brii said. "It is a great honor to be in the bed of our ruler, and it should not be a reward for such badly done duty."

"The Goddess woke you first," I said. "There has to be a reason for that."

"I don't smell flowers," Rhys said.

"Me neither, but maybe this isn't about Goddess work, as much as the fact that someone should have told me that sooner. I lived in fear of my aunt my entire life. I've been her victim of torture, and my cousin made my childhood a misery when my father wasn't watching."

"We need to know how much of the queen is in her niece," Ivi said, and he was very solemn, unlike his usual teasing self. I realized that maybe his teasing, like Rhys's humor, was hiding more serious things.

"Rhys needs the shower, and the beds are all taken, but the couches are big enough."

Rhys kissed me on the cheek. "Have fun." He moved past me to the showers, but put his weapons at the back of the shower, where the shelf had been designed for less lethal things, but it worked perfectly for weapons, as we'd all discovered.

"The couches are big enough for what?" Brii asked.

"Sex," I said. "Sex tonight, but tomorrow you have to persuade one of the other guards to be with you, because this only works if you go from my bed almost directly to someone else, right?"

"Will that not bother you?" Brii asked.

I laughed. "If I wasn't part fertility deity you wouldn't get sex tonight. Rhys did his duty very well tonight, and if I were truly mortal flesh I'd be a little sore, but I am not, and the power will rise between us and it will be good."

"So your orders are to make love to you now, but find another guard to sleep with as soon as possible?" Ivi asked.

I thought about it, and then nodded. "Yes, those are my orders."

Ivi grinned at me. "I like you."

I smiled back at him, because I couldn't help it. "I like you, too. Now let's go find the couches and prove just how much we like each other."

I heard the shower turn on behind us as we moved for the door.

CHAPTER TWENTY-TWO

THERE WERE ACTUALLY TWO LIVING ROOMS IN THE BEACH HOUSE. One was smaller and more intimate, if you could use that word for a space large enough to hold the dining room, kitchen, entrance, foyer, and a small sitting area off to one side. It was the Great Room, but the part that was a living room was smaller than the rest, so it was the small living room. The big one was a room to itself, with a bank of windows that ran from high-peaked ceiling to carpeted floor. It was one of the few carpeted areas in the house, so water tracked in here would be a problem, which was why it was isolated from most of the other rooms, and didn't have a door connecting to the beach. The long, wide sectional couch made a nearly full square in the room. There was only one narrow entrance on one end, and coffee tables built into the furniture at intervals, so you had a place to put your drinks, if the small golden wood table that sat to one side, next to a fully stocked bar, wasn't enough to set your drinks down.

The couches themselves were white, sitting in a sea of tan carpet. The color scheme was very close to Maeve Reed's main house. There were cool colors—whites, creams, tans, golds, and blues—in other parts of the house, but here there was nothing to distract the eye from the amazing expanse of ocean, and if you weren't bothered by heights you could stand near the windows and gaze down at sharp rocks that were pounded by the sea.

It was both a beautiful room and a cold one. It felt like a place created to entertain business associates, not friends. We were going to try to add some warmth to the decor.

The sky was still black against the glass. The sea stretched out, and almost oily in its ink-black shine, as it reflected the ripe moon.

The tan carpet was faded to a gray-white by the moonlight and the dark. The couches glowed almost ghostly in the moonlight. It was bright enough that it made thick shadows around the room. It took a bright moon to make shadows like that. The three of us walked into those bright shadows and our skin reflected the light as if we were white water to shine under the glow of the moon.

The house was so silent that I could hear the rush and murmur of the sea on the rocks below. We moved in a silence formed of moonlight, shadows, and the sighing of the sea.

I moved toward the couch that was closest to the glass wall, because to call it a window didn't do it justice. It was a wall of glass so that the sea stretched out forever until it met the curve of the world in a dark, moving circle that glowed and shimmered under the touch of the moon.

Something about the play of light made me want to see more of the view, so I passed the couch up and stood at the edge of the glass, where I could have that dizzying glimpse of the sea and the rocks, the water foaming silver and white in the dark light.

Brii began to take off his bows, arrows, and blades, laying them carefully on the long table to the side of the room.

Ivi came to me with his holstered gun and the sword at his belt. He came to me with the body armor vest still in place. Most of the men were tentative after so long without a woman, but Ivi grabbed my upper arms in an almost bruising grip and lifted me off the ground so he could kiss me. There was no bending down for this man; he made me come to him, and he was strong enough to pick me up off the ground and simply hold me where he wanted me.

The towel on my hair fell to the floor, so that my hair was wet and cold against our faces. He put one arm around my waist to hold me. The other hand he wrapped in my wet hair and pulled hard and sharp, so that I cried out for him, part pain and part something else.

His voice was harsh and fierce, already going lower as some men's do. "The others said you liked pain."

My voice came out breathy, strained with the hold he had on me. "Some pain, not a lot."

"But you like this," he said.

"Yes, I like this."

"Good, because so do I." He had to let go of my hair to pin me more tightly against his body as his other hand undid the Velcro of his vest. Then he flung me to the carpet and jerked his vest over his head in almost the same movement.

I lay there, breathless from the suddenness of it, and he'd hit just the right note so that I felt passive. The willing victim was a game I enjoyed if it was done right. Done wrong and he'd have a fight on his hands. The towel that had been covering me had come undone so that I simply lay on it naked and bare for the moonlight and for him.

He pinned my legs by kneeling on them, trapping my lower body, while he stripped off guns, sword, belt, and T-shirt. They made a pile around him like petals torn from an impatient flower.

He rose above me, putting more pressure on my legs, so that it was almost pain, but not quite. I had seen him nude, because most of us had no problem with nudity, but getting a glimpse of a man without his clothes is not the same thing as looking up the line of that same body as it kneels over you, and you know that this time everything that body promises is about to be yours.

His waist was long and slender. Even the muscles under all that gleaming skin were long and lean, as if no matter what he did he wouldn't bulk up. He was built like a long-distance runner, grace and speed mixed in with all that strength. His hair fanned out around him, and I realized it was moving on its own with no wind but his own magic to make it spread out around him like a body-long halo of white, gray, and silver, and the vines that traced that hair glowed more brightly, as if electric wire had been run to every line of vine and leaf so that they were painted in shades of green. The spiral of his eyes had begun to move, as if I would grow dizzy if I looked too long.

Whatever he saw in my face, it made him undo his pants, and push them down slender hips so that he revealed that last part of himself already hard and long and thick, as if his body had decided that the rest of him was slender enough and it would make up for it here. He pressed against the front of his own body, thick and long, and everything you could want in that moment.

He leaned over me, his knees still pinning my legs, so that he would have to move to use all that thick, quivering eagerness. He leaned over me, and his hair didn't fall forward, it moved to either side of us so that we were sheltered in the glow and movement of it. His hair made a sound like wind in leaves around us.

He pinned my wrists against the floor, and I was completely pinned, but he could not reach me. So I was trapped, but to no purpose that I could see.

He leaned his face over mine, and whispered, "Don't frown, Meredith. That's not the look I want on your face right now."

My voice was breathy, but I managed to ask, "What look do you want on my face?"

He kissed me. He kissed me as if he was eating me from the mouth down, all teeth and biting, and then when I was about to cry enough, he changed to a long, deep kiss, as tender and full of care as any I had ever had.

He raised his face just enough so I could see his eyes. They weren't spirals anymore, but just a glowing green as if he would be blind from the light. "That look," he said. "You said in the shower that you'd had all the foreplay you needed, so I won't bother tonight, but I want you to know that I am not like your Mistral. There are nights when gentle is good, too."

"But not tonight," I whispered.

He smiled. "No, not tonight, because I've seen you make a thousand decisions every day, Princess. Always in charge of something, always a choice to be made, always something to affect so many people. I've felt you needing to have a place where the decisions are made for you, and choice is not yours, some place where you can let go and stop being the princess."

"And be what?" I whispered.

"Just this," he said. He pinned my wrists with one hand and used the other to push his pants down to the middle of his thighs. Then he moved his knees from on top of my legs to use them to slide my thighs wider, so that he could begin to push against my opening.

He was almost too long for the angle he was using, so he had to use his free hand to move himself until he could slip the tip of himself inside. He was wide enough that even with my earlier sex, he had to push himself inside me, working his way in with his hips.

I raised my head enough that I could watch his body push its way into mine. There is always something about that first time that a man enters me that makes me want to watch, and just the sight of him so thick, so big . . . made me cry out, wordlessly.

He had almost his full weight on my wrists where he had pinned them. It hurt, but in that good way, in that way that let me know that the moment of decision was truly past. I could have said no, protested, but if he didn't want to let me go, I could not make him, and there was something about that moment of surrender that was exactly what I needed.

I cried out twice more before he worked his way as far inside as he was going. We ran into the end of my body before we ran out of the end of him. Then he began to pull himself back out, and then the push in, and finally I was wet enough, and he was ready enough. He began to push himself in and out in long, slow strokes. I'd expected the sex to be rough to go with the way he'd started, but once he was inside me, it was like the second kiss he'd given me, deep, tender, amazing.

He worked that slow, steady stroking until it spilled me over the edge and made me scream his name. My hands strained under his, and if I could have reached him I'd have painted his body with my nails, but he held me easily, keeping himself safe while he rode me and made me scream his name.

My body ran with light, my skin glowing to match his. My hair was like ruby lights reflecting on the white and dark of his hair, and my eyes adding shimmering gold and different shades of green to his, so that we lay in a tunnel of light and magic formed of the fall of his own hair.

Only after I was a quivering thing, all nerve endings, and fluttering eyes that could focus on nothing, did he start again. This time there was nothing gentle about it. This time he rode me as if he owned me, and he wanted to make certain that he touched every part of me. He pounded himself into me, and it brought me again with almost the first stroke, so that I screamed over and over again, as if every push of his body brought me. I couldn't tell where one orgasm stopped and the next began. It was one long line of pleasure, until my voice was hoarse with screaming and I was only dimly aware of my surroundings. The world had narrowed down to the pounding of his body and the pleasure of mine.

In the end, he gave one last push, and in that moment I knew he'd been more careful, because that last thrust got a real scream out of me, but the pain was mingled with so much pleasure that it ceased to be pain and just became a part of the warm, glowing edge of ecstasy.

It was only as he began to pull himself out of me that I realized he wasn't pinning my wrists anymore, but something was. I couldn't make my eyes focus enough to see, but when I pulled on my wrists there were ropes, but unlike any rope I'd ever touched.

He moved from on top of me and I realized I couldn't move my legs either. More of the ropes were laced around my thighs and lower legs.

It made me struggle harder to see, to focus, and to be aware. I hated to chase back the edge of so much pleasure, but I wanted to see what he'd used to tie me, and how he'd done it without moving his hands.

There were vines around my wrists, vines that led to more vines that had climbed part of the glass wall, so that the dark lines of them were silhouetted against the softening dark. It wasn't as dark as it had been when we started, but it wasn't dawn either. The darkness was fading but there was no true light. False dawn pressed against the windows, half-hidden by the dark lines of ivy vines.

Ivi got to his feet, using the back of the couch to steady himself, and even then he almost fell. "I haven't been able to pleasure a woman like that in so long. I haven't been able to call the vines for even longer. You are ivy-bound, Princess."

I tried to say that I didn't know what that meant, but Briac was standing by the vine-covered glass. He was nude, and I could see the ash-white of his skin, not moonlight skin like mine, but a gray-white that no one else in either court could boast. His shoulders were broader than Ivi's, and there was more meat and muscle to his body. Brii was still beautiful, graceful with his long yellow braid of hair trailing over one shoulder and down the front of his body so that it half hid the eager length of him, but he'd have had to unbind his hair to cover his grace completely. I lay there, bound hand and foot, unable to rise, or move, and there he stood over me nude and ready.

"This is not the way I would have come to you first, Princess Meredith," he said. He seemed almost embarrassed, which wasn't an emotion we allowed during sex much.

"He doesn't do bondage much, our Briac," Ivi said, and there was that teasing note that had become his speech, but that edge of sorrow that he'd had for so long was missing, as if there was no room for anything but that happy afterglow.

I pulled at the vines, and they moved against my skin, binding closer, twisting and alive, so that they tightened their grip as I tugged on them.

"Yes," Ivi said, "they're alive. They're a part of me, but they're awake, Meredith. Struggle and they tighten. Struggle too much and they'll tighten more than you want."

Brii dropped to his knees, then to all fours. He began to crawl toward me, and the vines on the floor writhed away from him, like small animals running from his touch. I couldn't help but move against the bindings just a little as he crawled toward me. The vines tightened, like hands reminding me to stop that, and I fought to be still as Brii was over me, still on all fours, so that I could see down the line of his body. See that he was hard, and ready, and I was going to need the work that Ivi had done between my legs to take him inside.

Brii leaned those full red lips, the most beautiful lips in either court, near my mouth and whispered, "Say yes."

I said, "Yes."

He smiled, then he kissed me, and I kissed him back, and then he began to push his way inside me.

CHAPTER TWENTY-THREE

HE STAYED UP ON HIS ARMS AS IVI HAD DONE. BOTH OF THEM WERE too tall to do the standard missionary position with me. Brii slid inside me more easily than Ivi had, but it wasn't because he was smaller.

"Goddess, she's so wet, but tight."

"Not as tight as she was before I had my turn," Ivi said. He moved up enough so I could see him past the sweep of Brii's shoulders. He looked down at me as the other man found his rhythm and began to dance his way in and out of me, his body pumping above mine, while Ivi held me for him.

Brii raised one hand from the floor where he was holding himself above me, and put his fingers on either side of my face. "I want you looking at me while I fuck you, Princess, not him." As if I'd insulted him by looking away, he proved that he might prefer gentle, but he had other speeds. He began to pound himself into me as hard and fast as he could, so that the sound of flesh hitting flesh, his labored breathing, and my small sounds of protest were all the world could hold.

It had been too soon since Ivi's good work, and Briac brought me quickly. One moment I was riding the building pleasure, the next my body was bucking and straining underneath him, fighting the orgasm, fighting the vines that held me down, my spine bowing, my neck thrown back so I screamed his name against the glass.

Briac rode my body until it quieted, and I was left blind and limp underneath him, and then and only then did he let his body do that one last thrust, so that he screamed wordlessly above me. Then he fell on top of me, limp, but his weight felt good and right. His heart pounded against my body, his breathing so harsh it sounded like he was still running as fast as he could as he lay there on top of me, too exhausted to move, too tired to do more than throw his body a little to the side so I wasn't smothered under his chest and stomach.

When he could finally move, he drew himself out of me, and that made me cry out again, and caused him to make a sound that was pleasure edged with pain.

He lay on his side beside me, and I could focus my eyes enough to see his own fluttering shut. He spoke in a voice that was hoarse and thick, "Goddess, that felt so good, almost too good."

"It almost hurts, doesn't it, after so long?" Ivi said, and I could see him now sitting on the couch, close enough that he'd had a ringside seat for the sex.

"Yes," Brii answered.

"Princess, can you hear me?" Ivi asked.

I blinked up at him and finally managed a breathy "Yes."

"Can you understand me?"

"Yes."

"Say something besides yes."

I gave a small smile and said, "What do you want me to say?"

He smiled. "Good, you really can hear me. I thought we might get you to pass out from pleasure."

"Not quite," I said.

"Maybe next time," he said.

That made me look at him a little harder, trying to chase back the amazing afterglow of it all. Dawn had come to the east, so there was white light to the western sky. The night had slipped away during all that sex.

"Didn't think there'd be next time," I said, and I realized that my voice was hoarse from screaming their names.

He smiled more widely, and his eyes held that knowledge that a man's eyes can after they've been with you in that most intimate of ways. "You ordered us to fuck someone else as soon as possible. You didn't order us never to fuck you again."

I couldn't argue with that, though it seemed like I should have, but I wasn't thinking quite clearly yet. My body still felt loose and liquid, as if I was only half inside it. I hadn't passed out, but it had been a near thing.

The vines began to unwind from my arms and legs, rolling away like they had muscles and minds of their own. I smelled flowers, but it was neither roses nor apple blossoms.

I looked past Brii, where he still lay on his side against the glass. There was a tree growing against the glass, just a few yards away from us. It had gray-white bark, and it rose at least ten feet above us. It was covered in white and pink blossoms, and the whole room smelled sweet with it.

I fought to support myself on my elbows enough to get a better look at it. I realized that the bark was the same ash-white color as Briac's skin. I'd always known he was a vegetative deity of some kind, but his name gave no clue. I stared up at the blossoming tree, then down at the man who was apparently passed out at my side.

"It's a . . ."

"Cherry tree," Ivi finished for me.

CHAPTER TWENTY-FOUR

WE WEREN'T SURE IF THE VINES AND THE TREE WOULD LAST, OR IF they would fade away like the apple tree had at the main house after Maeve Reed and I had had sex there. So, without really discussing it, we had breakfast in the formal living room around the table, under the spreading branches of the cherry tree with its blossoms and its breath of spring.

It was a longer walk for Galen and Hafwyn to bring the food, but everyone helped, and no one thought it a hardship as the first petals fell onto our plates. Before we had finished breakfast we were sitting in a room full of pink and white snow formed of petals, and where the blossoms had been there was the beginning of leaves, and the barest beginnings of fruit.

We talked quietly under the fall of blossoms and the growing greenery. And nothing we had to share seemed as bad, or as harsh, or as dangerous as it might have been, as if the very air were sweeter and calmer, and nothing could upset us.

I knew it wouldn't last, but while it did, we all enjoyed it. So, where Doyle and Frost might have been upset that they had slept through the night, they weren't. Rhys and I shared the dream about Brennan and his men, and we all discussed what it might mean, and what it meant that the soldiers whom I'd healed were healing others.

We talked of hard things, but nothing seemed that hard while the tree grew above us, and the light spilled across the sea. It was one of the most peaceful Sundays I'd ever known, full of quiet talk, touching, and being held, and even the news that Rhys had a sithen of his own here didn't cause alarm. It was as if we could have given each other any news, no matter how important or grim, and it simply wouldn't have been that important or that bad.

We had a blessed day, and though we'd planned on going back to the main house that night, somehow we didn't. None of us wanted to break the spell, for spell it was, or blessing. Whatever magic you wished to call it, we wanted it to last. It did last all that day, and all that night, but Monday morning always comes, and the magic of the weekend never lasts. Not even for fairy princesses and immortal warriors. More's the pity.

CHAPTER TWENTY-FIVE

I WAS SNUGGLED AGAINST THE SWEET SCENT OF FROST'S BACK, ONE arm across his waist, my hips curving around the firm roundness of his ass. Doyle lay against my back, spooning me just as perfectly. They were a foot and an inch or two taller than I was, so spooning meant we had to choose if we wanted our faces next to each other, or our groins. There was no way to have both.

Doyle snuggled in his sleep, one arm flung across me and over Frost's side. Of all the men, they touched each other the most in their sleep, as if they needed reassurance that not only I was there, but that the other man was, too. I liked that.

Doyle moved a little more and I was suddenly aware that his body was very happy to be pressed up against my ass. The sensation pushed me further out of the drowsy sleep. I couldn't see a clock, so I didn't know how long we had until the alarm sounded, but however long we had, I wanted to use it.

Music sounded. It wasn't the alarm. It was Paula Cole's "Feelin' Love," which meant it was my phone. I felt Doyle and Frost wake instantly. Their bodies tensed, muscles ready to spring out of bed for some emergency. I'd noticed that most of the guards woke like that, unless I woke them with petting and sex, as if anything else always meant some crisis.

"It's my cell phone," I said. Some minutia of tension slid away from their tensed muscles. Frost reached one long arm down to the side of the bed and began to rummage in the clothes pile, which was where all the clothes had ended up last night.

One of the interesting things about the Treo was that it could play an entire song, and that's what it was doing as Frost fumbled through the clothes. For me to reach the ground someone would have needed to steady me so I didn't fall out of bed, but Frost could reach the floor easily. There was no tension in his body as he finally held the phone back up in the air in my general direction.

We were far enough into the song to make me debate once more on the song as my main ring tone. It was fine until it played too far into the song in public. The sexually explicit lyrics didn't bother me, but I kept waiting for some little old lady or mother with small children to protest. So far no one had, or maybe I'd just gotten to the song in time.

I unlocked the phone and was suddenly talking to Jeremy Grey, my boss. "Merry, it's Jeremy."

I sat up, searching for the glowing face of the bedside clock, afraid I'd overslept. The blackout curtains in the main bedroom made the light not helpful."What time is it?"

"It's only six; you're hours from needing to be in the office." He sounded grim. Jeremy was usually pretty upbeat, which meant something was wrong.

"What's wrong, Jeremy?"

The men had both rolled over on their backs and were watching me. They were tense again, because they, like me, knew that Jeremy wouldn't call this early for anything good. Funny how no one ever wakes you up with good news.

"There's been another fey murder."

I sat up straighter, letting the sheet pool in my lap. "Like the other one?"

"I don't know yet. Lucy just called."

"She called you, not me," I said. "After the mess my presence made of the last murder, I think I'm probably persona non grata."

"You are," he said, "but if I feel I want you and your guard's opinion she's left me a very explicit message. She said 'Bring whatever employees you think will be the most helpful on this. I trust your judgment, Jeremy, and I know you understand the situation.'"

"That is an odd way for her to ask."

"This way when you show up, it's not her bad, it's mine, and I can make the case for needing you better than she can."

"I'm not sure Lucy's superiors aren't right, Jeremy. Her having to come save me made her lose the only witness we had."

"Maybe, but if a fey, especially a demi-fey, wants to run they will. They disappear better than almost any of us."

He was right, but . . . "That's true, but it was still a mess."

"Bring only guards who can do enough glamour to hide in plain sight. Bring more guards; two wasn't enough from what I saw on the news."

"If I bring more guards, it's more people to hide," I said.

"I'll have some of the other people meet us there, so we all show up in a mass. We'll hide you with numbers, and leave Doyle and Frost at home. They don't do good glamour, and they're too damn noticeable."

"They won't like that."

"Either you're Princess or you aren't, Merry. If you are going to be in charge, then be in charge. If you're not, then stop pretending."

"The voice of experience," I said.

"You know it," he said. "If I need you, meet Julian here." He gave me the address to meet so we wouldn't show up in a car that was associated with me.

"They won't let this many of us inside a crime scene, Jeremy," I said.

"Some of us don't need to be inside the crime scene to do our jobs, and it won't hurt our reputation to have more of our people on camera milling around with the police."

"Thinking like that is why you're the boss."

"Remember that, Merry. You have to earn the right to keep being the boss. Get off the phone, enjoy a few more hours with your boyfriend, but be ready to go earn the title Princess. Leave your two shadows at home, and bring ones who can blend in better when I call."

I hung up and explained to Doyle and Frost why they were not going with me if I had to go. They didn't like it at all, but I did what Jeremy had told me to do. I was the boss. He was right. Either I claimed the role or someone else would. I'd almost lost it to Doyle before, and now Barinthus. There were too many leaders among us and not enough followers. Doyle and Frost dressed in jeans and T-shirt and suit respectively. I chose a summer weight dress and heels. The heels were for Sholto who was coming to help guard me today. He was as good at glamour as any and could travel instantly from his kingdom to the edge where the sand met the surf because it was a place between and he was the Lord of that which passes between. He and King Taranis were the only sidhe left who could do magical travel.

The real problem was that only two of the guards were truly that good at personal glamour. Rhys and Galen could go with me as the main guards, but we needed more guards than that. I knew Doyle and Frost well enough to know that if they couldn't be with me, they would insist on more guards, which was fine, but who? Sholto was great at glamour and he was on his way, but who else? Instead of relaxing we spent a lot of the morning debating who would go with me.

Rhys said, "Saraid and Dogmaela are both almost as good at glamour as I am."

"But they have only been with us a few weeks," Frost said. "We have not trusted them with Merry's personal safety."

"We have to try them sometime," he answered.

Doyle spoke from the edge of the bed, where he was sitting as I got dressed. "They were Prince Cel's pet guards only a few weeks ago. I am not so eager to give them personal guard duty over Merry."

"Nor I," Frost said.

Barinthus spoke from near the closed door. "I found them competent guards here at the beach house."

"But that's just running the perimeter," Doyle said. "I would trust all the guards to do that. Merry's safety is a different type of duty altogether."

"We either trust them, or we need to send them away from us," Rhys said.

Doyle and Frost exchanged a look, and then Doyle said, "I am not as distrustful as that."

"Then you must let some of them guard Merry," Barinthus said. "They have already begun to suspect that they will never be trusted because of their association with Prince Cel."

"How do you know that?" I asked.

"They have spent centuries with a queen and a prince to answer to; they feel the need of someone to lead them. You have left many of them here at the beach house off and on these few weeks. I am who they have to follow."

"You are not their leader," Rhys said.

"No, the princess is, but your caution to keep them farther from her has left a vacuum of leadership. They are frightened by this new world that you have brought them to, and they wonder why you have not taken any of them as your ladies-in-waiting."

"That was a human custom that the Seelie Court adopted," I said. "It's not an Unseelie custom."

"True, but many of the ones with us now were longer at the Seelie Court than at our own. They would like something familiar."

"Or is it you who would like something familiar?" Rhys asked.

"I don't know what you mean, Rhys."

"Yes, you do." And there was something far too serious in Rhys's voice.

"I say again that I do not know what you mean."

"Coyness does not become you, sea god."

"Nor you, death god," Barinthus said, and there was an edge of irritation to his voice now. It wasn't anger. I'd rarely seen the big man truly angry, but there was some tension between the two of them that I'd never seen before.

"What's going on?" I asked.

It was Frost who answered. "Of those of us at your side, they are two of the most powerful."

I looked at Frost. "What does that have to do with the tension between them?"

"They begin to feel their way back to their full powers, and like rams in springtime they want to butt heads to see who is stronger."

"We are not animals, Killing Frost."

"But you would remind me that I am not truly sidhe. Nor was I one of Danu's children when she first came to the shores of our homeland. All this you remind me with my old nickname. I was the Killing Frost, and once even less than that."

Barinthus studied him. Finally, he said, "Perhaps I do see those who were once less than sidhe, but are sidhe now as lesser still. I do not mean to feel that way, but I cannot deny that I find it difficult to see you with the princess and about to be father to her children when you have never been worshipped and once were but a childlike thing to skip across the still winter's nights and paint the windowpanes with hoarfrost."

I'd had no idea that Barinthus thought that the sidhe who began life as non-sidhe were lesser, and I didn't try to keep the surprise off my face. "You never mentioned any of this to me, Barinthus."

"I would have taken anyone as father to your children if it would have put you on the throne, Meredith. Once you were on the throne, we could have solidified your power base."

"No, Barinthus, we could have taken the throne and been victim to assassination attempts until some of us died. The nobles would never have accepted me."

"We could have made them accept your power."

"You keep saying 'we,' Kingmaker. Define 'we,'" Rhys said.

I remembered Rhys's warning when I'd first entered the beach house.

"We as in us, her princes and nobles," Barinthus said.

"Except for me," Frost said.

"I did not say that," he said.

"But did you mean it?" I asked, and held my hand out to Frost, so he came to stand tall and straight beside me. I leaned my head against his hip.

"Is it true that you were crowned by faerie itself with the blessing of the Goddess herself?" he asked. "Did you truly wear the crown of moonlight and shadows?"

"Yes," I said.

"Was Doyle truly crowned with thorn and silver?"

"Yes," I said, and played with Frost's hand, rubbing my thumb over his knuckles, and feeling the solid comfort of his hip against my cheek.

Barinthus put his hands before his face, as if he could not bear to look at us anymore.

"What is wrong with you?" I asked.

He spoke without moving his hands. "You had won, Merry, don't you understand that? You had won the throne, and the crowns would have silenced the other nobles." He lowered his hands and his face looked tormented.

"You can't know that," I said.

"Even now you stand before me with him at your side. The one you gave up everything for."

I finally understood what was bothering him, or thought I did. "You're upset because I gave up the crown to save Frost's life."

"Upset," he said, and he gave a harsh laugh. "Upset—no, I wouldn't say I'm upset. If your father had been given such a blessing he would have known what to do with it."

"My father left faerie for years to save my life."

"You were his child."

"Love is love, Barinthus. What matters what kind of love it is?"

He made a disgusted sound. "You are a woman, and perhaps such things move you, but Doyle." He looked at the other man. "Doyle, you gave up everything we could have ever wished for to save the life of one man. You knew what would happen to our court and our people with a failing queen and no heir to the bloodline."

"I expected that there would either be civil war or assassins would kill the queen and there would be a new ruler of our court."

"How could you hold the life of one man above the better good of your entire people?" Barinthus asked.

"I think your faith in our people is too great," Doyle said. "I think that Merry crowned by faerie and Goddess or not, the court is too deeply divided with power factions. I think that the assassins wouldn't have stopped with the queen. They would have aimed at the new queen, at Merry, or at those closest and most powerful near her until she stood alone and helpless as they saw it. There are those who would have been happy to turn her into a puppet for their hand."

"With us at her side and in our full power they would not have dared," Barinthus said.

"The rest of us have been brought back into our power, but you have only regained a small portion of yours," Rhys said. "Unless Merry brings you back fully into your powers, then you are not as powerful as most of the sidhe in this room."

The silence in the room was suddenly heavier, and the very air was suddenly thicker, like trying to drink our breath.

"The fact that the Killing Frost may be more powerful than the great Mannan Mac Lir must rankle," Rhys said.

"He is not more powerful than I am," Barinthus said, but in a voice that held some of the slurring of the sea, like angry waves crashing on rock.

"Stop this," Doyle said, and he actually moved to stand between them.

I realized that it was Barinthus's magic making the air thick, and I remembered stories of him being able to make humans fall down dead with water flowing out of their mouths, drowned on dry land miles from water.

"And will you finally be king?" Barinthus asked.

"If you are angry with me, then be angry with me, old friend, but Frost had no say in the choices we made on his behalf. Merry and I chose freely."

"Even now you stand guard over him," Barinthus said.

I stood up, still holding Frost's hand. "Are you bothered that we gave up the crown for just one man, or are you bothered that we gave it up for Frost?"

"I have no quarrel with Frost as a man, or a warrior."

"Then is it really that he's not sidhe enough for you?"

Rhys stepped just enough around Doyle so he could meet Barinthus's eyes. "Or do you see in Doyle and Frost what you wanted with Prince Essus but were always afraid to ask for?"

We all froze, as if his words were a bomb that we could all see falling toward us, but there was no way to stop it. There was no way to catch it, and no way to run. We just all stood there, and I had moments for my childhood memories of my father and Barinthus to run through my head. It was quick flashes. A hand on someone's arm, a hand held a little too long, an embrace, a look, and I suddenly realized that my father's best friend might have been more than just his friend.

There was nothing wrong with love in our court no matter what sex you chose, but the queen didn't let any of her guard have sex with anyone but her, and one of the terms for Barinthus joining her court had been that he had joined her guard. It had been a way to control him, and a way to say that she had the great Mannan Mac Lir as her lackey and hers in every way, only hers.

I'd always wondered about her insisting that Barinthus join her guard. It hadn't been standard at the time for exiles from the Seelie Court. Most of the other sidhe who had come from that time had just joined the court. I'd always thought it was because the queen feared Barinthus's power, but now I saw another motive. She had loved her brother, my father, but she had also been jealous of his power. Essus was a name that people still spoke as a god, at least in the recent past, if you counted the Roman Empire as recent, but her own name, Andais, had been lost so completely that no one remembered what she had once been. Had she forced Barinthus to be her celibate guard to keep him out of her brother's bed?

I had a moment to think about Essus and Mannan Mac Lir joined as a couple both politically and magically, and though I didn't agree with what she'd done, I understood the fear. They were two of the most powerful of us. Combined, they could have owned both courts, if they'd been willing to, because Barinthus had joined us before we were cast out of Europe. Our internal wars had been our own business and no matter for human law, so they could have taken first the Unseelie and then the Seelie Court.

I spoke into that weighted silence. "Or was it Andais who made it impossible for you to have his love? She would never have risked the two of you joining your power together."

"And now there is a queen of faerie who would have let you have all you desired, but it is too late," Rhys said quietly.

"Are you jealous of the closeness you see between Frost and Doyle?" I asked it with a careful, quiet voice.

"I am jealous of the power I see in the other men. That I will admit to, and the thought that without your touch I will never come back to my power is a hard thing." He made certain to give me eye contact, but his face was a mask of arrogance, beautiful and alien. It was a look that I'd seen him give Andais. It was his unreadable face, and he'd never had to use it on me before.

"You flooded every river around St. Louis when Merry and you had sex only in vision," Rhys said. "How much more power do you want?"

This time Barinthus looked away, and would not meet anyone's eyes. That was answer enough, I supposed.

It was Doyle who stepped forward a step or two, and said, "I understand wanting to have all the old power back, my friend."

"You have regained yours!" Barinthus yelled. "Don't try to soothe me when you stand there full to bursting with your own power."

"But it is not my old power, not completely. I still cannot heal as I did. I cannot do many things that I once could do."

Barinthus looked at Doyle then, and the anger in his eyes had turned them from happy blue to a black where the water runs deep and there are rocks just under the surface, ready to tear the hull of your boat and sink you.

There was a sudden splash against the side of the house. We were too far above the sea for the tide to find us, and it was the wrong time of day for it anyway. There was another slap of water, and this time I heard it smack into the huge windows of the master bathroom attached to this bedroom.

It was Galen who slid from the doorway and walked farther into the bathroom to check on the sound. There was another burst of water on the glass, and he came back, his face serious. "The sea is rising, but the water is like someone picked it up and threw it at the windows. It is actually separating from the sea, and seems to float for a moment before it hits."

"You must control your power, my friend," Doyle said, his deep voice going deeper with some strong emotion.

"Once I could have called the sea and washed this house into the water."

"Is that what you want to do?" I asked. I squeezed Frost's hand and then moved forward to stand with Doyle.

He looked at me then, and his face showed great anguish. His hands ground into fists at his side. "No, I would not wash away into the sea all we have gained, and I would never harm you, Merry. I would never dishonor Essus and all he tried to do by saving your life. You carry his grandchildren. I want to be here to see the babes born."

His unbound hair writhed around him, and where most hair seemed to blow in wind, there was something of liquid in the way his hair moved, as if here in this room somehow the currents below touched and played with his ankle-length hair. I was betting that his hair didn't tangle either.

The sea quieted outside, the noise drawing away until it was just the quiet hush of water on the narrow beach below. "I am sorry. I lost control of myself, and that is unforgivable. I, of all sidhe, know that such childish displays of power are pointless."

"And you want the Goddess to give you back more power?" Rhys asked.

Barinthus looked up and that flash of black water showed for a moment, then was swallowed into something calmer, more controlled. "I do. Wouldn't you? Oh, but I forgot, you have a sithen waiting for you, regained from the Goddess only last night." There was bitterness to his voice now, and the ocean sounded just a little rough, as if some great hand stirred it with an impatient hand.

"Maybe there's a reason the Goddess hasn't given you back more of your powers," said Galen.

We all looked at him. He leaned in the doorway looking serious but calm.

"You have no stake in this, boy. You don't remember what I lost."

"I don't, but I do know that the Goddess is wise, and she sees further into our hearts and minds than we do. If this is what you do with only part of your power back, how arrogant would you be with all of it back?"

Barinthus took a step toward him. "You have no right to judge me."

"He is father to my children as much as Doyle," I said. "He is a king to my queen as much as Doyle."

"He was not crowned by faerie and the gods themselves."

There was a knock on the door. It made me jump. Doyle called out, "Not now."

But the door opened, and it was Sholto, Lord of Shadows and That Which Passes Between, King of the Sluagh. He came in with his unbound hair, in a white-blond cloak over a black-and-silver tunic and boots.

He wasted a smile on me, and I got the full impact of his tricolored eyes: metallic gold around the pupil, then amber, then yellow like aspen leaves in the fall. His smile faded as he turned to the other men and said, "I heard you yelling, Sea Lord, and I have been crowned by faerie and the gods themselves. Does that make this fight more mine?"

CHAPTER TWENTY-SIX

"I DO NOT FEAR YOU, SLUAGH LORD," BARINTHUS SAID, AND AGAIN there was that angry sound from the sea outside.

Sholto's smile vanished completely, leaving his handsome face arrogant, starkly beautiful, and totally unfriendly. "You will," he said, and his voice held an edge of anger. There was a sparkle of gold as his eyes began to shine.

The sea outside slapped against the glass again, harder, angrier. It wasn't just that it was a bad idea for the men to duel; it was dangerous for all of us here by the sea. I couldn't believe that Barinthus, of all people, was behaving so badly. He'd been the voice of reason for centuries at the Unseelie Court, and now . . . I'd missed some change in him, or maybe without Queen Andais, the Queen of Air and Darkness, to keep him in check, I was seeing the real him after all. That was a sad thought for me.

"Enough of this," Doyle said, "both of you."

Barinthus turned on Doyle, and said, "It is you who I'm angry at, Darkness. If you prefer to fight me yourself that will be fine."

"I thought you were mad at me, Barinthus," Galen said. That caught me off guard; I'd thought he would know better than to attract the big man's anger a second time.

Barinthus turned and looked at Galen, who was still in the bathroom doorway. The sea slapped against the windows behind him hard enough to shake them. "You didn't betray everything by refusing the crown, but if you want a piece of this fight, you may have it."

Galen gave a small smile, and moved away from the doorway. "If the Goddess had given me a choice between the throne and Frost's life, I would have chosen his life, just as Doyle did."

My stomach tightened at his words. Then I realized that Galen was baiting Barinthus, and the anxiety went away. I felt suddenly calmer, almost happy. It was such an abrupt change of mood I knew it wasn't me. I looked at Galen walking slowly toward Barinthus, his hand out almost as if he was offering to shake hands. Oh, my Goddess, he was doing magic on us all, and he was one of the few who could have because much of his magic showed no outward sign. He didn't glow, or shimmer, or be anything but pleasant, and you just felt like being pleasant back.

Barinthus didn't threaten again as Galen moved slowly, carefully, smiling, hand out toward the other man.

"Then you are a fool, too," Barinthus said, but the rage in his voice was less, and the next slap of ocean against the windows was also less. It didn't rattle the windows this time.

"We all love Merry," Galen said, still moving gently forward, "don't we?"

Barinthus frowned, clearly puzzled. "Of course I love Meredith."

"Then we're all on the same side, aren't we?"

Barinthus frowned harder, but finally gave a small nod. "Yes." That one word was low, but clear.

Galen was almost to him, his hand almost touching his arm, and I knew that if his glamour was working this well from a distance, that one touch would calm the whole situation. There'd be no fight if that hand once touched that arm. Even knowing what was happening didn't completely nullify the effects of Galen's charm, and I was just getting the backwash of it. Most of it was concentrated on Barinthus. Galen was willing him to calm down. He was willing him to be friends.

A scream sounded from outside the room, but it was inside the house. The scream was high pitched and terror filled. Galen's glamour was like most; it shattered with the scream and the adrenaline rush as everyone went for weapons. I owned guns, but hadn't packed one for the beach. It wouldn't have mattered, because Doyle pushed me to the floor on the far side of the bed, and ordered Galen to stay with me. He, of course, would go for the scream.

Galen knelt by me, gun out and ready, though not pointed, because there was nothing to point at yet.

Sholto had the door opened, staying to one side of the doorjamb so he didn't make a target of himself. He was on the queen's guard when he wasn't king of his own kingdom, and he knew the possibilities of modern weapons, and a well-placed arrow. Barinthus was pressed to the other side of the flattened door, the fight forgotten, as they did what they had trained to do for longer than America had been a country.

Whatever they saw out there made Sholto move forward at a cautious crouch, gun in one hand, sword in the other. Barinthus spilled around the door with no visible weapon, but when you're seven feet tall, more than humanly strong, nearly immortal, and a trained fighter, you don't always need a weapon. You are the weapon.

Rhys went next, keeping low, gun in hand. Frost and Doyle glided through the door armed and ready, and just like that it was just Galen and me in the suddenly empty room. My pulse was thudding in my ears, pushing at my throat, not at the thought of what might have caused one of my female guards to scream, but at the thought of the men I loved, the fathers of my children, maybe never coming back through that door again. Death had touched me too early for me not to understand that nearly immortal is not the same thing as truly immortal. My father's death had taught me that.

Maybe if I'd been queen enough to sacrifice Frost for the crown, I would have been more worried about the other women, but I was honest with myself. I'd only been trying to be friends with them for a few weeks, I loved the men, and for someone you love, you will sacrifice much. Anyone who says otherwise has either never truly loved or is lying to themselves.

I heard voices, but they weren't yelling, just talking. I whispered to Galen, "Can you understand what they're saying?"

Most of the sidhe had better-than-human hearing, I did not. He cocked his head to one side, gun now pointed at the empty doorway, ready to shoot anything that came through it.

"Voices, women. I can't understand what they're saying, but I can tell that one is Hafwyn, one of them is crying, and Saraid is pissed. Now Doyle, and Ivi, he's upset but not angry. He sounds panicked, as if whatever's happened bothered him."

Galen glanced down at me, frowning a little. "Ivi sounds contrite."

I frowned, too. "Ivi is never contrite about anything."

Galen nodded, and then was suddenly all attention at the door. I watched his finger begin to pull. I couldn't see anything around the corner of the bed. Then he raised the gun toward the ceiling and let out a breath in a low *whoosh*, which let me know how close he'd come to pulling that trigger.

"Sholto," he said, and got up, gun still in one hand, and held his other hand down for me. I took it and let him help me stand.

"What's happened?" I asked.

"Did you know that Ivi and Dogmaela had sex last night?" he asked.

I nodded. "Not exactly, but I knew that Ivi and Brii took lovers among the women who were willing."

Sholto smiled and shook his head, his face halfway between amused and thinking about something far too hard. "It seems that after last night Ivi assumed he could give her a little cuddle, and something he did seems to have terrified her."

"What did he do to her?" I asked.

"Hafwyn was witness and agrees with Ivi about what he did and did not do. Apparently, he merely came up behind Dogmaela, wrapped his arms around her waist, and picked her up off the floor, and she began to scream," Sholto said. "Dogmaela is too hysterical to make much sense. Saraid is being physically restrained from attacking Ivi, and the man seems honestly puzzled by the turn of events."

"Why would just being picked up make her scream?" I asked.

"Hafwyn says that it was something their old master, the prince, would do, but he would then fling them on the bed or hold them for someone else to do very bad things to them."

"Oh," I said, "it's a trigger event."

"A trigger what?" Sholto asked.

Galen said, "It's something usually innocuous that reminds you of abuse or violence, and suddenly it brings it all back up."

We both looked at him, both of us surprised, and unable to hide it. Galen gave me a sour look. "What, I couldn't know that?"

"No, it's just that"—I hugged him—"it was just unexpected."

"That I was that insightful is that big a surprise?" he asked.

There was nothing polite I could say to that question, so I hugged him a little more tightly. He hugged me back, and kissed me on top of my head.

Sholto was standing beside us now, and his eyes were all for me. There was that look that men get when they see a woman who is their lover and more. It was partly possessive, partly excited, and partly puzzled, as if something out in the other room was still on his mind. He held his hand out to me, and I left Galen's hand to go to him. Galen let me do it; we shared well most of the time, and even if we didn't, Goddess had decreed that Sholto was one of the fathers of the babies I carried. The fathers all got privileges. I just think that none of us had expected the genetic miracle of six fathers for two babies.

Sholto drew me into his arms, and I went willingly. He was the newest to my bed of all the fathers. We'd actually only had sex once I got pregnant, but as the old saying goes, once is enough. The newness meant that I wasn't in love with him. I didn't actually love him at all. I was attracted to him, I cared for him, but we hadn't had enough conversations to let me know if I loved him, or could love him. We liked each other, though; we liked each other a lot.

"I've seen the traditional King of the Sluagh's greeting to his queen," Galen said, "so I'll leave you to it. Maybe I can be insightful for Dogmaela." He sounded a little disgusted, but I let him go, because he had surprised me by being smarter than I'd given him credit for and that was my lack of insight.

Sholto didn't wait for Galen to close the door behind him before he showed me just how much he liked me with his kiss, his hands, and his body held as tightly to me as it could be with clothes still on. I let myself sink into the strength of his arms, the satin of his tunic, and the glint of the embroidery and the small jewels sewn into it, so that I ran my hands over his clothes as much as the body underneath them. I thought about him making love to me the way Ivi had done last night with most of his clothes still on so that the satin caressed my skin as we made love. The thought made me respond even more to his kisses, and sent my hands lower to trace his ass underneath the tunic, though I couldn't get as good a grip with one hand as the other because I had to reach around the sword at his waist.

Sholto responded to my eagerness, sliding his hands under my ass and picking me up. I wrapped my legs around his waist, and he walked us back the few feet to the bed. He lowered me to the bed, with my arms and legs still wrapped around him. He kept one hand on my back and the other caught our weight against the bed.

He drew out of the kisses enough to say in a breathless voice, "If I'd known this was the greeting I'd get, I'd have come sooner."

I smiled up at him. "I've missed you."

He grinned. He had one of the most handsome faces in either court, and the grin ruined that beyond-model-perfect perfection, but I loved that grin, because I knew that it was for me. I knew that no one else had ever made him look at them in quite that way. No one had ever made him as happy as he was in the moments we were together. Maybe I didn't love him yet, but I loved how he was when we were together. I loved that he let me see the great King of the Sluagh grin. I valued him letting down those years of arrogant shields so that I could see the man behind them.

"I love that you miss me." As if he'd read my mind, he raised up, forcing me to let him go just enough so he could reach down and begin to undo his pants. He left his sword, belt, gun, and holster in place, undoing only enough of his soft trousers to spill himself out into the light, hard and firm and as fine as any man in court.

Normally, I wanted more foreplay, but in that moment it worked for me. It was partly what Ivi and Brii had done with me last night, but it was also that Sholto had begun to condition me to the greeting.

He laid me back on the bed, my legs still hanging over the edge, and reached under my skirt until he found my panties. He drew them down my legs, slipping them all the way down over my high heels to drop to the floor. He raised my skirt and gazed down at me naked from the waist down except for the shoes. I didn't ask if he wanted me to remove the shoes, because I knew he didn't. Sholto liked me in heels.

He put his hands on either side of my hips and pulled me roughly to the firm length of his body. He angled in against me, raising my hips rather than touching himself to change the angle. He pushed himself inside me and I was too tight for him to do it all in one thrust. He had to work his way in, but I was already wet, just tight. I squeezed around him, tighter still, making his head fall a little forward so that his hair swept across my face. He hesitated above me, then he pushed harder, and I made him work for every inch until I orgasmed simply from the sensation of him being so big, so wide, filling me up so completely.

I screamed my pleasure, my head thrown back, my fingers clawing at his satin-covered arms, unable to find something to mark.

He picked me up off the bed with most of him still inside me. He held me in his arms while my body spasmed around him, and I clung to him. He shoved the rest of himself inside me in one long, hard thrust while he held me, and I screamed for him again.

He half collapsed on the bed, half crawled us into the middle of it. He let go of me with his arms, and only his lower body pinned me to the bed. He'd stopped moving once he was as deep as his body could go. He said, "You are my queen, and I am king. This is proof of that."

It was a very old saying among the nightflyers, of which his father had been one. They looked like huge dark manta rays with tentacles, and faces far from human. Among them, only the royals were able to breed, and able to bring the females to orgasm so easily. The female nightflyers reacted to a spine inside the penis that would have killed me, but luckily for both of us, Sholto didn't take after his father that much.

I spoke the next part of the ritual, because Sholto had taught it to me. "You inside me proves that you are royal and I am with child." If I hadn't been pregnant the reply would have been, "You inside me proves that you are royal and I will be with child."

He raised up enough to undo the belt around his tunic waist. He tossed the belt with its sword and gun to one side of us, not off the bed; within reach, but out of the way. He spoke as he began to wiggle out of his tunic with his body still pinning mine to the bed. "I don't remember you being that easy to pleasure, Meredith."

We shared well, all of us, but not so well that I could tell him that it had been partly Ivi and Brii last night that had helped make his entrance so amazing.

"I told you, I missed you."

He grinned again, then was hidden behind the rise of his tunic. He stripped off the undertunic of white linen next, and I could finally see his upper body. He was as muscled as any of the men except Rhys. He was broad of shoulder, simply beautiful, but there was a tattoo on his stomach, tracing up to his rib cage. The tattoo was of the tentacles that he would have had had he taken more after his father. Once they hadn't been a tattoo, but the real thing. Now he could be with me as smooth and human as any sidhe, or he could choose to be everything he could be.

Usually he asked me which I preferred, but one moment he rose above me with that flat and lovely stomach, the next tentacles writhed above me like some fantastic sea creature formed of ivory and crystal with lines of gold and silver running through all that pale beauty. He leaned over me, still hard and fast between my legs, but he leaned over for a kiss, pressing all that muscle and caressing against my body so that when we kissed he held me with more "arms" than any lover I'd ever had. The bigger tentacles were for heavy lifting, and wrapped around me like muscled rope but a thousand times softer, like velvet and satin and more. His more human arms were in the kiss, too, but it was all a part of him, all him hugging me, holding me, kissing me. Sholto loved that I didn't recoil at his extra bits. Once the sight of his uniqueness had disturbed me, no, honestly, it had frightened me, but somewhere in the magic that had joined us as a couple I had come to appreciate that different wasn't a bad thing. In fact, he could certainly brag that he could do things with me that none of the others could do without another man to help them.

The smaller tentacles, very thin and stretchy, had small reddish suction cups near the tips. They tickled between us, and I writhed toward their touch, eager for them to find their purpose. The small ends traced over my breasts until they came to my nipples, and then sucked on them hard and fast so that I made eager noises into his mouth as he kissed me. My hands traced along the muscled length of his back, and spilled over the hard velvet of the tentacles, caressing their undersides, where I knew they were sensitive. It made him begin to pull himself out from inside me, giving himself enough room so that one of the small tentacles could slide between my legs and find that small, sweet spot just under my hood, so that while he began to push his body in and out between my legs, working at the wetness and tightness, another of those small eager mouths sucked me.

He rose onto his arms, the bigger tentacles helping support his weight above me, as he sucked all three spots expertly. He knew I liked to watch him going in and out of me, so he parted all those extras like a curtain so I could raise my head enough to look down the length of our bodies. I had begun by enjoying watching him go in and out between my legs, but now I also liked seeing where he sucked my breasts and between my legs, so it was all him, all long, and firm, and giving me pleasure.

He had finally worked me open enough to move faster inside me. His body began to find its rhythm, and I felt the warmth begin to build between my legs from it, but the other building pressure of pleasure was coming faster.

I found my breath enough to say, "I'm coming soon." He liked to know.

"Which?"

"Upper," I said.

He smiled, and his eyes flashed to life, gold, amber, and yellow glowing above me, and suddenly his body was a glowing, vibrating thing. Magic struck gold and silver lightning along those extra parts of him. He caused my skin to glow, as if the moon were rising inside me to meet the glow and rise of him above me.

I had enough energy left to raise my hands and touch the moving bits, and my soft glowing hands caused colored lights to burst under his skin, one magic calling the other. But it was the vibrating of his magic along his skin inside me, outside me, and against me that finally pushed that first wave of warm, bursting pleasure over my body, so that I screamed, writhing underneath him. My fingers found the hard, solidness of the heavy flesh and marked them. I painted my pleasure down the colored lights of the heavy tentacles, and where he bled the red glowed so that it spattered against my skin like rubies scattered across the moon.

He fought his body to keep the slow, deep rhythm going between my legs. His head fell forward, his hair mingling with everything, and the hair filled with light so it was like making love inside something spun of crystal. And then between one thrust and the next he brought me, and we screamed together the light of our pleasure so bright that we filled the room with colored shadows.

He collapsed above me, and for a moment I was buried underneath the weight of him, with his heart pounding so hard that it seemed to be trying to come out of his chest where the pulse of it beat against the side of my face. Then he moved enough of his upper body so I wasn't trapped and I could breathe a little more easily. He pulled out from between my legs, the smaller pieces of him already faded, lying against me as if every bit of him were exhausted.

He lay on his side next to me while we both relearned how to breathe. "I love you, Meredith," he whispered.

"I love you, too." And in that moment it was as true as any words I had ever spoken.

CHAPTER TWENTY-SEVEN

SHOLTO AND I GOT DRESSED AND JOINED EVERYONE IN THE SMALL living room just off the kitchen and dining room. Since there were no walls to speak of, I thought it was just all the "great room," but the ones living here called it the small living room, so that's what we all called it.

Hafwyn and Dogmaela were on the biggest couch. Dogmaela was still crying softly into the other woman's shoulder. Their blond braids were intertwined and were so close to the same color that I couldn't tell at a glance which hair belonged to whom.

Saraid stood near the huge bank of windows with her shoulders hunched, her arms crossed over her chest, cradling her small, tight breasts. You didn't need magic to feel the anger rolling off of her. The sunlight sparkled in her golden hair. As Frost's was silver, hers was truly golden, as if the precious metal had been woven into hair. I wondered if her hair was as soft as Frost's.

Brii was standing beside her, his yellow hair seeming pale and unfinished next to her true gold. He tried to touch her shoulder, and she glared at him until he dropped his hand, but he kept speaking quietly to her. He was obviously trying to soothe her.

Ivi was near the sliding-glass doors talking quietly and urgently to Doyle and Frost. Barinthus and Galen stood to one side. The bigger man was talking to Galen and obviously upset. But it had to be about Dogmaela and Ivi, because if he'd figured out that Galen had almost rolled his mind with glamour he'd have been more upset. It was a serious insult for one highborn sidhe to try to bespell another. It said clearly that the spell-caster felt superior and more powerful than the one they were bespelling. Galen hadn't meant it like that, but Barinthus would most likely have taken it that way.

Cathbodua and Usna were on the love seat, with her holding him. Cathbodua's raven-black hair spilled only to her shoulders, part of it mingling with the black trench coat that she'd laid on the back of the love seat. The coat was a cloak of raven feathers, but like some other powerful items it could change, chameleonlike, into what worked best for the setting. Her skin looked paler against the pure blackness of the hair, though I knew it was no more white than my own. Usna was a contrast of colors compared to her. He looked like a calico cat, his white moonlight skin marked with black and red. Like the cat his mother had been shape-shifted into when she bore him, he was curled up in her lap, or as much of his six-foot-tall frame as would fit was curled up in her lap.

He'd undone his hair so that it spilled around her black clothes and her stark beauty like a fur blanket. Cathbodua stroked his hair idly as they both watched the emotional show before them. His gray eyes, the most uncatlike thing about him, and her black ones had almost the same expression in them. They were enjoying the turmoil in that dispassionate way that some animals have. Once he'd been able to turn into the cat he was colored to match, and once she could shift into the shape of a raven or a crow, and not have to depend on borrowing the eyes of some true bird for her spying. It made them both a little less human, or sidhe, and something more basic.

Of course, I hadn't realized until that moment that they'd been sleeping together. They'd been partners on guard duty, but until I saw the distant and somewhat scary Cathbodua petting him, I hadn't realized it was more. They had hidden it well.

Sholto seemed to understand, or maybe I looked surprised because he said, "You letting the other guards sleep together made them reveal their own liaison."

"Nothing makes either of them do anything. They chose to share because they thought it was safe."

Sholto nodded. "Agreed." He moved forward farther into the room, and since I had my arm in his, he moved me with him like it was the beginning of a dance.

Galen started toward us, smiling, and then Barinthus moved in a blur that I couldn't follow with my eyes. Galen was suddenly airborne and heading toward the big glass windows and the sea, and rocks, below.

CHAPTER TWENTY-EIGHT

GALEN HIT THE CORNER OF WALL JUST TO THE SIDE OF THE WINDOWS. The wall cracked with the impact of his body, crumbling around him like one of those cartoon moments where people go through walls. It wasn't a perfect outline of his body, but as he sagged against the wall, I could see where his arm had flung out and back trying to take some of the impact.

He was shaking his head, trying to get up as Barinthus strode toward him. I tried to run forward, but Sholto held me back. Doyle moved faster than I ever could to put himself in the bigger man's path. Frost went to Galen.

"Get out of my way, Darkness," Barinthus said, and a wave rose against the glass, spilling across it. We were far too high for the sea to reach us without aid.

"Would you steal a guard from the princess?" Doyle asked. He was trying to look at ease, but even I could see his body tensed, one foot dug into the floor in preparation for a blow, or some other very physical action.

"He insulted me," Barinthus said.

"Perhaps, but he is also the best of us at personal glamour. Only Meredith and Sholto can compare with him for disguise, and we need him to use his magic this day."

Barinthus stood in the middle of the floor glaring down at Doyle. He took a deep breath, then let it out in one sharp gust. His shoulders lowered visibly, and he shook himself hard enough to make all that hair ruffle like feathers, though no bird I'd ever known could boast so many shades of blue on them.

He looked across the room at me with Sholto's hand still holding my arm. "I am sorry, Meredith. That was childish. You need him today." He took another deep breath and let it out again so that it was loud in the thick silence of the room.

Then he looked past Doyle's still-ready form. Frost was helping Galen to his feet, though he seemed a little unsteady, as if without Frost's hand he might have been unable to stand.

"Pixie," Barinthus called out, and the ocean slapped against the windows higher and stronger this time.

Galen's father had been a pixie who had gotten the queen's lady-in-waiting pregnant. Galen stood a little straighter, the green of his eyes going from its usual rich green to something pale and edged with white. His eyes going pale was not a good sign. It meant that he was well and truly pissed. I had only seen his eyes that pale a handful of times.

He shook Frost's hand off, and the other man let him go, though his face showed clearly that he wasn't sure it was a good idea.

"I'm as sidhe as you are, Barinthus," Galen said.

"Don't ever try to use your pixie wiles on me again, Greenman, or the next time I won't miss the windows."

I realized in that moment that Rhys had been right. Barinthus was beginning to take on the role of king, because only a king would have been so bold to the father of my child. I could not let it stand unchallenged. I could not.

"It wasn't the pixie in him that let him almost bespell the great Mannan Mac Lir," I said.

Sholto's hand squeezed my arm, as if trying to tell me that he wasn't sure this was a good idea. It probably wasn't, but I knew I had to say something. If I didn't I might as well concede my "crown" to Barinthus now.

Barinthus turned those angry eyes on me. "What is that supposed to mean?"

"It means that Galen has gained powerful magic through being one of my lovers, and one of my kings. He'd have never come so close to fogging the mind of Barinthus before."

Barinthus gave a small nod. "He has grown in power. They all have."

"All my lovers," I said.

He nodded, wordlessly.

"You truly are angry that I have not taken you to my bed at least once, not because you want sex from me, but because you want to know if it would give you back everything you have lost."

He would not look at me, and his hair washed around him again with that sense of underwater movement. "I waited until you came back into the room, Meredith. I wanted you to see Galen put in his place." He looked at me then, but there was nothing I could understand on his face. My father's best friend and one of the most frequent visitors to the house we had lived in in the human world was not the man before me now. It was as if his few weeks here by the sea had changed him. Was this arrogance and pettiness what he'd been like when he first came to the Unseelie Court? Or had he already been diminished in power even then?

"Why would you want me to see that?" I asked.

"I wanted you to know that I had enough control not to send him out the window, where I could use the sea to drown him. I wanted you to see that I chose to spare him."

"To what purpose?" I asked. Sholto drew me in against his body so that I wrapped my arms around him almost absently. I wasn't sure if he was trying to protect me or just to comfort me, or maybe even just to comfort himself, though touch is more comfort to the lesser fey than to the sidhe. Or maybe he was warning me. The question was, warning me about what?

"I wouldn't drown," Galen said.

We all looked at him.

He repeated it. "I am sidhe. Nothing of the natural world can kill me. You could shove me under the sea but you couldn't drown me, and I wouldn't explode from pressure changes either. Your ocean can't kill me, Barinthus."

"But my ocean can make you long for death, Greenman. Trapped forever in the blackest depths, the water made near solid around you as secure as any prison, and more torturous. The rest of the sidhe cannot drown, but it still hurts to have the water go down your lungs. Your body still craves air and tries to breathe the water. The pressure of the depths cannot crush your body, but it still presses down. You would be forever in pain, never dying, never aging, but always in torment."

"Barinthus," I said, and that one word held the shock I felt. I clung to Sholto now, because I needed the comfort. It was a fate truly worse than death that he threatened Galen with, my Galen.

Barinthus looked at me, and whatever he saw on my face didn't please him. "Don't you see, Meredith, that I am more powerful than many of your men?"

"Are you doing this in some twisted bid to make me respect you?" I asked.

"Think how powerful I could be at your side if I had my full powers."

"You'd be able to destroy this house and everyone in it. You said as much in the other room," I said.

"I would never harm you," he said.

I shook my head, and pulled away from Sholto. He held on to me for a moment, then he let me stand on my own. It was how this next part had to be done.

"You would never hurt my person, but if you had done that terrible thing to Galen, stolen him as husband and father for me, it would be harming me, Barinthus. Surely you see that?"

His face fell back into that handsome unreadable mask.

"You don't understand that, do you?" I asked, and the first trickle of real fear wormed its way up my spine.

"We could form your court into a force to be feared, Meredith."

"Why would we need it to be feared?"

"People only follow out of love or fear, Meredith."

"Don't go all Machiavellian on me, Barinthus."

"I don't know what you mean by that."

I shook my head. "I don't know what you mean by any of the things you've done in the last hour, but I do know that if you ever harm any of my people and condemn them to such a terrible fate, I will cast you out. If one of my people vanishes and we can't find them, I will have to assume that you've done what you threatened, and if that happens, if you do that to any of them, then you will have to free them, and then . . ."

"And then what?" he asked.

"Death, Barinthus. You would have to die or we would never be safe, especially not here on the shores of the Western sea. You're too powerful."

"So, Doyle is the Queen's Darkness, still to be sent out to kill on command like the well-trained dog he is."

"No, Barinthus, I will do it myself."

"You cannot stand against me and win, Meredith," he said, but his voice was softer now.

"I have the full hands of flesh and blood, Barinthus. Even my father didn't have the full hand of flesh, and Cel didn't have the full hand of blood, but I have both. It's how I killed Cel."

"You would not do such a thing to me, Meredith."

"And moments ago I would have said that you, Barinthus, would never have threatened people I loved. I was wrong about you; do not make the same mistake."

We stared at each other across the room, and the world narrowed down to just the two of us. I met his gaze, and I let him see in my face that I meant what I'd said, every word of it.

He finally nodded. "I see my death in your eyes, Meredith."

"I feel your death in my heart," I replied. It was a way of saying that my heart would be happy to have his death, or at least not sad.

"Am I not allowed to challenge those who insult me? Would you make a different kind of eunuch out of me than Andais did?"

"You can protect your honor, but no duel is to the death, or to anything that will destroy a man's usefulness to me."

"That leaves little that I can do to protect my honor, Meredith."

"Maybe, but it's not your honor I'm worried about, it's mine."

"What does that mean? I have done nothing to besmirch your honor, only the pixie brat."

"First, never call him that again. Second, I am the royal here. I am the leader here. I have been crowned by faerie and Goddess to rule. Not you, me." My voice was low and careful. I didn't want it to break with emotion. I needed control in this moment. "By attacking the father of my child, my consort, in front of me, you proved that you have no respect for me as a ruler. You do not honor me as your ruler."

"If you had taken the crown as it was offered, I would have honored what Goddess chose."

"She gave me a choice, Barinthus, and I have faith that she wouldn't have done that if the choice offered was a bad one."

"The Goddess has always allowed us to choose our own ruin, Meredith. Surely you know that."

"If by saving Frost I chose ruin, then it was my choice, and you will either abide by that choice or you can get out of my sight, and stay out of it."

"You would exile me?"

"I would send you back to Andais. I hear she has been in a bloodlust since we left faerie. She mourns her only child's death in the flesh and blood of her people."

"You know what she is doing to them?" He sounded shocked.

"We still have our sources at court," Doyle said.

"Then how can you stand there, Darkness, and not want us all brought back into our power so we can stop the slaughter of our people?"

"She has killed no one," Doyle said.

"It is worse than death what she does to them," Barinthus said.

"They are all free to join us here," I said.

"If you bring us all into our power then we can go back and free them from her dungeon."

"If we rescued her torture victims we'd have to kill her," I said.

"You freed me and everyone else in her Hallway of Mortality when you left this last time."

"Actually, I didn't," I said. "That was Galen's doing. His magic freed you and the others."

"You say that to make me think better of him."

"I say it because it is true," I said.

He looked at Galen, who was glaring at him. Frost was just a little behind the other man, his own face the arrogant mask he wore when he didn't want anyone to read his thoughts. Doyle moved out from between Barinthus and Galen, but he didn't go far. Ivi, Brii, and Saraid were all standing a little apart from each other, the better to draw weapons. I remembered Barinthus's words that I'd left a vacuum of power and the guards at the beach house had turned to him because I neglected them, and seemed not to trust the women at all. I had a moment to wonder where their loyalty would lie, with me or Barinthus.

"Your magic filled the Hallway of Immortality with plants and flowers?" Barinthus asked.

Galen simply nodded.

"I owe you my freedom then."

Galen nodded again. He wasn't one for silence. The fact that he wasn't talking was a bad sign. It meant he didn't trust what he might say.

Rhys came in from the opposite hallway. He took one look at all of us, and said, "I see what the noise was that I heard. That was Jeremy. He needs us at the crime scene soon if we're coming. Are we?"

"We're coming," I said. I looked away from Barinthus to Saraid. "I'm told your personal glamour is good enough to hide in plain sight."

She looked startled, then nodded and even bowed. "It is."

"Then you, Galen, Rhys, and Sholto, come with me. We need to look human so the press doesn't interfere again." My voice sounded so sure of itself. The pit of my stomach was still clenched tight, but it didn't show, and that was what it meant to be in charge. You kept your panic to yourself.

I went to Hafwyn and Dogmaela still on the couch. Dogmaela had stopped crying, but she was pale and still shaken. I sat down beside her, but was careful not to touch. She'd had enough touching for one day apparently.

"I'm told your glamour would be up to the job, too, but I'll leave you here to recuperate."

"Please, let me come. I want to be useful to you."

I smiled at her. "I don't know what kind of crime scene this is, Dogmaela. It could be one that would remind you strongly of something that Cel did. For today, stay here, but in future you and Saraid will be part of my guard rotation."

Her blue eyes went a little wide, and then under the drying tears she looked pleased. Saraid came to us and dropped to one knee, head bowed low. "We will not fail you, Princess," she said.

"You don't have to bow like that," I said.

Saraid raised her head enough to give me those blue eyes with their white starbursts. "How would you like us to bow? You have but to ask and we will do as you prefer."

"In public don't do any of that, okay?"

Rhys walked wide around Barinthus, but was careful not to give his back to the other man. He was nonchalant about it, but if I noticed, I knew the other man did, too. "If you keep dropping to one knee in public, all the glamour in the world won't hide the fact that she's the princess and you're her guards."

Saraid nodded, then asked, "May I rise, your highness?"

I sighed. "Yes, please."

Dogmaela dropped to one knee in front of me as the other woman stood. "I am sorry, Princess, I did not give you the honor due your station."

"Please, stop that," I said.

She looked up, clearly puzzled. I stood and offered her my hand. She took it, frowning. "Have you noticed that the men don't kneel for me?"

The women exchanged glances. "The queen did not insist upon it always, but our prince did," Saraid said. "Just tell us which greeting you prefer and we will give it to you."

"A hello will be fine."

"No," Barinthus said, "it will not."

I turned and gave him a less-than-friendly look. "This is not your business, Barinthus."

"If you do not have their respect then you have no control over the sidhe," he said.

"Bullshit," I said.

He actually looked shocked, as if it wasn't a term he'd thought to hear from me. "Meredith . . ."

"No, I've had all I'm taking from you today. All the bowing and scraping in the world didn't make any of them respect Cel or Andais. It made them afraid of them, and that is not respect, that is fear."

"You threatened me with the full hands of flesh and blood. You want me to fear you."

"I'd prefer your respect, but I think you will always see me as the daughter of Essus, and no matter how much you might care for me you can't see me as fit to rule."

"That is not true," he said.

"The fact that I gave up the crown to save Frost's life has made you doubt me."

He turned so I couldn't see his face, which was answer enough. "It was the choice of a romantic, not a queen."

"And am I a romantic, and not a king?" Doyle asked, moving a little toward the other man.

He looked from one to the other of us, and then said, "It was most unexpected that you, Darkness, would make such a choice. I thought you would help make her into the queen we needed. Instead she has made you into something soft."

"Are you calling me weak?" Doyle asked, and I didn't like the tone in his voice at all.

"Enough!" I didn't mean to shout it, but that's how it came out.

They all looked at me. "I've seen our courts ruled by fear my whole lifetime. I say that we will rule here out of fairness and love, but if there are those among my sidhe who will not take fair treatment or love from me, then there are other options." I walked toward Barinthus. It was hard to be tough when I had to crane my neck so far up to meet his eyes, but I'd been tiny among them all my life and I managed.

"You say you want me to be queen. You say you want me to be harsh, and you want Doyle to be harsh. You want us to rule the way the sidhe need to be ruled, correct?"

He hesitated, and then nodded.

"Thank the Goddess and the consort that I am not that kind of ruler, because if I was I would kill you as you stand there so arrogant, so full of your power from only a month beside the sea. I should kill you now, before you gain more power, and that is exactly what my aunt and my cousin would do."

"Andais would send her Darkness to kill me."

"I already told you I am too much my father's daughter for that."

"You would try to kill me yourself," he said.

"Yes," I said.

"And you could only defend yourself," Rhys said, "by killing both Essus's daughter and his grandchildren. I think you'd let her kill you before you'd do that."

Barinthus turned on Rhys. "Stay out of this, Cromm Cruach, or did you forget that I know your first name, a much older name?"

Rhys laughed and it startled Barinthus. "Oh, no, Mannan Mac Lir, you can't play true naming with me. I am no longer that name, and haven't been in so long that it is no longer a true name at all."

"Enough of this," I said, my voice calmer this time. "We are leaving, and I want you, Barinthus, at the main house tonight."

"I will be glad of dinner with my princess."

"Pack an overnight bag. You're going to be at the main house for a while."

"I would prefer to remain near the sea," he said.

"And I don't care what you would prefer. I say that you will move into the main house with the rest of us."

He looked almost pained. "It has been so long since I lived near the sea, Meredith."

"I know. I've seen you swimming in the water of it happier than I'd ever seen you and I would have let you stay here by your element, but today you proved that it goes to your head like some rich liquor. You are drunk with the nearness of wave and sand, and I say that you will go to the main house and sober up."

Anger filled his eyes, and his hair did that odd underwater movement in the air again. "And if I refuse to move to the main house?"

"Are you saying that you will disobey a direct order from your ruler?"

"I am asking what you will do if I do not comply," he said.

"I will exile you from this coast. I will send you back to the Unseelie Court and you can find out firsthand how Andais sacrifices the blood of all the fey to try to control the magic that remakes her kingdom. She thought that if I left, the magic would stop and she would be able to control it again, but the Goddess herself is moving again. Faerie is alive again, and I think all you old ones have forgotten what that means."

"I have forgotten nothing," he said.

"That is a lie," I said.

"I would never lie to you," he said.

"Then you lie to yourself," I said. I turned to the others. "Come on, everybody. We have a crime scene to visit."

I started for the door and most of the people in the room followed me out. I called back over my shoulder. "Be at the main house tonight in time for dinner, Barinthus, or be on a plane back to St. Louis."

"She will torture me forever if I go back," he said.

I stopped in the doorway and the crowd of guards had to make an opening so I could see him. "And isn't that exactly what you threatened to do to Galen just minutes ago?"

He looked at me, just looked at me. "You are still moved by your heart and not your head, Meredith."

"You know what they say. Never come between a woman and what she loves. Well, don't threaten what I love, for I will move the Summerlands themselves to protect what is mine." The Summerlands was one of our words for Heaven.

"I will be there for dinner," he said, and he bowed. "My Queen."

"I look forward to it," I said, and that last I didn't mean at all. The last thing I wanted at the main house was an egotistical, angry ex-deity, but sometimes decisions aren't about what you want, but about necessity. Right now, we needed to go to a crime scene and try to earn the paychecks that helped support the mass of people we'd become. If only my title had come with more money, more houses, and less trouble, but I'd yet to meet a princess of faerie who wasn't in trouble of some kind. Fairy tales are true in one respect. Before you get to the story's end, bad things and hard choices are lived through. In a way I'd come to my happily ever after ending, but unlike fairy tales, in real life there's no ending, happy or otherwise. Your story, like your life, goes on. One minute you think you have your life relatively under control, and then the next minute you realize that all that control was just an illusion.

I prayed to the Goddess that Barinthus wouldn't force me to kill him. It would hurt my heart to do it, but as we walked out into the California sunshine and I slid my sunglasses on, there was something hard and cold inside me. It was a surety that if he pushed hard enough I would do exactly what I'd threatened. Maybe I was more my aunt's niece than I cared to think about.

CHAPTER TWENTY-NINE

DOYLE AND FROST, WITH USNA DRIVING, TOOK THE SUV, AND USNA used glamour to make him appear as me. It had surprised me that he had his driver's license, but apparently years before I was born he had left faerie to explore the country. When I'd asked why, he'd replied, "Cats are curious." And I knew just by the look on his face that that was all the answer I would get.

Usna wasn't good enough at glamour to walk through a crowd. One bump and the illusion would have shattered, which was why he wasn't going with me. There'd be a crowd where I was going. But we were hoping the more elementary illusion would lure the press from the outer gates, so we could drive off unmolested.

But his partner, Cathbodua, was good enough to go with us. There was a moment when she stood in the middle of the living room in her raven-feather cloak with that shoulder-length hair mingling with the feathers so that she, like Doyle, was dark enough that where one blackness ended and the other began the eye couldn't sort out. It made her skin seem to almost float against all the darkness.

Then the feathers smoothed out, and she was wearing the long black trench coat that it so often appeared to be. Cathbodua only had to soften her skin from the otherworldly paleness to a more human shade of pale. Most of the women had been so little photographed with me that they wouldn't even have to change anything but their eyes, hair, and some clothing. Saraid turned her golden hair to a brown-gold and her skin to a sun-kissed tan. Her blue-and-star eyes were simply blue. She was still beautiful, but she could pass for human. Even the fact that she was six feet even and naturally thin didn't make her stand out here in L.A. the way it would have back in the midwest. There were a thousand tall, gorgeous women here who had started out trying for acting and had had to settle for a day job.

Galen made his short curls a nondescript brown, and changed his eyes to match. He darkened his skin so he looked truly tanned, and he did subtle things to his face and body so that he looked ordinary. You'd seen a laughing, cute guy like him on every beach you'd ever been on. Rhys gave himself back the illusion of his missing eye, and painted both eyes to a good blue, but not too eye-catching. He simply piled his waist-length curls up under his fedora, left his signature trench coat at the beach house, and went in just the suit coat that he'd worn last to work, putting it over jeans and a T-shirt. The jeans were his, but the T-shirt he'd had to borrow. It fit through the shoulders, but lots of it was tucked into the stylishly faded jeans. He slipped back into his boots and he was dressed.

I came out of the bedroom with my hair an auburn that was almost brown. I'd also put it up into a French twist. The deep, chocolate-brown skirt suit was a little short for business, but I was short enough that long just wasn't good on me. I'd borrowed a holster and gun from Rhys and put them at the small of my back so I would be armed. It still left him a gun, a sword, and a dagger. I had my own folding knife in a thigh holster under the skirt. The knife actually wasn't just for defense; it was also so there would be some cold steel touching my naked flesh. Steel and iron help against faerie magic, but it's best if they touch your skin. There were a lot of fey, even sidhe, who couldn't have done glamour this detailed with cold metal touching their skin. My human and brownie ancestry helped me work magic no matter how much metal and technology surrounded me. The knife was nothing compared to the city itself. Out here by the ocean it was easier for the rest of them, but there were lesser fey who couldn't do much magic in the heart of any modern city.

The thought made me wonder about Bittersweet and whether Lucy had found her. I pushed the thought aside and checked the mirror one last time to make sure neither gun nor knife showed in the suit. The skirt was lightweight but flouncy, moving with me. I had a lot of skirts that were formfitting enough that even a small weapon showed against the material.

I walked back out into the great room. Galen met me, smiling. "I forgot you make your eyes brown, too."

"Green eyes are too unusual. Humans remember them."

He grinned at me, and moved to take me in his arms. I let him, pretty sure what he was going to say. "We should test the glamour and see if touching makes either of us lose our concentration."

We kissed, and it was a nice, thorough kiss. He drew away and I was staring up into a pair of dark brown eyes set in a face more tan than his would ever be by nature.

I smiled.

It was Rhys who said, "Come on you two, we all know our glamour holds up. Amatheon and Adair checked in. The press took the bait with Doyle and Frost, so we can go do some work." We followed him out the door, dropping each other's hands as we walked outside. I trusted the other guards that the main force of the press had gone away, but if we hung all over each other like lovers, no amount of glamour would keep them from snapping pictures, and not all glamour holds up to cameras. We don't know why, but even with the best of us sometimes a picture will reveal the truth when the naked eye will not.

Sholto had gone ahead of us all.

"All doors are in place."

"So you'll just appear," Galen said.

"Yes."

"How do you make certain someone isn't in the doorway when you appear."

"I can feel if it's empty," he said.

"Nifty."

"I didn't know you could do doorways," I said.

"Its a power that has returned since we were crowned."

"Don't tell Barinthus," Galen said.

"I will not." He'd been solemn when he said it. "But I will scout the area and if reporters seem aware you are on your way; tipped off, I believe they say."

"They do," I said with a smile.

"Then I will call if they have been tipped off." He'd gone with his blond hair looking short, his golden eyes as brown as Galen's and mine. Sholto even made his face less handsome so he wouldn't even attract attention as a too handsome human.

Rhys drove since it was his car. We put Saraid in the front with him, and the rest of us scattered in the back. We could actually see the distant flash of police lights when Rhys pulled over into a small parking lot. Julian or Jordan Hart leaned against one of the company cars. It wasn't until he turned and gave me that smile of his that I knew it was Julian and not his twin brother. They both had short, rich brown hair cut so it was short on the sides, but a little longer on top, where it was gelled into small spikes. But Jordan didn't have such a careless, devil-may-care smile. He had a good smile. They both did. They'd made enough money from modeling to first start their own detective agency and then to buy into the Grey Detective Agency. They were both six feet of tanned and easy handsome, but Julian was lighter, more of a tease. Though oddly it was the teasing brother who had found a monogamous relationship and done happily so for more than five years. Serious brother Jordan was still quite the ladies' man, though even in his single days Julian had never been a ladies' man. A gentleman's man, if that was a phrase, would have been more accurate.

He was wearing small-framed glasses with yellow-tinted glass that complemented his shades of brown and tan clothes. He came to me laughing. "You should have called, dear. I'd have worn another color so we wouldn't have matched."

I smiled and gave my cheek for a kiss, which I got and returned. His face still held that edge of laughter, but his eyes behind their almost-silly tinted glasses were very serious.

"You haven't been to the crime scene yet, have you?" I asked.

"No," he said, his voice as serious as his eyes, but if anyone was watching, his face still laughed and was pleasant. "But Jordan has."

Now I understood why his eyes were already a little grim. The twin brothers could let each other see what they were looking at, if they wanted to. When they'd been little they'd had no control over it, but they'd gone to the afterschool psychic programs along with all the other little gifted children and now they only shared if they chose. Whatever Julian's brother had shown him was bad enough to take the shine from his eyes.

He looked past me to the men with me, and the smile climbed back up into his eyes. There were other human wizards who would have had to ask before being certain who was hiding behind the glamour, but Julian really was that good, and so was his brother. So he went to Galen and exchanged a cheek kiss like he had with me and a handshake with Rhys. The fact that he knew who to kiss and who to just shake hands with said that the disguises weren't really fooling him. That was not good, since some police were now wizards, but most didn't specialize in "seeing" the truth.

Julian hesitated at the women, which meant that it wasn't what they looked like to his physical eyes that let him know who to kiss. It was something more mystical than that. He didn't know the female guards well at all, so he shook their hands. He was actually more careful of the women than the men.

Of course, even Julian hadn't quite been his exuberant self since more than half of Kane and Hart's detective agency had gotten eaten by a very big, bad piece of magical beastie called the Nameless. We—my men and I—had eventually entrapped it, but Kane and Hart had been ground down to only four employees, which was why the Grey Detective Agency was now the Grey and Hart Detective Agency. Both agencies had been going after the same niche market, so it made sense to join forces, and maybe Julian and Jordan Hart just felt that mixing their human magic with our not-so-human magic might be healthier for their remaining employees.

Adam Kane, Julian's longtime boyfriend, had lost his younger brother Ethan in the fight. I think Adam would have agreed to anything in those first few weeks. Even now Adam was doing mostly office work, seeing clients, but not much fieldwork. I wasn't sure whether that was still grief, or whether Julian couldn't stand the thought of endangering him. Eventually, if it had to be asked, Jeremy would do it, because at the office he was the boss. It was actually nice that I wasn't the boss every damn where.

"It's actually quicker to walk from here," Julian said. His hands went to his jacket pocket and started to lift a pack of cigarettes out, then he hesitated. "Do you mind if I smoke as we walk?"

"I didn't know you smoked," I said.

He gave a brilliant smile, flashing the perfect white teeth that he'd gotten as a model and that now made him picture-perfect when he was working with the local celebrities. "I quit years ago, but lately I've felt the need again." Something passed over his face, some thought or emotion, and not a good one.

"Is the crime scene that bad?" Galen asked, proving that he'd noticed the expression, too.

Julian looked up almost absentmindedly, as if he weren't really seeing the here and now. I'd seen that look before when he was seeing through his brother's eyes. "It's bad enough, but not so bad it makes me want to smoke."

I debated on whether to ask him what *was* bad enough to send him to smoke, as he lit a cigarette and began to stride down the sidewalk. He walked as he usually did, as if the sidewalk was a runway and everyone should be looking at him. Sometimes they did. Rhys moved ahead of us, with Saraid by his side. Galen and Cathbodua took up the rear position behind Julian and me. I realized that we could use all the glamour we wanted, but they were clearly being bodyguards. That would be a clue that Julian and I weren't what we seemed.

He seemed to notice that when I did, because he offered me his arm, and I took it. He began to touch my arm too much, and smile down at me too much. He was playing the part of wealthy lover and businessman or celebrity who needed the bodyguards. I played with him, bumping my head against his shoulder, and laughing at comments that weren't funny at all.

He leaned over and spoke quietly, smiling brilliantly. "You always were a quick study on undercover work, Merry."

"Thank you, you, too."

"Oh, I'm very good under the covers." And he laughed. He also tossed his half-smoked cigarette into the first trash can we came to.

"I thought you needed the cigarette," I said, smiling up at him.

"I'd almost forgotten that flirting is better than smoking." He leaned over me, putting one arm across my shoulders to draw me in against his body. I'd had a lot of practice walking like that with people about six feet tall, though he moved differently than most of my men. I slid my arm around his waist, underneath the jacket, brushing against his own gun that was at the small of his back so it didn't ruin the line of his suit coat. We strolled up the street like that, our hips rubbing against each other as we walked.

"I didn't think you liked flirting with women," I said.

"I'm an equal-opportunity flirt, Merry, you should know that."

I laughed, and this one was for real. "I do remember that, but not usually this much for me."

He kissed the skin of my temple, lightly, but there was an intimacy to it, a reality to it that he'd never used when undercover on my arm. There had always been an edge of teasing with it. It let you know he didn't mean it, so you wouldn't hold it against him later.

Julian was always touching people, and that gave me a thought. I leaned into him even more tightly and spoke quietly for his ears only. "Are you not getting much touch lately?"

It startled him enough that he stumbled and caused our easy rhythm to falter. He caught himself and me, and we continued our almost lazy stroll up the sidewalk toward all the blinking lights.

"Isn't that awfully direct for fey culture?" He whispered it against my hair.

"Yes," I whispered back, "but we'll be at the crime scene in minutes, and I want to know how my friend is doing."

He smiled, though I was close enough to know that it left his eyes empty. "No, I'm not getting much touch at home. Adam seems to have buried his heart with his brother. I'm starting to look around, Merry. I'm starting to shop seriously, and I realized it's not just sex, it's the touch I miss. I think if I could get more touch I would be able to wait out his grief better."

I stroked my hand across the flat planes of his stomach, and he gave me a speculative look. I smiled up at him and said, "You can have touch, Julian. Our culture doesn't see touch as necessarily sexual."

He laughed then, an abrupt and happy sound of surprise. "I thought you saw every touch as sexual."

"No, sensual, but not sexual."

"And there's a difference?" he asked.

I traced my hand across his stomach again, while my other hand clung to his waist. "Yes."

"Which is this?" he asked.

That made me frown. "You don't like women, remember?"

He laughed again, and put his hand over mine where it rested on his stomach. "Yes, but you won't share your men."

"That would be a question for the individual men," I said.

He raised his eyebrows at me. "Really?"

His expression made me laugh. "See, you'd rather sleep with them than with me."

He rolled his eyes a little and made a waffling gesture with his hands, then grinned at me. "True." He leaned down, still smiling, but his next words didn't match. "But if I cuddle you Adam will forgive me, while he might not forgive me a man."

I studied his face from inches away. "It's that bad?"

He nodded, and lifted my hand off his stomach so he could lay little kisses on my fingers as he spoke. "I love Adam more than I ever thought I'd love anyone, but I'm not good without attention." He let my hand fall and leaned our faces as close together as the height difference and my heels would allow. "It's a weakness of mine, but I need touch, and flirting, something."

"Come to the house for dinner tonight and we'll do a big cuddly pile while we watch something on the movie-size TV."

His steps hesitated, and he almost broke rhythm but caught himself, so neither of us lost a step. "Are you sure?"

"Trust me, as long as it's not sexual you can get touch."

"And if I wanted it to be sexual?" he asked.

That made me frown at him, and he looked away, not meeting my gaze. He pretended he was looking at the police and all the emergency vehicles, but I knew he was hiding his face from me, because whatever was in his eyes in that moment he didn't want to share.

I stopped him, by stopping my own walk. I turned him to face me. "You told me once that your commitment to Adam was your first happiness, that you'd fucked and worked, but never been happy, not really."

He gave a small nod.

"If you tell me your priority is to keep your commitment to him, then I'll help you keep it, but if you're telling me that it's over and you want sex, that's a different conversation."

I watched the pain in his eyes. He drew me into a hug that left no daylight between our bodies. He'd never hugged me like that, and seldom other men unless he was teasing and trying to see if he could make them uncomfortable. But it wasn't a hug about sex, or teasing. He held me too tightly and too desperately. I held him back and spoke with my face pressed to his chest. "Julian, what's wrong?"

"I'm going to cheat on him, Merry. If he leaves me this alone for much longer, I'm going to cheat. I think that's what he's waiting for, so he can use it as an excuse to break up."

"Why would he want to do that?" I asked.

"I don't know, maybe because Ethan always hated the fact that his only brother was gay. He always hated me and blamed me for turning his brother into a fag."

I drew back enough to try to see his face, but he curled around me so I couldn't. "Ethan didn't believe that. Adam's always liked men."

"He had a few girlfriends here and there. He was engaged once before me."

I touched his face and turned him to look at me. "Is he making noises about being into women again?"

He shook his head, and I realized there were tears glittering behind those tinted glasses. He wasn't crying yet, but he was a blink away from it. "I don't know. He doesn't want me to touch him. He doesn't want anyone to touch him. I don't know what's in his head anymore."

The tears trembled on the thickness of his eyelashes. He kept his eyes wide so the tears wouldn't fall.

"Come over for dinner. You can at least have some touch."

"We're supposed to have dinner together tonight; if it works out I might not need the touching from anyone else."

I smiled up at him. "If you don't show up, then we know you and your main squeeze are having fun, and that will be great."

He smiled at me, and wiped hastily at the unshed tears. He was gay but he was still a man, and most of them hated to cry, especially in public. "Thank you, Merry. I'm sorry to bring this to you, but my other friends, they're mostly gay men and . . ."

"They see it as a chance to poach you," I said.

He made that waffling motion again. "Not poach, but I am learning how many of my friends would be happy to be in my bed again."

"That's the problem with staying friends with most of your exlovers," I said.

He laughed and this time it sounded happy. "What can I say? I'm just a friendly guy."

"So I've heard," I said. I hugged him, and he hugged me back, more a friend hug this time. "Have you talked to Adam about couple's therapy?" I asked.

"He says he doesn't need therapy. He knows what's wrong with him. He lost his damn brother and he's allowed to mourn."

Rhys made a throat-clearing sound and we turned to him. "We have to show ID and get through the line." He was utterly neutral as he said it, but I knew that he'd caught some of what we'd been doing. One, all fey have better-than-human hearing, and two, after a thousand years you get to read people.

"I'm sorry," Julian said. "I am being unprofessional and that's not acceptable." He stepped away from me, straightening his jacket, smoothing his lapels, and gathering himself at the same time.

Galen leaned in and said, "We'll cuddle you without wrecking your marriage."

"Oh, that is a blow to the ego," Julian said with a smile. "That you're not even tempted to seduce me."

Galen grinned. "I don't think I'd be the one doing the seducing."

Julian grinned back at him. Cathbodua frowned and said, "I will not be cuddling anyone but Usna tonight."

"How sad for you," I said.

Cathbodua frowned harder. I shook my head, but said, "No one has to cuddle anyone they don't want to cuddle. It's all about touching because you want to, not because you're forced to."

She exchanged a look with Saraid. "That is very different from the prince."

Saraid said, "Happily so."

Julian glanced from one to the other of the women, and then said, "Were you honestly thinking that Merry would force you to touch me when you didn't want to?"

The women just looked at him. Julian shivered. "I don't know what your life was like before this, but I'm not into force. If my charming personality doesn't make you want my company, then so be it."

The women exchanged another look. Cathbodua said, "Give us a few more months of this new world and we may even believe that of both you and the princess."

"Tell Jeremy to keep all the female guards off undercover duty for a while," Julian said.

I thought about how either of the women might have taken the little walk with Julian. Would it have seemed like force, a kind of sexual abuse? So many walking wounded to take care of, and I'd just offered to help take care of Julian. But I didn't mind that last, because I knew how weak you could grow from lack of attention, until you began to look at strangers while the person who was supposed to love you neglected you. Humans saw it as a weakness on the part of the cheater, but I knew through my first fiancé that a person can leave a relationship in more ways than just walking away. You can leave your partner so bereft of attention that it's like not being in love at all.

If we could help Julian through this rough patch with Adam, then we would. I understood that you could die a little bit every day from lack of the right touch from the right person. I'd spent three years without the touch of another sidhe. I didn't want to see anyone else go through that if I could help them. And Adam wouldn't see me as a threat, because I was a woman.

We fished out our IDs and waited for someone in charge to give us permission to cross past the uniforms. We were private detectives, not police detectives, and that meant that no uniform was going to just say, "Come on down."

We waited in the brilliant sunlight while Julian held my hand and I held his back. I'd have rather helped him with his need than seen more dead bodies, but I wasn't getting paid to touch my friend, I was getting paid today to look at the dead. Maybe we'd have a nice divorce case next. That was sounding pretty good as we followed the nice police detective through the crowd of police and rescue workers. They were all avoiding each other's eyes. I'd learned that that was a bad sign—a sign that whatever lay ahead was disturbing to the people who saw a hell of a lot of disturbing things. I kept walking, but now holding Julian's hand wasn't just so he could get some touch for the day; it was because touching made me feel just a bit braver.

CHAPTER THIRTY

THERE WAS NO HAND-HOLDING AT THE CRIME SCENE. WE WERE ALL civilians being allowed into a police investigation. I was a woman and not all human, so I had to uphold the honor of both my sex and my ancestry.

The first victim was curled before the fireplace. It wasn't a real fireplace, but one of those plug-in electric ones. The killer, or killers, had positioned the body in front of it to match the illustration that Lucy had shown us safe in its plastic evidence wrap, tagged and bagged. She, because it was a she, had been dressed in the same ragged sack clothing as the illustration. It was a story I remembered reading as a child. I'd liked stories about brownies because of Gran. The brownie fell asleep before the fire and was caught napping, literally, by the household children. Gran had said, "Na brownie worth 'er salt would fall asleep on th' job." The rest of the story was about the children going with the brownie to fairyland and I knew that was made up, because I'd been there as a child and it was nothing like the book.

"Well, another childhood memory ruined," I said softly.

"What did you say?" Lucy asked.

I shook my head. "Sorry, but my grandmother read me this book as a child. I was thinking about reading it to my own kids, but maybe not now." I stared down at the dead woman and forced myself to look at what they'd done to her face. There was a brownie in the story, so they'd made her into a brownie by taking her nose and her lips, and paring her down to what they needed to make the picture.

Rhys came up beside me and said, "Don't look at her face."

"I can do my job," I said, and I didn't mean to sound defensive.

"I mean, look at all of her, not just her face."

I frowned, but did what he asked, and the moment I could see her bare arms and legs without the horror of her face getting in the way I understood what he meant. "She's a brownie."

"Exactly," he said.

"She's been butchered to look like one," Lucy said.

"No, Rhys means her arms and legs. They're longer, shaped a little differently. I would bet she's had some kind of electrolysis to get rid of the more-than-human body hair."

"But her face was human. They cleaned up the blood but they carved her face down to that," Lucy said.

I nodded. "I know of at least two brownies who have had plastic surgery to give them a nose and lips, a human face, but there's no good procedure for the arms and legs being a little thin, a little different."

"Robert lifts weights," Rhys said. "It gives more muscle tone and helps shape the limbs."

"Brownies can lift things five times their size. Normally they don't need to lift weights to be stronger."

"He does it just so he looks more human," Rhys said.

I touched his arm. "Thank you. I couldn't see anything but the face. They cleaned it up and hid the blood but it's obviously fresh wounds."

"Are you saying she really was a brownie?" Lucy asked.

We both nodded.

"There's nothing in any of her background that says she's anything but a native Los Angeles human."

"Could she be part brownie and part human?" Galen had come up behind us.

"You mean like Gran?" I asked.

"Yes."

I thought about it, and looked at the body, trying for dispassionate. "Maybe, but she'd still have to have a parent who wasn't human. That shows up in census records, documents of all kinds. There's got to be some record of her real background."

"A surface check said human, and she was born here in town," Lucy said.

"Dig deeper," Rhys said. "Genetics this pure aren't that far away from a fey ancestor."

Lucy nodded and grabbed one of the other detectives. She spoke gently to him and he went away at a fast walk. Everyone likes something to do at a murder scene; it gives the illusion that death isn't that bad, if you keep busy.

"The electric fire looks brand-new," Galen said.

"Yes, it does," I said.

"Was the first scene like this?" Rhys asked.

"What do you mean?"

"Staged with props brought in to make the illustration work."

"Yes," I said, "but a different book. A different story altogether, but yeah, props brought in so the staging was as perfect as they could make it."

"The second victim isn't as perfect as this one," Galen said.

We both agreed that it wasn't. We were assuming that this was Clara and Mark Bidwell, who lived at this address. They fit the height of both, and overall description, but honestly, unless they could be identified by dental work or fingerprints we couldn't be certain. Their faces weren't the faces smiling down at us from the pictures on the wall. We'd assume that it was the couple who lived here, but it was an assumption. The police were assuming it, too, so I felt better about that, but I knew it was breaking one of the first rules that Jeremy taught me: never assume anything about a case. Prove it, don't assume it.

As if my thought had conjured him, Jeremy Grey stepped into the room. He was about my height, five feet even, and was dressed in a designer suit in black that made his gray skin a darker, richer shade of gray, and though it would never be a human skin tone, somehow in the black suit it seemed like one. He'd stopped wearing all gray just this year. I liked the new colors on him. He'd been dating a woman seriously for about three months. She was a costumer at one of the studios and took clothing rather seriously. Jeremy had always dressed expensively in designer suits and shoes, but somehow everything fit him better. Maybe love is the best accessory of all?

His triangular face was dominated by a large hooked beak of a nose. He was a Trow—that was his race—and he'd been cast out centuries ago for stealing a single spoon. Theft had been a very serious crime back then among any of the fey, but the Trow were known for their puritanical views on a lot of things. They also had a reputation for stealing human women, so they weren't puritanical about everything.

He moved as he always did, gracefully; even the plastic booties over his designer shoes couldn't make him anything but elegant. Trow did not have a reputation for elegance, but Jeremy did, and it always made me wonder if he was the exception to his people, or if they were all like that. I'd never asked, because it would be reminding him of how he lost everything so long ago. You could ask after tragically dead relatives more politely among the fey than about their exile from faerie.

"The man in the bedroom is human," he said.

"I'll have to go back and look again, because honestly, all I could see were the facial cuts," I said.

He patted my arm with his gloved hand. We'd had to put on all the protective gear but if any of us touched anything we'd have gotten yelled at. It was strictly look but don't touch. Though honestly, I wasn't really tempted to touch.

"I'll walk you through," he said. That let me know he wanted to talk to me alone. Galen started to follow me, but Rhys held him back. Jeremy and I moved through the strangely dark apartment on our own. It was decorated in shades of brown and tan. That was typical coloring for an apartment, but even the furniture was shades of brown. It was all very somber and vaguely depressing. But maybe I was projecting.

"What's up, Jeremy?" I asked.

"One Lord Sholto is out in the hallway with the rest of your non-licensed people."

"I knew he'd be along," I said.

"Warn a Trow next time the King of the Sluagh is expected."

"Sorry, didn't think."

"But Lord Sholto just confirmed the call I got from Uther. I've got him across the street with eyes on this place."

"He saw something?"

"Not about the case," Jeremy said, and ushered me into the bedroom where the second body lay. The man had had his face treated the same as the woman, but now that I could look away from the faces, I realized that Jeremy and Rhys were right, he was human. The legs, the arms, and the body build were all proportional. He was wearing a robe that the killers had cut up to resemble the rags the brownie wore in the story, but it didn't come close to the perfect match of the victim in the other room.

The killers had left an illustration behind, and it did match, but they'd had to improvise the set pieces. They had him flat on his back to match the image of the brownie drunk on faerie wine. Again it was a mistake. Brownies didn't get drunk, bogarts did, and if a brownie went bogart it became very dangerous, sort of a Jekyll-and-Hyde type of problem. A drunk brownie did not pass out peacefully like a human, but I'd found that a lot of the fairy stories were like that: parts were dead-on and parts were so far off it was laughable.

"They brought the book with them, or they chose this illustration late, so late that they couldn't get all the props they needed to make it match."

"I agree," Jeremy said.

Something about the way he said it made me look at him. "If it's not about the case, then what could Uther have seen that would be important?"

"Someone on the press out there did a little math and decided that the short woman hanging all over Julian had to be the princess in disguise."

I sighed. "So they're out there waiting for me again?"

He nodded. "I'm afraid so, Merry."

"Crap," I said.

He nodded again.

I sighed. I shook my head. "I can't worry about them now. I need to be useful here."

He smiled at me, and patted my arm again. "That's what I needed to know."

I frowned at him. "What do you mean?"

"If you'd said something different, then I was going to assign you to the party circuit and leave you off the real cases."

I looked at him. "You mean send me to the celebrities and would-be celebs who just want the princess at their house?"

"It pays extremely well, Merry. They make up cases for us, and I send you or your beautiful men and they get more press attention. It works for everyone, and we're making money in an economy where most agencies aren't."

I had to think about that for a moment and then said, "So you're saying the extra publicity is actually bringing in more money than if we didn't have it?"

He nodded and smiled, showing the white, straight smile that was the only "cosmetic" work he'd had done on coming to L.A. "You're like any celebrity in one way, Merry. The moment the press doesn't care enough to make your life miserable you are on the downslide."

"The weight of the press following me crashed through a window last week," I said.

He shrugged. "And that made worldwide news, or did you avoid the television all weekend so you wouldn't see it?"

I smiled. "You know I avoid the shows where I'll see myself, and we had other things to do this weekend besides watch television."

"I guess if I had as many girlfriends as you have boyfriends I'd be too busy to watch TV, too."

"You'd be exhausted, too," I said.

"Are you insulting my stamina?" he asked, smiling.

"No, I'm a woman, you're a man. Women rule on the multiple orgasms, men not so much."

That made him laugh. One of the uniforms said, "Jesus, if you can laugh looking down at that then you really are cold-blooded bastards."

Lucy spoke from the doorway. "I think I hear your patrol car wondering where you are."

"They're laughing at the body."

"They aren't laughing at the body. They're laughing because they've seen things that would make you run home to your mommy."

"Worse than that?" he asked, motioning to the body.

Jeremy and I both nodded and said, "Yes."

"How can you laugh?"

"Go get some air," Lucy said, "now." And she made the last word very firm.

The uniform looked like he wanted to argue, thought better of it, and left. Lucy turned to us. "Sorry about that."

"It's okay," I said.

"No, it's not," she said, "and the press have found you, or think they have."

"Jeremy told me," I said.

"We're going to have to get you out of here before the press looking for you gets bigger than the press about the bodies."

"I'm sorry about this, Lucy."

"I know you don't enjoy it."

"My boss has just informed me that I make more by going to pretend crimes for parties for celebrities than when I do real crimestopping."

Lucy raised an eyebrow at Jeremy. "Really?"

"Absolutely," he said.

"Still, we need to have you show yourself outside so the press hounds don't mess up our investigation."

I nodded. "Did you find out anything more about the woman, the brownie?"

"It turns out she's been passing for human, but she's actually full-blooded brownie. You were right about the plastic surgeon needing to know her background before he reconstructed her face. Why is that so important?"

"Fey heal differently from humans, much faster. If a plastic surgeon didn't know she was a brownie, her skin could actually heal faster than he could work," I said.

"Or," Jeremy added, "there are some metals and man-made medicines that are deadly to us, especially the lesser fey."

"Some anesthesia doesn't work on us at all," I added.

"See, this is why I wanted you here. None of the rest of us would have thought of the doctor and what it would mean if she were full brownie. We need a fey officer to help us deal with things like this."

"I heard you were recruiting pretty heavily trying to get one of us to come on board," Jeremy said.

"For scenes like this, and just for community relations. You know how it is, the fey don't trust us. We're still the same humans who chased them out of Europe."

"Not the exact same ones," he said.

"No, but you know what I mean."

"I'm afraid I do."

"Has anyone come forward to join?" I asked.

"Not that I've heard."

"How human looking would they have to be?" I asked.

"To my knowledge, they aren't limiting it to a particular type of fey. They just want someone on our force who is fey. Most of us feel that that would help smooth things. I mean, we've got what amounts to a pedophile ring using the fey who look like children."

"It's not pedophilia," Jeremy said. "The fey are consenting and are usually hundreds of years old, so very legal."

"Not if money is exchanged, Jeremy. Prostitution is still prostitution."

"You know the fey don't understand that as a concept," he said.

"I know that. You see regulating sex the same as regulating what you can do with your own bodies, but it's not that. Frankly, and I'll never admit this in public, but if the fey involved look like kids and can satisfy these perverts, more power to them. It keeps them away from the real kids, but we need to talk to the fey involved with the pedophiles to see if they know if any children are involved."

"We protect our children," Jeremy said.

"But some of the older fey don't see under eighteen as children."

"That is another cultural difference," Jeremy agreed.

"If you made an exception for the adult fey who catered to the pedophiles, they would help you find the ones who are still targeting children," I said.

Lucy nodded. "I know they look like kids, fresh meat, some very human, and they get treated like fresh meat, but if they defend themselves with magic it can turn into a federal crime."

"And what started out as maybe their first arrest for prostitution is suddenly use of magical force, which is a lot more serious jail time," I said.

"Or what about the fey who killed a man trying to rape him in jail, and now he's up on murder charges?" Jeremy said.

"He smashed the man's head like an egg, Jeremy," Lucy said.

"Your human legal system still treats us like monsters if we don't have diplomatic immunity and a celebrity princess."

"That's not fair," I said.

"Not fair? There's never been a sidhe in jail in this country. I'm one of the lesser folk, Merry. Trust me when I say that the humans have always treated your people as different from the rest of us."

I wanted to argue, but I couldn't. "Did you ask the plastic surgeon if he's done more fey?"

"No, but we can," she said.

"The demi-fey at the first scene looked typical, but check and see if they were doing anything to pass for human."

"They couldn't. They're the size of Barbie dolls or smaller," Lucy said.

"Some demi-fey can shift to a larger size, between three and five feet tall. It's an uncommon ability, but if you could make yourself that tall you could strap down the wings, depending on the kind of wings they are."

"Really?" Lucy asked.

I looked at Jeremy. "One of your silent film stars was a demi-fey who hid her wings. I knew a saloon worker who did it, too."

"And none of her customers found out?" Lucy asked.

"She used glamour to hide them."

"I didn't know the demi-fey were that good at glamour."

"Oh, some of them are better at glamour than the sidhe," I said.

"That's news," Lucy said.

"There's an old saying among us that where the demi-fey go faerie follows. It implies that the demi-fey are the first of us to appear, and not the sidhe or the old gods grown small, but actually they are the first form of us."

"Which is true?" she asked.

"To my knowledge no one knows," I said.

"It's the fey version of the chicken and the egg. Which came first, the demi-fey or the sidhe?" Jeremy said.

"The sidhe will say that we did, but honestly, I've never met anyone old enough to answer the question."

"Some of the demi-fey who were killed had day jobs, but I assumed that they were demi-fey. It didn't occur to me that they could pass for human."

"What are the jobs?" I asked.

"Receptionist, owner of their own lawn-care business, florist assistant, and dental hygienist." She frowned at that last one. "I did wonder about that last one."

"I'd look at the receptionist and the dental hygienist," Jeremy said.

"What about the rest of them?" I asked.

"One of them worked at the lawn-care business with the boss, and the other two were unemployed. As far as I can tell, they were flower faeries full-time, whatever that means."

"It means they tended their special flower or plant and didn't feel the need for money," Jeremy said.

"It meant they had enough magic to not need a job," I added.

"Is that typical of the demi-fey, or unusual?" she asked.

"It depends," I said.

Her cell phone rang. She slipped it out of her pocket, said a few "Yes, sirs," then hung up. She sighed. "You better go and show yourself, Merry. No hiding with magic. That was my immediate supervisor. He wants you out so the press will disperse. There's so many of them they're afraid they can't get through to take the bodies out."

"I'm sorry, Lucy."

"No, the information was all stuff I couldn't have gotten with just human cops. Oh, and he said to take your men with you just in case."

"He means the sidhe, not me, right?" Jeremy asked.

She smiled. "We'll go on that assumption. I'd like to keep at least one of you here until we clear the scene."

"You know that the Grey . . ."

Julian added, "And Hart."

Jeremy smiled at him. "Grey and Hart Detective Agency is happy to help."

"I sent Jordan home. He's a little more of an empath than I am, and the residual emotions were getting to him."

"That's fine," Lucy said.

"If you hurry he's just outside in the hallway," Julian said.

I studied his pleasant face and asked, "Does he need a ride?"

"He won't ask for one, but if you go out at the same time he'll take the ride from you, Merry."

"All right, then I'll go and I'll drop Jordan off at the office so he can type up his report and I'll maybe see you tonight after dinner."

He nodded. "I hope you don't see me."

"Me, too," I said and went to the other room to get Rhys and Galen, who as licensed detectives were allowed past the apartment door, and pick Saraid and Cathbodua up from the hallway, which was as far as the police would let her get without a detective license. It was also why Sholto wasn't allowed at the murder scene. I hoped Jordan was still in the hallway. Julian wouldn't have mentioned him if he wasn't badly shaken. I couldn't sense emotional debris from murder scenes, and any time I watched the effect of it on an empath I was glad all over again that it wasn't one of my gifts.

CHAPTER THIRTY-ONE

WE FOUND JORDAN IN THE STAIRWELL LEADING DOWN. HE WAS sweating and pale, his skin clammy to the touch. I'd been afraid we'd missed him when he wasn't in the hallway, but he actually leaned on Galen going down the stairs, which meant he was in bad shape. Jordan wasn't the touchy-feely one of the Hart brothers.

He had the same short-on-the-sides, spiky-on-top hair as his brother, but his jacket was a reddish-brown tweed over the brown slacks, and his shirt was a tomato red. All the extra color must have looked good when Jordan started the day, but now it just emphasized the sick paleness of his skin.

We'd all dropped the glamour so when we stepped out into the sunlight there were cries of, "There she is!" "Princess!" "Princess Meredith, over here!" One reporter did actually ask a question about something else. "What's wrong with Hart? Why does he look ill?"

A female voice rang out, "Is the murder that gruesome?"

It was nice to know that the mass of humanity on the other side of the police barriers wasn't all here just for fairy-princess pictures. People were dead; that should have been more important.

A man in a suit stepped forward and yelled in a voice used to yelling above noise, "The princess and her people aren't authorized to answer any questions about the crime." He turned to a pair of uniforms near him, and they started walking toward us. I was betting that they were supposed to be our escort to our car. I glanced out at the crowd of reporters. They had spilled into the street until even if the police hadn't blocked off the road there wasn't room for a moped, let alone a car. We were going to need more uniforms.

Then there was movement across the road, almost a restless roll of the press, like water when you stir it with a big enough stick. Uther waded into the mob. Maybe we wouldn't need more uniforms. One nine-foot-tall Jack-in-Irons might just be enough.

It wasn't just Uther's sheer size that was impressive. His face was part human and part that of a boar, complete with tusks that curled up and out so big that they'd begun to do that spiral curl that only long years will give to tusks. The last time Uther had helped with crowd control the press had parted like the proverbial Red Sea, as some did now, too, but others turned to him, and started shouting questions at him, too. But they weren't about the murder, or me.

"Constantine, Constantine, when's your next movie coming out?"

Another reporter yelled out, "How big are you?"

"Did they just ask what I think they asked?" I asked.

Jordan's knees went out from under him, and Galen picked him up in his arms and carried him toward the edge of the barricades. Rhys touched his hand to the man's forehead. "He's in a bad way."

"What is wrong with him?" Sholto asked.

"Wizard's bane," Rhys said.

"Oh," Sholto said.

"What?" I asked.

"It's an old term for wizards who overextend themselves. I figured it was a quicker explanation to Sholto."

"Which I've just made longer," I said with a smile.

Rhys shrugged.

I saw Uther shaking his great tusked head, and even without hearing him I knew he was denying that he was this Constantine. Apparently Uther wasn't the only Jack-in-Irons in L.A., and whoever the other one was, he'd made a movie. I loved Uther as my friend and coworker but he didn't exactly have a face made for the movies.

One of the EMTs who had managed to get here before the crowd converged came up to us. He was medium height with blond hair that had streaks of color that humans didn't have, but he gave off that wave of competence that the best healers seem to have. "Let me look at him." He touched Jordan's face as Rhys had, but also took his pulse, and checked his eyes. "Pulse is okay, but he's in shock." As if on cue, Jordan began to shiver enough that his teeth started to chatter.

We ended up having to take him to the back of the ambulance. They put him on the gurney. He started panicking when they surrounded him, and he reached out to us. "I need to talk to you guys before it fades." I knew what he meant; Jordan, like a lot of psychics, could only hold on to his visions for a short time, and then details would begin to fade.

The EMT named Marshal said, "There isn't room for all of you in here."

As the physically smallest I crawled in, took his hand, and tried to stay out of the way. Marshal and his partner wrapped Jordan in one of the insulated blankets, and started making up an IV.

Jordan started pushing at them. "No, not yet, not yet."

"You're in shock," the EMT said.

"I know that," Jordan said. He grabbed my hand and stared up at me with his eyes too wide, showing too much white like a horse about to bolt. "They were so afraid, Merry, so afraid."

I nodded. "What else, Jordan?"

He looked past me to Rhys. "Him, I need him."

"If you let us put the IV in," Marshal said, "we'll let in your other friend."

Jordan agreed, they hooked him up, and Rhys crawled in with us. Galen did his bit by distracting the EMTs so we could talk. Saraid, her hair flashing like metal in the sunlight, joined him, smiling and at ease to distract. Cathbodua stayed by the open doors of the ambulance on guard. Sholto joined her. We just might have enough guards today.

Jordan looked at Rhys, his face wild with fear. "What did the dead tell you?"

"Nothing," Rhys said.

"Nothing?" Jordan asked.

"Whatever killed the brownie made it impossible to speak with the dead."

"What does that mean?" I asked.

"I mean they took everything. There's no spirit, ghost, if you will, to talk to."

"Not all the dead like to talk to you," Jordan said, but he was calmer now, either from the fluids or from getting his way.

"True," Rhys said, "but this wasn't a choice. They're just gone. Both of them as if they never existed."

"You mean whatever killed them ate their souls," Jordan said.

"I won't debate semantics, but yeah, that's what I mean."

I said, "That's impossible, because that would mean they've been taken out of the cycle of death and rebirth. Nothing but a true God could do that."

"Don't look at me for answers on this one. I'd have said it was impossible, too."

Jordan let go of my hand and grabbed Rhys's jacket, wadding it in one fist. "They were so afraid, both of them, and then there was nothing. They were just snuffed out like a candle. Poof."

Rhys nodded. "That would be how it might feel."

"But you didn't say how afraid they'd be. Oh, my dear God, so afraid!" He looked up into Rhys's face as if looking for comfort, or confirmation. "There were wings, something with wings. Angels wouldn't do this, can't do this."

"Angels aren't my gig," Rhys said, "but there are other things with wings. What else did you sense, Jordan?"

"Something flew because she was envious. She always wished she could fly. I got that very clearly, as if it had been a wish since childhood, and beauty. She thought whatever was flying was beautiful."

"And the man?" Rhys asked.

"He's just fear, all fear, but fear for his wife more than himself. He loved her." Jordan said it like "loved" should have been in all capital letters.

"Did the woman know what magic they used against her?"

Jordan frowned, and had that distant look that I'd seen on his face before, as if he were looking at things I'd never see. "She thought beautiful and wings, and wished she could fly, and then her husband came in and there was love and there was fear. Such fear, but she died too quickly to fear for her husband much. They killed her first. There was confusion about the man. Two killers, two, one female, one male. They're a couple. Sex, lust, killing made them feel both, and love. They love each other, too. They don't know that what they're feeling isn't right. It's love for them, and out of that love they do horrible things, terrible things." He gave frightened eyes to both of us, looking from one to the other. "This wasn't the first time. They'd had this feeling together before, the power rush of the kill together before . . . they've killed . . . before."

His voice was trailing off, his eyes losing their franticness. His fist began to open, and he fought to hold onto Rhys's jacket. "Man, woman, couple . . . killing. Power . . . they want power . . . magic. Enough to do something."

"To do what?" I asked.

His hand slid away from Rhys to flop boneless on top of the blanket. "To do . . ." And he passed out.

Rhys called out, "Marshal, did you put something besides fluids in the IV?"

Marshal appeared at the doors of the ambulance, giving a longer-than-necessary look at Cathbodua all black and Goth and scary by the doors. Sholto looked much less scary, though I know he wasn't. He nodded. "I put something to calm him down. It's standard for psychic shock. They calm down, and the shock goes away. He'll be fine when he wakes up."

"He'll also have no memory of what he picked up from the murder upstairs," Rhys said.

"I had one psychic stroke out from severe shock. I know you lost some information, but it's my job to keep him alive and well, and I did my job."

Rhys was angry enough that he just got out of the back of the ambulance without another word. I think he didn't trust himself to talk to Marshal anymore.

"Could he really have hurt himself if this had continued?" I asked.

Marshal nodded. "The odds are against it, but I took that chance with one psychic and he's still in rehab learning how to tie his own shoes. I'm not going to let that happen to another person, not if I can help it. It's my job to keep everyone healthy, not to solve crime. I'm sorry if it made it harder on you guys."

I touched Jordan's face. The sweat was already drying on his skin. He was warmer, and his breathing had evened out into something like normal sleep. "Thank you for helping him."

"Just doing my job."

I smiled at him. "Will you transport him to the hospital?"

"I will if the crowd ever thins enough, and I'm told that that won't happen until you leave, Princess."

I nodded. "Maybe not, but he needs someone to ride with him to the hospital. His brother is upstairs. I'll call him, and I need your word that you won't transport Jordan until his brother is with him."

"Fine, I give you my word."

I shook a finger at him. "I'm a princess of faerie. We take the giving of our word very seriously. You seem like a nice guy, Marshal the EMT. Don't give me your word unless you really mean it."

"Are you threatening me?" he asked.

"No, but magic works around me sometimes, even here in L.A., and that magic takes your word of honor very seriously sometimes."

"You're saying that magic works around you whether you want it to or not?"

I wanted to take it back, because I didn't want the press to get hold of that fact, but Marshal had helped my friend, and he seemed like a nice guy. It would be a shame to have him hurt just because he didn't understand what his word was supposed to mean to the power of faerie.

"Talk to the reporters and I'll say you made it up, but yes, sometimes. You seem like a nice guy. I'd hate for you to have a problem with some stray bit of magic. So you have to stay here until Julian, his brother, gets here."

"Or something bad could happen to me?" He made it a question.

I nodded.

He frowned as if he didn't believe me, but finally nodded. "Okay, call the brother. I think the crowd won't thin out too fast."

I slid out of the ambulance. Cathbodua fell in at my side in that practiced bodyguard move that I'd begun to take for granted. Sholto mirrored her on the other side. I used my cell phone to call Julian. He'd want to know that his brother was doing this poorly anyway; of course, I'd forgotten that both brothers were powerful psychics.

He picked up his phone about the time I saw him through the crowd of cops. He was already on his way to his brother's side. I flipped the phone closed and waved at him. He waved back, pocketing the phone he'd been about to answer. They were psychics. They didn't need telephones.

CHAPTER THIRTY-TWO

UTHER JOINED US AT THE BARRIERS ALONG WITH OUR UNIFORMED escorts. This pair of policemen was male, one young and African American and the other on the far side of fifty and Caucasian. In fact, he looked like he'd been dropped on the scene by a casting agent who'd filled the order for an older white cop, a little overweight, a little jaded, and very world-weary. His eyes said he'd seen everything and been impressed by none of it.

His partner was a rookie, and seemed bright and shiny in comparison. The young officer was Pendleton; the older one was Brust.

Pendleton stared up at the nearly giant-sized fey. Brust gave Uther the same dull look he'd given everything else, and said, "You coming with the princess?"

"Yes," Uther said in a deep, rumble of a voice that sounded perfect for his size. He'd taken voice lessons to get rid of the speech impediment that the tusks had given him so that he could sound like he was speaking the queen's English when he wanted to. He did it mostly because it hurt people's heads to hear someone who looked like him speaking like a college English professor. It amused him, and most of the rest of us.

"I think with four guards and us we've got this," Brust said.

I moved in smiling. "I'm sure you do, Officer Brust, but Uther is also a coworker and we need to discuss the case with him."

Both officers looked the big guy up and down. I'd seen the looks before, and so had Uther. He said, "Would you prefer that I quote Keats, Milton, or the football scores? What works for you so you don't think I'm as stupid as I look?"

Pendleton said, "We don't . . . I mean, I don't . . . We didn't say anything like that."

"Save it, Penny," Brust said, and looked up at Uther. He said in a voice as dry and serious as any I'd heard, "So you're saying you're not just another pretty face?"

"Brust," Pendleton said, and sounded offended on Uther's behalf. It made me shave years off Pendleton's age, or he'd joined the force later than he looked. His offense was civilian businessman offense, not cop offense.

Uther laughed his rumbling chuckle. "No, I'm not just another pretty face."

Brust actually gave a little smile. "Then by all means help us move these fine citizens back."

Pendleton looked from one man to the other, puzzled that they'd somehow bonded. I understood it. Uther knew what he looked like, and he hated it when people pretended that he didn't. He liked people who honestly weren't bothered by his appearance, but the ones who were bothered but pretended they weren't always made his hackles rise.

"Come on, big guy," Rhys said, "let's see if we can clear out some of this crowd for the nice policeman."

Uther smiled down at him. "I don't think you're going to be much help, little man."

Rhys grinned up at him. "One of these days I've got to take you into a mosh pit."

Galen made a happy sound. "Only if I get to go," he said.

"What is a mosh pit?" Saraid asked.

Cathbodua surprised us all by answering. "It's an area at a music concert where people dance oddly and often get hurt." She gave a small smile of her own. "I think Uther in one of them would be worth seeing."

"I didn't know you liked modern music," I said.

"I doubt you know much of anything that I like, Princess Meredith."

I could only agree. Uther moved out in front of us and the reporters did back up, because he was simply that physically intimidating, but some of the reporters started asking him questions. Again, they seemed to believe he was this Constantine person.

Rhys and Galen stayed wedged on either side of me, with Brust in front, Pendleton in back, and Saraid and Cathbodua to the sides and back of all of us. Sholto stayed at my side as Julian did on the way up, but there was still no hand holding, not until we were clear of the crime scene.

Uther finally came to a stop, because the press was so thick that it was either stop or start stepping on people. Brust used his shoulder mic, probably calling for more help to clear the crowd. I was going to be persona non grata at crime scenes after this, and there was nothing I could do about it.

Uther tried to make things better. "I am Uther Boarshead. I work for the Grey and Hart Detective Agency. I do not make films."

One female reporter shoved a recorder at him, and said, "Your tusks are bigger than his, more curved. Does that mean that other things are bigger, too?"

I asked Rhys in a low voice, "What kind of movies does the other guy make?"

"Porn," he answered.

I stared at him.

Rhys grinned, and nodded. "Yep."

"Recent films?" I asked.

"Apparently the films are popular. The big guy has been getting asked for autographs and propositioned when he's in public."

I stared at him in horror, because Uther was a very private person.

I couldn't think of many things that would bother him more. I also couldn't think of a way for it to stop. Most people would just see the outer packaging, and this Constantine was probably the only other Jack-in-Irons in L.A. It was like being the body double for Brad Pitt. People wanted it to be him, and so they didn't believe you when you said that it wasn't.

"I take it his costar is fey, not human," I said, moving in close to Rhys so the reporters just feet away wouldn't hear.

"His main leading ladies, yes, but he's done some with humans."

I looked at Rhys, and his one eye sparkled with appreciation of my surprise. I said, "Rhys, I couldn't be with Uther and not be hurt, and I'm only part human."

"My understanding is that the humans are more fluffers and foreplay."

Galen leaned in and said, "I don't know, I thought the fey-on-fey films were more shocking. Watching all that go on in such a small place . . ." He made a face. The sidhe are not easily squicked, so the fact that he made that face said a lot about the squick factor of the film.

"You watched them?" I said.

"Uther wanted to see them, and he didn't want to watch alone. He invited the men at the agency over to sort of hold his hand."

I wanted to call and tell Lucy what we'd learned from Jordan but I didn't dare do so this close to running recorders and sharp-eared reporters.

Sholto drew me in against his body abruptly. Saraid's hand just appeared and was holding the arm of a man with a tape recorder in his hand. "Please, do not touch the princess," she said, in a voice that did not match her brilliant smile.

"Sure, sorry," he mumbled.

She let go of his arm, but he stayed so close to Galen that if we did get to move forward he'd have to move so Galen could step forward at all. The reporter said, "Princess Meredith, what do you think of the reporters going through the window of your cousin's deli?"

"I hope no one was hurt."

A woman screamed from just in back of him, "Meredith, did you ever sleep with Uther?"

I just shook my head.

A wave of policemen moved in and began pushing them back, helping us move forward. Sholto kept me pressed against him. Shielding me from as much of the cameras as he could. I was happy to be moving, and happier not to be trapped with the questions. I was used to sex questions about me and the men in my life, but Uther and the other detectives at the agency, except for Roane, whom I'd actually dated, were off that list. I liked it better that way.

CHAPTER THIRTY-THREE

UTHER RODE IN THE FAR BACK OF THE SUV WITH HIS KNEES TUCKED to his chin and his upper body bent until his head was almost between his shins. He looked squished and totally uncomfortable. Jeremy had driven him to the scene in the van, where he fit in the back, but the boss man had to stay behind and continue to try to help the police. I sat in the middle seats with Galen on one side and Sholto on the other. Saraid rode in the small jump seat that was the last seat in the back, which was one of the reasons Uther was wedged so close. Cathbodua rode in front with Rhys. I turned as far as the seat belt would let me so I could see Uther.

He looked like what he was, someone impossibly tall shoved into a normal-size space. But the unhappiness on his face wasn't about the fit; he was used to trying to fit into a world made for smaller folk.

"How did I miss this whole Constantine problem?" I asked.

He made an *umph* sound. "You and I once discussed you helping me lift my long fast. You said no, and I respect that. If I started talking to you about pornographic movies featuring another Jack-in-Irons, I feared you might misconstrue my motives."

"You thought I'd take it as flirting?" I asked.

He nodded, settling his lips around the curve of his curling tusks the way another man might settle a toothpick. It was a thinking gesture for him.

"Bragging perhaps, or even seduction. I've had more human women proposition me since Constantine's movies than ever in my life." He crossed his big arms over his chest.

Galen turned beside me so he could see the big man, too. "And why is that a problem?" he asked.

"You watched the films. No human woman could survive."

"Now, that's bragging," Saraid said, turning toward him.

"It isn't," he said. "It's truth. I've seen what my brethren can do to a human woman. It was one of the worst things I'd ever seen done to a human by a fey, and that includes the nightflyers of the sluagh." He remembered Sholto too late and gave a glance his way. "I mean no offense, Lord Sholto."

"None taken," Sholto said, managing to turn so he could both see the big man better and have an excuse to touch my thigh through my hose. Was it nerves, and if so, why? Why did the conversation make him nervous?

Sholto continued, "I, too, have seen what the royals of the nightflyers do to human women. It is . . ." He simply shook his head. "It is the reason I forbade them from seducing outside our kingdom."

"Seduction, you call it," Saraid said, and gave him a less-than-friendly look. "There are other names for it, Shadow Lord."

His triple yellow and gold eyes gave as cold a look as her blue, which is harder with a warmer color, but Sholto managed. "I am not a product of rape, if that's the story that the Unseelie sidhe tell."

There was a tightening around the eyes that said he'd hit the mark, but all she said out loud was, "You were a babe. How do you know how your birth came about?"

"I know who my father was, and he was not one to take his pleasure unwilling."

"So he says." Saraid glared at him.

His fingers began to rub back and forth on the hose that stood between him and my skin. I knew why he needed touch now. "Said, for he died before ever we came to this country. There are pleasures among the nightflyers that do not exist elsewhere."

She made a face, the face Sholto had been seeing on sidhe women from the moment he couldn't hide the tentacles and extra bits. That old pain was still there etched in his handsome face. He could truly be sidhe now and have it just as a tattoo, but he didn't forget how he'd been treated when he could do no more than hide it with glamour.

I laid my hand on the side of his neck. He actually startled at the touch, and then seemed to realize that it was me and relaxed into it.

"I do not think there are many among even the Unseelie who would take one of you, spine and all, and call it pleasure," Saraid said.

"Sholto's father was not one of the royals, so the spine wasn't there to be an issue," I said. I curved my hand around his neck so my fingers could rest at his hairline and the warmth of the back of his neck under his ponytail.

"So he says." Saraid glared at him again.

Galen's voice was mild as he said, "So any sidhe woman who would bed a nightflyer would be a pervert of the worst sort?"

She folded her arms across her chest and nodded. "To sleep with any of the sluagh is one of the few evils."

"I'm a pervert then," I said.

She looked startled, raising her eyes to me. "No, of course not. He is no longer the Queen's Perverse Creature. He can be as sidhe as any other with his new magic."

I laughed then, and said, "Have all of you female guards been imagining him coming to my bed only with his sidhe body and none of his nightflyer parts?"

Saraid was surprised again and didn't try to keep it off her face. "Of course."

I leaned into Sholto, cuddling against his body as much as my seat belt and the turning in the seat would allow. "There are things that his extra bits can do that usually takes four men to accomplish, and even then the arms and legs get in the way."

Saraid looked ill.

Sholto wrapped his arms around me and pulled me close, his head resting against my hair. I didn't have to see his face to know he was wearing a satisfied expression.

Galen put a hand on the other man's shoulder. I felt Sholto tense a little, and then he relaxed again, though I knew he was puzzled. Galen had never shared a bed with the two of us. In fact, none of the other men had. Sholto wasn't close enough friends with any of the other men to be that comfortable with them.

"Sholto saved our lives by getting us to Los Angeles before Cel could come after Merry," Galen said. "No one else among all the sidhe still have the power of transporting that many others by magic except for the King of the Sluagh. He helped Merry take vengeance for her grandmother's murder."

"After he killed the grandmother," Cathbodua said, finally joining in from the front seat.

Rhys said, "You weren't there. You didn't see the spell turn poor Hettie into a weapon to kill her own grandchild. If Sholto hadn't killed her, Merry might be dead now, or I'd have had to kill my old friend. He saved me from that, and he saved Merry. Don't talk about something unless you know what you are talking about." His voice was as grim as I had ever heard it. He had been a frequent visitor at my Gran's bed-and-breakfast, and had helped keep her company the three years I had had to hide away from even her.

"If you say it is the truth, then I will believe you," Cathbodua said.

"I will take oath on it," Rhys said.

"That won't be necessary," she said, but she glanced back at all of us, and said, "I apologize, King Sholto, but perhaps Saraid or I should tell you why we have such a hatred of the nightflyers."

"I know that Prince Cel had made friends of a sort with one of the dispossessed royal nightflyers." He pressed his face into my hair as he spoke, as if it were too awful to look straight at.

"You knew the prince was using him to torture us." Saraid's voice was outraged, and her anger translated into a flash of warmth as her magic began to rise.

"I killed him when I found out," Sholto said.

"What did you say?" Saraid asked.

"I said, when I found out, I killed the nightflyer who was helping the prince torture you. Did you not wonder why it stopped?"

"Prince Cel said he was rewarding us," Cathbodua said.

"He stopped because I killed his playmate and made of him an example so that no one else among us would be tempted to try to replace him in Cel's fantasies. He told me before he died that the prince had made for himself a spine of metal so they could tear and rape together." The slightest of tremors went through his body, as if the horror of it was still with him.

"Then we owe you a debt, King Sholto," Cathbodua said.

A sound escaped Saraid. I turned in Sholto's arms and found tears gliding down her face. "Thank Goddess, Dogmaela was not here to find out that our prince's kindness was not a softening of him, but the action of a real king." Her voice never showed the tears I could see. If you'd just heard the voice you wouldn't have known.

"It was that kindness, that promise of never doing that again to her, that helped him persuade Dogmaela to participate in a fantasy that required cooperation," Cathbodua said.

"Do not tell," Saraid said. "We swore to never tell such things. It is enough that we endured them."

"There are things the queen made us do," Rhys said, as he turned onto a side street, "that we never speak of either."

Suddenly Saraid was sobbing. She put her hands in front of her face and cried as if her heart would break. Between sobs she said, "I am so glad . . . to be here . . . with you, Princess . . . I could not do it . . . could not endure . . . I had decided to let myself fade." Then she simply wept.

Uther laid an awkward hand on her shoulder, but she didn't seem to notice. I touched her hand where it lay against her face, and she turned and held my fingers with hers, still hiding her crying from our sight. Galen reached across and touched her shining hair.

She wrapped her hand more tightly around mine, and then she lowered her other hand, her eyes still closed with her weeping. She held out that weeping hand. It was a moment before Sholto and I realized what she was doing. Then, slowly, hesitatingly, he reached out and took her hand.

She grabbed onto him and held both our hands tightly as she shook and cried. It was only as the weeping began to quiet that she stared up at us, at him, with eyes shining blue and stars with tears. "Forgive me for thinking that all princes and all kings are like Cel."

"There is nothing to forgive, because the kings and princes are like that at the courts still. Look what the king did to our Merry."

"But you are not like that, and the other men are not like that."

"We have all suffered at the hands of those who were supposed to keep us safe," Sholto said.

Galen stroked her hair as if she were a child. "We've all bled for the prince and the queen."

She bit her lip, still clinging to our hands. Uther patted her shoulder. "You all make me glad that Jack-in-Irons are solitary faerie and beholden to no court."

Saraid nodded.

And then Uther said, "I'm the only one who can reach you for a hug. Will you take it from someone as ugly as me?"

Saraid turned to look at him, and Galen had to move his hand away so that she could. She looked surprised, but she looked into his eyes and saw what I'd always seen: kindness. She simply nodded.

Uther slid his big arm across her shoulders. It was as careful and gentle a hug as I'd ever seen, and Saraid let herself fold into that hug. She let him hold her, and buried her face against his wide chest.

It was Uther's turn to look surprised, and then he looked pleased. His kind might be solitary faeries, but Uther liked people, and solitaire wasn't his favorite game. He sat in the back, crammed into the tight space but he got to hold the shining, beautiful woman. He got to wrap her tears in his strong arm and hold her against a chest that was as deep, with a heart that was as big, as any I'd ever known.

He held Saraid the rest of the way home, and in a way she held him right back, because sometimes and especially for a man, being able to be someone's big strong shoulder to cry on helps you not need to cry so very much yourself.

On that drive Uther wasn't alone, and neither was Saraid. Sholto and Galen held me. Cathbodua even put a friendly hand on Rhys's shoulder. The sidhe had lost the knack of comforting each other with touch. We'd been taught that that was something for the lesser fey, a sign of their weakness and the sidhe's superiority. But I'd learned months ago that that was just a story to mask the fact that the sidhe no longer trusted each other enough to touch like that. Touch had begun to mean pain instead of comfort, but not here, not for us. We were sidhe and lesser fey, if you could call a nine-foot-tall man lesser, but in that moment we were all just simply fey and it was good.

CHAPTER THIRTY-FOUR

WE PULLED UP IN FRONT OF WHAT I'D STARTED TO THINK OF AS home, but it was Maeve Reed's estate in Holmby Hills. She had assured us through e-mails and phone calls that she wanted us to stay as long as we needed to. I worried that eventually she'd grow tired of us all, but for today, and until she got back from Europe, it was home.

The reporters who had followed us from the crime scene merged with the ones whom the neighbors were letting camp on their property, for a fee of course, and we were all home. Rhys hit the button that opened the gates in the tall stone wall and in we went. It had become automatic to ignore the shouted questions from the reporters who rushed forward. They stayed off the edge of Maeve's property. I kept waiting for one of them to notice that they never, ever crossed that invisible line, but so far they hadn't.

We were within our rights, and so was Maeve, to prevent trespassing. We were even allowed to use magic to prevent it as long as said magic wasn't harmful. We'd simply reinforced Maeve's own wards, and the reporters stopped every time just like we wanted. It was nice that something was doing just what we wanted.

I'd called Lucy on the ride over, and told her everything Jordan had told us. It helped, but not enough. Julian texted me and told me that his brother was fine and wouldn't have to be held overnight at the hospital. Marshal the EMT wasn't the only one who had started treating shocky psychics more seriously. Marshal had just been the first medical professional to admit why. I appreciated that.

Rhys pulled up in front of the big main house because we'd moved into it from the guest house, giving the guest house over to our newer members. I'd asked Maeve's permission before the move, but again it left me wondering what we'd do when she rightfully wanted her house back. I put the thought away, and concentrated on the more immediate problems like a magical serial killer, and would Barinthus defy me or would he be here for dinner, or . . .

Then the big double doors opened and Nicca and Biddy were there waving at us. He had his arm across her shoulders and she had hers around his waist. He was just a shade taller than her six feet of sidhe warrior. His long brown hair was in two knee-length braids on either side of his handsome face, but it was the smile in his brown face that made him truly beautiful. Biddy's smile echoed his, though she was pale, her black curls cut short around her face. They both had brown eyes, and the baby probably would, too. She'd just started to show a little, though unless you knew what you were looking for under her shorts and tank top you wouldn't know it was a baby.

Her bare arms and legs were long, and showed muscles moving smooth under her skin as she came around to my side of the car. Nicca got Rhys's door. He was a little less muscled than she was, though not by much, but the easy happiness that they seemed to feel for each other made me happy every time I saw it. They were the first of us to get officially married, and it seemed to agree with both of them.

Biddy didn't get the door for Cathbodua. She had seen where I was and got the back door, which actually meant she was letting Galen out first. "Welcome home, everybody," Biddy said. She glowed not just with the pregnancy, but with love. Whenever I was around them I had hopes that the rest of our sidhe would pair up and it would be the beginning of a lot of happily ever after for a lot of our people.

"Good to be home," Galen said as he scooted out. Nicca got the door on the other side and Sholto scooted out, too. They both put their hands back in for me, and there was that awkward moment when the two men looked across the car at each other. But it was Galen, and most of the time he made things easier, not harder.

He did a little half salute and said, "You're on the side with the house."

Sholto smiled at him, because he was a good king, and good leaders appreciate people who make things easier. "Is that the system you've worked out? Whoever is closest to the house gets to help her out?"

"If she's in the backseat," Galen said, "but if she's in front, then Biddy or Nicca or whoever gets to the passenger side helps her out."

Sholto nodded. "Very logical." He offered me his hand and I took it, letting him help me scoot over the seat. Nicca and Biddy were already at the back to help Uther out. You could fold the seats we were in down, but why make him squirm through when you could just open the back?

Saraid actually took Uther's hand to get out of the back of the SUV. It pleased him that she took his help. She was tall and muscled and trained in both weapon and magic, which meant she didn't need the help, but she'd taken his comfort and now she gave it back to him, by letting him help her.

I could hear the high, excited barking of the dogs inside. That, too, was a happy thing. The faerie hounds had vanished with our magic fading, but when the Goddess returned some of the magic she also returned some of our animals. The first to return were the dogs.

Biddy laughed. "Kitto is trying to keep them still, but they've all missed their masters and mistress."

Rhys was at the door first, and tried to keep the door closed enough so he could slip inside without the furry horde getting past him, but it was a losing battle. They flowed out around him, nine of them, all terriers, staying to mill about his feet. He bent over to touch the heads of the black-and-tan terrier pair, a breed that hadn't existed in centuries but was the founding breed of most of the modern terrier breeds. The rest of them were all white with red markings, the original colors of most faerie animals.

Galen was almost covered in small lapdogs and tall, graceful greyhounds. For whatever reason, he'd gotten more dogs than any other sidhe. The lapdogs capered around his legs, and the greyhounds nuzzled him for petting. He did his best to give them all attention.

Sholto let me have my hands free to greet my own dogs. There were only two dogs for me, but they were slender and lovely. Mungo was taller than the modern standard allowed, but Minnie was within range, though now her belly was swollen tight with puppies. She was due any day, and she would be the first of the dogs to give birth. One of the best dog vets in the area had started making house calls. We had a camera set up and a live feed on the computer. The computer savvy of us had come up with the idea to charge people for watching the birth of the first faerie dogs born in more than three centuries. Apparently, we were having a lot of people sign up for it, some because of the dogs, and some because they hoped to see me and the men on camera with the dogs, but whatever the motive it was surprisingly lucrative, and with this many people to take care of we needed it to be.

I touched the silky ears of my dogs, and cupped their long muzzles in my hands. I put my forehead to Minnie's forehead because she liked it. Mungo was a little more aloof, or maybe he just thought forehead bumps were beneath his dignity.

Then the air was full of wings, as if the most beautiful butterflies and moths had suddenly decided to have a ball above our heads. Most of them were the demi-fey who had followed me into exile. They were the afflicted of their kind and had been wingless in a society that saw that as worse than crippled. But my magic, along with Galen's, Nicca's, and Kitto's, had both nearly killed them and given them the wings they'd never had before. But there were demi-fey among them who had been in exile in L.A. for decades or more. The first ones had come quietly, almost afraid, but when they were welcomed we'd more than doubled our numbers.

Royal and his twin sister Penny hovered above me. "Welcome

home, Princess," she said. She was wearing a small robe like she'd borrowed the dressing gown of someone's doll, except there were slits in it for her wings.

"It's good to be home, Penny."

She nodded, her tiny antennae trembling as she moved. She and her brother were both dark of hair and pale of skin, and had the wings of an Ilia Underwing moth. It matched the tattoo I had on my stomach, because something about bringing out Royal's wings and saving his life had taken me to another level of power, and all great magic leaves its mark on you.

Royal hovered beside my face, his wings moving more than any real moth to keep his heavier body airborne, though there had been that famous physics paper on the moth that proved that none of the demi-fey should be able to fly. He touched my hair and I swept it aside so he could sit on my shoulder. It was like a signal for the other demi-fey to flutter around us. They poured over Nicca's braids and started swinging on them like they were ropes. He seemed to have an affinity with them, maybe because Nicca had wings of his own. They were a tattoo when he wished, but if not, they rose above his body like a magical sail on some boat that would take you only to beautiful, magical places.

I'd had him as a lover, both when the tattoo was the only thing he had and he'd never had real wings, and after the new wild magic of faerie made the wings real so that they rose above me shining with magic. He'd been the child of a sidhe and a demi-fey who could be human sized.

A flock of the smallest of the demi-fey, most of them ghost pale with white hair like cobwebs around their pointed faces, fluttered around Sholto speaking in high, twittering voices, asking for permission to touch the King of the Sluagh. He nodded his assent and they climbed in his ponytail like it was a playground and perched on his shoulders three deep on either side. None of them were bigger than my palm, the very smallest of the small. Royal was on the other end of their size range at ten inches.

Penny, Royal's sister, hovered by Galen and asked permission to climb aboard. Galen had only recently allowed any of them to touch him casually. He'd had a bad experience with them at the Unseelie Court. People think it's funny to be afraid of something so small, but bear in mind that the Unseelie demi-fey drink blood as well as nectar. Sidhe blood is sweet to them, and royal sidhe is sweeter still. Queen Andais had once chained Galen down and given him over to those tiny mouths. Prince Cel had paid their queen, Niceven, to take more flesh than Andais had ordered. The experience had given Galen what amounted to a phobia of them. Ironically, the demi-fey liked the feel of his magic, and would hover around him in butterfly-colored clouds, but they'd learned not to touch him without asking. Penny settled onto his shoulder in her little robe, one hand in the deep green of his curls. Galen had begun to trust Penny.

Rhys had so many of the smaller fey on his shoulders, giggling under his hair, that they looked like children peeking out from between drapes, or leaves, like a storybook. That made me think of our two murder scenes, and it was as if the sunlight were a little dimmer.

"You're sad suddenly," Royal said near my face. "What did you think of just now, our Merry?"

It was always tempting to turn your head when one of them talked, but when they were sitting on your shoulder, turning your head completely knocked them off, so you had to turn just enough to meet those dark almond-shaped eyes, but not as much as I would have if he'd been standing beside me.

"Am I so easily read, Royal?"

"You gave me wings. You gave me magic. I pay attention to you, my Merry."

That made me smile. The smile made him move in against my face so that his body curved into the line of my cheek, tucking his thighs underneath my chin. His small arm went wide around my cheek so that his bare upper body was pressed against my face, and that would have been all right. I might have been able to enjoy the hug—and if most people had been watching they would have seen it as innocent comfort, like being hugged by a child—but I knew better. And if I'd had any doubts, his face was now very close to my eye and there was nothing innocent in his handsome miniature face. No, it was a very grown-up look on a face not much bigger than my thumb.

I would have been okay with that, but it was Royal, and he had to push it. His body tucked a little too close to the line of my jaw, and I could feel that he was happy to be pressed against me.

It was considered a compliment among the fey if just being close to someone aroused you, but . . . "I'm glad to see you, too, Royal, but now that you've paid the compliment, a little breathing room, please."

"You should come play with us, Merry. I promise it would be fun."

"I appreciate the possibilities, Royal, but I don't think so," I said.

He pressed himself more tightly against me, putting a little hip into the hug.

"Stop that, Royal," I said.

"If you'd let me use my glamour it wouldn't disturb you. It would entrance you." And his voice held that edge of sultry bass that only a larger body with the deep chest to match should have given him. What few outside faerie realized was that some of the demi-fey had the most glamour of us all. I knew from experience that Royal could make me think he was a full-sized lover, and that his glamour could bring me to orgasm with very little effort. It was a gift, his talent.

"I forbid you that," I said.

He kissed the side of my face but he did move his lower body enough that I wasn't quite so aware that he was there. "I wish you hadn't forbid it."

Galen called from the door. "Are you coming inside?" He was frowning a little. I wondered how long I'd been standing there talking to Royal.

"You may not use your glamour but you've distracted me again," I said.

"The fact that I distract you isn't glamour, my goddess of white and red."

"Then what is it?" I asked, tired of the games.

He smiled, obviously pleased with himself. "Your magic calls to mine. We are both creatures of warmth and lust."

I frowned at him.

Sholto loomed over me, and certainly over Royal. "I do not think the princess is a creature of any kind, little man." The flock of tiny fey in his ponytail stopped playing hide-and-seek in his long fall of hair, as if they were listening.

Royal looked up at him. "Perhaps the word 'creature' is ill chosen, King Sholto. It was perverse of me to forget the queen's pet name for you."

Sholto was suddenly very still beside me. He had hated Queen Andais calling him "her Perverse Creature." He had confessed to me he feared one day being just that as the Killing Frost and the queen's Darkness. Feared one day he would simply be the queen's "Creature."

"You are like some winged bug I can smash with a careless swat. Your glamour can't change that, or give you the full-sized women you seem to prefer."

"My glamour has given me full-size, as you call it, more than once, King Sholto," Royal said. Then he smiled, and I knew just from his expression that whatever he was about to say I wouldn't like it. "Merry can speak to my glamour and just how much she enjoyed it."

Sholto's face showed just how unhappy that made him. He turned that scowl to me. "You didn't," he said.

"No," I said, "but if I hadn't been stopped I might have. If you've never had a demi-fey who carried sex magic try their wiles on you, then you don't understand. It's more powerful glamour than most of the sidhe still have."

"Remember, King, we hide in plain sight from the humans as real butterflies, moths, dragonflies, and flowers. They never see through our disguises, and that's not always true with sidhe glamour."

"Then why don't you help trail people for her detective agency?" Sholto asked.

"We could if they would stay in certain parts of the city, but they tend to go places with too much metal." Royal shivered, and it wasn't a good shiver.

Two of the tiny fey still riding in Sholto's hair took to the air as if the thought was too frightening even for listening. The three left in his hair hid like children hearing the monster under the bed.

"It is beyond most of us to travel through some parts of the city," Royal said.

"So your glamour is only good for soft things," Sholto said.

Royal looked at him, but a smile curved his delicate lips. "Our glamour is very, very good with soft things."

"I believe Merry when she says something, so if she says you are that good at it, then I believe her, but I also know she's forbidden you to try your wiles on her again."

"It's my week to take Queen Niceven's weekly donation. I think Merry will want me to use my glamour for that."

Sholto had only to move his eyes to come back to my face from the little man on my shoulder. "Why are you still donating blood to Niceven through her surrogates?"

"We need allies at the courts, Sholto."

"Why do you need them if you never plan to go back and rule?"

"Spies," Royal whispered. "The demi-fey are the proverbial flies on the wall, King Sholto. No one looks at us, no one notices how often we are about."

He looked from one to the other of us. "And I thought it was Doyle's spy network that was getting such accurate information."

"The Darkness has his sources, but none as sweet as Merry has," Royal said, and I knew he was playing it up to see if he could irritate the other man. Royal took great pleasure any time he could make one of my full-sized lovers jealous. It pleased him inordinately.

Sholto frowned at him, then laughed. The sound startled Royal and me. The little man on my shoulder jumped, while I was simply puzzled. The fey in Sholto's hair flew skyward and went over the house and away into the blue.

"What is so funny, oh King of the Sluagh?" Royal asked.

"Does your glamour make men jealous, too?"

"As for Merry's reaction to me, so your jealousy, King Sholto. Neither is magic."

Sholto's face sobered and he studied the little man, not unhappily, but he truly studied him. He did it long and hard enough that Royal hid his face in my hair. I'd noticed this was a social gesture for all the demi-fey. They did it when they were embarrassed, afraid, being coy, or even simply out of other things to do. Royal didn't like being the object of such concentration by Sholto.

Mungo bumped my hand and I petted his sleek head. For the dogs to react meant that it wasn't just Royal who was getting tension from Sholto's reaction to the demi-fey.

I stood and petted my dogs, letting some of the tension bleed off into the gesture. "We should get inside," I said at last.

Sholto nodded. "Yes, we should." He offered me his arm and I took it. He led me inside as Royal whispered in my ear, "The sluagh like the goblins still eat us like prey."

It made me stumble up the small steps to the porch. Sholto caught me. "Are you all right?"

I nodded. I could have asked Sholto, but if the answer was yes, I didn't want to know, and whether it was yes or no, it was still an insulting question. How do you ask a man who you are supposed to love and who is the father of your child if he commits a little cannibalism on the side?

"You're afraid to ask," Royal whispered like one of those cartoon devils on my shoulder.

That made me lean in against Sholto and whisper just inside the door, "Do the sluagh still hunt the demi-fey?"

He frowned and then shook his head. He looked at Royal, now hiding more seriously in my hair. "We do not hunt the small ones for food, but sometimes they are very irritating and we have to cleanse our faerie mound of them. How my people clean our house of them is their own business. I don't tolerate them in my kingdom, because you're right, you forget they are there, and I don't tolerate spies."

Royal slid completely behind my neck so that he put his arms and legs on either side of my neck and held on as if I were the trunk of a tree.

"Hide all you want, Royal, but I won't forget you're there," Sholto said.

I could feel Royal's heart thudding against my spine. I was about to be sympathetic, but then I felt him lay a kiss against the back of my neck. It can be a very erotic spot, and as he laid soft kisses against my skin, I felt that totally involuntary reaction low in my body. I made him move.

CHAPTER THIRTY-FIVE

I WAS IN THE BEDROOM CHANGING FOR DINNER WHEN THERE WAS A knock on the door. "Who is it?"

"It's Kitto."

I was down to my dark brown bra with its lace trim, and still in my skirt, hose, and heels, but he was on the list of people who I didn't have to hide from. I smiled and said, "Come in."

He peered around the door as he opened it, as if unsure of his welcome. I'd managed a few minutes alone and he knew I valued my rare privacy, but I hadn't seen him in two days, nearly three, and I'd missed him. But the moment I saw his black curls and his huge almond-shaped eyes with their swimming blue color, like looking into one of those perfect pools that dotted the neighborhood, I smiled more widely. The thin black of his elliptical pupils no longer detracted from the beauty of his eyes for me. It was just Kitto's eyes, and I loved all of his face, the delicate bones in that soft triangle. He was the daintiest of all my men. He was four feet even, more than a foot shorter than I, but it was four feet of broad shoulder, narrow waist, tight ass, and everything he needed to be male, just done in a perfect miniature package. He was wearing designer jeans and a tight T-shirt that showed off the new muscles that weight-lifting had given him. Doyle made all the men work out.

My face must have shown how pleased I was to see Kitto, because he smiled in return and ran to me. He was one of the few men in my life who didn't try to be cool, or in charge, or even worry about being manly. He simply wanted to be with me and didn't try to hide that. There were no games with Kitto, no hidden agendas. He simply loved being with me, in the way that most people outgrow, but since he had been born before Rome became a great city, he would never outgrow the childish enthusiasm that he had for life, and I loved him for that, too.

I had a moment to brace my heels before he flung himself on me, climbing me like a monkey to wrap his legs around my waist, his arms hugging me tightly, and it just seemed natural to kiss him. I loved that I could hold him as the other men held me. I let our combined weight carry me backward to the bed, so I was sitting on the edge of it while we kissed.

I had to be careful when I slid my tongue between his teeth, because he had a pair of retractable fangs tucked neatly against the roof of his mouth, and they weren't just there for decoration. His tongue was thinner than human tongues, red and black-tipped, and it, like his eyes and the thin play of rainbow scales down his back, marked him as part Snake Goblin. He'd been the product of rape. His sidhe mother had never acknowledged him, but left him outside the goblin mound, even though at that time the sidhe were still food for the goblins. She hadn't left Kitto to be saved by his father's people. She'd left him to be killed by them.

He was also the least dominant of my men, so I knew that I had to be the one to pull his T-shirt out of his belt and let my hands trace the smooth coolness of the scales that traced his spine. But the moment I undid some of his clothing, his small, strong hands slid down the back of my skirt so he could cup my ass and trace the edge of the dark brown lace panties that matched the bra.

I pulled his T-shirt up and he raised his hands so I could lift the shirt off and let it fall to the floor. He was suddenly nude from the waist up, still sitting in my lap. I liked his new muscles and the fact that he was tanning, ever so slightly, like a wash of brown over all that paleness. Goblins didn't tan, but the sidhe could sometimes, and when he'd discovered that he could tan, he'd started sunbathing by the pool.

"You're beautiful," I said.

He shook his head. "Not sitting this close to you, I'm not." His hands started for a button of my skirt, and then he hesitated. I understood, and I undid the belt of his pants so he'd feel free to undo my buttons and zipper. He folded the top of my skirt down, and then hesitated again. I could see his eagerness to take the skirt down, but I'd have to cooperate by lying back on the bed so he could slip it over my hips. He was still in his pants, and among the goblins whoever undressed first was the submissive, and that could mean even more among the goblins than at a human BDSM event.

I undid the button of his jeans, and started the zipper. He rose on his knees on either side of my thighs so I could work the zipper down, and now I could lie back on the bed and let him slip the skirt over my hips and down my legs, so that I lay looking up at him in only the lingerie, hose, and heels.

He gazed down at me and his face said more than any words how beautiful he found me. "I never dreamed that I would be allowed to see a sidhe princess like this, and to know that I can do this," he said, and he traced his fingers along the mounds of my breasts where the bra met the whiteness of my flesh. I drew a breath for him. He smiled, and put his hand down the front of my bra until he found a nipple and played it between two fingers, rolling it, pinching it, softly, until I made a small happy noise for him.

He smiled more, and put his hands to his opened pants, then hesitated again. This time I helped by saying, "Take off your pants, Kitto. Let me see you without them."

I wasn't specific enough in my wording, because he didn't just wiggle out of his jeans; the silky blue of his underwear went with the outer pants. He crawled back to me nude, his body already growing eager. I lay on the bed, my knees still over the edge of it, my heels not touching the ground, and watched him, my eyes drawn to that part of him that was oh so male.

He leaned over me so that just his mouth touched mine, and we kissed. It started out gentle, but grew until he had to draw back from me, saying with a hoarse whisper, "You're going to cut yourself on my fangs."

"You said that the poison only works if you concentrate. Otherwise they're just teeth."

He shook his head. "I'm not willing to risk you and the babies." He laid his small hand on my still-flat stomach and said, "I won't risk them."

I watched the gentleness in his face, no, the love. He wasn't one of the fathers and he knew that, but for him more than for any of the other men it didn't seem to matter. He was also more excited about decorating the nurseries than most of the other men, including some of the fathers.

I ran my hands up his bare arms and across his shoulders, until he looked down at me, and the gentleness was edged with something not so gentle. That suited me and my mood just fine. I showed him with my hands, my arms, and my kisses that I appreciated his care for me, my babies, my life, all of it. But I kept the kisses more careful, because Kitto was right. It wasn't worth the risk.

I was down to nothing but my thigh-high hose and the high heels with him on all fours above me. I slid down the bed so that I could slide my hands around his hips and my mouth around that bit of him that dangled so temptingly over me. His entire body reacted to my mouth sliding over him, his spine bowing, and his head dropping, his hands digging into the bed like a cat kneading its claws. His breath came out in a soft explosive sound, as if he wanted to say something but I'd stolen his words away.

I put my hand at the small of his back, my nails digging in just a little, as I held my upper body off the bed and wrapped my other hand around the base of him so I could get a better angle. It wasn't that Kitto was small, but he wasn't as well-endowed as some of the other men in my life. But there is a certain joy in giving oral sex to a man who doesn't make you have to fight to deep throat all of him. I put my mouth down until I met his body and there was no more of him to go in my mouth. My hands wrapped around his hips and waist so that I could enjoy being that deep on him and not having to use my hands, but only my mouth to suck and swallow so that it was an almost continuous motion of my mouth around the long, wide, quivering, length of him.

My nails dug into his back, and he cried out for me. He found his words, and said, "Stop or I'll go. Please stop or I won't last."

I took my mouth off him long enough to say, "Go, go in my mouth."

"I need to bring you pleasure first."

"I do enjoy this."

He shook his head and would have pulled away farther, but I kept him above me with a flexing of nails in his back. "Please, Merry, please let me."

I licked a long wet line up his stomach, and let go of him so I could move underneath his body and reach his nipple. I licked the edge of it until it hardened under my attentions. I put my teeth in a seal around his nipple, sucking on him, and then using my teeth to stretch his nipple out from his body. He made small eager noises for me.

His voice was breathy as he said, "Please, let me go down on you."

I bit him hard enough to leave a red ring from my teeth in a mark around his nipple, hard enough for him to cry out above me. Kitto liked to be bitten, as much as he liked to bite.

He shuddered above me. His whole body quaked with reaction to the bite. When he could control himself enough to speak, he asked, "Please, may I go down on you?"

"I've gone down on you before," I said.

"But second, after I've pleasured you." He stayed on all fours beside me, waiting for me to give him permission.

"Why is it so important that I go first, other than that it's fun for me?"

He knelt on the bed, sitting back on his heels. "You know how goblins view oral sex?"

"Powerful goblins don't give oral sex, they receive it from less-powerful goblins. It's a mark of dominance to get head, but not ever give it."

He smiled. "Exactly. Some powerful goblins will give oral sex to their strumpets, but only in private, only where no one else will ever find out."

I had two other part-goblin lovers, the very powerful twins Holly and Ash. One of the twins was a pervert among goblins because he loved going down on women, but he only did it when the three of us were alone. He knew that his brother would never tell, nor would I, but if anyone found out it would lessen his status among them.

"You can pleasure me, but only after I've pleasured you first."

"I won't tell, Kitto."

He shook his head. "You are sidhe and that means magic, but the goblins view all of you as softer, weaker. I would never do anything to endanger you."

I stayed on my back, but propped myself up on my elbows. "Are you saying that if the goblins found out that I pleasured you orally before you touched me that it would lose me status among them?"

He nodded, and he was very serious. "There are those among the goblins who think Kurag, the Goblin King, is besotted with you and that is why the goblins are your allies. They don't believe him when he says you are wise and powerful."

"And if they found out that I let you be dominant to me it would hurt my case?"

He nodded again. "And it would lessen Kurag's hold on them. Goblin kings never step down, or die of old age, Merry. They're murdered by their successor."

"The ones most likely to succeed him are Holly and Ash, and they are my allies, too."

"There are some among the goblins who think you are only sleeping with the twins to keep them from killing Kurag."

"Why would I care enough about Kurag to do that?" I asked.

"There are those at our court who think the twins would not honor the treaty Kurag made with you, and then the goblins would be free to ally themselves with whomever they wished when the Unseelie has a new ruler."

"Andais isn't going to step down," I said.

"Not for anyone but you," he said.

"I don't want the throne," I said.

"Then she will be queen until someone assassinates her. I fear that whomever takes the throne may always see you as a threat to their holding the crown."

"Because faerie and Goddess crowned me and Doyle."

"Yes, and you are the queen's bloodline."

"Maybe faerie will pick a new ruler for them."

"Maybe," he said, but he sounded doubtful.

"But what does all the politics have to do with the oral sex in the privacy of our own bedchamber?"

"Until things are settled at both the Unseelie and the goblin courts I don't want to do anything that might cause a problem for you."

I studied his solemn face. "You mean that. That until both courts are sure of their rulers, you pleasure me first."

He nodded.

I sighed, and then smiled. "It's not a hardship; you are very orally talented."

He smiled, and there was nothing humble about the expression on his face. "I was a strumpet passed from one powerful keeper to another for sex. I had to be good at my only job so they valued and protected me."

"I've never asked before. How did you happen to have no master or mistress when Kurag offered you to me?"

"The husband of my last mistress had grown jealous of me, and since that was a sign of weakness, my mistress had to either get rid of me, or challenge her husband to a duel."

I looked at him. "That is a bit of goblin culture that I didn't know."

"Weakness is not tolerated among us."

"You're as sidhe as you are goblin, maybe more," I said.

He gave a little smile that I couldn't decipher. "Maybe, but for now, please let me go down on you?"

"And when you've made me scream your name, what then?"

"Then I would very much like to fuck you." He said it all formally, but the wording was goblin. Goblins didn't make love, they fucked. In truth, they made love, some of them, but when asking in public, they fucked.

"No one can hear us, Kitto."

"I want to go down on you, and then I want to fuck."

I sighed again, and nodded. "Yes," I said.

"Yes," he said.

I smiled at the slow spread of happiness on his face. "Yes."

"Do we want to make them wait dinner on you?"

"Why do you ask?" Because I knew he'd have a reason.

"Because if I bring you more than twice by mouth, and then fuck you as long as I want to, they'll have to wait dinner."

I knew it was not an idle boast. "I guess it will have to be a quickie," I said.

He glanced at the bedside clock. "An hour, that will be a quickie."

There was more than one reason that I loved having Kitto in my life.

CHAPTER THIRTY-SIX

KITTO REMINDED ME THAT HIS TONGUE WAS NOT ATTACHED TO THE same muscles that the rest of my lovers had in their mouth and throat. He reminded me that his tongue was longer and thinner, had a partially prehensile tip, and was forked. It meant that he could do things with his tongue that just weren't possible with someone who was more humanly equipped.

He licked, and touched, and sucked until I screamed his name to the ceiling, and then he pressed his mouth to me again and used his tongue in a series of fast flicking movements that only seemed to work after I'd been brought at least once before, but boy did it work that second time. I drove fingernails into his hair, feeling the silky curls under my fingers, and driving my nails just a little into his scalp. The small pain of it seemed to urge him on to new heights, and encouraging him earned me a third orgasm.

My eyes fluttered back into my head so that I was blind, my hands fallen away from him limp at my side as my body rode the aftershocks of his talented mouth. I felt the bed move, felt his body spreading my thighs wider. I tried to open my eyes to watch him enter me, but I still couldn't make my body work enough to do it. He'd outdone himself tonight.

But the sensation of him entering me while I was that wet, that eager, that swollen with pleasure made me writhe underneath him. I couldn't help but move as he pushed himself inside me. He knew he wasn't as big as some of the men in my bed, but his prep work made up for it, and he wasn't small by any means. He pushed all that thick, aching hardness into me one slow inch at a time, until I was making small eager noises before he buried himself inside me as far as his body and mine would allow. Then he began to pull himself out of me, just as slowly, just as controlled.

My body didn't want controlled, or slow. I began to dance my hips underneath him so that I was taking in his length and pulling away from him, so that all his carefulness was undone by my eagerness.

He made a sound low in his throat, almost a cry, and then he gave up on slow and careful. He started moving to the rhythm I had set, and we began to dance together, his body into mine, my body over and around his, until we did dance on the bed in that most intimate of dances.

He was short enough that he could lie down on me and we could still look into each other's eyes. I wasn't trapped under him; we could both still move, and writhe for each other. I felt that sweet heavy pleasure begin to build between my legs, and my fingers found his back. My breathing sped and I had to fight to keep the dancing rhythm of my hips meeting his body. Between one stroke, one rise and another, the sweet heaviness spilled up and over, and I shrieked my pleasure, my neck bowed, my nails set into his back as I painted my orgasm on his skin, and my hips bucked underneath him, and I felt somewhere in all that pleasure his body lose its own rhythm. He fought to keep it, trying for another orgasm, but I squeezed him tightly inside me, and that was his undoing. His body shoved into mine in one last deep thrust that brought me screaming, nails digging into his body as if he were the last solid thing in the world, and everything else had washed away on the pulsing of our bodies, the ecstasy of him inside me, and me wrapped around him.

He collapsed on top of me, his head cradled in the bend of my shoulder. I lay on my back, his heartbeat pounding against my chest as he fought to catch his breath. I had to swallow twice past my own pulse before I could whisper, "They'll have to wait dinner a little while."

He nodded, wordlessly, and then took a deep, shuddering breath and said, "Totally worth it."

I could only nod wordlessly as I stopped fighting for enough air to talk and relearn how to breathe all at the same time.

CHAPTER THIRTY-SEVEN

I WAS DRESSED FOR DINNER, WHICH HAD BECOME A SEMI-FORMAL occasion, which meant I was a little overdressed for the police forensics lab, magical division. Jeremy had phoned before we could actually eat because he'd been called by one of the police wizards to come and give an opinion on Gilda's confiscated wand. The one that had made a policeman fall down and not wake up for hours.

Jeremy wanted some of us to look at it, because he thought it was sidhe workmanship. He'd offered for me to stay home and eat because he really needed some of the older sidhe guards, Rhys had gone early to commune with his new sithen, and Galen was, like me, too young to know much about our older enchanted sidhe items. But the three of us were the only ones with private-detective licenses. The others could only come as bodyguards. The reporters going through the window had been on all the news and YouTube, so the police believed that I wouldn't go out without a shitload of guards. So I was "protected" and Jeremy got the sidhe he wanted to look at the wand. The only downside was I had to eat something quickly in the car, and the yellow high heels dyed to match the yellow, belted dress, complete with crinoline to make the skirt sit right, were the wrong shoes for standing on the concrete floors.

The wand was in a Plexiglas rectangle. There were symbols literally pressed into the case. It was a portable anti-magic field so that if something was found the police could put it inside the case and negate it until forensics could figure out a more permanent solution.

We all stood around staring down at the wand, and by all I meant the two police wizards, Wilson and Carmichael, plus Jeremy, Frost, Doyle, Barinthus (who had shown up just as we were leaving), Sholto, Rhys, and me. Rhys had cut his sithen exploration short to solve crime.

The wand was still two feet long but now it was only two feet of pale white and honey-colored wood, clean and free of all the sparkle that Gilda was so fond of, and that I remembered clearly. "It doesn't look like the same wand," I said.

"You mean the star tip and the flashy outer covering?" Carmichael asked. She shook her head, sending her brown ponytail bobbing over her lab coat. "Some of the stones had metaphysical properties that helped amp up the magic, but it was all just to make it pretty and to hide this."

I stared at the long, smoothly polished wood. "Why hide it?"

"Don't look at it with just your eyes, Merry," Barinthus said. He towered over all of us in his long cream trench coat. He was actually wearing a suit under the coat, though he'd left the tie off. It was the most clothes I'd seen him in since he got to California. He'd put his hair back in a ponytail, but even contained, the hair still moved a little too much for ordinary hair, as if even standing here in this very modern building with all the latest, greatest scientific equipment around us there was still some invisible current of water playing with his hair. He wasn't doing it on purpose; it was just his hair this close to the ocean, apparently.

I didn't like that—it sounded like an order—but I did it, because he was right. Most humans have to work at seeing magic, doing magic. I was part human, but in one way I was all fey. I had to shield every day, every minute, to not see magic. I had shielded heavily when I entered this area of the forensics labs because it was the room where they kept the really powerful magical items that they didn't know what to do with, or were in the process of de-magicking, or figuring out a way to destroy that wouldn't blow up other things. Some magic items once made are difficult to destroy safely.

I had upped my shields because I didn't want to have to wade through all the magic in the room. The anti-magic boxes kept the things from working, but didn't keep the wizards from being able to study them. It was a very nice bit of magical engineering. I took a deep breath, let it out, and dropped my shields just a little bit.

I tried to concentrate on just the wand, but of course there were other things in the room, and not all of them reacted to just vision. Something in the room called out, "Free me of this prison and I will grant you a wish." Something else smelled like chocolate, no, hard cherry candy, no, it was like the scent of everything sweet and good, and with the scent there was a desire to find it and pick it up so I could have all that goodness.

I shook my head and concentrated on the wand. The pale wood was covered in magical symbols. They crawled over the wood, glowing yellow and white, and here and there a spark of orange/red flame, but it wasn't fire exactly, it was as if the magic were sparking. I'd never seen that before.

"It's almost like the magic has a short in it," I said.

"That's what I said," Carmichael said.

Wilson said, "I thought it might be extra power like little pieces of magical battery meant to up the spell." He was tall, taller than all the men except for Barinthus, with short pale hair that was going from gray to white. Wilson was barely thirty. His hair had gone gray after he'd detonated a major holy relic meant to bring about the end of the world. Anything meant to bring about the end of the world that might actually do it was always destroyed. The problem was that destroying something that powerful wasn't always the safest occupation. Wilson was on the magical equivalent of the bomb squad. He was one of a handful of human wizards across the country certified for high-holy-relic disposal. Some of the other magic bomb techs thought Wilson had literally had a decade of his life span blown away with his old hair color.

He pushed his wire-framed glasses more firmly up his nose. He still looked like a really tall bookish computer nerd, and he was except that he was a bookish magic nerd, and according to the other magic techs either the bravest of them or one crazy motherfucker. I was quoting. The fact that only Wilson and Carmichael were still working on it and that it was in this room meant that the wand had done something unpleasant.

"Did the policeman who Gilda hit with this wand die or something?" I asked.

"No," Carmichael said.

"No. What have you heard?" Wilson asked.

She frowned at him.

"What?" he asked.

I said, "This room is only for things that scare the police. Major relics, things designed to do bad things that you haven't figured out how to de-magick or destroy yet. What did Gilda's wand do to earn a place here?"

The two wizards looked at each other.

"Whatever you hold back," Jeremy said, "may be the key to deciphering this wand's power."

"Tell us what you see first," Wilson said.

"I've told you what I think," Jeremy said.

"You said this might be sidhe workmanship. I want to know what some sidhe think of it." Wilson looked from one to another of us; his face was very serious now. He was studying us the way he'd study anything magical that interested him. Wilson had the unsettling tendency to see the fey as another type of magical thing sometimes, as if he'd study us to see what we'd do.

The men looked at me. I shrugged and said, "Magical symbols in white and yellow are crawling over the wood with those odd sparks of orangey red. The symbols aren't static but seem to be still moving.

That's unusual. Magical symbols glow sometimes to the inner eye, but they aren't this . . . fresh, like the paint hasn't dried."

The men with me nodded. "That's why I thought it might be a sidhe creation," Jeremy said.

"I don't follow," I said.

"The last time I saw magic that stayed that fresh, it was an enchanted item made by one of your people's great wizards. They hide the core of the magic behind metalwork, or living greenery that is kept fresh by the magic, but it's all pretend, Merry. It's just meant to hide the core."

"I understand what you're saying, but why does that make it sidhe workmanship?"

"Your people are the only ones I've ever seen who could keep magic interlaid over something this fresh and vital."

"We've never seen anything able to do this," Wilson said.

"What makes it sidhe?" I asked.

"It isn't," Barinthus said.

We looked at him.

Jeremy looked a little uncomfortable, but he looked at the tall man and asked, "Why isn't it sidhe magic?"

Barinthus managed to look as disdainful as I'd ever seen him. He didn't get along with Jeremy. I'd thought it was personal at first, but realized it was some prejudice Barinthus had against Jeremy being a Trow. It was like a racial thing for Barinthus, as if a Trow wasn't worthy enough to be the boss of us.

"I doubt I could explain it in a way you would understand," Barinthus said.

Jeremy's face darkened.

I turned to Wilson and Carmichael, smiling, and said, "Could you excuse us for a minute? I'm sorry, but if you could just step over there somewhere."

They looked at each other, then at Jeremy's angry face and Barinthus's haughty figure, and they went to stand away from us. No one wants to be standing right next to the seven-foot-tall man when he starts a fight.

I turned back to the seven-foot-tall man. "Enough," I said, and I poked a finger into his chest, hard enough to move him a little. "Jeremy is my boss. He pays us most of the money that clothes and feeds all of us, including you, Barinthus."

He looked down at me, and two feet is enough distance to make haughty work really well, but I'd had all I was taking from this ex–sea god.

"You aren't bringing in any money. You don't contribute a damned thing to the upkeep of the fey here in L.A., so before you go all high and mighty on us, I'd think about this. Jeremy is more valuable to me and to the rest of us than you are."

That got through the haughtiness, and I saw uncertainty on his face. He hid it, but it was in there. "You didn't say that you needed me to contribute in that way."

"We may be getting Maeve Reed's houses for free, but we can't keep letting her feed the army of us. When she comes back from Europe she may want her house back, all her houses back. What then?"

He frowned.

"Yeah, that's right. We are more than a hundred people, counting the Red Caps, and they're camping out on her estate because the houses already won't hold everyone. You don't get it. We have what amounts to a faerie court, but we don't have a royal treasury, or magic to clothe and feed us. We don't have a faerie mound to house us all that will just grow bigger as we need it."

"Your wild magic created a new piece of faerie inside the gates of Maeve's land," he said.

"Yes, and Taranis used that piece of faerie to kidnap me, so we can't use it to house anyone until we can guarantee that our enemies can't use it to attack us."

"Rhys has a sithen now. More will come."

"And until we know that our enemies can't use that new piece of faerie to attack us, too, we can't move many people in there."

"It's an apartment building, Barinthus, not a traditional sithen," Rhys said.

"An apartment building?"

Rhys nodded. "It magically appeared on a street and moved two buildings so that it could appear in the middle of them, but it looks like a rundown apartment building. It's definitely a sithen, but it's like the old ones. I open a door one time and the next time there's a different room behind the door. It's wild magic, Barinthus. We can't move people in there until I know what it does, and what plans it has."

"It is that powerful?" he said.

Rhys nodded. "It feels it, yes."

"More sithens will come," Barinthus said.

"Maybe, but until they do, we need money. We need as many people as possible bringing in money. That includes you."

"You didn't tell me that you wanted me to take the bodyguarding jobs he offered."

"Don't call him 'he'; his name is Jeremy. Jeremy Grey, and he's been making a living out here among the humans for decades, and those skills are a hell of a lot more useful to me now than your ability to make the ocean come up and smash into a house. Which was childish, by the way."

"The people in question don't need bodyguards. They simply want me to stand around and be stared at."

"No, they want you to stand around and be handsome and attract attention to them and their lives."

"I am not a freak to be paraded for cameras."

"No one remembers that story from the fifties, Barinthus," Rhys said.

One reporter had called Barinthus the Fish Man because of the collapsible webbing between his fingers. That reporter had died in a boating accident. Eyewitnesses said that the water just came up and slapped the boat.

Barinthus turned away from us, his hands going into his coat pockets. Doyle said, "Frost and I have both guarded humans who didn't need guarding. We have stood and let them admire us and pay money for it."

"You did one job and then you refused after that," Frost said to Barinthus. "What happened to make you say no after that?"

"I told Merry it was beneath me to pretend to guard someone when I should be guarding her."

"Did the client try to seduce you?" Frost asked.

Barinthus shook his head; his hair moved more than it should have, like the ocean on a windy day. "Seduction is not crude enough for what the woman did."

"She touched you," Frost said, and just the way he said it made me look at him.

"You say that like it's happened to you, too."

"They invite us to the parties to do more than guard them, Merry, you know that."

"I know they want media attention but none of you told me that the clients had gotten that out of hand."

"We're supposed to be protecting you, Meredith," Doyle said, "not the other way around."

"Is that why you and Frost are back to guarding mostly just me?"

"See," Barinthus said, "you've distanced yourself from it, too."

"But we help Meredith with her investigations. We didn't just stop doing the parties and then hide away by the sea," Doyle said.

"Part of the problem is that you haven't picked a partner," Rhys said.

"I don't know what you mean by that."

"I work with Galen, and we watch each other's backs, and make sure that the only hands that touch us are the ones we want touching each other. A partner isn't just to watch your back in a battle, Barinthus."

That arrogance that Frost hid behind was back on Barinthus's face, but I realized that for him it wasn't just a version of a blank face.

"Do you honestly believe that no one among the men is worthy to partner with you?" I asked.

He just looked at me, which was answer enough, I supposed. He looked at Doyle. "Once I would have been happy to work with Darkness."

"But not now that I've partnered with Frost," he said.

"You have chosen your friends."

I wondered for a moment if Barinthus had a crush on Doyle, or did his words mean only what he said. The fact that I'd never realized he was more than my father's friend had made me question a lot of things.

"It's okay," Rhys said. "You and I have never gotten along."

"It doesn't matter," I said. "Old news. If you want to stay here, then you need to contribute in a real way, Barinthus. You're going to start by explaining to Jeremy and the nice police wizards why that isn't sidhe magic." I gave as good eye contact as I could with a two-foot height difference. I guess with the three-inch heels it was a little less, but it was still a neck-craning moment. It's always hard to look tough when you're looking that far up at someone.

His hair flared out around him for all the world as if it were underwater, though I knew it would be dry to the touch. It was a new show of growing power, but I'd already noticed that it seemed to be an emotional reaction for him.

"Is that a no, or a yes?" I asked.

"I will try to explain," he said at last.

"Fine, good, let's get this done so we can go home."

"Are you tired?" Frost asked.

"Yes."

Barinthus said, "I am a fool. You may not look it yet, but you are with child. I should be taking care of you. Instead I am making things harder for you."

I nodded. "That's about what I was thinking." I led the way back to the police and Jeremy. We all gathered around the wand again. Barinthus didn't apologize, but he did explain.

"If it was truly sidhe workmanship it would not have the power flares. If I understand what electrical shorts are, then that's accurate.

The flaring points mark weak spots in the magic, as if the person who enchanted it didn't have enough power to make the magic smoothly. The flaring points are also as Wizard Wilson says, moments when the power grows stronger. I believe one of those power flares is what harmed the policeman who was originally hurt."

"So if you had made it, or another sidhe, then the magical marks would be smooth and the power would be even," Wilson said.

Barinthus nodded.

"Not to be rude," Carmichael said, "but aren't the sidhe less powerful than they once were magically?"

There was that uncomfortable moment when someone says something that everyone knows, but no one is supposed to talk about. It was Rhys who said, "That would be true."

"Sorry, but if that's true, then why couldn't this be a sidhe with less control of his, or her, magic? Maybe it's the best the wizard could do?"

Barinthus shook his head. "No."

"Her logic is sound," Doyle said.

"You see the symbols; you know what they are for, Darkness. We are forbidden such magic, and have been for centuries."

"These symbols are old enough that I'm not familiar with all of them," I said.

"The wand is designed to harvest magic," Rhys said.

I frowned at him. "You mean to make your own magic grow more powerful?"

"Nope."

I frowned harder.

"It's designed to steal other people's power," Doyle said.

"But you can't do that," I said. "Not that we're not allowed to do it, but it's not possible to steal someone's personal magic. It's intrinsic to them, like their intelligence, or their personality."

"Yes and no," he said.

I was beginning to be tired, really tired. I hadn't had any real pregnancy symptoms, but suddenly I was tired, achingly so. "Can I have a chair?" I asked.

Wilson said, "I'm sorry, Merry, I mean, of course." He went and got a chair.

"You look pale," Carmichael said. She started to touch my face like you'd check a child for fever, then stopped herself in mid-motion.

Rhys did it for her. "You feel cool and clammy. That can't be good."

"I'm just tired."

"We need to get Merry home," Rhys said.

Frost knelt by me, with me sitting he was about eye level with me. He put his hand against my face. "Explain to them, Doyle, and then we can get her home."

"This wand is designed to take magic from others. Merry is right, the magic cannot be stolen permanently from someone, but the wand is like a battery. It absorbs magic from different people and gives the wand's owner more power, but she would have to feed the wand new power almost constantly. The spell is clever, and harkens back to the older days of our own magic, but it has the marks of something other than sidhe. Our magic, but not."

"I know what it reminds me of," Rhys said. "Humans. Humans who were my followers, but who could do some of our magic. They were good, but it never translated exactly."

"The marks aren't carved on the wood, or painted," Carmichael said.

"If it was sidhe magic, then we could trace the symbols on the wood with our finger and our will, but for most humans they needed something more real. Like the fact that our followers saw the marks of power on us and thought they were tattoos, so they painted themselves with woad for protection in battle."

"But that didn't work," Carmichael said.

"It worked when we had power," Rhys said, "and then when we lost enough power it was worse than useless to the people whom we were supposed to protect." Rhys looked so unhappy. I had heard both him and Doyle tell stories of what had happened to their followers when they had lost so much power they could no longer protect them with magic.

"Is there a human who could trace those symbols?" I asked. Sitting down had helped.

"With nothing but will and word, I doubt it."

"What else could he or she have used?" Carmichael asked.

"Body fluid," Jeremy said.

We all looked at him. "Remember, I learned wizardry back when the sidhe were still in power. When the rest of us could find a piece of your enchantments, we copied it using body fluid."

"There's nothing visible on the wood. Most body fluids would leave something visible behind," Carmichael said.

"Saliva wouldn't," Wilson said.

"Spit works," Jeremy said. "People always talk about blood or semen, but spit is good, and it's just as much a part of a person."

"We haven't swabbed the wood directly because we weren't sure how the spells would react to it," Wilson said.

"Whoever made it has left you DNA," I said. I was feeling much better. I stood up, and threw up all over the forensic lab floor.

CHAPTER THIRTY-EIGHT

ONCE I THREW UP I WAS FINE. I WAS APOLOGETIC ABOUT THROWING up in the lab, but luckily the floor wasn't actual evidence. Carmichael gave me a breath mint and we left. Rhys drove us home, and made arrangements to pick up the other car tomorrow. I was the only other person who could drive, and none of the men seemed to want me to do that. I guess I couldn't blame them.

I leaned back in the passenger seat and said, "I thought I was supposed to get morning sickness, not evening sickness."

"It differs from woman to woman," Doyle said from the backseat.

"You knew someone who got evening sickness?" I asked.

"Yes" was all he said.

I turned in the seat and he was Darkness in the dark car, but the streetlights shone as Rhys drove. Frost was beside him, helping make the contrast even greater. Barinthus was on the far side and managed to make it clear that he didn't want to be that near Frost.

"Who was she?" I asked.

"My wife," he said, and looked out the window, not at me.

"You were married?"

"Yes."

"And you had a child?"

"Yes."

"What happened to them?"

"They died."

I didn't know what to say to that. I had learned that Doyle had been married, had had a child, and had lost them both, and I hadn't known any of that minutes before. I turned around in the seat and let the silence fill the car.

"Does it bother you?" Doyle asked quietly.

"I think so, but . . . How many of you have had wives and children before this?"

"All of us except for Frost, I think," Rhys said.

"I had both," Frost said.

"Rose," I said.

He nodded. "Yes."

"I didn't know you had a child with her, though. What happened?"

"She died."

"They all died," Doyle said.

Barinthus spoke from the dimness of the backseat. "There are moments, Meredith, when being immortal and ageless is not a blessing."

I thought about that. "As far as we know, I'm aging just a little less than humanly normal. I'm not immortal or ageless."

"You were not immortal as a child," Barinthus said, "but then you didn't have hands of power as a child."

"Are you all going to be sitting in some rocket-powered car a century from now telling our children about me?"

No one said anything, but Rhys took one hand off the wheel and laid it over mine. I guess there really wasn't anything to say, or nothing comforting. I clung to Rhys's hand, and he held it all the way home. Sometimes comfort isn't about words.

CHAPTER THIRTY-NINE

I TOOK OFF THE HIGH HEELS AS SOON AS WE WERE THROUGH THE door. Then it was like a comedy routine, with all the men trying to help me up the stairs. Julian and Galen stepped out of the living room into the foyer. Galen was all concern when he heard that I'd been sick, but both he and Julian had trouble not laughing when they heard that I'd thrown up in the forensics lab.

I frowned at them both but I hugged Julian, because I knew that him being here meant that his dinner with Adam hadn't gone well. "Sorry I wasn't here to cuddle during movies tonight."

Julian laid a brotherly kiss on my cheek. "You were off crime-fighting. I forgive you." He made a joke of it and his smile was genuine, but his brown eyes held a sad shadow.

I stepped back from him and Galen picked me up.

"I can walk," I said.

"Yes, but now they'll stop arguing and follow us while you get ready for bed. I have more news. And so does Julian."

Galen had already started for the stairs, and with a call to Julian he used the speed his long legs could give him. Julian had to hurry to catch up.

Rhys actually caught up with us on the stairs before anyone else did. He explained as he ran to keep up, "Doyle and Frost are talking to Barinthus. We've never been friends, so I thought I'd come help tuck you in." He grinned and gave a lascivious eyebrow waggle.

It made me smile, which was why he'd done it. "What's happened now?" I asked.

Galen kissed my cheek as he got to the top of the stairs. "It's not bad news, Merry, but you could probably do without it."

"Just tell me," I said.

"Julian," Galen said.

"Jordan came out of the meds saying one sentence over and over again: 'Thumbelina wants to be big.' He just kept repeating it, but when he was completely out from under the meds he didn't remember saying it, or what it meant."

"Did you tell Lucy?"

He nodded. "But it could be nonsense. You know that."

"It could be, but the murderer has been copying children's books. Maybe this is the next book," I said.

Rhys opened the bedroom door and Galen carried me in. The bed was already turned down, with a silk robe laid out for me.

I leaned my head into the bend of Galen's neck, letting the warmth and scent of his skin soothe me. I whispered, "I had to stand up to Barinthus. I told him Jeremy was more useful to me than he was."

"Sorry I missed it," Galen whispered.

Rhys said, "She really let him have it."

"Did you hear what they said?" Julian asked.

Rhys nodded. He looked at the other man. "Just like Galen and I heard your conversation with Merry on the sidewalk, so I know that you being here is a bad sign for your dinner with Adam."

"Damn, how good *is* your hearing?" Julian asked.

Galen set me on the bed. Then he knelt in front of me. "Mistral is talking with Queen Niceven in the mirror in the main room. She's insisting that you feed Royal tonight or the alliance is over between you and her."

I looked at him. "One feeding and she'd cancel the alliance," I said.

He nodded. "We've been talking to her for most of the time you've been gone."

"What's happening at the court to make her want to be rid of us so badly?"

Galen glanced back at Julian, who took the hint and said, "I think you need to handle things here and sleep tonight, Merry. Thanks for the offer of a cuddle, but you have other things you need to do more than me."

"We'll cuddle you," Rhys said.

Julian looked at him, frowning.

Rhys grinned. "I told you, Galen and I heard what you told Merry. If you're that desperate for some touch, Galen and I can do it."

Julian looked from one to the other of the men. "Thanks, but I'm not sure what's being offered."

"We'll put you in the middle," Galen said.

"Strictly as friends," Rhys said.

Julian looked at me then, and his expression was pained. I laughed. "You'll get your cuddle, but you will be stuck between two of the prettiest men around and no sex."

He opened his mouth, closed it, and finally said, "I want the touch, but I'm not sure if I should be insulted or complimented."

Rhys and Galen both laughed. "It's a compliment," Rhys said, "and we can send you back home with your virtue intact."

"Won't you be sleeping with Merry tonight?" Julian asked.

"Not tonight. Mistral hasn't seen her in two days, almost three, so we'll step aside for him. Not sure who the other man will be, but we've bunked with her recently, and I think tonight won't be about sex."

"I feel strangely fine now," I said.

Rhys gave me a look. "I still wouldn't push it. This is the first morning sickness you've had, so I'd take it easy."

"I didn't know you could get morning sickness in the evening," Galen said.

"Apparently you can," I said, and didn't elaborate on the conversation in the car. I reached up under my skirt for the tops of my thigh-highs. I wanted them off and then I'd brush my teeth. Strangely, I really wanted to brush my teeth soon. The breath mints that Carmichael had given me only went so far.

Mistral came through the door cursing under his breath. His hair was a uniform gray like rain clouds, but unlike Wilson's, his had always been that color. His eyes were the shade of sickly yellow-green that the sky turns just before the heavens open up and the tornado eats the world. It was the color his eyes went when he was very worried, or very mad. Once long ago when Mistral's eyes had been that color the sky had mirrored them, so that his anger or anxiety had changed the weather. Now he was simply more than six feet of muscled warrior. He was the most masculinely handsome of my men. He was very handsome, but you would never look at his face and think pretty, or beautiful. He was entirely too male-looking for that. He was also the only one with shoulders broader than either Doyle or Frost. Barinthus had him on sheer physical size, but there was always something about Mistral, Lord of Storms, that made him big. He was a big man who took up a lot of space. Now he was a big, angry man. The only thing I caught completely in the rush of very old Gallic was the name Niceven, and a few choice curses.

Galen said, "I take it Niceven wouldn't change her mind."

"She wants out of this alliance for a reason." He made a visible effort to master his temper and came to me. "I have failed you, Merry. You have to feed that creature of hers tonight."

"Let me try to talk to her," Rhys said.

"You think you can do what I could not?"

"I can tell her that Merry got sick tonight. Niceven's had children. Maybe she'll cut Merry some slack for that."

Mistral sat down on the bed beside me, face all concern. "Are you well?"

"I seem to be now. I guess I couldn't get by without a little morning sickness."

He hugged me very gently, as if afraid I'd break. Mistral liked his sex pretty rough, so to feel him hold me like I was made of eggshells made me smile. I hugged him back a little more firmly. "Let me brush my teeth and then we'll see how I feel." And that's what we did. I took the robe that had been laid on the bed into the bathroom, brushed my teeth, and took off the hose, and my dress. I came back out with the robe belted in place and the room empty except for Rhys. He was sitting on the side of the bed looking less than pleased.

"How do you feel?"

"Fine," I said.

He gave me a look.

"Really, I'm fine; whatever caused me to be sick seems to have passed."

"I'll have the cooks make a list of the food you ate tonight. Some women just can't eat certain foods while pregnant."

"Could your wife?" I asked.

He shook his head, smiling a little, and stood up. "No, I won't talk about that. What I will talk about is that Royal is outside. He seems genuinely embarrassed that his queen is insisting on this, even knowing you were ill earlier this evening, but he's worried that she'll call him home if he refuses to be a good little surrogate for her."

I came to him, putting my arms around his waist. He returned the favor, and with him only six inches taller than me the eye contact was comfortable. "Kitto made mention that Kurag is wanting out of our alliance, and Kitto is being careful not to give him any excuse for it. Is there something happening at the Unseelie Court that I should know about?"

"You didn't want to rule the Unseelie Court, so it's not your problem."

"That would be a yes. Something is happening."

"Not that you need to know about, though."

I studied his face, trying to read something behind the smiling pleasantness of it. "Why are the goblins and the demi-fey both wanting to sever ties with me?"

"When they thought you were going to be queen they wanted to align themselves with you, but now they want to be able to align with whoever wins the race."

"The Unseelie Court still has a queen," I said.

"Who seems to have been driven mad by the death of her son."

I hugged him, putting my face against his chest. "Cel was going to kill me. I had no choice."

He rested his head against my hair. "He would have killed us all, Merry, and she would have let him. The fact that you had enough power to do it is amazing and wonderful, and let's face it, she wasn't the most stable cookie in the box to begin with."

"I didn't mean to leave our court in such disarray. I just wanted us safe."

"No one blames you, Merry."

"Barinthus does, and if he does so do others."

He kissed my cheek and held me close, and again that was answer enough. I could have asked questions about how bad it was, and what we could do, but the only thing we could do was to go back and take the throne, but we'd rejected the crowns of faerie once. I hadn't found that you got second chances at such offers. Even with the crowns on our heads, the chances that Doyle and I could hold the throne against all the factions that Andais had allowed to rise in her court was slim. I wanted to stay safe and have our babies. They and the men I loved meant more to me than crowns and even the Unseelie. So I let him hold me and I didn't press for details because I was certain they would all be bad ones.

CHAPTER FORTY

ROYAL MIGHT HAVE BEEN EMBARRASSED ABOUT HIS QUEEN'S LACK of manners, but he couldn't hide the fact that he wanted to be with me. Of course, in fey culture to hide the fact that you found someone attractive, especially if they were trying to be attractive, was an insult. I wasn't exactly trying to be attractive, but I wasn't trying not to be either.

I lay in the white robe against all the pale creams and gold of the bed. Royal floated above me on his wings of red and black and gray. They were a blur of color, and even though the wings were the wings of a moth, they moved more like those of a dragonfly, or a bee, much faster than the moth he resembled. He lowered himself slowly toward me until his wings blew my hair across the pillow in a red wave. He landed in the middle of my chest. His weight was not so much that I minded, but solid enough that I knew he was there. He knelt between the mounds of my breasts, his knees touching some of that soft flesh. He was wearing one of the gauzy loincloths that some of the demi-fey were fond of. It was the grown-up real version of the clothes that the killer had put on the demi-fey at the first crime scene.

He folded his wings behind his back, so that the darker and plainer outer coverings slipped over the startling brightness of the red-and-black stripes. He gazed up at me, and with a face that small with bobbing black antennae he should have been cute or silly even, but Royal had always managed to be neither of those things, from the first moment I met him.

"You look solemn, Princess. Are you well? I heard you were ill earlier."

"And if I said I was ill, what would that change?" I asked.

He lowered his head and sighed. "I would still feed, but I would be sorry for it." Even as he said it one tiny hand traced the edge of my breast where it touched the edge of the robe.

"Your actions give lie to your words, Royal."

"I am not lying, but I have never lied to you about the fact that I find you beautiful. I would have to be blind and unable to touch the silk of your skin not to want you, Princess Meredith."

I told the truth. "I feel well enough now, but I am tired, and I think sleep would do me good."

"If I could make love to you for real I would make it last all night, but since I can only do what the Glimmer does, I will make it enjoyable but not take so long."

"Glimmer. What does that mean?"

He looked uncomfortable. "You will not like the answer."

"I still want to know."

"There are humans who have a fetish for the small folk such as me, and there are even demi-fey who have the same interest for the big folk. I have seen the images on the computer and am told there are films."

"But . . . how? I mean, the size difference."

"Not intercourse," he said, "but mutual masturbation, or the demi-fey rub themselves on the man's penis until they both go. That seems to be the most popular image on the computer." He seemed very serious as he told it, and not intrigued by it, as if it was just fact and not about sex at all.

"And it's called Glimmer?"

"A Glimmer Fetish if it's a big person liking a demi-fey."

"What's it called if the demi-fey likes the big person?"

He lay down on his stomach between my breasts so that his head was just above them and his feet just below them. "Wishful thinking," he said.

That made me laugh, which made my chest rise and fall and slid the robe a little to both sides so that he was suddenly lying with more of my bare breasts on either side of him, not quite to nipples showing, but the mounds of my breasts framed him. He put a hand out to either side. "May I use glamour now?"

Royal was one of the demi-fey who was very good at glamour, so we'd worked out a system between us. He had to ask before he could pull his glamour on me. I wanted to know the moment my mind was clouded, because he was good enough that I couldn't always tell. Some of the men had shared my bed when Royal fed for his queen, and he was good enough at the glamour that it worked on them, too. They didn't like it, and he was the only demi-fey to act as Niceven's surrogate who had me to himself, because the men found him disturbing, or the men who didn't find Royal disturbing disturbed Royal. Doyle was willing to stay, but the demi-fey didn't like him, none of them. It was the same for all the men who could throw off the glamour. The demi-fey found it hard to concentrate around them enough to feed. So, Royal and I had the feeding to ourselves with the knowledge that at a prescribed time one of the guards would knock on the door and interrupt.

Niceven's original plan had been to have one of her surrogates who could shift to nearly my own height make a bid to get me pregnant and try to be king of the Unseelie, but I was already pregnant and Royal didn't have a bigger form.

"May I use my glamour now so that we will enjoy the feeding as much as we can?"

I sighed and again it made him rise and fall on my breasts. He caressed his hands on the soft mounds of them almost like a swimmer. He laid his head against my chest and said, "I love the sound of your heart like this."

"Whatever fetish this is, I think you have it."

He raised his head and looked at me. "Only for you."

I gave him the suspicious look that comment deserved.

"Must I take oath for you to believe me?" he asked.

"No," I said, "and yes, you may use glamour, but behave yourself."

He grinned at me and there should have been no heat possible in a man his size. He should have looked more like a cat curled between my breasts, sexless, and pretty, but a cat couldn't look at you like that. And then he dropped his shields much as I had in the lab, but where my shields kept me from seeing magic everywhere Royal's shields kept him from befuddling the world with his magic.

One moment I was puzzled by how a man the size of a doll could make me nervous and the next he was sliding down the side of my body, spilling back my robe until he bared my breasts. I'd always kept him away from intimate things, but tonight I'd forgotten to negotiate as firmly as usual. I knew vaguely that there was a reason not to let him put that tiny rosebud of a mouth on one of my nipples, but while I was still trying to form the thought of why, he set his mouth around me, and from the moment he began to suck I couldn't remember why he wasn't supposed to do it, or rather, I no longer cared.

I'd had demi-fey suck fingertips, and from such innocent kisses they could make you feel as if they were sucking on much more intimate things. Now he was on something intimate and it was as if there was a line from there all the way to that most intimate of places where a man can suck on a woman. But it was more than that; it was as if I could feel his body all along the edge of mine. Royal could use his glamour to give the illusion that he was bigger. I could feel the weight of him against the side of my body, so warm, so real, as he sucked on my breast.

I had to put my hand on the delicate brush of his wings to make certain he was only so big and no more. He flicked his wings against my fingers and suddenly they, too, felt bigger, as if they rose above his back like sails on a ship, but sails that were brushed with velvet scales and flicked delicate and beautiful against my hand.

He bit me just enough to make me cry out for him and suddenly the world smelled of roses. Wild roses and summer heat filled the world. I had to open my eyes to make certain we were still in the pale bedroom with its satin and silk. Rose petals began to fall from nowhere onto the bed.

His hands cupped my breast, mounding it up so he could get a better seal on my nipple, and his hands felt bigger, his mouth kissing me hard and harder as he drew my nipple out to one long, harsh line, but the pain was just right, just what I needed to cry out for him again. I thought it was his glamour when he was suddenly staring down at me, his body on top of mine. I'd felt his glamour make him seem big enough to do all that. I opened my eyes to find his wings rising above us both in a spill of color and movement. His face was still a delicate triangle, but it was as big as my own, and he was still beautiful, but as I watched him lean in for a kiss I realized it wasn't illusion.

Rose petals fell on him, framing him in a rain of pink and white as he kissed me—a real kiss with lips big enough to do it right. One of my hands found the back of his neck and the curls of his hair while my other hand traced the line of his back until I found where his wings joined his body, and we kissed, gently and long, and his body settled closer to mine. I realized that he had grown bigger but his clothing had not. He was nude against my body and I was nude under the robe as we kissed.

He rose from the kiss enough to say, "Please, Merry, please. I may never get my wish again."

"What did you wish?"

"You know what I wished." His hand slid down between our bodies until his fingers found my opening. He slid a finger inside me and even that small entering made me catch my breath and writhe for him. He smiled down at me. "You're wet."

I nodded. "Yes." I slid my own hand between our bodies and found him hard and long and big enough to please any woman. I wrapped my hand around him until he shuddered above me.

"Please," he said.

"Yes," I said, and I let go of him and moved my hips up to meet his body.

He opened his eyes and gazed down at me. "Yes?" he asked.

"Yes," I said.

He smiled and then he raised his body enough and used his hand to guide himself to my opening. I lifted my hips to help him find his way and suddenly he was sliding inside me. "So tight, but so wet." He rose on his arms so he could push a little more with his lower body. The movement gave me a clear view down the line of our bodies so I could see him pushing his way inside me, see his body going inside mine for the first time.

I cried out, "Goddess!" The rain of petals thickened like soft, perfumed snow except this snow was warm and silken against our bare skin.

Royal pushed his way inside me until our bodies met and then he shuddered above me, his wings fanning out to frame the pale beauty of his body. He looked down at me and said, "You're lying in a bed of rose petals." And then he began to make love to me, his body going in and out of mine. He put one of my legs up over his shoulder to get a slightly deeper, slightly different angle and it was as if he'd known that would help him hit that spot just inside me. He began to glide himself over and over that spot as he rose above me, his wings flicking out to their widest as he buried himself the deepest in my body.

My breathing sped up, and I felt that heavy sweet sensation growing inside me. His breathing was faster, his body getting more frantic. I breathed out, "Almost, almost there."

He nodded as if he'd understood or even heard me. He fought his body, his breathing, everything to push himself in and out of me just a few more strokes, and between one and the next he spilled me over the edge and I was screaming his name, my hands finding his sides, his back, holding on to him, as he brought me writhing and shrieking underneath him.

My skin glowed brightly enough to paint his winged shadow

against the ceiling. He cried out above me, and thrust himself one last time inside me. We screamed together and then he held himself on his arms, his head down like a winded horse. His wings began to fold back behind him.

I saw movement in the room and realized that Mistral and Frost had seen at least the end of our lovemaking. Royal collapsed slowly on top of me, and it was only as he folded in against me so warm, and his head touched the pillow beside my head that I realized that in this form he was taller than Kitto. He was my height.

I held him, my hands careful with the edge of his wings as we both waited for our heartbeats to slow. I felt something cooler than the body fluid we'd just shared and it was on my shoulder. I petted his curls and he raised his face enough to look at me. He was crying. It was his tears against my skin.

I did the only thing I could think of to do. I kissed him, and we held each other until we could move enough to clean up in the bathroom. We'd been debating who would share my bed along with Mistral tonight. I knew who had my vote, if the storm lord would allow it, and maybe if he wouldn't. Maybe as with Barinthus it was time for me to stop being nice to everyone and ask for what I wanted, and in that moment I couldn't think of anything I wanted more than to keep Royal with me. Maybe it was his own glamour, or maybe it was the Goddess with her fall of rose petals, but whatever the reason, he was one of the men I wanted beside me as I slept tonight.

CHAPTER FORTY-ONE

I HAD FALLEN ASLEEP WITH ROYAL ON ONE SIDE, SLEEPING ON HIS stomach as you had to do when you had moth wings on your back. Mistral wouldn't share the bed with him, not even with the rose petals still on the sheets to prove that it was the Goddess who had decreed that Royal was supposed to be brought into a larger form. It wasn't really Mistral's fault, but I'd had enough of trying to make everyone feel good about themselves at the expense of my own feelings. There was no way to be fair about it. Either I cast Royal out with the afterglow of the amazing sex, his new form, and the blessing of the Goddess still riding both of us, which made me sad to think about, or I told Mistral either he shared with whom I wanted to share with, or he slept without me. He wouldn't relent, and I was left, as with Barinthus, to stand my ground.

The bed was big enough so that Frost and Doyle slept on one side and Royal on the other. They both saw Royal being brought into his larger form as another blessing. So did most of the men, but for Mistral it was two days without me and then the demi-fey got the sex that he somehow thought was his right. I'd informed him that I wasn't up to his level of rough sex that night, and that hadn't gone over well either.

I'd woken to Frost beside me, one arm flung out and his silver hair flung across the bed so that Royal's wings flickered awake in a pool of silver as if his wings were a piece of exotic jewelry set in a base of melted silver. Doyle was on the other side of Frost, propped up on one elbow watching me when I opened my eyes. He'd put Frost next to me the night before saying, "Rhys wasn't touching your skin directly. I'm thinking that may be why he was awake to guard your dreaming vision. I will give up the chance to touch you this one night to guard your safety."

Frost had tried to protest that he wanted to help guard me, but Doyle had been insistent, and as in most things, when the Darkness was insistent he got his way with the other men. Mistral and Barinthus were the two exceptions to that rule and even they usually let him persuade them.

I lay there covered in silver hair cradled between the warmth of Frost and Royal and watched over by my Darkness. It was a good way to wake up, and I was glad I hadn't vision-traveled to the desert again. The news was already traveling about a mysterious black Humvee that was showing up and helping our troops. The media were speculating that it was a new special forces Hummer that was impervious to bullets and bigger things. The black coach was doing what I'd asked it to do. Maybe that's why I didn't have to rescue anyone else personally.

I wrapped the happy waking around me like a comforting blanket on a cold night even though the early California morning wasn't actually cold, but rather chilly at best. But what Lucy wanted me to come see so bright and early made me feel cold down to my bones.

It was a small rose garden in the back of an older home. The rose bushes were all hybrid teas and were planted in a perfect circle, with only one small archway leading into it, a bench to one side for sitting and admiring, and a small musical fountain in the very center of it. I would have been happy to sit on the bench and listen to the water's song, letting the scent of roses wash over me, except that under the perfume of roses were other smells, ones that I hadn't wanted to smell again. The smell of roses would still remind me of the blessings of the Goddess, but this memory would pair it with blood and the smell of fear as the dead had given up their last moments of life, so that there was about the rose-scented morning a hint of charnel and outhouse.

Lucy said, "If they were human sized it would be a massacre, but they're so tiny that even twenty of them doesn't seem as real."

I wasn't sure I agreed, but I let her statement stand. But if the bodies had been bigger the killers wouldn't have been able to hang them between the roses like some macabre clothesline. The dead demi-fey hadn't even begun to change color yet. They were all pale and perfect like little dolls, except that what child would tie their dolls up by their wrists and string them up between rosebushes so that the bound bodies formed a circle with the roses? But the killers had left the archway open so that people could walk back and forth without stooping. There was a demi-fey male hanging from the archway's top like some gruesome ornament. Their throats were pale and whole, untouched.

"There's not as much blood. How did they die?" I asked.

"Look at their chests," she said.

I started to say that I didn't want to, but I squared my shoulders and bent closer to one of the female victims. She had a cloud of pale blond hair like spun sunshine. Her tiny eyes were a blue as bright as the sky above us, but beginning to cloud a little. I forced myself to look at the gauzy purple dress she was wearing and there was a pin through her chest. It was one of those long slender pins like you'd use for pinning a butterfly to a mount as you waited for it to die and for rigor mortis to give you the fanned wings and perfect display you wanted.

I stepped back from the body and looked at the double row of hanging victims. They were dressed like the first demi-fey victims in the gauzy dresses or kilts, depending on the sex of the fey in question, but they were the children's book versions of the gauzy clothes covering everything. I knew, from very recent experience, that the demi-fey were very grown-up, and most of them liked to show more skin. Standing here in the cool morning air seeing the lifeless bodies with their wings flared out behind their bodies it was hard not think about

Royal and how he'd risen above me with his wings framing him. I wondered if any of these demi-fey had been able to grow bigger?

"We have some hints that one of the killers is a demi-fey, but how could another demi-fey do this to their own kind?" Lucy asked.

"Whoever it is hates being a demi-fey. The pin through the heart like they were really the butterflies they resemble and not people shows a real hatred, or disdain," I said.

She nodded and handed me the plastic-wrapped illustration. It was a scene from *Peter Pan* where his shadow is hanging up. It was not exact, not even close. "This one's different," I said.

"It's not a close copy," Lucy said.

"It's almost as if the killers wanted to do this murder, this way, and searched for an image that would justify it, but the murders came first in the plan, not the picture."

"Maybe," she said.

I nodded. She was right; I was guessing. "If you don't want my guesses then why am I here, Lucy?"

"You have somewhere better to be?" she asked, and there was an edge of hostility to it.

"I know you're tired," I said, "but *you* called *me*, remember?"

"I'm sorry, Merry, but the press is crucifying us, saying we aren't working hard enough because the victims aren't human."

"I know that's not true," I said.

"You know it, but the fey community is scared. They want someone to blame, and if we can't give them a killer then they'll blame us. It didn't help that we had to arrest Gilda on charges of magical malfeasance."

"Bad timing," I said.

She nodded. "The worst."

"Did she give up the name of the person who made her wand?"

Lucy shook her head. "We offered to drop the charges if she'd give up the name but she seems to think that if we can't find the manufacturer, we won't be able to prove what the wand did."

"It is hard to prove magic in a court. Your wizards will only be able to explain the magic on this one. Magic is easier to prove when you can demonstrate it for the jury."

"Yeah, but there's nothing to see when someone sucks some of your magic, or at least that's what the wizards tell me," Lucy said.

Rhys joined us in the circle. "Not the way I wanted to start the day," he said.

"None of us wanted this," Lucy snapped at him.

He held up his hands as if to say "ease up." "Sorry, Detective, just making conversation."

"Don't just make conversation, Rhys, tell me something that will help catch this bastard."

"Well, from Jordan we know it's bastards, plural," he said.

"Tell me something we don't know," she said.

"The elderly lady who lives here lets the demi-fey come and dance in her rose circle at least once a month. She sits in the garden and watches them."

"I thought it was against the rules for them to let humans watch," Lucy said.

"Apparently her husband was part fey so technically they counted as fey."

"What kind of fey was he?" I asked.

"I'm not sure he was, but the woman believes it, and who am I to tell her that there's a difference between being a little bit fey as in artistic or crazy and being descended from the fey?"

"Is she senile?" I asked.

"A touch, but not badly. She believes what her beloved husband told her, that he was the product of a fey lover whom his mother had for a brief time."

"Why can't it be true?" Lucy asked.

Rhys gave her a look. "I've just spent the last hour looking at pictures of him. If he was part fey it was way back in the family tree, nothing recent."

"You can tell just by looking?" she asked.

He nodded.

"It leaves a mark," I said.

"So it's another circle where people would know the demi-fey came regularly."

"Jordan said that there was something with wings at the murder scene, and the brownie who died had thought whatever was flying was beautiful."

"A lot of pretty things fly," Lucy said.

"Yes, but look at them. When they were alive they were beautiful."

"You keep saying that maybe a demi-fey did this, but even if one of these guys hated themselves enough to do this, they couldn't get twenty of them to hold still while they did all this." She didn't try to keep the disbelief out of her voice.

"Don't underestimate the demi-fey, Lucy. They have some of the most powerful glamour left to us, and they're insanely strong for their size, more so than any other type of fey."

"How strong?" she asked.

Rhys answered, "They could toss you around."

"I don't believe that."

"It's true," he said.

"One of them could knock you on your ass," I said.

"But could a pair of them do this?"

"I think they'd need at least one half of the pair to be regular size," I said.

"And they could control this many demi-fey, control them enough to do this to them?" she asked.

I sighed, and then tried to breathe less deeply. "I don't know. Honestly, Lucy, I don't know anyone powerful enough to make this many fey of any kind allow themselves to be tied up and murdered like this, but if they were dead before the pins went in, dead by magic somehow, I know some fey powerful enough to kill this many at once."

I leaned in and spoke quietly to Rhys. "Could a Fear Dearg do this?"

He shook his head. "They never had enough glamour to work the demi-fey like this. It's one of the reasons they liked humans so much. It made them feel powerful."

"Don't whisper. Share with the class," Lucy said.

I moved closer to her, just in case one of the many police in the garden overheard and made problems with her for failing to do another part of her job. "Have you found Bittersweet yet?"

"No."

"I'm sorry you lost her because of what happened with the reporters."

"It's not your fault Merry."

"I'm still sorry."

"Why did they go so far from the illustration this time? There's only one shadow hanging up and there are twenty of them here."

"Maybe they wanted to kill more of them," Rhys said.

"Why?"

He shook his head. "I have no idea."

"Neither do I, damn it," she said.

To that the only thing I could add was "Me either." It wasn't helpful, and until we found Bittersweet to help give us an eyewitness account we were stuck.

CHAPTER FORTY-TWO

I WAS BACK AT THE OFFICES TAKING CLIENTS LATER THAT DAY AS IF nothing unusual had happened. It seemed like after seeing those hanging bodies I shouldn't have had to do anything else for the day, but life doesn't work like that. Just because you start the day off with nightmares doesn't mean you don't still have to go to work. Sometimes being a responsible grown-up sucked a lot.

Doyle and Frost were standing at my back for the client sessions. I was never allowed to see anyone alone. I'd given up arguing about it. This was one battle I was not going to win, and sometimes wisdom is saving your energy for the battles you can win. Rhys had two hours before he had to be on a stakeout, so he was sitting in a chair in the corner of the room. It was part of our ongoing theory of "more guards were better."

But when I saw who went with the name on my list I was glad they were all there. The client name was John MacDonald, but the man who walked into the room was Donal, who I'd last seen in Fael's Tea Shop the day Bittersweet disappeared and Gilda's wand knocked down a policeman.

He was still tall and overly muscled with long blond hair and a very nice set of ear implants so he had a graceful curve to his ears. They were actually a good match for Doyle's except that his were black and Donal's were human pale.

"The police have been looking for you," I said, my voice calm.

"I heard," he said. "May I sit down?"

Rhys was on his feet. Even though he didn't know who Donal was, he'd picked up on our tension. "After we search you for magic and weapons, yes," Doyle said.

Rhys put the man up against the wall and searched him very thoroughly top to bottom. "He's clean." Rhys sounded like he wished he'd found some excuse to be rough with the man, but he did his job and stepped back.

"Now you can sit down," I said.

"If you keep your hands where we can see them at all times," Doyle added. Rhys followed Donal as he went for the chair and took up a post to his left shoulder.

Donal nodded as if he'd expected that, then sat down in the client chair with his hands spread flat on his thighs.

I studied his face and told my too-fast heartbeat that it was being silly, but one of Donal's friends had almost raped me, and nearly gotten me killed. It had been Doyle's magic that had saved me, but it had been a near thing, not to mention that they'd tried to steal some of my life essence. It had been a nasty spell.

"If you know the police are looking for you, why not just turn yourself in?" I asked.

"You know that I was part of the group that worked with Alistair Norton."

"You were one of the people helping him steal the life essence of women with fey ancestry."

"I didn't know that's what the spell was doing. I know you don't believe me, but the police did. I was stupid, but stupid doesn't make you guilty."

"Since your friend tried to rape me I'm not going to be very sympathetic. I would think the police might like you better than we do."

His eyes flicked to Frost and Doyle at my back—he fought not to glance back at Rhys—then back to me. "You may hate me, but you understand magic better than the police and I need you to help me explain to them about the magic."

"We already know everything about your friend and what he tried to do to me, and did successfully to a lot of other women."

"Liam, my friend, was involved with it, too. The police never found out because he's one of their wizards. If they'd known, he'd have lost his certification with them."

"You mean the Liam that they never found was one of theirs."

He nodded. "But his real name isn't Liam. He always used that when dealing with other sidhe wannabes, because he wanted a name that showed his heritage."

"What heritage?" Doyle asked.

"I don't know if it's true, but his mother always told him that he was from a one-night stand with a sidhe. He's tall enough, and his skin is paler than human normal, like yours," he said, looking at me. "And his," he said, indicating Frost.

"How old is your friend?" I asked.

"He's under thirty, like me."

I shook my head. "Then his mom was either lying or delusional."

"Why?"

"Because I'm the last child born to the sidhe and I'm over thirty."

Donal shrugged. "I just know what he said, and what his mother told him, but he was obsessed with the fact that he was half sidhe." He touched his ear implants. "I know I'm pretending, but I'm not sure he did."

"What's his real name?" I asked.

"You'll call the police and that will be that, if I tell you, so I'll explain first and then give you his name."

I wanted to argue, but finally nodded. "We're listening."

"Liam still wanted fey magic so he could be sidhe enough for his heritage so he began to try to design a spell to steal magic from other people."

"You mean their essence, like your other friend was doing?"

"No, not exactly. He wanted magic, not life force. I was naive last time, or maybe I wanted to be fooled, but I knew when Liam started saying similar things it was going to be bad. He found a way to create wands that help people with magic steal other people's magic. It won't help people without magic, but it's designed for wizards and other fey."

"Did you say wands?" I asked. I felt Doyle go very still beside me, and Frost moved around the desk to join Rhys at the man's side, not like bodyguards but more like prison guards.

Donal gave Frost a nervous glance, but said, "Yes, and I've seen it work. It's not a permanent stealing. It's like the wand takes a charge and their magic is a battery. They regain their power, and the wand loses power."

"So you have to keep recharging it," I said.

He nodded.

"How do you steal power?" I asked.

"Touching them with it, but he theorized that he could steal more power if he was willing to kill them. He seemed to believe that if he could take the person's soul all their magic would go into the wand."

"Did it work?" Doyle asked.

"I don't know. When he started talking crazy I cut ties with him, I didn't want anything to do with him. After what happened with Alistair, I'd learned that sometimes it's not just crazy talk. Sometimes people you thought were your friends will actually do the terrible things they talk about. It's not bragging; sometimes it's just crazy."

"Why not go to the police?" I asked.

"And tell them what? I barely got away without charges from the last time, so I'm a person of interest when things get weird, but more than that I wasn't sure he was going to test his theory. I couldn't tell the police I thought he might do it; what if he never did? He was one of their wizards, for the love of Goddess. They'd believe him over me."

"So you came to us because you're afraid to go to the police."

"Yes, but more than that, you understand magic and power better than they do. Even their other wizards aren't quite the same as you are."

"What changed your mind? What made you think to tell us?" I asked.

"The fey murders. I'm afraid that my ex-friend is behind them."

"What makes you think that?"

"It would take a lot of power to kill the supposed immortal, right?"

"Does your friend have that kind of power?"

"No, but his girlfriend does. She's this little thing and you think she's harmless and cute. A little sick, but cute."

"She's sick as in crazy?"

"Well, yeah, but I mean the relationship is sick. I mean, she's a demi-fey and he's my size."

"She's not one who can change size?" I asked.

He shook his head. "But she wants to, and she hates all the fey who can hide what they are since she can't."

"Isn't her glamour good enough for her to hide?"

"She can pretend to be a butterfly, but she isn't really good at glamour, or people always seem to see through her illusions. I've known others who were much better at it."

"So the wand wasn't for him, it was for her," I said.

He nodded. "Yes, and it worked. She was more powerful the last time I saw them. She used glamour on me, made me . . . want her, see her as bigger, but she wasn't. I . . ." He was obviously embarrassed.

He leaned on the desk, stretching his hand out, beseeching me. "I did things. Things I didn't want to do." He shook his head. "No, no, you're not going to believe me. I can see it in your eyes."

I wanted him to tell us everything he knew and I would tell the police he'd come to us. We were allowed to use magic to help our clients. Hell, it was one of the things our agency was known for, and I knew I was justifying what I would do next.

I stood up so I could reach across the desk and touch his hand. "It's okay, I know what it's like to have the powerful demi-fey affect you."

He looked at my hand on his. "May I hold your hand?"

"Why do you want to?"

"Because I'm elfstruck and just holding your hand would be more than I ever thought I'd get."

I studied his eyes. There was pain there and it was real. I thought about it, and knew that the more he touched me, the more likely he was to tell me everything. If he was truly elfstruck for the touch of my body, he'd give up every secret he'd ever known. I said, "Yes."

He took my hand in his, and there was a tremble to his hand as if it was much more important than it should have been. Frost touched his shoulder, but instead of being afraid, Donal stared up at him as if the touch was wonderful. He did have it bad.

"My therapist says that I got messed up because I got to watch elf porn when I was twelve. He says that's why I'm elfstruck, and why all my interests are the sidhe, because I watched them glow on screen when my sexuality was just forming." He turned from Frost to me, and his eyes were tormented. "Once you've seen a pair of you light up a room, how can any human compare?"

I blinked at him. "I'm sorry. I didn't know any sidhe had made porn."

Rhys answered, "There are a few who came out when Maeve Reed did, but they didn't have her acting ability."

I looked back at him. "Are you saying that there are currently sidhe who are acting in porn?"

He nodded. "Hell, there's even Glimmer porn."

"Royal mentioned it last night," I said.

"I'll just bet he did," Rhys said.

I gave him an unfriendly look.

"Sorry," he said.

I held Donal's hand and felt his happiness at such a small touch. To be elfstruck for a human was truly terrible. It meant that nothing and no one satisfied the need. Humans had wasted away for lack of our touch, but it was usually a human whom we'd captured and taken to faerie and then released, or someone who'd escaped but found that you never really escaped faerie. That was in the old days, long before I was born, but the human was ruined for regular life. They longed for things that humans couldn't give them.

Then I thought of something. "Rhys, how did you find out about Glimmer porn?"

"When we watched Constantine's movies there were a few extra films with fey."

"That's why she wanted to be big," Donal said, "so they could have sex for real. She was a camera girl for a while."

"What does a camera girl do?"

"They have an online site where you can watch demi-fey do things to themselves and with each other, and sometimes with humans. You subscribe like to any porn site."

"And that's what his girlfriend did for a living?" I asked.

"They met through the site. She broke the rules by dating a client and they fired her."

"So a camera girl is a demi-fey."

"Not just demi-fey, humans, too. They're just girls you can pay and they'll act out your fetish," Rhys said.

Donal nodded.

"And how do you know all this, Rhys?" I asked.

"I have a house outside faerie, Merry, remember? When you're not allowed to touch anyone else, porn is a wonderful thing."

I glanced at Doyle. "I thought the queen didn't even let the guards pleasure themselves."

"She made that rule for only her most trusted men. With time and distance, I think only the men she thought she might want again someday."

"Should I be insulted?" Rhys asked.

"No, happy. At least you had a release."

Rhys nodded. "Fair enough."

"Did you see them kill anyone?" I asked.

"No, I swear I would have gone to the police."

"So why are you sure that they did it?"

"It was when I found out who some of the demi-fey were who died. She hated the ones who could hide and play human, and she hated the ones who were more powerful than she was, but only sometimes. Sometimes she was their friend, but other times she seemed to hate them. She really earned her name."

"What name?" I asked.

"Bittersweet. Sometimes she'd call herself Sweet and she would be, but other times she called herself Bitter, and she was crazy mean."

I had one of those moments when things fall into place. She hadn't been our witness, she'd been one of our killers, but why had she hung around? Why not stay away?

"She pretended to be a witness to the first murders," I said.

"She might not have been pretending," Donal said.

"What do you mean?"

"If she was Bitter and did bad things, when she came back as Sweet she'd be puzzled. I would never do such horrible things, she'd say. I thought it was an act at first, but at the end I realized that she honestly didn't remember."

"Can demi-fey go bogart?" Rhys asked.

"I thought only brownies did the Jekyll-and-Hyde thing," I said.

"She was half brownie," Donal said. "She said she was like Thumbelina, born to a full-sized mom, but the size of her thumb. Her sister is normal sized, but looks like a brownie."

I remembered Jordan's message as he came out of his drug-induced sleep. "Thumbelina wants to be big." "What about her dad?" I asked.

"A demi-fey who can be human sized. She's got a brother like that, too."

"What's her sister's name?" I asked.

He gave it, but it wasn't our victim. I had another thought. "Did her mother and sister have the surgery to build up their face?"

"They look human, noses, mouths, the whole thing. And the fey heal much better than humans, so their surgery actually looks good."

"So her mother and sister, though brownies, can pass for human?"

He nodded. "If her father and brother could hide their wings, so could they."

"She's the only one who can't shape change?" I asked.

He nodded. He began to rub his thumb across my knuckles. I fought not to pull away from him, but if he was elfstruck and had become so through just seeing movies, then his whole life had been ruined by some of our people.

I looked at Rhys. "Have you seen the sidhe porn?"

"Some," he said.

"Could that be enough to make a human elfstruck?"

"If they were susceptible, being a child would make it worse." He looked at the man in our client chair and he just nodded. He believed it, too.

"Give us Liam's real name," I said.

"You believe me?"

"I do."

He smiled and looked relieved. "Steve Patterson, and it's just Steve, not Steven. He always hated that his whole first name was a nickname."

I took my hand back and he let me go reluctantly. "I have to call the police and tell them his name."

"I understand." But his eyes had filled with tears and he turned to gaze up at Frost, who still had his hand on his shoulder. It was as if any touch from us was better than no touch.

I called Lucy and gave her everything we had. "You believe this Donal wasn't involved?"

I looked at him gazing up at Frost as if he was the most beautiful thing in the world. "Yeah, I do."

"Okay, I'll let you know when we have Patterson. I can't believe he's one of our own. The media are going to go apeshit."

"Sorry, Lucy . . ." but I was talking to empty air. She was on her way to catch our murderer and we were left with Donal who had been doomed from the age of twelve to want only us. Who knew that our magic worked so well on film? And was there any cure for it?

CHAPTER FORTY-THREE

PATTERSON WASN'T HOME OR AT WORK OR ANYWHERE THAT THE POlice looked for him. He'd packed up and simply vanished. But a whole human man was easier to find in L.A. than a demi-fey smaller than a Barbie doll. They finally put their pictures up on the news as persons of interest who might have information on the killings. They were afraid of what the fey community might do if the news got out that they were our suspected killers. I had mixed feelings because saving the taxpayers the cost of a trial had its appeal.

That night I dreamed about the last murder scene. But it was Royal suspended from the top of the arch, his body limp in death, and then he'd opened his eyes, but they'd been clouded like the eyes of the dead. I woke covered in sick sweat, calling his name.

Rhys and Galen had tried to pet me back to sleep, but I couldn't go back to sleep until they woke Royal up and brought him to me. I had to see him alive before I could go back to sleep.

I woke up sandwiched between Rhys and Galen, with Royal on the pillow by my head curled up and looking somewhere between a child's daydream and a very grown-up fantasy.

He woke with a lazy smile and said, "Good morning, Princess."

"Sorry I woke you last night."

"That you care enough about me to worry so is not a bad thing."

"It's too early to be talking," Galen mumbled into his pillow and then snuggled lower in the bed so he could hide his eyes against my shoulder.

Rhys just rolled over and threw an arm across my waist and part of Galen. I could feel that Rhys was awake, but if he wanted to pretend he could.

Royal and I lowered our voices and he moved down the pillow so he could snuggle against the side of my face and whisper into my ear. "The other demi-fey are jealous," he said.

"Of the sex?" I whispered.

He traced his hand along the curve of my ear the way a bigger lover might caress a shoulder. "That, but to be able to grow in size is a rare gift among us. None here in this house can do it except for me. They are wondering if a night with you would do the same for them."

"What do you think?" I asked.

"I don't know if I want to share you with them, but I am like all new lovers, jealous and infatuated. We've even been approached by some demi-fey who are not ours. They want to know if 'tis true that I've gained such a power."

Rhys raised his head, done with pretense. "What did you tell them?"

Royal sat up next to my face, wrapping his arms around his knees. "That it was true, but they didn't believe me until I showed them."

"So you can do it at will," Rhys said.

He nodded happily.

"What do you think would happen if we went down to the Fael and you changed in front of everybody?"

"Merry would be pestered silly by other demi-fey wanting to be big."

I looked at Rhys, and Galen raised his head. "No, Rhys, no."

"It's been two days and the police still have no clue where they are," Rhys said.

"You are not going to make Merry into bait for these monsters."

"I think that's up to Merry," Rhys said.

Galen turned his unhappy face from him to me. "Don't do it."

"I think Bittersweet wouldn't be able to resist," I said.

"That's exactly what I'm afraid of," he said.

"We'd have to run it by Detective Tate," Rhys said.

Galen propped himself up on both elbows and looked down at all of us. "You woke up screaming, Merry. That's just from seeing their victims. Do you really want to put yourself out there as a potential victim for them?"

In truth, no, but out loud I said, "I know I don't want to go to another murder scene, especially if I could flush them out into the open."

"No," Galen said.

"We'll discuss it with Lucy," I said.

He went up on his knees and even nude and lovely he was so angry that it wasn't sexy. "Does my vote not count at all here?"

"What kind of ruler would I be if I kept myself safe and let more of the fey die?"

"You gave up the damned crown for love; well, don't do this for the same reason. I love you, we love you, and this human has some of the most powerful enchanted items that the oldest among us have seen in centuries. We don't know what he's capable of, Merry. Don't do this. Don't risk yourself and our babies."

"The police may not even let me play bait. They seem worried I'll get hurt just by the media."

"And if the police say no, you'll still go down to the Fael and have Royal show off, won't you?"

I didn't say anything. Rhys looked at me, not Galen. Royal just sat there as if waiting to see what the sidhe would decide as his kind had done for centuries.

Galen got out of bed and picked his clothes up from the floor where they'd been dropped last night. He was as mad as I'd ever seen him. "How can you do this? How can you risk everything like this?"

"Do you really want to see another murder?" I asked.

"No, but I'll survive it. I'm not sure I'd survive seeing your body in the morgue."

"Get out," I said.

"What?"

"Get out."

"You can't unman her before a battle," Rhys said.

"What the hell does that mean?" Galen asked.

"It means that's she's scared and doesn't want to do this, but that she'll do it for the same reason we picked up a weapon and ran toward the fighting and not away from it."

"But we're her bodyguards. We're supposed to run toward the problem. She's who we're supposed to guard. Doesn't part of that job mean keeping her from taking risks?"

Rhys sat up, pulling the sheet into his lap and a little off me. "Sometimes, but in the old days we rode into battle beside our leaders. They led from the front, not the rear. The only failure for a king's guard was not dying at their side, or them dying before we did."

"I don't want Merry to die at all."

"Neither do I, and I'll bet my life that I can keep that from happening."

"This is insane. You can't, Merry, you can't."

I shook my head. "I hope I don't have to but you having hysterics doesn't make me feel any better about it."

"Good, because you shouldn't feel better about it. You shouldn't do it at all."

"Just go, Galen, just go," I said.

He went, his clothes still bundled in his arms, nude and beautiful from the back as he walked out the door and slammed it behind him.

"I'm scared," I said.

"I'd be worried if you weren't," Rhys said.

"That's not comforting," I said.

"Being the leader isn't about comfort, Merry. You know that better than any leader we've had since we landed in this country."

Royal was just suddenly big enough to hold me. He wrapped his arms around me, his wings flicking out behind him, fanning the red-and-black underwing as the moth would to scare a predator away. "Tell me not to show off my new power and I will hide it away."

"No, Royal, we want them to know."

He pressed his face to mine and looked at Rhys. "Is it really that dangerous?"

"It could be," he said.

"My vote with the green knight won't change your mind, will it?"

"No," I said.

"Then I'll do what you want, my princess, but you must promise that nothing will happen to you."

I shook my head, my hands tracing up his back to the strange stiff delicateness of his wings. "I am a royal of faerie. I can't make a promise I know I can't keep without being foresworn."

"We'll talk to Doyle and the rest," Rhys said. "Maybe they'll have a safer plan."

I agreed. Royal held me, but in the end no one had a better plan.

CHAPTER FORTY-FOUR

ON WEDNESDAY WE WENT TO THE FAEL AND HAD ROYAL SHOW OFF his new talent. A hurried towel thrown his way by Alice the barista and he was covered enough for human law. The flock of demi-fey in the tea shop had been beside themselves fluttering around him, and when he told how it had happened they came to me. I was covered in little hands, little bodies, all wanting to touch me, to swing from my hair, and crawl on my clothing. I had to drag one little female out from my blouse where she'd nestled between my breasts.

I had a moment of claustrophobia; so many little bodies. Doyle, Rhys, and the rest helped me step out of them, and we went home with the trap baited. I was never anywhere, not even in the house, without at least four guards with me. I was protected, but what we hadn't thought about was that I had friends in L.A., people I cared about, and we hadn't protected all of them.

I was getting ready for bed. Doyle was watching me brush my teeth, which I thought was a little too much caution, but since we didn't know everything that Steve Patterson's magical items could do I didn't argue, though never having a minute to myself was getting old and it had only been three days.

My cell phone rang in the bedroom. I called, "Can someone get that?"

Frost came with my phone, holding it out to me. The ID said it was Julian. I picked up and said, "Hey, Julian, can't get enough of me at work?"

"This isn't your friend." It was a man's voice, but I didn't recognize it.

"Who is this?" I asked. I had one of those moments where you know something bad is about to happen, but there's nothing you can do because the mistake was made days ago.

"You know who it is, Princess."

"Steve, right?"

"See, I knew you'd know."

The men had gone very still listening.

"Do I ask how you got Julian's phone?"

"You know that, too," he said, and his voice was too controlled. Not cold, but it lacked fear, or excitement. I didn't like that he had no affect on the phone.

"Where is he?" I asked.

"That's better. He's with us. Humans are so much easier to take with my magic than the fey."

"Let me talk to Julian."

"No," he said.

"Then I think he's dead, and if he's dead you have nothing to bargain with."

"Maybe I just don't want to let you talk to him."

"Maybe, but if I don't talk to him then he's dead. Something went wrong with your plan to kidnap him and he's already dead." My own voice sounded matter-of-fact and not excited or scared either. Maybe after a while so much happens that you just don't have enough energy to get excited at the beginning of the emergency. Maybe that's what was wrong with Patterson too.

I heard a sound on the other end that I wasn't sure of, and then Julian's voice, "Merry, don't come. They're going to . . ." I knew the next sound, flesh hitting flesh. I'd heard enough to remember.

"I've gagged him again. I promise you that I won't kill him if you come and make Bittersweet big like your Royal."

"I can't guarantee that the magic will work for every demi-fey," I said.

"She's part brownie. She has the genetics inside her for being bigger, and both her father and her brother can do it. She can be whatever she wants to be." Now there *was* emotion in his voice. This he wanted to believe. This was his lie to himself, that there was a way to be with his lady love in a real way that wouldn't kill her. He needed to believe that, just as I needed to believe that he wouldn't kill Julian.

"I can try, but Julian goes free whether it works or not."

"Agreed," he said, and his voice was back to no affect. I was almost certain he was lying. "Come alone," he said.

"I can't do that. You know that."

"You've seen Bittersweet's work. She's very creative, Princess." There was another sound that I wasn't certain of, and then a sound from a man. It wasn't a scream, but it wasn't a good sound either.

I heard the higher-pitched voice of a woman. "Scream for me, human, scream for me!"

Julian's voice came thick and low with effort. I knew the sound of strain in his voice as he fought not to scream. "No." He said it calmly and clearly.

Steve's voice rose. "No, Bitter. If you kill him, she won't make you big."

Her voice was a high-pitched whine now. "I'll just cut this part off. He won't miss it."

"If you hurt him too badly there won't be anything to save," I said, and it was my voice's turn to be emotional. Fuck.

"Bitter, you want to be big, don't you?"

"Yes." And her voice was already changing. "Oh, God, what have I done? Where are we? What's happening? Steve, what's happening?"

"You need to come tonight. No police or he dies. No guards or he dies."

"They won't let me come without guards. I'm pregnant with their children. They won't let me come alone." We'd already had that talk days ago, and Galen had won this one point. If the bad guys called and wanted me to meet them alone I wouldn't do it.

Bittersweet was crying, and from the sound of it she was on his shoulder near his ear as she sobbed. At least this side of her personality wouldn't hurt Julian. In fact, I raised my voice and said, "Bittersweet, it's Princess Meredith. Do you remember me?"

"Princess Meredith," she said and her small voice was closer to the phone, "why are you on the phone with Steve?"

"He wants me to make you bigger."

"Yes, like you did for Royal," she said and her voice was calming as she talked more.

"He says if I don't do it he'll kill my friend."

"He just wants us to be able to love each other."

"I know, but he says that you'll torture my friend if I don't do it."

"Oh, I could never . . ." and then she saw something and started to make little screams. "Blood, blood on me, what did I do? What's happening?" Her voice got farther away and Steve was back on the phone.

"I need you to meet us tonight, Princess."

"She needs help, Steve."

"I know what she needs," he said, and again there was emotion in his voice.

"Let Julian go."

"You should have guarded your friends and lovers better, Meredith."

I started to say that Julian wasn't my lover but Doyle touched my arm and shook his head. I trusted his judgment and said, "Believe me, Steve, I know we screwed up."

"Meet us tonight. You can bring two guards, but if I sense that they're casting spells then I will shoot your lover in the head. He's human; he won't heal."

"I know he's human," I said.

"With all the talent in your bed, why take a human?" he asked.

I thought that wasn't an idle question for Steve. "He's my friend."

"Do you love him?"

I hesitated because I wasn't sure which answer would keep Julian safest.

Doyle nodded.

"Yes," I said.

"Then come with just two guards and it can't be the Darkness or the Killing Frost. If I see either of them I'll just shoot him."

"Okay, I won't have them with me as my guards. Now where do I meet you?"

He gave me an address. I wrote it down on the paper that Frost brought from the bedside, and repeated it to him so there wouldn't be a mistake. Lives have been lost over a transposed number more than once.

"Be here at eight. By eight-thirty we'll assume you're not coming and I'll let Bitter do what she wants to him." He lowered his voice and whispered, "You saw the last bodies. She's getting better at killing. She enjoys it now. She's picked her illustration and it's not from a child's book."

"What are you talking about?"

"It's a textbook, a medical textbook image. Don't be late." The phone went dead in my hand.

"Did you hear that last part?" I asked.

They had.

"Fuck, I didn't think Julian was in danger. Why him?"

"That day you snuggled up to him on the street they must have been watching," Rhys said.

"There were police wizards at the scene. Rhys, he might have been working his own crime scene."

"Makes sense."

"And if they were watching the house they know he stayed over and didn't leave until morning," Doyle said.

"He's been living with another man for more than five years. Why wouldn't they assume he was sleeping with one of you?"

"Because Steve Patterson is heterosexual and he'll think girl before he thinks boy because of it," Rhys said.

"A medical textbook. She's going to butcher him."

Rhys leaned in the doorway as Frost and Doyle looked at each other. "The question is, are they already at this address or will they move Julian to the meeting spot?" Rhys said.

"Do we tell Lucy? Do we tell the police?" I asked.

The men exchanged a look. Doyle said, "If we don't bring the police in we can simply kill them. They don't want me at your side, that's fine. I am the Darkness. They won't see me until it's too late."

"If we just plan to kill them, it's easier," Rhys said, "simpler."

"What gives Julian the best chance to get out of this alive and whole?" I asked.

They exchanged a look among them again. "No police," Doyle said.

Rhys nodded. "No police."

Frost hugged me, and whispered it into my hair. "No police."

And just like that the plan changed again. We wouldn't call the police. We'd just kill them. I should have been human enough to be bothered by that, but I kept hearing Julian's voice over the phone and her voice asking him to scream for her. I kept seeing their victims. I remembered my dream with Royal dead in it. I thought about what they planned on doing to Julian and might be doing to him right this minute. I didn't feel bad as we planned how to find the address, scout it undetected, and decide how best to save Julian. If we could take them alive, we would, but we only had one priority: Julian as unhurt as possible, and the only dead: Steve and Bittersweet. Beyond that it was all fair game.

Rhys was right. It was much simpler.

CHAPTER FORTY-FIVE

THE ADDRESS WAS A HOUSE IN THE HILLS. IT WAS A NICE HOUSE, OR had been before the bank got it and the housing market crashed. Apparently our serial killers were squatting in the house. I wondered what they'd do if the estate agent brought prospective buyers around unexpectedly. Probably best that that didn't happen.

Sholto came back to L.A. He was the Lord of That Which Passes Between. The tree line and the yard of the house was a between place, just like where the beach met the ocean, or where a cultivated field abutted a wild place. He could bring more than a dozen soldiers to the edge of the yard itself. But that was as close as he could get. Doyle had been in charge of scouting the area and had found the house thick with magical wards. They might be crazed serial killers but they knew their magical wards. It was a mix of human and fey magic, as good as any he'd seen in years, which was high praise.

It meant we would have to be inside the wards and just trust that either we wouldn't need Sholto and his backup, or that we could stall until they smashed through the walls. He was going to bring the Red Caps because the magical wards wouldn't stop them. They'd just avoid the windows and doors, which were the most heavily warded, and make new doors in the walls themselves where there were no wards. Demi-fey were strong, but they didn't think about that kind of brute force any more than humans did. It was an edge for us, but we needed more.

Frost was coming with Sholto and the Red Caps. Doyle would go in ahead with Cathbodua and Usna, who were the other two guards about whom he actually said, "They hide almost as well as I do. I would trust them to do this." Again, high praise.

The question was, who would go in as my two overt guards? Barinthus asked to go. "I have failed you, Merry. I have been arrogant and unhelpful, but for this I am ideal. I can take more damage than even most of the sidhe. I have used diplomacy for centuries but it's not because I lack skill with any weapon." Doyle had backed him on that.

Barinthus had added, "And I am proof against most magic no matter what it is."

I'd studied his face, not sure if he was just bragging again.

"I am the sea made into flesh, Merry. You cannot set the sea on fire. You cannot drain it dry. You cannot even poison all of it. You can hit it, but the blow does you no good. Being by the ocean has given me back much of my power. Let me do this for you. Let me prove that I was worthy to be Essus's friend, and that I am yours."

In the end both Doyle and Frost agreed that he was a good choice and so he was one.

"The other one has to be me," Rhys said. "I'm third in charge and almost as good with weapons as the two big guys here, better with an axe. And I'm almost back to my old power level. I can kill fey with a touch of my hand; you've seen me do it."

"Have you tried doing it when faerie wasn't touching either you or the victim?" I asked.

We'd all had to think about that. In the end he'd gone out into the yard in a section that hadn't become fey and found an insect. He made sure the demi-fey were okay with him doing it, and then he touched it and told it to die. It rolled over on its back, twitched once, and died.

"Now if only I got back my healing powers, too," he said.

Doyle had agreed, but for this night's work death was better. By six that night we had our plan in place, and enough people to make it work. That was why kings and queens needed hundreds of people. Sometimes you needed soldiers.

Sholto would give us a little time and then he would take everyone out to the yard and the wall and he'd lead them to the edge of the other yard miles away. I knew he could do it, and then we'd have all the help we needed, but there would be a few minutes when it would be up to the handful of us who were going to be there first. Barinthus and Rhys as my guards, and Doyle, Usna, and Cathbodua, who had the best chance of going undetected into the house.

Some of our demi-fey mingled with the local insects on the edge of the property in the bank of wildflowers near the house. They were supposed to let us know if Bittersweet went too bitter too early and started to cut Julian up. It was the best we could do.

Doyle, Cathbodua, and Usna went in one of the cars before we did. Doyle wrapped me in his arms and I put my head against his chest so that I could hear the slow, deep beat of his heart. I breathed in his scent as if I would memorize it.

He raised my face so he could kiss me. There were a thousand things I wanted to say, but in the end, I said the most important one. "I love you."

"And I you, my Merry."

"Don't get killed," I said.

"Nor you."

We kissed again, declared our love again, and that was it. The first of the people I cared about the most left to try to get past some of the most powerful magical wards they'd seen in centuries outside of faerie itself. If they could get inside before we arrived, they would take our bad guys and rescue Julian, but if they thought it would set off alarms before they could save Julian they would wait. Barinthus would accidentally on purpose set off all their wards like a false alarm, and Doyle, Cathbodua, and Usna would breach the wards at the same time. When they reset their wards we'd have extra people inside. That was the plan.

I had to kiss too many people good-bye when it was our turn to leave. Too many "I love you's" and too many "don't die on me's." Galen was wordless as he held me and kissed me good-bye. He would come with Sholto and the others, and he would fight this battle. Once they had kidnapped Julian he hadn't even argued, and he hadn't once said, "I told you so." For that I loved him more than his willingness to shed blood to save Julian. We'd all do what we had to do to save our friend, but most of the men wouldn't have been able to resist an "I told you so."

Rhys drove, and Barinthus had the backseat to himself. I had the shotgun seat though no real shotgun. I was carrying my Lady Smith because they'd told us not to bring the police, or more than two guards; they hadn't said not to bring weapons, so we were all loaded for Dragon.

I was also wearing a folding knife in a thigh sheath under my summer skirt, not because I thought I'd use it to cut someone, but because cold steel cuts through most glamour. If I'd had less human or brownie blood in me, I might not have been able to bear the knife next to my skin, but I wasn't just one thing. I was the sum of my parts. I kept thinking calm thoughts as Rhys drove up into the hills. I hoped that what little dinner I'd eaten wasn't something my new baby-rich body didn't like. I didn't want to throw up all over the bad guys, or then again, maybe I did. It would certainly be distracting.

In a pinch I could fake morning sickness. I held the thought in reserve, and prayed to Goddess and Consort that Julian wasn't hurt badly and that we would get out safe, and none of us would get hurt. That was my prayer as we drove into the growing dusk.

There was no smell of roses to accompany the prayer.

CHAPTER FORTY-SIX

WE WERE TWENTY MINUTES EARLY WHEN RHYS PULLED INTO THE small gravel parking area. What do you do when you arrive early at the kidnappers' rendezvous? Do you get out? Do you wait? What would Miss Manners say about it? I was betting it wasn't in any of her books.

Rhys got out first, then Barinthus. He got the door for me and gave me his hand as I stepped out. I had a little jacket on over the skirt and summer blouse to hide the Lady Smith at the small of my back. Rhys and Barinthus were both in lightweight trench coats to hide their guns, knives, swords, and for Rhys a small axe at his back. Some of the weapons were even magical holy items. I had left mine at home, because the sword that had come to my hand had only one purpose and that was to kill and kill messily. We would at least pretend we were here for something else. If the police did get called we had to be able to at least fake the thought that we'd come to rescue Julian and not to kill Steve and his little girlfriend. I was betting we'd get to all the above, but we needed wiggle room in case one of the neighbors called the cops.

We went to the door as if we were visiting. It felt almost wrong to ring the doorbell and wait for them to answer. Doyle had called us in the car and they hadn't risked the wards for fear of getting Julian killed before they could rescue him. So when we went through the door Barinthus would throw off enough magic to set off every ward they had. If we timed it right they would get in at the same time. I trusted Doyle to time it right.

Rhys rang the doorbell. They had put me between the two of them. I'd been given my orders to not show myself until Rhys said differently. I couldn't see anything but that the door opened.

Rhys's matter-of-fact voice was my first hint that . . . "The barrel of a gun isn't a very friendly way to start a visit."

"Where is the princess?"

"Wave to the man, Merry."

I waved above his wide shoulders.

"Fine, come inside, but if you try any magic your friend will be dead before you can get to him. Bittersweet is with him now."

I didn't like the sound of that, but I followed Rhys back through the door. The moment I passed it the wards flared along my skin so powerfully magic that they took my breath for a moment. I'd never felt anything like it, not even in faerie itself.

Barinthus came through last and did what we'd planned. He flared his magic like throwing wide a cloak to make certain you tripped the alarm. But it wasn't noise that these alarms made, it was magic.

Rhys kept me behind him, shielded by his body. "You've got your wards set too sensitive for Barinthus. Easy, he was Mannan Mac Lir. That's a lot of magic to get inside these wards."

If Barinthus hadn't been so bloody spectacular in physical appearance it might not have worked, but it was hard to stare up at a seven-foot-tall man with hair every shade of blue of the world's oceans and elliptical pupils in his blue eyes like some deep-sea creature and not understand just how much magic was standing in front of you.

Bittersweet came whirring down from the balcony that looked out over the huge open living room. It was one of the biggest great rooms I'd ever seen. I saw her past Rhys's shoulder as he and Barinthus tried to talk Steve Patterson into lowering the gun.

She had a bloody knife in her hand almost as big as she was, and just from the look on her face I knew she was Bitter, and not Sweet. We were about to meet her Hyde face-to-face.

"She's coming at our backs, Rhys," I said quietly.

"I'm worried about the gun," he said between smiling lips as he tried to calm Patterson down.

I turned to face her, and yelled out, "I'm here to help you be able to make love to Steve." It was the only thing I could think of that might get through the bloodlust I saw on her face.

It did make her hover in the air on her furiously beating wings. Blood dripped heavily and thickly off the tip of the improbably long knife. It had to have a wooden or ceramic handle around all that metal or she wouldn't have been able to hold it.

"They're here to help us, Bitter. They'll help you be big enough for everything we want."

She blinked again as if she heard him but couldn't understand. I wondered if we were too late for reason. Had her mental illness eaten her to the point where bloodlust was more important to her than love?

"Bittersweet," he said, "please, honey, can you hear me?" I wasn't the only one worried about her.

"Bittersweet," I said, "do you want to be with Steve?"

Her tiny face screwed up with concentration and then finally she nodded.

"Good," I said. "I'm here to help you be with Steve the way you want to be with him."

Her face was emptying out or filling up. The rage was leaking away, but more personality was coming into her eyes, her face. The knife fell from her hands to clang on the floor and spatter blood so that some droplets hit my skirt. I did my best not to flinch. It wasn't the blood; it was the thought of it being Julian's.

Bittersweet looked at her hands and the fallen knife and wailed. That was the only word for it. It was one of the worst sounds I'd ever heard come from someone. It held despair and torment and utter hopelessness. If the Christian Hell exists, then people should make that sound there.

"Steve, Steve, what did I do now? What did you let me do? I told you not to let me hurt him."

"Bittersweet, is that you?"

"For now," she said, and she looked at me. There was weariness in her face. "You can't make me big, can you?"

"I might be able to, but the Goddess would have to bless us."

"There is no blessing here," she said. "The Goddess doesn't talk to me anymore." She landed on the floor and looked up at me. She was nude, but there was so much blood I hadn't been able to tell until she got close. What had she done to Julian? Were Doyle and the others inside the house? Were they rescuing Julian?

She held her hand out to me. I knelt down. Rhys said, "Merry, I'm not sure that's a good idea."

"Put the gun down," Barinthus said.

The men danced their three-way gun dance, but for me the world had narrowed down to the small blood-drenched figure on the carpet. I offered her my hand and she wrapped a small hand around one finger. She tried to call her glamour and roll me as she could some humans, but she truly didn't have enough power. It was as if she'd gotten the appearance of her demi-fey father, but her magic was brownie. It was so unfair.

"You can't save us," she said.

"Bittersweet, she'll make you big. We can be together."

"I know there's something terribly wrong with me," she said, and she was calm as she said it.

"Yes," I said. "I think you'd get an insanity plea pretty easily from any jury."

She smiled, patting my finger, but it wasn't a happy smile. "I can see into that other part of my mind now. It wants to do such terrible things. I'm not sure what I've done and what I just dreamed of doing." She patted me again. "That other in me wants you to make her big, but once you do she's going to cut the babies out of you and dance in your blood. I can't stop her, do you understand?"

I stared at her, trying to swallow past my pulse. "I think so."

"Good. Steve doesn't understand. Doesn't want to believe."

"Believe what?" I asked.

"That it's too late." She smiled that sad, weary smile and then it was a totally different smile. She bit my finger and I reacted by jerking my hand, sending her flying skyward with my blood on her mouth. She went for the knife on the floor and a lot of things happened at once.

Steve yelled something and the gun went off. It was thunderous in the enclosed room and I was partially deaf as I watched her pick up the blade and come straight at me with that evil smile on her face. I didn't try to draw the gun and shoot a target so small and so fast. I called my hands of power, my hand of flesh and my hand of blood. She slashed at me and I gave her my left arm to cut while I touched her legs with my other hand, the hand of flesh. A knife came from above and spitted her through the back, pinning her to the floor in front of my knees.

I turned toward Rhys and Barinthus and found Barinthus on the ground bleeding. Rhys had his gun out and pointed. The other man was on his back on the floor.

Doyle leapt from the balcony where he'd thrown the knife from, and landed in a crouch on the balls of his feet and his hands. He came to me, taking off his shirt to wrap my bleeding arm. It didn't hurt yet, which meant it was probably going to be deep.

Bittersweet's body was dead before my magic began to roll her flesh inside out. She ended as a ball of unrecognizable flesh curled around the bisecting blade. The full hand of flesh could melt a body into a mass and the worst thing was that it didn't kill the immortal. You could stop them, but for death you needed a blade. I was glad she'd died first.

"I'll live. See to Barinthus," I said.

Doyle hesitated, then did what I asked. Rhys was checking for a pulse on Patterson. He made sure the gun was kicked away from his hand, but when he turned and saw me looking, he shook his head. Patterson was dead.

I heard sirens. The neighbors had called because of the gunshots. Of all the times for someone in L.A. to call the cops.

Doyle helped Barinthus sit up. The big man winced and said, "I'd forgotten how much it hurts to get shot."

"It's not fatal," Doyle said.

"It still hurts."

"I thought you gave me the lecture about how the sea can't be hurt," I said.

He smiled at me. "If I hadn't said it, would you have let me come?"

I thought about it. "I don't know."

He nodded. "It's time I pulled my weight," he said.

Cathbodua flew from the balcony, her raven-feather cloak looking more like wings than ever before. She knelt by me. "How bad is it?"

"Not sure," I said. "Is Julian . . . ?"

"He'll live and he'll heal, but he is hurt. Usna is with him now." She held pressure on the makeshift bandage. Doyle was applying pressure on Barinthus's side, and Rhys had put his gun out of sight and had his detective's license out in plain sight when the police hit the door.

They didn't shoot us, and they didn't arrest us. It helped that we had so many wounded and that I was Princess Meredith Nic Essus. Every once in a while it doesn't suck to be the celebrity.

CHAPTER FORTY-SEVEN

I HAD TO HAVE STITCHES IN MY ARM, BUT THEY WERE THE KIND THAT dissolved into the wound because the other kind of stitches would be grown over by the body before the doctor could get them out. I wasn't sure I healed that fast but I was glad the doctor knew enough about the fey to take the precaution.

Lucy was as mad as I'd ever seen her. "You could have been killed."

"He worked for the police, Lucy. I was afraid if we called you guys in it would get back to him."

"None of our people would have talked to that serial-killing son of a bitch."

"I couldn't risk Julian, especially since it was my fault that they took him."

"How was it your fault?" she asked.

"I put myself out as bait and we protected ourselves and our demi-fey, our fey, but we didn't think to guard Julian and the others."

"Why did they take him?" she asked.

"He comes over and gets a little skin-hunger fix now and then."

"Is that code for sex?"

"No, it's exactly what it sounds like. He comes over to get cuddled and we send him back home with his virtue intact. He slept over the other night for the first time and apparently the bad guys saw him leave in the morning. They assumed he was another lover."

"Don't you have enough already?"

I nodded. "Some days too many."

"They didn't find out that Julian is gay?"

"Doyle said that when someone is heterosexual they think that first."

She nodded as if that made sense to her. "You know that Lieutenant Peterson is screaming for us to arrest someone."

"On what charges? Forensics can look at the blood patterns, but she attacked me. If Doyle hadn't used his knife when he did it would be a lot worse than this." I motioned at the bandaged arm.

"And I've seen Barinthus down the hallway. The doctors say that he'll live, but that if he'd been human he wouldn't have."

"It's hard to kill an ex-god," I said.

She patted my shoulder. "You know we do know our job, Merry. We could have backed you on this."

"Your boss's boss doesn't even like me at a crime scene for fear I'm going to get hurt by some overzealous reporter. Do you really think he'd have agreed to me walking in there to save Julian?"

She looked around the room, then leaned in and spoke quietly. "I'll deny this if asked in public, but no. They'd have never let you go in."

"I couldn't let my friend die because we screwed up and didn't put a guard on all my friends." That made me think. "How is Julian doing?"

"He's still in surgery. It looks like he's going to pull through but he was cut up some. You don't want to see the picture the little psycho bitch was using this time. It was a medical text on anatomy." Lucy shuddered. "She hadn't gotten too far when you got to him, but it would have been the worst of the lot, and they weren't going to kill him first."

"She wasn't pretending that she was killing to gain power or magic. She'd admitted to herself that she liked the pain and the killing."

"How do you know all that?"

"She told me some of it before she died."

"What, she did a villain speech?"

"Something like that."

"Patterson is the one who made Gilda's wand. She knows everyone who bought items from him and she's agreed to help us track all of them down for leniency."

"Is she going to see jail?"

"One of the serial killers was a police employee, Merry. We're having enough bad PR with the fey community without jailing the Fairy Godmother of L.A."

"How are the fey reacting to Gilda ratting them out for the magical items?"

"She says it's for their own good. The items are a danger to the community and she had no idea that her wand was evil." Lucy made air quotes as she said evil.

"To hear Gilda, she's crusading to destroy the work of the evil serial killer personally."

"I trust Gilda to land on her feet in the public eye," I said.

"Jeremy and the gang are out in the waiting room. Adam, Julian's life partner, went all to pieces."

"He hasn't really recovered from his brother's death yet."

Lucy looked solemn. "I remember that one. You're having a hell of a year, Merry."

What could I say to that? I agreed with her.

There was a knock at the door and Doyle, Frost, and Galen came in. "I think that's my cue to give you some alone time." She said hi to all of them and left us to it.

Doyle took my good hand in his. "I almost let her kill you."

"We almost let her kill you," Rhys said and put a hand on my thigh under the sheet.

Galen just stood there looking down at me.

"You going to say 'I told you so'?" I asked.

He shook his head. "I saw what she did to Julian, and I saw the picture she was trying to copy. We couldn't let someone do that to Julian."

"But if we hadn't baited them in the first place he wouldn't have been a target."

"Or if we'd thought to put guards on our human friends and coworkers it wouldn't have happened," Rhys said.

Doyle nodded. "I thought of 'us' as only the sidhe and fey in the house with us. I forgot that our family is larger than that. It's Jeremy and everyone at the agency. It's Lucy and some of the other police officers. It's the soldiers whom you saved and whom Goddess seems to have such an interest in. I have to stop thinking like a god who only had a small section of land and start thinking bigger."

I winced a little at the wording. "All Steve wanted was for Bittersweet to be big enough to be his lover for real."

"But what did Bittersweet really want?" Rhys asked.

"Death," Doyle said.

"What?" I asked.

"She saw me, Merry. She saw me on the balcony, I know she did, and she still went for the knife. She still attacked you and gave me her back."

"Maybe she just didn't think you could hit a target that small from that distance at that angle with a blade," Rhys said. "Most of us couldn't have risked that throw so close to Merry."

"I do not miss," he said.

"But maybe the demi-fey didn't know that, Doyle," Rhys said.

"But why attack Merry then, why not attack you? She saw you draw your gun, and her lover was there to be saved. Why didn't she try to save him? Why did she attack Merry and give me her back if she didn't want to die?"

"I think part of her wanted to die," I said, "but I think part of her just enjoyed causing pain. Bittersweet told me just before that other part rose and went crazy. She said that part of her wanted to be made big and then it would cut the babies out of my body and dance in my blood. She said she couldn't control it."

"So you think she wanted to die and it was suicide by Doyle," Galen said.

I shook my head. "No, I think she knew we would kill them both and she wanted to do the most harm, to cause the most pain to all of us that she could. I think she felt that killing me and the babies would hurt you all worse than anything else she could have done."

We were all quiet, hearing the rush and hush of the hospital around us. "I'm glad they're dead," Galen said.

I let go of Doyle's hand to reach out to him. His eyes were shiny with unshed tears. He leaned over my hand and kissed it. "I'm sorry we fought."

"Me, too."

"I'll never like you taking chances but I promise not to unman you before battle again."

I smiled and Rhys patted him on the shoulder. Doyle leaned over and laid a kiss on my lips. "We will have at least two of us in the room all night."

"The killers are dead, Doyle."

He smiled, and smoothed my hair back from my face. "There are always more killers, my Merry, and when I saw her strike you with the blade twice before I could get my aim certain I thought my heart would stop."

"I'd already touched her with my hand of flesh."

"But I did not know that." He kissed me again and said, "Frost is letting Adam cry on his shoulder about Julian. It seems that the near-death experience has helped Adam see the errors of his way. I think Julian will not have to come to us for cuddling when he gets out of the hospital."

"How did Frost end up holding Adam's hand?"

"I saw him coming," Doyle said with a smile.

"Me, too," Rhys said.

"Me, three," Galen said. "I'll hold Julian's hand if he needs it but Adam's treated him badly and I'm mad at him for it."

As if on cue Frost came through the door. Doyle moved back to give him room to do his own kissing. "Adam wants to thank you for risking everything to save the man he loves."

"He loves him now," Galen said.

"Don't leave me alone with Adam again. I saw at least two of you duck back around the corner."

"We'll take first watch," Doyle said. Frost nodded. And they did. And when their four hours were up Galen and Rhys were there, and then Amatheon and Adair, Usna and Cathbodua, Saraid and Dogmaela, Ivi and Brii, until I woke with light streaming around the curtains and it was Doyle and Frost again. "The doctor says you can go home today," Doyle said.

"You're here. I'm already home." They both kissed me and we were touching when the doctor came in to finally let me get up and go home.

Some nights I sleep between my Darkness and my Killing Frost. Some nights it's Rhys and Galen, and Mistral has finally agreed to share my bed with Barinthus. Barinthus is helping Mistral get more comfortable with the world outside of Maeve Reed's house and grounds, and Mistral seems willing to share me with Barinthus though we haven't crossed that barrier yet. I'm not sure what Mannan Mac Lir would do if sex with me gave him back as much power as it's given Rhys and Doyle.

Some nights Royal joins us, some nights Adam and Julian come for dinner. Jeremy and his new human girlfriend have come a few times, too. She's a little uncomfortable with all the touching, so we don't touch Jeremy on the nights he's with her. Uther and Saraid are making friends, and if it turns into more, well, that's up to them.

Brennan and his unit are coming back to the States soon. They want to visit and that seems right, too. I haven't had any more dreams where I visit the desert, but something tells me the Goddess isn't done with that, or me. The government flagged the dirt sample at the lab. They want to know where we got it. They don't believe the truth. I'm finally showing, and strangers keep trying to touch my tummy like I'm some kind of lucky Buddha statue. I'm told they do that to all pregnant women, but I've seen women walk away smiling, and men shake Galen's hand as if they were friends. Maeve Reed says she's coming back from Europe soon. We need more money, more jobs for more of us. Even in the midst of such magic and so many blessings the real world calls and I think that's the message that Goddess was trying to get out. The sidhe in Europe were forced to be little more than just another ethnic group. The sidhe in the United States hid themselves away in their hollow hills and remained apart from the humans. I think we're supposed to be of the world, not apart from it, but we're still supposed to be sidhe. We're still supposed to be magic, and help the people around us see that they're magic, too; it's just a different kind of magic.

ABOUT THE AUTHOR

LAURELL K. HAMILTON is the *New York Times* bestselling author of the Meredith Gentry novels: *A Kiss of Shadows, A Caress of Twilight, Seduced by Moonlight, A Stroke of Midnight, Mistral's Kiss, A Lick of Frost,* and *Swallowing Darkness,* as well as seventeen acclaimed Anita Blake, Vampire Hunter novels. She lives in St. Louis, Missouri. Visit her website at www.laurellkhamilton.org.

ABOUT THE TYPE

This book was set in Electra, a typeface designed for Linotype by W. A. Dwiggins, the renowned type designer (1880–1956). Electra is a fluid typeface, avoiding the contrasts of thick and thin strokes that are prevalent in most modern typefaces.